The Blackguard of Windless Woods

Highlander: The Legends, Volume 5

Rebecca Ruger

Published by Rebecca Ruger, 2023.

ISBN: 9798859686957
Thhe Blackguard of Windless Woods
All Rights Reserved.
Copyright © 2023 Rebecca Ruger
Written by Rebecca Ruger

Prologue

"Make yer pleas now, villain, or send yer chants to whatever god ye adhere to. The Blackguard of Windless Woods stands before ye, ready to send ye to yer maker."

The squirrel that was originally the intended target of the eager, sword-wielding lad was long gone, having scurried away at the first swing of the wooden weapon. The large rock upon which the critter had paused was now the focus of the lad and gave no reply to the instruction.

Not wanting to break his makeshift weapon, the lad swiped left to right but did not allow any part of the blade to touch the stone. He shifted his feet, swinging around his left hand, threatening the rock with his squat quarterstaff, likewise fashioned crudely and replaced often as was required to keep pace with his frequently zealous practice.

He didn't much care for the staff, being that it had no sharp end. Though his sword edge was blunted, at least it had a point. The quarterstaff was only ever a flat topped piece of wood, and for the life of him, ten year-old Dougal Kildare had yet to learn how this piece would provide a foundational skill that was supposed to inform the use of various other weapons, sword included, as had been promoted by his instructor, Walter of Sandsting.

With a sigh of dissatisfaction for what little fight he could muster against a rock, Dougal turned his back on it. He scanned his gaze over the woods surrounding him, presently finding no other suitable prey. Not for the first time, the quiet of this section of the forest near Templeton Landing beguiled him. He paused and closed his eyes, listening, waiting.

As expected, no sound came to him. He would never understand it, the silence within the forest, and only in this area, far removed from the castle and the village, beyond the range of limestone hills, past the barren moors fringed by smaller, softly rolling hills and steep-sided valleys. There were other woodland tracts dotted throughout Kildare land, but it was only in this part, near a curiously quiet stream and amid a copious stand of pine, birch, and rowan trees that no sound intruded. 'Twas not so densely populated with trees and brush to have cancelled out all other noise, to have stopped the wind at some point where the trees grew so closely together that they refused to admit the wind. 'Twas only a mysterious section of woods where, for no apparent reason, no sound intruded.

His mother had given it that designation, *the windless woods*, said it had been like that for years, as far back as she could recall, to when she was a child herself, and then beyond that she was sure. But it was more than only windless, was possibly haunted or sacred, Dougal was certain, and his mother had never disputed this.

The Blackguard part, Dougal himself had imagined.

Though he was only a bastard child, his sire was the mighty Tearlach of Templeton, the Butcher of Glencarnie, so named for what ravages he visited upon the Maules and Monroes after they'd risen in insurrection against the Earl of Strathearn. Tearlach and his Kildare army had devastated several areas around the strath of the River Spey, sparing neither person nor place, and not leaving unchecked church, monastery, or even the lowliest crofter's cottage or most innocent of souls. 'Twas warranted, necessary even, Dougal had oft been told and since made to believe, that masterful and complete subjugation was the purest form of power, that those who would oppose the earl or Tearlach himself presented a danger of becoming a tool in the hands of enemies, or enemies themselves. After Glencarnie, one needed only whisper the name of the Butcher and compliance was soon at hand.

How mighty his father was!

As his son, even though acknowledged only by gruff nods and dark glowers as of yet, Dougal was fairly certain he would one day require a moniker as terrifying, as dread-inducing as his father's. He planned to be just like him, a bringer of fear but not one who ever entertained such a weakness. That, young Dougal was sure, would earn greater favor from the man who was impressed with bravery and might, and not with any simpering, hopeful words of adoration. Tearlach Kildare didn't want admiration, he wanted to dominate and control by means of cold hard fear, as any great leader should.

At length, Dougal skipped on away from the windless wood to the tidy but flawed hovel he and his mother called home. Theirs, which was one of many tightly clustered huts situated amid a sodden morass, was of un-mortared stone, windowless, chimney-less, a bank of earth serving as its back wall, more cheerless than not. They shared it with his mother's parents, a brooding and uncharitable couple who were gone now, over to Nairn to visit another daughter and her kin. Dougal savored these times, when his grandparents were gone, either of them being difficult to love. His grandfather seemingly had neither use nor liking for Dougal while his grandmother was ever critical and cool to her own daughter.

Dougal shoved his thin shoulder against the door that never moved easily save by the wind of a storm and breathed first the soggy stench of wet peat, where it only smoldered in the hollow in the middle of the earthen floor, as if the peat had not the strength to burn properly.

Sitting cross-legged on the ground, Aimil Beaton lifted her gaze from the kettle where boiled the fish Dougal himself had caught that morning. On a scarred wooden platter next to the fire sat pieces and chunks of what remained of the rye bread that had served as their first meal of the day. Without a word, Aimil dusted off the lone stool in the hut and patted it twice.

Dougal sat on the stool, it being low to the ground so that his knees were higher than his thighs. It took him a minute to realize that his mother had yet to speak to him. Always, Aimil greeted him with words. "Come, my love," or "Sit, my love," were often the first things out of her mouth when he returned from his adventures of the day.

She stared now at the boiling broth inside the kettle, her jaw tight.

Dougal asked no questions, wondering if he'd neglected some chore or task, to have wrought her silence. When he could stand it no more, when she neither moved nor spoke and another few minutes had passed, he cleared his throat. "Màthair?"

"Yer father will come for ye today," she said, her voice cracking. "Ye will go with him now, be trained as a knight."

The house was bleakly lit, with naught but the red coals of the fire to give light. A single tear, sliding away from his mother's eyes, reflected that weak light.

Dougal's gray eyes widened while his heart skipped a beat. All that he'd ever wanted would now be his, all his enthusiastic dreams come true—his mother's dream as well, for she had long petitioned for his father to accept Dougal as his rightful son.

"But then why do ye cry, màthair?" he asked.

She shook her head, her dull long hair falling over one shoulder, and did not face her son.

"I...I have erred, my love," was all she said. "I should have fled with ye years ago, nae wished ye to be acknowledged."

The reversal of her stated intentions and dreams, which had given birth to the vigor of Dougal's own hope, came as a shock to Dougal. "But...?"

Finally, Aimil lifted her tired face to him, a strange and wild pleading in her green-eyed gaze. She leaned forward from her perch on the ground, clutching Dougal's hand into her own.

"Ye must resist all that he would force upon ye," she hissed. "Dishonor and deceit, any wickedness to match his own. Those things that he considers virtuous are most certainly nae. Cursed, he is, an evil-doer and tormentor," she said, "and cursed ye'll be, my love, if ye dinna heed me in this."

"But ye said yerself," countered Dougal, "tis my right to be named his son—"

"Named as such," Aimil said, making a distinction as she never had before, "*named* by word but pray nae by deed. Vow to me, lad. Say ye'll nae turn yer back on what is guid and right." She wept openly now, thumping a dirty finger against his narrow chest. "Ye ken what is guid, my love, just here in your heart. Dinna turn yer back on decency, certainly dinna resist or reject guid love."

Though nearly alarmed by her sudden shift, further thoughts upon the matter while he lay awake that night contemplating the brightness of his future from this day forward suggested to Dougal that his mother had only been sorry to be losing her only child. Of course, she would wish for her son to be as fearsome and brave as Tearlach Kildare. Naturally, she would want him to be formed in the image of so powerful a man.

Chapter One

THE SUN WAS JUST RISING over the hills beyond the loch, painting the pre-dawn fog with streaks of gold when he arrived at the water's edge. 'Twas not yet full summer; the mornings did not come vibrantly and sharply. A grayness hung about, tinting the water and the hills and the air itself, including that sun-streaked mist.

Dougal Kildare scraped his hand over his mouth and jaw and yawned wide and long, hoping to dispel the last vestiges of sleep. He forced his eyes wide open, focusing on the path, this one new to him—same as was yesterday's, same as would be tomorrow's when they made camp somewhere closer to their objective.

He took a leak in the scrub brush at the fringe of the loch, watering a woody plant whose leaves had just begun to bloom, and then went to his haunches at the water, briefly startled by his own reflection. He stared down at the image painted on the smooth surface of the water, at the grimly set features, the only expression worthy of the face that stared back at him, nearly half of it blighted by an inescapable and gruesome scar.

Infuriated as he frequently was by the unsightly reflection, Dougal whisked his fingers across the calm water, dispelling the hated image, the one that he'd gained years ago at Falkirk. *Lucky to be alive* didn't pacify him as it initially had. He scooped up handfuls of water and scrubbed his face and hands, gargled and spat, and took himself off, away from the water, his mood soured with the sun barely risen.

The Blackguard of Windless Woods. Bah!

Too often, any notice of his own face compelled memories he'd rather stayed dead and buried. Not memories of the combat or the crushing defeat that set the Scots back years by his reckoning, but of what had followed. He'd worn the scar initially as a badge of honor, a short-lived endeavor, that. Dougal quickly learned that badges of honor, such as they were, were received more favorably when they were not so grisly. People began to sneer and grimace at the sight of him. A woman, standing beside her young daughter at the market at Aberdeen a month after Falkirk, had covered her daughter's eyes with her hand, before she'd spun herself and her child around, as if merely facing him would subject them either to damnation or a similar affliction, as if it might be contagious.

That hostility had seemed slight in comparison to his reception at home. His mother had wept for three days. His uncle had, at first, been able to lift his gaze only so far as Dougal's neck, unwilling to contemplate the general savagery of his nephew's face. Even that had not wounded Dougal so much as the reaction of Brigid Faucht, his betrothed once upon a time.

Betrothed no more. Her subsequent refusal to wed had come as no surprise, not after the revulsion she'd shown, which she'd been unable to hide, and to which Dougal hadn't been sure she'd expended so much effort. Her father, being a large landowner under the banner of the MacDonnells, desiring peace with the Kildares as well as irrigation upgrades Dougal's father had included in the marriage contracts before his death, would not allow her to withdraw her pledge. She'd taken matters into her own hands then, lifting her skirts for "a prodigious number of men, of all backgrounds and occupations"—this, according to Dougal's captain, Walter, revealed with a grimace of his own for being the one to give Dougal this news.

Brigid had gotten her wish. Dougal himself had called off the betrothal. And he knew no sense of peace or any greater pleasure for the comeuppance Brigid had known, finding herself unwed and then with child. She'd married eventually the tanner's lad, had several more bairns by now, was no more the pampered daughter of a great and wealthy patriot, but the ragged wife of a man who favored ale more than his wife, who then—in an irony too great to be misremembered—had himself been disfigured by the war, losing both his right arm and his left eye in battle.

Dougal had learned but quick how fickle were women, and more unkindly, how he was now perceived by them. No more the proud and handsome son of the laird, whose attention and affections were once sought with great fervor, but now only a figure that evoked both pity and horror, either of which rankled him to no end.

Ah, but wasn't life simpler now, he regularly tried to convince himself. No ties, no binds, no comedy or tragedy. Naught but war, the type of struggle he preferred, completely impersonal, no engagement necessary but for that of his sword.

Born the bastard of a northern mormaer and a milk maid and having few prospects but enough anger to start his own war,

Dougal felt he'd always been destined for the sword. He'd only risen to chief by default, when no legitimate son of his sire had lived long enough to assume the role. His father likely twisted and turned in his unholy grave at the thought of his by-blow ruling Templeton Landing, his precious true-born sons turned to dust in their graves upon some nameless battlefield, only God knew where. Dougal regularly allowed himself to entertain plenty of satisfaction over this, his sire being an out and out despicable person. His mother had never said as much, but Dougal imagined he understood the truth, that he was likely the product of rape. He'd heard enough of the whispers. But praise be, possibly the only thing his mother had ever fought for in her life, that her son be recognized as the Kildare chief's son. If she hadn't pursued as much, Templeton Landing and the fate of the hundreds of souls who called it home would have fallen into the hands of his greedy uncle, Padean, the only Kildare male remaining. Honest to Christ, Dougal sometimes believed the only reason his father had acknowledged him, setting up his successful petition to inherit when Tearlach Kildare finally flopped over, was because his own heir and a spare were so lacking in every regard—dull-witted, naturally unsightly and regularly unkempt, with humors as foul as their sire, and proficiency in any action constantly lacking. His father's brother, Padean Kildare, had not much to recommend him either, but since Padean had sampled Tearlach's wife before the wedding—unbeknownst to Dougal's father at the time—that one was no more in any line to inherit anything.

All gone now, Tearlach, his awful wife, and their two sons—or mayhap the firstborn had actually been Padean's son, didn't matter now. Only Padean and Dougal's mother remained, wisely giving each other a wide berth at Templeton Landing when last Dougal had been home.

Gone, too, and longer than had been gone his sire, were the dreams Dougal had lived with as a child.

That was then, when his father had seemed to a very young Dougal an invincible and honorable man, one whom he should be pleased to emulate.

Dougal's life, he thought of late, could be split into fragments or seasons defined by his thinking and beliefs at the time. As a small child, the bastard son of the mormaer, he'd revered his father from afar, longing for even the smallest scraps of attention; when he'd first been recognized by his father, his heart had sung with pride as he endeavored to be exactly what his father wished of him, and precisely as his larger-than-life father was; after several years in his father's company, and as he matured, Dougal had understood there was nothing inside Tearlach Kildare worthy of his adoration or his attempts at emulation—the man owned a dark heart and a dangerous mind. Dougal labeled another fragment of his life as a season, when first his sire had died, when Dougal, escaped from the burden of his sire's expectations could become his own man, but oh, how he'd failed himself then. This last and current season of his life was all the years after the dishonor that had wrought the disfigurement, and subsequently learning to live with himself, with what he was, his father's son after all.

A blackguard he was, but not as he'd imagined himself, a man with a sword to be venerated, one by which the mere mention of his name would have chased English from the land or brought fear and compliance to any other misbegotten person bent on evil deeds. Blackguard he was for how he had conducted himself, for what trouble he'd brought himself—the black deed that had resulted in his scars—simply because his heart was, he'd discovered, as dark as his father's. He was not a better man than his father, he was the same man, with a stormy cruelty flowing in his veins.

He shook himself internally and visibly, chasing the demons of unrest from his mind.

He thought of home, Templeton Landing, which he hadn't seen now in more than a year. He'd been pleased years ago, upon his father's demise prior to Falkirk, to have installed his mother as chatelaine of the enormous keep, had been pleased as well to reduce his Uncle Padean's circumstance to that of bailiff. Ah, but his joy had been short-lived, and he'd never believe otherwise, that his own misfortune had not been fate seeking its due. Wishing ill upon another will only bring it back to you, he'd since learned. For every wish he'd eventually had that his father would die a slow and gruesome death, Dougal had been repaid in full, and in reverse. His father had breathed his last between the legs of another defenseless maid while Dougal was the one sentenced to a slow and gruesome death, day after day since the English hadn't been so kind as to kill him on any of the numerous occasions he'd given them the chance.

Shucking these vexing thoughts with a brutal finality, Dougal headed back to the Kildares' makeshift camp, turning his mind to the most recent orders of his king.

It was only three days ago that he stood shoulder to shoulder with Robert Bruce, Scotland's newly crowned king—self-coronated, the likes of which Dougal had never perceived but with which he could find no fault. Only the bold and true would endure and must therefore command both respect and authentic constancy. Still, few were the smiles shared by any of the king's retinue, knowing what challenges they would face. The period immediately after Robert Bruce's enthronement was one of concentrated activity, as the newly made king made his way north, intent on fortifying his power base by whatever means necessary.

Before he left for Banff, Robert Bruce charged Dougal Kildare and his small but formidable army with making for Midlothian, where it was said several of the Anglo-aligned Scots lurked around, either securing fealty of the people or forcing it upon them.

"Specifically, we should not allow those adherents of Edward to command any position along the old Roman road," Robert Bruce had said. "It will only strengthen their ability to transport arms, men, and supplies. At all costs, we must hold what fortifications we can in that region."

Dougal's role then, and that of his party of twenty men, would be to rout any English or Edwardian supporters wreaking havoc along the path of that old Roman causeway, from which they were now but half a day. Dougal had attended the king's coronation at Scone with only twenty men-at-arms, his appearance as any other knight, noble, or thane, being more ceremonial than convened for military might. But with his orders from the king, he'd sent word home to Templeton Landing that another seventy men should march toward Midlothian, awaiting further instruction at the barely visible remains of an ancient Roman fort near Dalkeith.

By the time the sun had reached a loftier position in the sky and had chased away the fog almost completely, Dougal was riding beside his captain, Walter, across a hilltop heath, watching as Randolph returned from his forward reconnaissance. The speed at which flew the sure-footed courser beneath the scout alerted the waiting men that already something was afoot.

Walter reminded Dougal that might not necessarily be the case.

"He does this," Walter groused, his mouth curled with some disfavor, "comes in all hellbent and then says naught but he passed a wagonful of nuns on the way."

Dougal recalled that specific occasion and several others as Walter remembered, equally ordinary—save for one aspect of that particular encounter. "Ah, but that young novice, hanging off the rear of the wagon, was she nae making eyes at him? Forgetting God and vows of chastity just to wink at our Rand?"

His captain snorted. "He's barmy," he further complained. "Might well be a fine scout, but outside those reports, I dinna ken he speaks so much truth. Cut it in half, whatever he says. Closer to reality, I wager."

Dougal smirked and waited.

Randolph, being of an age with Dougal's ten and twenty years, though no more clever than a lad half as old, was sound in battle and despite his hulking size, able to creep silently upon his deerskin brogues when needed. True, sometimes he tried Dougal's goodwill, as he presented more questions than answers, and his typical expression showed his face scrunched up to such a degree as to ask even more questions.

He reined in sharply and directly in front of the two men leading the rest of the quiet party, and reported immediately to Dougal, "Nae Kildares waiting near the Roman ruins, nae one. Do ye ken the missive was received? Mayhap yer uncle withheld them?" Without waiting for answers to these queries, he then stated, "Sure and we've got trouble ahead. More than two dozen

English, but less than four. Freshly shod horses carrying armored men, says their imprint in the muck. Moving slow, creeping through the forest, making some attempt to conceal themselves. Four miles south, heading toward the river."

Dougal's brows drew down over his crisp gray eyes while Walter immediately challenged Randolph's report.

"And do I need to take an ax to that information? Or is what you say God's truth as you ken it?"

"Nae, sir," Rand answered smartly. "And they've carts, loaded heavy, at least two. Do you ken they're moving with siege engines?"

"Unlikely that," Walter surmised. "Nae with so few men. Come with hundreds, then aye, those wagons might be transporting machinery, but nae for so few."

Dougal concurred though imagined it mattered little what they moved inside those wagons. He was under orders to secure the area along the ancient Roman trail. A shame his own men from Templeton Landing had not yet reached the assigned location, but he could not wait. He and this unit would have to investigate the doings near the River Esk now, outnumbered if a meeting should occur.

"Let's move," he said, spurring his horse into motion, his blood always roused to exhilaration at the thought of meeting and besting any who would fight against freedom.

ELEANOR MACADAM'S EYES widened as she stared out from the rooftop battlements. The sight of the gathered army, small though it was, ignited a fear in her belly that she'd not ever known. *Small* was relative. While she saw perhaps only fifty mounted men organized within a quarter mile of Bowyer House—named for the man or family who had originally built the tower house more than a century ago—fifty was easily twice as many as all the people now huddled inside the small castle.

For as long as she'd lived here, nigh on two years now since her father had personally and indignantly delivered her here, Eleanor had never heard the horn that had sounded only an hour ago. 'Twas an eerie, low peel of noise, which had wailed for a full thirty seconds before breath was drawn and another deep blast came, raising gooseflesh on Eleanor's arms. Within minutes, the peasants from the adjacent cottages began flooding into Bowyer House. Presently, they occupied the hall above the ground floor, those who would not fight. Those that would—the castle guards and the male peasants—were stationed strategically within the house and yard and here about the battlements.

"But what do they want?" Eleanor asked the captain of the guard, Dickson, who stood beside her, likewise staring out from the embrasure. "And why are they only sitting there?"

"Want?" He repeated, his tone annoyed. "What do any English want? Subjugation! Suppression! And by any means possible." He snorted his disdain, squinting out toward the tidy lines of mounted cavalry and foot-soldiers staring down Bowyer House. "*Jesu*, but dinna say they're only waiting on the rest of their army," said the grizzled old man in charge of Bowyer's defenses.

Dickson—surname unrecalled, he'd told Eleanor some time ago—was a robust and irritable soldier, with little patience for ineptitude and even less for anything that might be construed as dereliction of duty. He acted as both castellan and captain of the house guard, all of the tiny staff here being utilized similarly, in dual roles. Though the MacAdam holding was not robust either in value or population, Dickson took his role as guardian seriously, and managed what he called "a tight ship". He had a soft spot for Eleanor, though, of which she was aware—a sentiment which she ardently returned but tried not to take advantage of—and which she partly believed was born of pity, for how she'd been abandoned here by her sire, shortly after *the incident* in Northumberland several years ago, an ill-advised episode that had come on the heels of her mother's passing.

Bowyer House, as a fortress, was neither large nor well-secured, being naught more than a wooden-palisaded tower house that would quickly fall to any besieger with half a brain in his head and at least forty men in his command. Eleanor's father, Anker MacAdam, had been born here at Bowyer House but had acquired the Ancrum Castle and estate in Northumberland in right of his wife, Matilda, and now, according to Dickson's sometimes irritable rantings, owed allegiance to both kings and needed to pick a side. Anker MacAdam's lack of attendance upon either Bowyer or Eleanor suggested that he'd chosen fealty to the English over any faithfulness to his country of birth or the daughter he'd left there.

Possibly—or more probably—she should be devastated by her father's apparent lack of feeling toward her, but truth be told she could conjure little in the way of gentle emotion toward him, not anything that wasn't fear or fright, for his towering rages and heavy hand. Dickson might well be crusty, but he had never treated her ill. Though he raised his voice often, 'twas only his general manner, and never once had he raised his hand. Her father, to the contrary, had only ever behaved dreadfully toward both Eleanor and her dear mother. For years and years....

"Ye get inside now, lass," said Dickson. "Naught but trouble coming our way."

"Dickson, what was the point of teaching me how to use a bow and arrow," Eleanor countered levelly, "if I'm not to be allowed to put the painstaking instruction to use?"

His gray and bushy brows lifted clear into the middle of his forehead as he stared down at her from his great height. "'Twas naught but distraction, that, to keep ye busy after..." he let that trail off and frowned anew. "If ye ken for one minute I'll be stationing ye here with the six archers we do have—"

"Pray do not fear what my father would think or feel if something untoward should happen to me—"

Dickson scoffed at this, in his inimitable way, with a hand swung wildly and his expression sour. "It's nae that man's reaction I concern myself with," he shouted at her, "but my own, should something happen to ye. Now git."

"Dickson—"

"Dinna argue, lass," he begged, throwing back his head with exasperation, "and dinna be taking any more of my time with this nonsense. Go."

With an aggrieved huff, Eleanor swung around so swiftly her skirts twirled widely about her. She made her way back inside but only, she told herself, to see that all the denizens of Bowyer were settled as comfortably as possible. She didn't care what Dickson said, it made no sense to not use every available weapon at their disposal. And since she had suffered through extensive training with the bow, under Dickson's sometimes impatient tutelage, she wasn't about to sit by idly while her own home was attacked.

They were going to attack, were they not? That small, standing English army. What else could they be about, striking that menacing formation directly in front of the tower house?

She dashed down the straight stone steps from the rooftop and gained the spiral stairs from the floor below, rushing down several more flights until she reached the hall. Here, indeed, all of Bowyer's small peasantry population was gathered, all women and children save for ol' Henry Oliver who, though blind now for decades, had once been a falconer on the Isle of Man, and who could still direct his faithful hound, Magnus, and supervise his peregrine falcon, Manx, but certainly could not be expected to raise a sword toward the enemy.

The hall of Bowyer House was occupied by only one table, there being no need for another since the board was more than thirty feet long, plenty large enough to accommodate the few who supped regularly inside the house. Goldie, the brewer who also assisted on wash day, sat with her two lads, her lips thinned with anxiety while her sons made quite a ruckus, slapping hands upon the scarred wood, trying to smack the hand laid before it was yanked away. They giggled uproariously every time they hit the mark, both being too young to recognize their mother's vacant stare or the bloodless dread of her countenance. Beyond Goldie, a heavily pregnant Ellen, wife to one of the castle guards, Eduard, wore a path in the timber floor with her pacing. Curstag and Floireans, the elder women of the village, weavers by occupation though they effectively kept quite a bevy of livestock between them, busied themselves with tatting as they sat across the wide board from Goldie. The household staff, Cook and Lucy and Moira, seated next to Goldie's boys, were the first to take note of Eleanor's coming, lifting worried gazes at her.

In answer to the unspoken question, Eleanor shrugged, unwilling to subject any to more panic. "Nothing happens," she said. "They only sit there and even Dickson cannot say why. Mayhap they'll send a man forth and we will be made to know their intent."

"Come to slaughter us all," Cook predicted, bringing more than one frantic pair of eyes her way, "and mark my words."

"Now, Cook, we do not yet—"

"'Tis how they play, those godless barbarians," Cook asserted. "First they distress us with fright, sitting and waiting and wondering, and that's 'fore they charge and we're now too fractured of mind to resist."

Eleanor didn't imagine that Dickson or any of his trained men would succumb to spinelessness simply because the enemy at their door hadn't made known their intent swiftly enough. Eleanor was no soldier, of course, but imagined that no matter how long they were made to wait for what seemed inevitable, she would have no trouble gathering all her strength and will to survive when the time came, come what may.

"They'll nae make us wait too long," Henry said, in his quiet voice, so well suited to the gentle man he was. "Ye'll nae have time for dread to expand." He turned his face marginally in Eleanor's direction. "And where will you be, lass?"

Eleanor lifted her chin. "Upon the battlements, bow in hand."

Henry chuckled good-naturedly, as if he were only entertained and not concerned. "Best keep to the far side, lass, away from that one."

"I will remind him," she argued, knowing full well that Henry spoke of Dickson and what the captain's reception would be to her return, "that I am the daughter of Anker MacAdam, the rightful heir to Bowyer House, that it is my duty to protect and—"

Henry's more robust chuckling cut her off. "Aye, you tell him that, lass."

Bother that, she thought, and took herself off, back up the stairs to her own chamber, to claim her bow and the arrows Gowan, the fletcher, had helped her make—and those with the feathers Henry and his falcon had helped her amass.

With her mother gone and her father so joyously diminished in her life, without siblings or other family to call her own, Eleanor had nothing to lose. If she would not rise to the occasion in defense of her friends at Bowyer—the only family known to her, truth be told—should she not deserve to perish most shamefully and horribly herself?

Chapter Two

"Like hares in their shallow nest," Walter observed, squinting his eyes to take in the scene in the glen below them.

Laying on the cold, hard ground beside Walter, likewise propped up on his elbows, Dougal considered the situation below. Despite a stand of trees about halfway down the beinn upon which he was perched, he had a mostly unhindered view of the tower house to his left and east, and those English cavalrymen, sitting about four hundred yards away, to his right, having come from the west, it would appear.

To get here, to this middle high ground, the Kildares had needed to take out a few of the English scouts. Easy work, that, which had not required but a few of his own men dismounting and stealthily creeping up on those men. Six down, sixty to go, by his reckoning.

'Twas not an unfair assessment Walter had made. The many-storied tower house was surrounded by a stake wall of dried and crisscrossed, speared timber but boasted few other defenses. Depending upon the depth of the timbers in the ground, the palisade might easily be torn down simply with heavy rope and a few strong destriers. Fire was always an option as well. There was neither a gate nor a gate house, simply an opening in the middle of that tall fence, allowing people, horses, and whatnot to come and go freely. In light of this visit by an English army, the

22

denizens of the tower house had brought a wagon to fill that gap, turned on its side and wedged against the stake wall.

Dougal narrowed his eyes now, determining that the wall walk atop the tall but slim castle did not show more than a dozen defenders that he could see.

"And there'd be the hawk," Walter said next, throwing a grimace toward the sitting English.

"We can take out half their number with our archers before they make their first foray," Dougal decided.

"We can nae," Walter said. "Without the lads from Templeton, we've only Boyd and Eideard and Elon with us, and between them, mayhap only one full quiver."

"Bluidy hell."

"Still, we'll bring it closer to a fair fight," Walter acknowledged.

They still hadn't met with the rest of the Kildare army and thus were only twenty-two men against the roughly estimated four dozen English. Dougal didn't fear the odds, but then was not so reckless that he would go into such a skirmish overly confident and without a well-developed scheme to assure the greatest chance at success.

A body crawled up next to them. Dougal and Walter turned to find Randolph returned from his latest expedition, scouting the east side of the tower, where they hoped to find entrance.

"Aye, it's locked down," he said, "but nae impenetrable."

"Aye and give me a shield and I'll get in there," Walter said, "talk the peace with them inside to see us all entombed with them, fighting from the same wall."

"You canna go," Dougal argued. Walter was about as far from a diplomat as was ever born or grown. Tact and subtlety were not in his repertoire. "It will be my job to see us admitted and—"

"*Jesu*, and that'll be all they need to see," Walter blurted with the aforementioned lack of tact, "you and your mug scaring the bejesus out of them. They'll ken they've met hell already and the fight nae yet begun."

Dougal rolled his eyes and clamped his jaw. Only Walter could get away with such an incendiary remark and not find himself skewered. He crawled backwards a few lengths and then stood and went down the north face of the hillock, advising Randolph to remain there, keeping watch. This braeside was not so steep and was peppered with hearty pine trees, the ground-hugging kind, and one particularly thick grove, which effectively hid the rest of his men from plain view.

Walter had followed and chirped at him, wanting to know what he was planning.

"To show my plaid and the crest on my shield," Dougal said, retrieving another dagger from his saddlebags, and tucking that into his calf-high boot. "Get inside to advise of our presence."

"Might better arm yourself with a white flag," Walter surmised. "And you canna go off by yourself—you with nae heir and nae male kin but that manky uncle of yours, and—"

"Take a breath, captain," Dougal demanded impatiently. Walter was sometimes more haivering nursemaid than second-in-command. "Station Boyd and the twins just on that ridge. If those cavalry move, start picking them off." Hopefully, they'd march only the talking head forward first, making a request for a surrender without a fight. Dougal wouldn't allow it, but the civility of it would give him and his men time to get inside.

Dougal mounted his big bay destrier, taking a moment to adjust his belt and sword once seated, and to right the pleats in the red and green and saffron plaid. He plucked his tri-cornered shield from where it hung over his steed's left flank and instructed Walter, "Wait ten minutes before assembling the men at the base of the beinn behind me. Give Randolph a horn and leave him where he is to call out any warning of movement. If they move before we've gained entry, have at it. Let the fight be met."

Annoyed now, Walter grumbled, "Aye, aye, I ken all that. But dinna get dead in the meantime. I'm nae making those words to your mam."

Dougal gave his captain a tight nod, briefly meeting Walter's severe blue gaze before turning the destrier around. This last bit was said always, prior to any and every occasion of battle. There was some glad familiarity to the grave warning.

He went to the foot of the beinn and rode in an enlarged circle, giving wide berth to the tower house so that he could come at it straight from the east, while the English gathered there, due west.

At home, at Templeton Landing, the battlements were vast, with four towers and many covered walkways, having different levels, and several warrens equipped with murder holes. This tower house had only one roof and thus only one parapet, the crenellated wall showing but few defenders.

He approached the postern gate, such as it was, more of the wooden fence met by a twenty-foot span of the crumbling remains of an old stone wall, not tall enough that a man couldn't climb over it, and housing a wooden gate that looked as if any person—Dougal, if he wanted to—could simply crash his shoulder into it to splinter the thing open.

Dougal kept his gaze sharp, along the fence and about the rooftop battlement, where a sudden scrambling took place as his presence was noted. He paused then, lifting his gray eyes to the figures on the parapet, being far enough outside the useless gate that he was easily seen. He held up his hands, to show that he carried only the shield and had not drawn his sword.

He counted four people standing in the embrasures, though more might be huddled behind them. They were only silhouetted forms, the sun being overhead and slightly behind them, the hazy rays shining directly into Dougal's face.

Something was called down to him but not loud enough for him to hear. He nudged the destrier a few paces forward but stopped again when he saw the unmistakable outline of a bow being lifted over the merlons and settled inside the gap between, the bearer taking aim.

To be expected, he allowed generously.

The arrow that flew at him in the next moment was certainly not expected, and dreadful aim aside—it flew past him on his left, easily missing the mark by a dozen feet—Dougal's charity deserted him. He'd not yet spoken one word; they had no cause to assault him as of yet.

A flurry of noise and motion took place up there, impolite arguing and someone raising their hands in exasperation.

The outrageousness only continued, when a voice—decidedly female and sounding as if the speaker might be cringing and wincing—called out, "Sorry!"

Bluidy hell.

ELEANOR GASPED AT YOUNG Mànas and threw her hands in the air. "Sweet St. Andrew! Why did you fire at him?"

The red flush of excitement on Mànas' face faded to a bloodless dread. "Sorry. I-I was—it slipped."

"Oh, my God!" Eleanor cried. "He's wearing a Scots' tartan, showing a Scots' crest. Why would you have—can you at least wait until we hear what he has to say?"

"Aye, now"—he cleared his throat, his doleful eyes and slim shoulders drooping— "now we can."

Eleanor leaned into the bay of the embrasure, knowing a keen embarrassment for that discourtesy. "Sorry!" She called down to the mammoth man atop an equally impossibly large horse.

Dickson, now made aware that something was afoot on this side of the roof, came from the opposite side, around the low stone and timber wall of the rooftop enclosure, which housed the stairwell and on this day, an assortment of weaponry brought up from the ground floor armory. He yanked a gawking Samuel away from the crenel and showed his face there.

"What ho?" He called gruffly and without preamble to the man below.

"Sir Dougal Kildare, laird of Templeton Landing, knight to the one true king, Robert Bruce, sent at his behest to keep fast the ground of Lothian. At your service."

Eleanor's eyes widened. Mànas had just tried to kill a knight of the realm!

Dickson apparently needed further accounting. "Come by yourself?" He called down, his gravelly voice carrying well. He then grumbled to those close to him, "Dinna reckon nae value in that."

"I have an entire unit with me," replied the man, sitting straight and tall in the saddle. "Come recently from the king's coronation and searching out the enemy in this region. You have the English at your door, and by all accounts, neither the numbers nor the proficiency—if that first volley should be any indication—to withstand a siege."

"First volley?" Dickson questioned, leaning back and sending a scathing glance over those gathered around him. "Did one of you eejits shoot at—"

"Who holds this tower?" Interrupted the man below, not inexplicably sounding a wee irritated.

"*I* hold this tower," called down Dickson, with greater aplomb than he might normally reckon. "Bowyer House you've come upon, sir, stronghold of Sir Anker—"

"Have they sent forth their messenger as of yet?" The man wanted to know.

"They have nae," answered Dickson, exhibiting a similar irritation for the continued interruptions. "And when they do—"

"I will meet them. Is the lord nae in residence?"

"He is nae."

"Then 'twill be you and I who meet them, sir," said the man. "Come."

"Bluidy..." Dickson grumbled, straightening from where he'd leaned out over the wall. He hitched up his belt, which rocked his sheathed sword against his leg, wearing a pensive frown but did not meet anyone's gaze. Briefly he peered back out over the wall and past the postern gate, surveying the trees and hills all around. When he next turned, he caught Eleanor staring at him.

"I dinna ken we've much choice," he reasoned, his tongue working around the inside of his mouth and over his teeth, moving his lips and whiskered cheeks as it did.

"But he's come to help us," Eleanor said, wondering at Dickson's hesitation.

"Says he," Dickson grumbled, his suspicion made clear. "Tomag!" He called and his brows drew even more sharply together when the lad, unofficially Dickson's second-in-command, moved just one step into his captain's line of vision, three feet away. "Aye," he said and took the lad by the shoulder and said something to him that only Tomag could hear.

Tomag nodded once and then again, his eyes, more long than wide, blinking steadily. "Aye, captain," he said when Dickson had finished.

Pivoting on his heel, Dickson called out gruffly, "Hold tight, lads. I'll nae be long."

Eleanor returned her attention to the man, Dougal Kildare of Templeton Landing, knight of the realm, who'd by his own account had recently witnessed the king's coronation. How very extraordinary, that he should arrive now, on this day, and at this moment, as an army gathered outside Bowyer House.

She could not say for certain that the man himself was extraordinary, or not. Little could be discerned from her vantage point of nearly thirty yards away, certainly not with the man wreathed in sunshine as he was. The light did not land usefully on him with any intent to make his visage known in detail, but rather sprayed him with a glow that in some manner could be mistaken as a halo, but more precisely which served to conceal the man's face from Eleanor's heightened curiosity. If questioned at this very moment, she could only affirm that he was broad in the shoulders and owned a rich voice, powerful she might have said. And apparently he was an angel sent by God.

She jumped when next Dickson barked at her.

"God's teeth, lass!" Dickson called just before he exited the rooftop, finally realizing her presence fully. "I said to ye nae five minutes ago, to get below and stay below!"

"I will, Dickson," she promised—lied—to him. "Hurry now!" She urged, wanting him gone so that she could race to the front of the tower's ramparts and see everything.

It was another few minutes before Dickson had saddled his steed and exited the rear gate. Eleanor and a dozen more watched as he and the knight walked their horses around the front, pausing just outside where the overturned wagon now served as a closed gate. They did not ride forward but remained side by side upon their horses exchanging words, their backs to all the watchers on the wall, while they waited the messenger from the assembled army, who presumably had come with the intention of subduing Bowyer House.

Eleanor pressed one hand to the edge of the merlon, squeezing into the open crenel with Mànas to see what she could. Though Mànas was a fine lad, dear in many regards, the same could not be said for the scent of him. Eleanor held her breath and backed away, and then had her attention caught by what Tomag was about in the next opening. He'd nocked an arrow but did not aim this far and away at the army that soon would ride straight toward them but stood close to the wall and directed the path of the missile almost straight down.

"Good heavens, Tomag," she whispered, "whatever are you about?" He appeared to be about to shoot at Dickson.

"Keeping the knight honest, lass," replied Tomag, without turning to address her, without moving at all. "Captain said ye can nae ever be sure."

"Oh," she said, supposing this might be true. Nothing should be taken at face value.

"If he makes one wrong move," Tomag continued, one eyed closed while he kept his target lined up properly, "Captain says to make sure it's his last."

Eleanor grimaced at this, hoping Tomag had a steadier hand and employed greater discernment than Mànas had a wee bit ago.

She moved beyond, to his far side, ignoring his reiteration of Dickson's parting command, that she remove herself from the roof.

Though she could not hear what was being said at this distance, she could clearly see and hear the low rumble of Dickson's conversation with the knight, both men owning voices that resonated deeply. Neither looked at the other, both staring forward yet, and yet Eleanor judged that Dickson was satisfied the knight was who he said and that his intention was as stated, to flush the English from the region.

Finally, after they'd sat below for nigh on a quarter hour, a trio of mounted men moved forward from the whole of the English army. Having never been in any situation even remotely similar to this circumstance, Eleanor was surprised to be overwhelmed with a sense of dread. She clutched nervously at her bodice and let her gaze dart back and forth between the coming messenger of the enemy and Dickson, so vulnerable just now as he rode out to meet them.

Please let the knight not only be truthful but valiant as well, she prayed quickly, only concerned about her captain's well-being at the moment.

They met, three English and the two Scots in the middle of the lane, two hundred yards away. From what Eleanor could see, it looked as if one of the English tried to hand deliver a written missive. The offer was rebuffed by Sir Dougal, who appeared to wave his hand dismissively before he pointed his finger at the letter-bearer. Lord only knew what he said, but Eleanor suspected it was not kindly given—he thrust his forefinger first at the man, then at the army behind him, and then beyond, all very curtly, quite obviously an order and not only an invitation to leave.

For his part, the messenger appeared to take umbrage, growing taller in the saddle as indignation straightened his spine, Eleanor might have guessed. He snapped at the reins, turning his horse swiftly around, briefly struggling to do so as he was flanked so tightly by the other two men, and he could not reverse the animal's direction so easily. A wee scramble ensued before all three faced away, returning to their army.

Dickson and Sir Dougal turned their heads and their horses at the same time, both swinging around to the right before they urged their steeds into a slow canter as they returned to Bowyer House.

Eleanor breathed again, having not realized she'd stopped a moment ago when the parties met. She raced from the wall and the roof, dashing down the spiral stairs, wanting to meet them at the back gate.

Only Dickson returned, dismounting and walking his horse through the gate before Daniel, one of the two guards stationed in the rear yard, closed the gate after him and dropped the brace.

Dickson appeared decidedly less anxious than when he'd left the yard minutes ago. Curiously so. Eleanor might almost have guessed he wore a grin. Or he did until once more, he realized her presence, she being somewhere she didn't belong.

"*Jesu*, lass," he snapped then, though with little of his customary bite, "will ye heed me in this? Get inside."

"I cannot, Dickson," she countered. "Not until you tell me what transpired. What do they want? Where did the knight go?"

"Fetching his own army, or parts thereof," replied Dickson, "from where they'd hidden on the far side of the eastern hills."

As Daniel and the other guard, Alasdair, gathered close to hear the news as well, Dickson handed off the reins to Beetle, a lad of no more than ten and two, so named for his pitch black hair, which often reflected a metallic blue in the right sunshine, and his nearly black eyes. A person might well guess at Beetle's origins as they might his history; he was simply there in the yard one day several years back, Dickson said, and the captain—never reluctant to put hands to work—had bade him help the stablemaster.

"More will come, lad," said Dickson to the spindly youth. "Look lively there, eh?"

"What did the messenger say?" Eleanor persisted, wanting to throttle Dickson for making her wait. "You're nearly smiling, Dickson. Are they giving up their pursuit of Bowyer House?"

Passing his gaze over Alasdair and Daniel, Dickson shook his head and faced Eleanor squarely now. "Sure and they're coming, lass. Nae escaping that. But they'll nae charge gleefully into the fray, nae now, nae after the message the knight, Sir Dougal, gave to the messenger."

His grin actually grew, as if he had not just said that they were about to be put to a siege.

A wee alarmed, hoping the knight did not provoke the English to behave more brutally than would be necessary to simply capture and garrison Bowyer House, Eleanor asked in a very small and slow voice. "What did he say to them?"

Dickson lifted his hand, as if to calm her fears. And then he chuckled outright before he answered. "I'm nae saying it, lass," Dickson cautioned, including the two hovering soldiers in his gaze, "I'm only repeating it. And I'd nae repeat it—delicate ears and tender sensibilities and what have ye—but damn if it weren't splendid. The goblin messenger—white as a ghost he was—tries to give the knight the terms of surrender, nae doubt that's what he conveyed, but the Kildare knight dinna even look at it. Tells the lad—his words exactly, God smite me here— *Set that parchment ablaze, take it back to the vermin in charge of this misadventure, and shove it as far as you can up his arse.*" Dickson waved his hand in front of his red cheeks and his broad smile, as unaccountably merry as Eleanor had ever seen him. "But that's nae all," he went on, still grinning broadly. "Tells him dinna stop to put that fire out or he'll personally chase that fiery missive up the commander's arse with his boot. He dinna even blink—voice like a demon as he delivers that dire warning—and I can scarce contain my own shock, nae the chortle that wants to burst. God's teeth, lass," he said. His laughter died slowly, a wee melancholy softening his face. "Shite, how I miss fighting shoulder to shoulder with the bold ones."

Alasdair and Daniel exchanged looks that Eleanor could not fully comprehend, though she supposed there might have been some admiration for the knight's dangerous insolence. Eleanor was not so much entertained as she was awash with a fresh fear. Suddenly the knight sounded more devil than angel.

"Dickson...is he—can we trust him?"

This caused Dickson to sober instantly. He leaned close and pointed his finger at Eleanor. "Mark me, lass. He's just what we need to hold Bowyer House. A score of men come with him, and I'll wager they fight as if they were forty men. Still," he said, all evidence of his untimely good humor erased, "when the fighting is done, we'll want him gone but quick. I dinna say demon lightly. Guid fighting man have we, but ye, Eleanor MacAdam, canna sit with one such as he at the boards for supper. I'll nae have it."

Chapter Three

An alarm sounded then, an exclamation at the end of Dickson's odd statement. Eleanor startled and blanched at the ominous wail from the horn. Whatever fleeting jauntiness Daniel and Alasdair had known with Dickson's tale of the odd encounter was lost. As neither of them had yet to see a score of years and had not once lifted their swords in an actual fight, they briefly paled.

"*Jesu*, but here they come," Dickson breathed. His pallor, too, did not escape a draining.

While Eleanor looked eagerly at Dickson, expecting at least one more command that she hie to the hall, and at most that he issued some assurance that all would be well, he stared blindly at her, his brows knitted. He lifted his hand and clutched at the padded brigandine covering his chest.

"Dickson!" She urged.

"To the wall, lads," he said—not with any large and angry exhorting, but with a sudden shortness of breath that frightened Eleanor.

His face twisted in some agony, and the hand gripping the leather breastplate squeezed with greater force and then he slumped to the ground, his legs giving out under him.

Eleanor, closest to him, sank with him, making a frantic grab for him to keep him from falling hard.

Chaos reigned for the next few seconds. Men hollered from the wall, shouting that the English were coming. Mànas specifically cried out to Eleanor, asking where the knight had gone. Daniel and Alasdair had been forced into motion by Dickson's slumping to the ground. Gently, they laid him onto his back. A thunderous noise was heard and felt, the ground vibrating beneath Eleanor's knees, telling of the advance of fifty mounted Englishmen.

At Dickson's side, Eleanor shook his shoulders, trying to get him to open his eyes. Tears gathered instantly for the ashen color of Dickson's face. "Dickson, please," she cried, to no avail. He hadn't been shot at, hadn't suffered any wound. He'd grabbed at the left side of his chest, might have suffered a contraction of his heart. She laid her head against his chest, and closed her eyes to the world, to all sight and sound. And heard, or felt against her ear, the beat of his heart.

"We must get him inside," she decided, her voice breaking, lifting her anxious face to Daniel and Alasdair. "You'll have to carry him. Bring him up to the hall. I'll ready the women within."

Leaving the guards to the frantic business of wrestling with Dickson's not inconsiderable weight, Eleanor rose shakily to her feet and raced inside and through the passageway, past the kitchen and scullery, climbing a set of stairs and bursting into the hall, drawing a panicked and abbreviated wail from Moira.

"Cook, Lucy, Moira!" She called. "Clear this table. Dickson has fallen, must be brought in, tended here."

Ellen wailed, clutching two hands at her rounded belly. "Och and they'll slay all of us now."

"It hasn't started yet," Eleanor told her. "'Tis Dickson's heart." When they only stared at her, she clapped her hands forcefully. "Move. Now. Daniel and Alasdair bring him now. His heart is failing."

They did move, sluggish with confusion at first until Eleanor clapped her hands again and they scurried from the bench and began removing what little littered the table boards, including Goldie's lads.

"What have you for the heart?" Eleanor asked Curstag and Floireans, the closest thing Bowyer House had to a healer. The elder women said nothing but nodded and they, too, rose from the table and left, presumably to fetch whatever herb or medicine would be most useful.

She rushed to the archway to the stairs, where Daniel and Alasdair now appeared, struggling and wincing to carry their captain. Goldie and Ellen gasped at the sight of Dickson's lifeless body.

Eleanor reached for Dickson' hand but Alasdair said sharply and breathlessly, "To the gate, lass. The knight comes with his army. Open the gate."

Her eyes popped wide for a moment, recalling the other calamity about to befall Bowyer House, but then quickly sped outside. She sprinted across the bailey, crashing into the gate, her hands fumbling with the brace, the wooden crossbeam being almost too heavy for her to lift. She tried to get under it, to shove it up and away, but knew no success. She stood at the end of it, and wedged her feet into the ground, pushing with both hands and all her might and finally the weighty drawbar moved, an inch at a time until finally the gate was no longer barred.

Eleanor plunged forward, laying both hands on the smooth wood of the door, thrusting it open and rather spilling into the area beyond when the door swung more easily than expected.

There was no one within sight of the back gate to have witnessed her ungainly stumbling out into the tall grass, but they were close. Figures and shadows moved in the trees fifty yards ahead, the cacophony of this army's coming enough to drown out the noise at the front of Bowyer. A score of mounted men rode into view, many wearing the same plaid as had the knight, Dougal Kildare. She could not find him now in this throng and hastily scurried out of the way of the opening, standing outside the safety of the inner bailey, near the edge of the door as the party rode on into the yard. She hoped to God they were who they said, and that the truth of their intent had been given honestly.

Nervously, swallowing the dryness in her throat, Eleanor drew but little comfort from those aforesaid details that identified them as Scotsmen, their plaids and the few crested shields she noticed. Several of them made a point to meet her gaze, either judging the extent of her fright or wanting to show their brutal battle miens, one meaner than the next.

Recovering herself, though yet speechless with now two different fears, she spun around inside when the last horse cleared the gate, and these men began to dismount. She yanked at the door to pull it closed, which had required much less force to push it open but now stubbornly refused her efforts. After a moment of struggling, a strong hand joined hers at the door. Another hand took hold of her upper arm, not entirely gently, and moved her out of the way as the door was smoothly drawn closed. She was released and two hands were used to slide the drawbar into place.

The man, whom she thought might have been the first man to come, who'd announced himself then as Dougal Kildare, turned and faced the yard, ignoring Eleanor to point at one or more of his men.

"Four stay here. Hold this against any who come," he said. "At all costs. Half dozen out front and wait for my signal." And then once more and without a hint of tender propriety, the knight circled long fingers around Eleanor's upper arm, turning her to march her toward the keep. "I presume you are the MacAdam daughter," he said as he propelled her along. "Where is your man, Dickson?"

"Dickson has fallen," She rushed out, staring ahead as they moved into the house. "Just now, something attacked him, his chest. He is being tended in the hall."

The knight showed no sympathy for Dickson's condition but said in his low and deep voice. "Take us to the roof. Tell me what you can." The remainder of his small army, those he'd not deployed elsewhere, followed them in to the lower passageways.

Her fear of not obeying and suffering repercussions from this cold and savage man far outweighed her nearly immobilizing fright. She began to speak at once, thankful that she spent so much more time with Dickson and the house guard than she did in the kitchens or about any domestic chore. "We've fourteen men, not any of them having ever seen a siege or battle." After she pointed to a darkened archway on the right, she was pushed in that direction and was prodded ahead swiftly, up the twisting and dimly lit stairs, the hand on her arm unrelenting. Her words, all the information spewed, was given with the urgency felt in the speed she was directed to maintain. "You'll want to speak with Tomag, if you should have questions. We've only six archers and you, yourself, can now attest to their exact fledgling expertise." She was a wee breathless now. "There is a store of arrows, twelve gross, at the top of the stairs. A few axes and spears stay there as well. All from the nearby village are accounted for, inside the hall."

At the door to the roof, he halted her with a tug of his hand, allowing the men who followed to pass by them, going immediately out onto the roof, disappearing from sight.

In the brief moment that they did, Eleanor got her first full look at the knight, Dougal Kildare. Even as she understood after several years living in England that her world was tiny, she knew for certain she had never encountered a man such as this. Man. Beast. He was both of these, less so handsome than he was so very sinister for the merciless scars that ravaged one side of his face from temple to chin. But then he was so...vital, so potent of energy, his gray eyes intense, as piercing as surely a wolf's eyes must be. Through the wool of her sleeve she could feel the strength and heat of the man's fingers.

Dougal Kildare released her arm, meaning to follow his men. "We'll handle it from here."

He made to exit the stairwell and arrive at the ramparts, but Eleanor would not let him. She reached for his arm, finding only the sleeve of his tunic, but that was enough to return his attention to her.

"With so few men?" She asked, reluctant to expose her doubt, but then unable to prevent it. There were still more than fifty enemy men lined up out front and this knight hadn't come with more than a score of soldiers.

He seemed to take no offense, or it was hard to tell since his expression was already carved of stone and so pitiless. "I dinna foresee any difficulty, lass."

Her consciousness was fleetingly under the spell of him and his brutal façade.

She would have argued, might have at any other time uttered, *My home, my fight*. But she did not. She would not invalidate his coming by being needlessly shrewish at this time. More importantly, she wanted to be with Dickson, should be with him now, rather than anywhere else.

"I will go to my captain," she informed him. "Should I—?"

"You should do only that," Dougal Kildare said briefly, curtly, "and leave the fight and all its necessary machinations to me and mine."

Eleanor nodded, dismissing his condescension as the device of a stranger. Little fault would she find with the angel who looked every bit the devil, who'd simply appeared out of nowhere to lend them aid against the forthcoming siege.

She pivoted to descend the stairs. Somehow she had no doubt that Bowyer House and all its feeble residents were in good hands, now under the governance and protection of Sir Dougal, a more fearsome and formidable knight she'd surely never met.

AS HE HAD NOT WITH the bonny lass with the striking green eyes and the wealth of russet hair who'd admitted him to the yard, Dougal didn't waste time on introductions atop the wall. Walter, Boyd, and Elon were at the front wall by the time he reached there himself. Boyd and Elon were already firing from their small supply of arrows. Walter was peppering a young lad with questions about which of the residents *could* shoot with any proficiency when Dougal arrived. Upon his approach, he'd already taken note of one stunned lad, more interested in the queries Walter put to another than the bow held loosely in his own hand as the English cavalry rode hard to the gate.

Without a word, Dougal swiped the bow from the lad's apparently useless hand, snarling at him when the lad startled and then looked about to fuss over the thievery.

"Works better when you hang it over the wall and attach an arrow to it," he grumbled, and then proceeded to do just that. He let fly one after another, assessing the situation just south of Bowyer House at the same time.

The enemy messenger he'd flayed verbally ten minutes ago said he rode under the banner of de Havering, and that they had an army one hundred strong. At the time, Dougal had sneered at this, knowing Rand wouldn't have mistaken his estimation so grossly. The clearly intimidated envoy, being naught but a red-cheek lad with doleful eyes, had stuttered and explained that half the army had been set up here for days now, that two additional units had recently joined them.

Dougal now accepted this as truth, assuming that Rand's estimation had been based on the tracks of those late-coming units, and that the envoy hadn't exaggerated their total number. Dougal saw with his own eyes easily one hundred Englishmen coming hard at this house, half of them mounted. Bowyer House, the recently incapacitated Dickson had said. A shame that, whatever affliction had felled the man before the fighting had begun. Brief had been their exchange, but Dougal knew a seasoned warrior when he met one. He would not have objected to fighting alongside that big bear of a man, and might have welcomed his presence if only to direct his own floundering men. As they'd ridden out to meet the messenger, Dickson had mentioned that his unit should be construed as castle guards, with no experience in battle, having been culled from Bowyer's village farmers and laborers.

After he'd dropped four men from their galloping steeds and had now seen the larger picture of what they faced, Dougal was not greatly appeased. This was not an advancing army of five hundred men, with a dedicated unit of bowmen. Like as not, they behaved as did Dougal's army, shooting when time allowed or necessity demanded but mostly being men-at-arms, ready and willing to engage in hand-to-hand combat, which in the end, decided most battles. If they were mostly trained as cavalry, expecting to fight in that manner, they would be disappointed, as Dougal had no plan to send out his own men on horseback only to be slaughtered by the superior numbers of de Havering's Englishmen. They needed first the archers to slim those numbers, to a more manageable size, to a fight upon equal footing or something close to it.

Dougal turned and found the owner of the bow he'd just used directly behind him, watching. Just watching.

"Bluidy hell," he muttered, grabbing the lad by the collar and thrusting him into the spot where he'd stood, pressing the bow back into his hand. "Keep at it," he commanded and then advised his captain, Walter. "Stay here. I'll meet the lads below and we'll cover the front ground." There was no way the pitiful timber wall would hold for very long. He called out for a few of his men to follow him, wanting to receive the English there with a larger number and resolution.

He descended the circular stairs two at a time, bursting out into the bailey in less than half a minute. The four lads he'd bade hold the rear gate whirled all at once at his sudden exit from the keep. "They're coming up hard, too many to fell with arrows alone," he advised, even as he began moving around toward the front. "Hold that gate!" He called out over his shoulder as he jogged around to the front. He spared only a moment to check the front entrance to the tower house, pleased to find it barred to entry. Like the gates—one being naught but an overturned wagon—it would not hold forever, but it was secure for now, which might prove advantageous in a bit, at least as a measure to slow their advance if it came to that.

Approaching the front gate and the charging army, Dougal nudged at the side boards of the overturned wagon, testing its give, but then noticed for the first time that the Bowyer men had not only set the wagon here to close the opening. They'd fortified their improvised device by setting thick timbers vertically into the ground, which stood right behind the wagon. Freshly turned dirt surrounded the standing tree trunks, the timber only standing four or so feet above the earth. How deep they went Dougal could only imagine but a quick push against one did not move the pillar at all.

"Clever," he mused, supposing the wagon would not simply be shoved out of the way.

Facing the oncoming army, only seconds now to spare before they were upon them, he rallied the men at his side to remain strong. "Stand fast, lads," he encouraged. "They canna all come through at once."

And so they did not. Could not. It was a curious affair, one not well conceived by de Havering or anyone in his company. The stockade wall was just high enough that even the most advanced fleet-footed courser could not leap over it. And though the wagon acting as a door was not as tall, it was bulky enough that no Englishman dared to bound over that.

So they came all across the glen in a great rush of speed only to stop with resounding force, horses whinnying and snorting, hooves lifted off the ground with so swift a restraint. And an entire five seconds passed, in which time the Englishmen only sat there, unsure how to proceed. But then they were fairly easy targets for the archers on the ramparts and as a slew of arrows rained down on them, they then did move, the more clever of them realizing they would have to dismount if they stood any chance of gaining entry or avoiding being felled from above. Many rushed to the wall on foot and began to climb while others charged directly at the wagon, thinking it would give easily with so many shoving.

Because the wooden palisade was not solid but filled with gaps, it allowed Dougal and his men to thrust their swords between slats and spaces to attack those attempting to climb. While he did this, he kept an eye on the wagon, knowing when it gave enough, being chopped and hacked at with swords, splintering on one end just enough so that one man could pass through at a time. He hollered out to Boyd and Luca, two of the men on the ground here with him, to shift their attention with him to those coming through and they met them, one by one, as they burst into the bailey.

And now the fight was on and there would be no help in this position from the archers on the wall. Never would they take chances with their own men in such close proximity to the enemy. But this was natural to Dougal, this was the purest form of battle, he'd always thought, this was why he trained his men so rigorously, for hours on end. Neither he nor his men fought with shields when this close but preferred to have their sword in one hand and their dagger in the other.

In instances such as this, in smaller skirmishes, he kept a running tally in his head of the dead. Mayhap twenty would be felled all told by arrows as they raced across the glen toward Bowyer, and they'd lose two or three more, discharged from their steeds when the one in front of them crashed and they couldn't pull up in time and they and their horse literally tripped over them. Eighty remaining, give or take. So now he remained aware of each man driven to the ground with sword or dagger by him and his men here, four, five, six of them. And more who fell, being clogged near the gate and that wagon, easily targeted yet by arrows shot from the battlements, another three or four and five, six more. And suddenly, the dozen MacAdam fighters and his own twenty were fighting against only sixty enemy soldiers. Dougal liked those odds so much better.

He struck his sword into the face of a gap-toothed Englishman whose eyes would forevermore stay wide, and just as he withdrew the weapon, he caught sight of a flaming arrow coming down. At the same time he gave one last yank to remove his sword from the enemy's head, Dougal followed the arrow's trajectory, watching as it pierced the chainmail and lodged in the chest of the soldier just now squirming his way through that foot of space where the wagon had been forced away from the wall. The man screamed as fire lit up his chest and face, but did not move, was wedged there in the opening, his knuckles white as he gripped one of the boards of the wagon.

Walter, that would have been, who'd sent that fiery missile. How he loved his fire in the midst of a skirmish! Oh, and how perfect, that the man's body, quickly aflame, his screams dying with him, prevented any other from coming through that access point.

Dougal wholly expected and was not disappointed to see more flaming arrows flying through the air.

He raised his sword and brought it down on the next man to come through the gate, swiping it across his neck, through chain mail and flesh.

Fifty-nine, fifty-eight, fifty-seven enemy combatants remaining, Dougal amended, as more climbed the wall and were quickly taken down either on their ascent or descent.

A huge and roaring man briefly stood tall at the top of the stockade fence, somehow missed being struck by an arrow from above though a grand target he made for that short moment, and then leapt down directly in front of Dougal. His bare arms were as thick as the spiked club he carried. His yellow hair streamed out from under his helm and he bared his teeth, showing that they'd been file to points.

What manner of beast was this? Dougal wondered, never having seen the like.

They danced around each other, the man tossing his weapon from hand to hand to demonstrate his dexterity.

"'Tis only the first wave," crowed the evil giant, easily half a foot taller than Dougal, as he swung the club one-handed, from left to right along the ground, meaning to take out Dougal's legs.

Dougal jumped up, the thorny club passing harmlessly beneath his feet. Making his knees loose, he moved with more agility around the beast.

"The baron Hastings will join the effort," taunted the pointy-toothed troll, gloating as does a man who expects to prevail. "His uncle is Pembroke, a more formidable foe than de Havering could ever hope to be. Hastings' army numbers five hundred and he bears down now," he said as he delivered his next strike.

The attack was lazy, again one-handed and across his body, but then that was only the start of his intended swing. He swung it high and joined his other hand with it over his head, meaning to bring it straight down onto Dougal.

They lunged forward at the same time, the man's eyes wide with fury as he realized his error, making himself so vulnerable that Dougal simply aimed directly at his chest, his thrust easier, swifter. A crunching sound was heard as his sword passed through bones, exiting the man's back. Neither of them moved, Dougal holding his sword steady, the club still raised over the man's head, their eyes locked. Dougal inhaled the stench of sweat and death and burning flesh as blood began to spill from the mouth of the giant on the end of his sword. At the same time the club fell from his hands, Dougal lifted his foot and kicked the troll off his blade, watching as he fell straight back, raising a bit of dust from the dry earth as he crashed onto it.

His chest heaving, Dougal turned to face whoever came next.

Bluidy saints. Pembroke's nephew was coming.

This was only the beginning then.

Chapter Four

A s sudden as had been their charge, so too had been their retreat. It happened only moments after the troll had fallen,
though Dougal could not say if the two things were related. But
some Englishman, just reaching the top of the stockade fence,
surveying the carnage inside, had called out a command to retreat. His second call of "Retreat!" had been interrupted by an
arrow spearing his neck. He'd toppled backward off the fence.

Hours later as a moonless night descended over Midlothian
like a blanket, covering the glen all around Bowyer house in absolute blackness. Dougal had ordered that torches be lit along
the bailey, in drum barrels near the wall. They needed to be able
to detect even the slightest movement from outside the wall.
Though he expected little in the way of action overnight, he was
not in the habit of giving full rein to his assumptions. Aye, armies
rarely pursued a siege overnight as it was too easy to fall prey
to whatever defensive devices might be conceived by the intended victims in their own home, but he would take no chances.
The English making camp a quarter mile away might well be
sore about the fight they met today; possibly, having expected to
sail right through the meager wagon gate, having assumed they
would at this hour control Bowyer House, they might well be
feeling a wee desperate and then nothing should be assumed of
them.

He had discussed as much with Walter earlier, just as dusk settled an hour after the attack had begun.

"I reckon we've lessened their force by half," Walter had greeted his laird proudly when Dougal had returned to the ramparts.

They'd stood at the prow of the battlements, overlooking the yard below, littered with bodies of those who'd attempted to gain ground near that wagon, which had since been wedged back into place and fortified with stacked wood meant for the hearths and sacks of seed that Bowyer might not be able to afford but which had a good weight and stacked nicely. Beyond the improvised gate in the vast sea of short grass lay more bodies, dead or dying. While Dougal had ordered the archers that any of them still moving should be put out of his misery, he'd also instructed that no Englishman intending to recover any body was to be targeted. He was not a savage but respected the unwritten laws that governed warfare as much as he was able.

"Thirty-seven I counted as dead," Dougal had remarked to Walter, "which means we are still outnumbered but in a better position than three hours ago." They discussed the complete inferiority of the fight put to them today. No archers were employed to wreak havoc on the ones shooting at them; they'd made no plan to actually get inside the fence, previously considered useless but now known as having some advantages; Dougal wondered if it were only a test of the defenses, or if, mayhap, his hostile words to the messenger had merely riled de Havering beyond sense.

"They dinna expect the fight you gave there at the gate," Walter had commented. "Thought they'd march right in. That did the trick today, but tomorrow, they'll come all at once, would be my guess."

"And God help us then," said Dougal, telling Walter of what he'd learned. "One of them, before he was slain, gave up that they're expecting more—and dinna the king, himself, mention the Earl of Pembroke, Aymer de Valence? Aye, it seems his nephew, a baron Hastings, is or was expected to meet with this pup, de Havering, to join their forces."

"And moving on then, to join with Pembroke in his pursuit of the Bruce?" Walter asked, considering the latest intelligence that had been made to them.

"That I canna say. But 'twas said this baron will have five hundred fighting men, if the troll who delivered the news should be trusted."

Walter's cheeks had ballooned briefly before he blew out a troubled breath. "God's teeth, lad, but that we canna fend off." He'd scratched at his jaw, four fingers and his thumb bent to the task. "Might better remove these people to safety."

Aye, it was likely suicide, to stay. "We've orders from our king, Walt," he'd reminded his captain. "Nae to save lives, specifically, but to hold the old Roman road. But aye, we might send out the denizens, herd them off to the north."

"A slipping away is best undertaken overnight, innit? Sneak 'em out the back door?"

Dougal had considered this, chewing the inside of his cheek. "Might they suspect that? Might they nae be waiting out yonder?"

"They may nae," Walter said with some consideration, his brown and gray brows drawn down once more. "They dinna ken that we've been advised of more coming. They'll ken that we expect to manage tomorrow same as we did today. There's no reason to send the folks running."

Having agreed with that reasoning, Dougal had directed, "Send out Elon and Rand, scout the area straight north, all the way to the causeway where we came in. If it's clear, we'll ferry them out overnight."

"Aye," said Walter. "And what of Niall? Will we take him home?"

To Dougal's complete shock, they'd lost only Niall today, who'd been struck down near the gate only seconds before that order to retreat had been called out. Though the loss struck him hard, Niall being a gentle soul with a large family of adoring sisters, Dougal considered it nearly inconceivable that the lad had been their only casualty. Plenty of cuts and scrapes they'd endured but nothing as serious as Niall's loss.

"We dinna ken when we'll get home," Dougal had reminded Walter. "I'll inquire within where they bury their dead here at Bowyer. His sisters will appreciate that he's nae alone in the hills or glens somewhere but buried with in the company of these MacAdams, assuming there's a *màthair* MacAdam among them."

Walter had nodded grimly. "And I've got this now. The Bowyer lads went in to fetch some victuals and ale for us. We'll catch our sleep in shifts up here."

With a nod, Dougal had sent one more glance out across the land, noting how quickly dusk had turned to night. He left his captain and the rooftop and now headed inside, meaning to formally—belatedly— introduce himself to the lady of the keep, the MacAdam daughter. He would also inquire after the condition of her man, Dickson, and then advise that if Elon and Rand gave an all clear sign, she and her people could be ferreted away on foot, to safety. Likely, living in the area, she would know the closest place where they might find sanctuary.

The spiral stairs, which he'd been up and down now several times all through the day and evening, opened up at each floor. He stepped out from the stairwell on the second floor and strode through a short corridor which brought him to the hall. The chamber was not great in size, was relative to the size of the round tower house, was nothing like the great hall at Templeton Landing. The ceiling was not vaulted, and the chamber was not filled with a dozen long trestle tables, had but a low stone ceiling and only one long board raised as a table. The hearth, which split the chamber in two and whose chimney rose straight up and intersected the roof as well, was lit with a small fire, and because only a few other candles were employed, the room was dim and dreary, not unlike those who occupied it.

Weary they were, he decided, their day no less harrowing than had been his, for how unaccustomed they were to a battle brought to their door, for their being no training that could ever prepare someone to sit and wait, to hear but not truly know what went on. At the table sat two very old women, each busy with some sewing or embroidery work, their faces bent over their task, their visages as still as their hands were not. At the other end of the table sat an elderly man, who Dougal nearly instantly recognized as blind for how he sat, his gaze fixed on nothing as he stroked the fur of an old hound, whose head rested contentedly in the old man's lap.

Beyond the table and those who sat at it, two women sat on the floor, their backs to the wall. One was heavy with child, her hand protectively cradling her unborn bairn as she slept in the corner. The woman next to her had her bairns with her as well, two wee, dark-haired lads, one on each side of his mother, both their heads nestled in her lap. Her own head was tipped back against the white-washed wall, her eyes closed, one hand resting on the head of each of her lads.

Dougal approached the table silently on his leather-shod feet and addressed the old women, even as he was aware of the blind man's head turning and following his progress.

"I'm looking for your mistress," he stated.

If they were startled by his coming, or by his speaking to them, he could not say. Both women turned their wizened faces toward him, their expressions unchanged, giving no hint that they entertained any curiosity about who he was or why he asked after their mistress.

"Above stairs," said one of them, much heavier than the other one, with a bosom so large it rested on the table in front of her as if it, too, was weary, and needed rest. "With the captain, third door down."

He nodded his appreciation and pivoted to return to the stairwell.

"Be ye the knight?" Asked the blind man.

Dougal turned back around, closing the distance between him and the man so that he could keep his voice low.

"Aye, Dougal Kildare, sir, at your service."

"And so ye've been, all day by my reckoning." said the man, who never stopped stroking the dog's fur. "That ye, with the raucous grunt delivered with each blow that fell?"

"It might have been," Dougal allowed, knowing that Boyd and Elon, and any other man who'd fought beside him at the gate today might have been guilty of letting loose guttural roars with each swing of the sword. 'Twas something Walter had taught him years ago, when he'd been given leave to abandon his wooden sword and had first started training with the real thing.

See that one over there? Walter had asked way back then, of another lad making a lot of noise each time he thrust or swiped with his sword. *He's working harder, putting everything he has into the exercise, as you will need to do in a fight. There'll be a time for stealth, nae doubt, but when there is nae, exert great energy, more power from every part of your body.* 'Twas all part of his education, something Dougal now passed on to the men he trained these days. He'd since discovered that his most powerful swings or thrusts put him off balance if he did *not* open his mouth and eject a forceful grunt.

Presently, he supposed it should not surprise him that the blind man, whose other senses might be heightened to compensate for his lack of sight, would have heard those death-bringing growls from here.

"And where do we stand," asked the man, "we poor citizens of the absent MacAdam?"

"We'll ken better on the morrow," was all Dougal would reveal, but thought to add, "after we make some adjustments to the inadequate wall." He remarked then on the man's telling comment. "The MacAdam has nae completely abandoned ye, has his daughter here in his stead." He posed the statement almost as a question.

The blind man harrumphed, his thin upper lip curling with distaste. "Nae here in his stead. Cast out, she was, away—dinna want her wicked ways festering in and around his new wife and bairns."

Wicked ways piqued Dougal's interest but only fleetingly before he disqualified his curiosity. None of his business, he decided, even as what little he'd seen of the MacAdam daughter had not given him any hint, nary a whiff, of *wicked ways.*

"Your name, sir," he requested, meaning to change the trajectory of their short conversation.

"Henry Oliver, sir, born, raised, and fought on Man. Reduced to this," he said, lifting a hand slowly, turning it over, as if that explained *this.* "Here now at the benevolence of the MacAdam lass, and God bless her soul."

"Aye, we'll see on the morrow what He has in mind for her and all of ye," Dougal observed. "Keep the faith, Henry." With that, he departed, reaching the stairs unimpeded then and easily finding the chamber to which the big-bosomed woman had directed him. He rapped softly, neither meaning to alarm anyone nor possibly wake a resting Dickson.

When no one answered and the door was not pulled open, Dougal rapped again a wee louder now and then slowly, quietly pushed open the door. The chamber was alight with a golden glow and much warmer than either the rest of the house and certainly the rooftop. His eyes went immediately to the bed, where slept the sickly man. Dickson was pale and still, but neither condition was so great as to be concerning. Next his gaze traveled to the lass, asleep in a large, cushioned chair very close to and facing the narrow bed. The chair looked to have been pulled away from a similar one near the hearth and now was turned away from the tall fire, so its occupant rested in shadows.

Dougal moved closer to the opposite side of the bed so that he could stare directly at the chestnut-haired lass, the only movement of her body the small rise and fall of her chest, pushed by her tranquil breathing. A thick fringe of dark lashes fanned her cheeks, and her lips were without a single crease but softly parted as she slumbered. He thought she might be dreaming, noting how her eyes moved behind her lids. Her hair hung over one shoulder, a long tail falling across one half of her chest. One hand laid in her lap, palm facing up while the other rested upon the arm of the chair, her fingers loose, not quite gripping the arm though they curled over the end of it.

Either exhaustion had overwhelmed all else or the lass was one of those fortunate few who could sleep anywhere and at any time.

He was pleased to examine her for a moment, his gaze slanted with cynicism as it raked over her. It was simply a matter of his own history that he looked upon her with unkind eyes, expecting to find fault though he could not. Ah, but when she woke, he would. She would open her mouth, would speak of petty matters, would reveal her flaws, whatever they might be, would harangue him to save her above all others, mayhap at the cost of others. She would lie and conspire and practice spiteful intrigues, would be reviled by his disfigurement, and he would know her character, would be reminded that the more beautiful they were the more devious they should be considered, self-interested to the point of greed and to the detriment of all they came in contact with.

And this one was exquisite.

And yet....

Wicked ways. Nothing about her serenely sleeping visage implied a wickedness, either the exciting or the evil variety. He watched her until he was befouled with a sense of trespass, for having scrutinized her so thoroughly without her knowledge, for having made decisions about her without her input.

With some mind to permit the courtesy of fairness, he recalled how outstanding she'd been upon first meeting. Her home was being assaulted and the captain of her guard had just fallen, and he himself had handled her gruffly and yet she'd been able to concisely relay pertinent information—as any woman he'd ever known would most certainly *not* have been able to do—without hysterics or drama and with nary a tear in sight.

Dougal cleared his throat, meaning to wake her gently. She did not wake as serenely as she'd slept but snapped upright at the sound as if he'd struck her. Her left cheek was creased where it had lain against the tall arm of the chair and her hair was flat on one side and then mussed on the other, and still she exuded perfection.

She glanced up and down his person, her green eyes widening before they settled.

"Oh," was all she said before giving her agitated attention to the man in the bed between them. She did not touch him needlessly, thereby waking the resting man, but examined his face anxiously before she exhaled slowly and turned her regard to Dougal. She shushed him with a finger to her full pink lips and then stood and rose from the chair, beckoning Dougal forward to the hearth.

"Please, sit," she invited in a whisper, indicating the second big arm chair. "You must be exhausted. Have you eaten? Oh, gosh, I should not have fallen asleep—how could I?—when you and your men must need...something." She wrung her hands together at her waist.

He was not exhausted but he seized at that excuse to sit and remain in her company, refusing to acknowledge intrigue as his reason to not simply say what he'd intended and be gone.

But then she did not stay with him but darted to the door and through it, leaving him alone and a wee stupefied for her swift departure. Dougal sighed heavily and allowed the small fire to hold his attention, wondering what she was about.

And when she returned a minute later, she said, her voice still hushed, though quickened by some excitement. "Oh, gosh, I just left without telling you of my intention. I went to the kitchen and begged a meal from Cook. Already, she's sending up platters to the ramparts and will send along a tray here soon."

She stoked the fire quietly, bringing the flames to life, improving the golden glow of the chamber. And then she scurried about. Though she moved hastily, mayhap governed by nervous energy, she did not tromp about making any great noise. She relocated a small table to his chair side with nary a sound and then poured a cup of ale from a pitcher at the bedside and handed that to him, before disappearing behind the chair, only to reappear with a tray laden with bread and cheese.

"It's...it's a few hours old," she said in her soft voice, showing a little grimace. "Would you rather wait—"

"'Tis fine," he said and meant it. He'd eaten far worse over the years whenever the army was too long afield, moldy and bug-riddled rations, and meat that was naught but shoe-leather. "I canna stay." There was much to be done overnight.

"You don't need to," she said levelly, still whispering, her voice sweet. "But eat now, while it's quiet. And tell me what happens."

She set the tray on the small table and then surprised him by going to her knees and sitting on the floor just beyond the table, close enough to the hearth that she was awash in the warm and favorable light as she faced him. Slumber had painted her in tranquility, a sleeping beauty. Her present animation, though tinged in apprehension, brightened her eyes and brushed her lily-white face in gold, coloring her delicately curved lips a tempting shade of rosy satin.

He'd lost the thread of their short discussion for a moment and so she filled the silence between them.

"I am Eleanor MacAdam, by the way," she said, a wee breathless now. "We've not been introduced," she added.

He nodded, recovering himself from the golden spell she'd unwittingly cast, and sat straighter in the chair, reaching for a chunk of the bread. But he only held it in his hand. "Dougal Kildare, lass."

"Yes, I was there at the wall when first you arrived. But however did you know of our predicament? Who sent you? Or were you following that English army already?"

He shook his head now, answering succinctly, "As I'd stated, we'd been charged with protecting the old Roman road and all the properties along it, as needed." He bit into the soft and warm cheese and continued, "'Twas only guid fortune that had my scout finding the English tracks."

"Eat, please. More," she invited quietly, even as her smile was generous for the wee grimace he'd shown for having talked while chewing. "Sir, pray do not bother with unnecessary comportment when you sit her now covered in blood that I recognize is not your own but that of those who meant us harm."

He made to stand, having forgotten that he was an unholy mess of blood and gore, having not intended to remain within, to sit. Eleanor MacAdam rose up onto her knees and stretched her hand forward. She did not touch him, was not close enough to do that.

"Please, stay," she implored kindly. "You have saved us! You may drip blood on the rug and may even spit out crumbs while you speak, and I vow to you I will not mind."

He couldn't help it and he couldn't recall the last time, if ever, he'd been so overtaken by a want to smile with genuine amusement. Little did he allow the grin to evolve though, being more bewildered by her odd charm and then not unaffected by the magnificence of her solicitous smile.

He swallowed and cleared his throat, adopting a meaningful scowl as advance warning of his next words. "Today was only the beginning, I fear."

Her face hardened, her lips thinning, surprising Dougal for the quick display of anger.

"Oh, those bloody English," she cursed. "They simply will not cease with their absurd greed and want of bloodshed!" Her eyes widened once more and she sent him a stricken glance. "Did any—was anyone killed today?"

Already, he'd judged her and even as he understood that some of his opinions might be offensive or merely incorrect, he was convinced she was a gentle soul. So then he was loath to nod and tell her the truth, though he did.

"Aye, we lost a fine Kildare lad."

"What was his name?" She asked, her lower lip quivering a wee bit.

"Niall, he was. I was meaning to inquire if we might lay him to rest here. I dinna ken when next we'll make it back home." He hadn't imagined that he'd ever exposed his own softness to a stranger, to a woman no less, but heard himself say, "Raised by his sisters, he was, and I'd like to tell them he was nae left alone...but with or near others."

She'd sat back down on her heels and now gasped, her eyes alighting with purpose. "Oh, but of course. We have no crypt here, but the graveyard sits on the hill to the north, between the keep and the village." She laid her hand over her heart, splaying her fingers as she exhaled and showed him a very small and bittersweet smile. "My mother rests there. She will keep him in good stead, I promise."

That was all he needed to hear, adding to his previous judgment of her. She was genuine, he decided, and did not only promise as much to quiet his concern. She was pleased to offer the location, pleased to be of service to him and the lost lad.

Dougal suppressed a yawn, not quite sure why he wasn't in any hurry to take his leave. The bread and cheese and ale had satisfied the greater part of his gnawing hunger. He didn't need to wait on more food. He inclined his head sideways, toward the bed where lay the still-sleeping Dickson. "You and your captain are...close?"

"Dickson is...everything to me," she said, turning her face fully in that direction, availing Dougal to fine view of her delicate profile.

There was something pleasing about a beautiful woman's face in profile, the mystery of it, a greater dignity to it, he imagined, the soft lines flowing smoothly from forehead to chin. Mayhap he only enjoyed this view because it allowed him to stare so brazenly at Eleanor without causing embarrassment.

"All these people," she continued, "here at Bowyer, they are my family, or rather the only people who—" she stopped suddenly and drew in a breath before facing him and finishing, not with what she'd been about to say though. "They are all my family."

"And that'll be next, lass," he said then, recalling finally the reason for his visit. "The evacuation of the keep."

"But we—you—thwarted their efforts today. Surely tomorrow, their numbers reduced, will be reckoned in our favor...will it not?"

He shook his head, considering how to best transport the gravely ill man, Dickson, with the evacuees. A travois, he presumed, affixed to a mare who was not skittish, mayhap one of the war horses of his men, his own perhaps, well-suited to commands, accustomed to creeping stealthily about, unable to be spooked and either turn over his passenger, or take off with the unhealthy man flying dangerously behind him.

His thoughts were interrupted by a quiet scratching at the door, which opened immediately and revealed a young lass bearing a tray. Her tired eyes went round at finding a battle-worn and blood-covered knight sitting so cozily in the chamber and near the fire. Eleanor jumped to her feet and claimed the platters, asking the lass to remove the tray of bread and cheese Dougal had half-emptied.

The savory aroma that came in with the tray caused Dougal to leave off with any polite resistance. He leaned over the steaming meat pies and roasted vegetables on the warm trencher, which also put him closer to Eleanor as she'd resumed her seat upon the floor.

"The truth is, lass," he said next, "there might come tomorrow, soon enough if not then, more trouble than what we kent today. Another force is expected to join this one—five hundred strong if the account be worthy. We canna defend against that many—even if the remainder of my army does arrive from Templeton Landing."

"But then...we should all leave. You and your men as well."

"I have my orders from my king."

"But if there's little hope in—"

"I ken what my orders are," he repeated.

"To remain here? To face an army you've just said you cannot hope to survive? Is that what Robert Bruce said to you? Die for me?"

Stunned by her quiet outburst, whispered though her outrage was, Dougal could only stare at her.

Her expressive eyes fastened onto his, showing a generous amount of irritation. "I'll never understand that kind of sacrifice—"

"'Tis an honor to—" Dougal began, equally annoyed that she would call into question his willingness to die if need be to honor a vow made to his king.

"It makes no sense," she countered firmly, raising her voice above a whisper for the first time. "If Bowyer House is to be lost, so be it, but should you as a man fighting for freedom, not want to live to fight another day? Why sacrifice yourself for a lost cause? Move on, Sir Dougal, if that be the case, and fight elsewhere to greater effect. Do not squander your usefulness merely for the sake of a vow made to your king in so unsettling and unstable a time."

When he could only stare, nearly aghast as he was rarely made, his hand arrested on the trencher, she went on.

"Imagine if you will, sir, that all honorable men think as you do and we lost them, all the stalwart, valiant, indefatigable, and most capable men, those who would fight most steadfastly for our freedom. But we lost them to honor, they having no wish to dissatisfy their king. How careless, is it not?"

Clenching his teeth, he gave no answer, unwilling to school her properly, which would by necessity include having to raise his voice quite loudly.

She shrugged then and said, "Very well, we will disagree in perpetuity on that point. Likely that will prove short-lived, though, since you either mean to compel me away to safety or will soon be off upon your magnificent steed, looking for the next castle and persons to save—oh, pardon me," she said, barely attempting to hide a grin, "looking for the next opportunity to honor your king."

"I-I dinna..." he started and then stopped, never before in his life having been so befuddled and exasperated by a person so swiftly. He couldn't recall a time, ever in his life, when he'd stuttered.

"It's very simple, sir," she said, coming to her feet. "Armies so often fight for the wrong reasons. You are...you are simply amazing, for what you have done. You have worked miracles today where there should have been none and I will forever be grateful, but sir, do not fight only or solely for your king. Fight for freedom and fight for us," she said with some passion, thumping her fist now lightly at her chest, "for all those who cannot fight. Make the right choices in that regard, I beg you, because any sacrifice—your death, sir, should it come to that because you made a vow to your king—would be a monstrous loss to Scotland's freedom." She blew out a frustrated breath. "If nothing else, think of yourself. I promise you your king is not thinking on you."

Much like his previous stuttering, Dougal experienced another first in a long time, he being utterly speechless.

Chapter Five

Well, now she'd done it.

The knight stared at her, his scowl deep, his eyes darkened by distaste.

"I'm sorry," she rushed out. "Oh, I'm so sorry. That was ill-mannered and so very—" She stopped abruptly, quieted by the brutality of his silent regard. He sat with his disfigured cheek facing the fire, which was made ominous by light and shadows dancing in and over the rugged landscape of his left cheek. And yet, despite his scar, despite the present smoldering anger of his gaze, there was a radiance about him, as if the deformities actually heightened how complete was his human experience. Rolling her lips inward while her pulse raced, Eleanor bowed her head and whispered one more heartfelt apology before she moved away from him and the hearth, taking the chair again at Dickson's bedside.

Sweet Mother of God, what had made her behave so? And toward a man she'd only just met, one who'd no doubt saved many lives today? She knew little of the world, but understood the basic tenets of knighthood, This man teemed with those qualities, likely instilled in him since boyhood, that truth, honor, and freedom should come before all else. Eleanor bit her lip, staring blindly at her lap, considering that this particular knight might struggle with gentility and possibly humility, but she had no right to call into question his honor, or the reasons behind whatever actions he might take.

She straightened in that chair and rested her gaze on the sleeping Dickson, her hands curled stiffly around the arms of the chair and attempted once more to apologize. "Pray forgive me, sir. I ought not to have disparaged your...anything about you. I am in a highly nervous state and unable, it seems, to exert proper restraint upon my feelings."

Because their chairs did not face each other, she could not know his reaction to this but felt for certain that his gray eyes must be stricken with fire right now. When he spoke, after a full half minute had passed, his voice was chilly, hardened, all that earlier lethargy gone.

"Perhaps I used the word *honor* too lightly, too frivolously," he stated. "Bowyer House itself is nae important, frankly, nae ye nor these people. Ye just happen to be here. I fight at the king's behest because what he says is true. If the English gain control of this path from south to north, if they are able to move arms and men uncontested, with ease through my Scotland, then nae hope survives for any of us."

He stood from the chair and though Eleanor did not look at him, she heard his sword and sheath scrape against the chair as he moved. She held herself rigidly, yet regretting her eruption, challenging his motivation.

"So many more will die if I do nothing now, here. So nae, I canna give it up so easily. And if I die, I die in the name of Scotland's freedom and nae only at the behest of my king."

She nodded, her face tipped down at her chest. When he moved again, Eleanor lifted her face and pushed her hands through her hair, moving all of it off her face. The braw knight was headed for the door.

"Sir Dougal," she said, a pleading note in her voice. "I only—"

He ignored this, interrupting her. "If my scouts say 'tis clear in the north, then ye and the others will be moved out," he said, staring at Dickson in the bed and not at Eleanor. "Make whatever arrangements ye need, and be prepared— soon, I should imagine. Travel light, though ken ye likely will nae be returning, ever, if it comes to it."

Eleanor opened her mouth but said nothing. The brave knight was gone, had exited the chamber, leaving the door open in his wake.

All the stiffness that she'd been forced to adopt in the face of his dangerously quiet fury drained away, as if a cork had been pulled from her anxiety, so that she drooped and deflated, sinking bonelessly into the chair. Her gaze rested on Dickson's weathered and coarse hand, where it lay above the tidy blankets covering him from chest to toe.

The hand twitched and moved, startling Eleanor to greater awareness.

She sat forward and clutched at the hand. "Dickson?"

Many parts of his face moved. His eyes, fringed sparsely with thin lashes, fluttered. He ran his tongue over his teeth while his mouth remained closed. His brow crinkled with apparent discontent.

"All sounded fairly sweet...for a while," he said, not yet opening his eyes. "I kent mayhap I was witnessing a wooing for how courteous was the knight and how honeyed was the lass...when first he came."

Eleanor spit out a choked chuckle, relief overwhelming any other emotion. Dickson was well. So then she took him to task for his flawed idea.

"A courting?" She asked, the outrage now feigned for Dickson's benefit. "Was your brain addled along with your heart? He's rather terrifying—"

"Och, and dinna let the scars frighten ye, lass." He smiled and finally opened his eyes, though he did not turn them upon the closely hovering Eleanor.

"Bah, his scars are not terrifying," she refuted. "His scars are...are just scars. 'Tis all the rest of him, so tightly wound, as if he struggles hourly or by the minute to hold a beast in check."

"Aye, there is that," Dickson affirmed. "That's how I ken he was a fine warrior. All that coiled energy, wanting to spring."

"But Dickson, he had his fight today and yet was still coiled."

"That was nae fight, lass, nae what I heard all day, nae what he's looking for."

Eleanor frowned, mildly irritated. "Good God, Dickson, how long have you lain awake, pretending to sleep?"

"Only on and off throughout the day," he said, rolling his head on the pillow until he faced her. His blue eyes settled with some measure of softness upon her, even as he confessed, "I ken ye'd drive me mad with yer enthusiastic tending and restless fretting. I dinna ken I had the stamina to lie here trapped and all day hear, again and again, *how do ye feel*?"

"You mean old man," she chastised lightly, "allowing me to be tortured all day with fear. You could have said at least once to me that you were all right and *then* pretended to sleep the rest of the day."

"Aye, I suppose I might have, if I'd kent that," he mused, entirely unremorseful.

"But how *do* you feel, Dickson? Curstag gave you foxglove, said that should settle any ill humors."

"Aul guid, lass," he assured her. "But give this mean auld mon a hand, will ye? Help me sit up."

She did so, with one hand holding his and tugging and the other under his shoulder to lift. She smiled slyly while she did this. "Floireans was here as well and suggested that you might want to *chasten your flesh and cut away not only the fire of sin but the heat of indiscretion*. I assume you will understand her meaning more than I can fathom."

"Cut off her tongue, I might rather," was Dickson's response, not unexpected, to Floirean's absurd admonishment.

Eleanor rearranged the pillows behind Dickson when he was sitting up, until he waved his hand with annoyance, dismissing her. "Exactly what I feared ye'd be about all day, this kind of fussing. Now ye tell me, lass, why'd ye give the knight grief the way ye did?"

"I knew you weren't going to let that go unmentioned," she said, settling back into the chair at his side.

"Do ye imagine that will bring back yer brothers, either one of them?" Dickson asked. "Ken ye'd save the knight from death by goading him to a greater purpose?"

"I was...wrong, Dickson, to have said...anything to him." She rose again and refilled the cup that had sat all day on the bedside table, handing it to Dickson, who might be parched. "But no, of course I did not think that would bring back either Robert of John. And I'm not saying I believe that's how they perished, recklessly, seeking glory and not considering the ones left behind," she said as she sat once more. "Not to say that thoughts of Robert and John hadn't crossed my mind when the knight so casually stated his willingness to die. God's bones, how it used to hurt Mother's heart, how cavalier her lads talked about death and dying, almost as if they went seeking to be immortalized by dying a glorious death. Recall how mother suffered. It just struck me as preposterous, that Sir Dougal—or any of his men—should die for a lost cause."

"Aye, and if it's lost," said Dickson, sounding a wee bit heartier as their conversation went on, "then off ye'll go. Listen to the lad and get yerself gone."

"Are you coming with me, Dickson?" When he gave her a look suggesting she knew very well what his answer would be, she stated firmly, "Then I'm not going."

"Ye're a pain in my arse, lass," he grumbled, "always have been. Ye'll go, if I have to strap ye to a steed myself to see ye gone."

Curtly, as if she'd bristled over his fake rudeness, knowing full well he would not deal well with any melancholy or the exposure of tender feelings, she barked out the truth, "You know you're all I have, Dickson, the only one who cares about me. And you know how selfish I am, so don't even think about me leaving you or you staying, or heaven forbid, you dying. I will neither concede to departing without you nor will I allow you to succumb to some pesky heart ailment."

Ignoring this, as she might have supposed he would, Dickson argued, "Bowyer House is nae worth staying for, lass. You'll be made a prisoner and we can nae account for the behavior of your captors."

"It is not about the house, Dickson," she scoffed. "I'm not an idiot to plant my feet so stubbornly for stone and timber and not any memory worth preserving. But if you won't go then neither will I. I won't leave your side—"

"This here is what'll put me in the grave," he contended hotly.

"Hush. Of course it will not," she said easily. "I will go, and soon, as the knight suggested, and make arrangements for the others, but I'm not leaving Bowyer House unless you do. You're saddled with me, Dickson. And before you get all up in arms over what you might think is only stubbornness, I will qualify my resistance with: if you change your mind and decide to depart, then I will happily abandon Bowyer." She showed another grin. "But if it makes you feel better, I will kick and scream and protest so that you feel you're getting your way."

"Ye're making light, lass, and 'tis nae the time—"

"I do not make light, Dickson," she said, suddenly grave. "Not at all. I listened all day with a sickening and expanding dread to the battle just outside our door. I heard men slay and be slain. I heard the desperate screams and final shrieks and I could not see, so then it was so easy to imagine it might have been Robert or John, what they'd...sounded like. It might have been dear, sweet Mànas or our stalwart Tomag or even that brash and braw knight, Sir Dougal. I trow my heart lived outside my body all day long. I half expected at any moment the wall would be breached and the door thrown open. I expected this very door here to crash open, splintering against the wall, with marauders come calling, brandishing swords, evil spewing from their eyes." Tears fell and her voice and chin quavered. "And how would I save you? I have only my knife and you never would teach me how to use that...and...and how would I save you?"

"Ah, *Jesu*. There now, lass," Dickson said, as gentle as she'd ever heard him. "Dinna fash nae more. Nae more. C'mon now, ye're breaking my heart all over again."

Eleanor nodded jerkily and lifted her watery eyes to Dickson. "I don't like feeling so helpless, Dickson."

He seized on this. "That's why I want ye gone, lass. Nae trapped here."

"Will you come with me?" She pleaded, her voice wobbly.

His thick shoulders sank a bit as he blew out a breath. "Ye believe it's all about glory, but it's nae, lass, nae entirely. But aye, there is pride, and it's how we're trained, lass. I canna die sitting in a bed, canna flee when I have an ounce of strength left in me to fight. I will nae surrender, nae ever. I'll go when comes the time with sword in hand, and God willing, it will drip with the bluid of my enemies. If I can rise, if I can walk, it'll nae be to leave, it'll be to fight. But lass, I canna fight right if I have to be worrying about ye."

She understood now. Suddenly, she knew how and why her mother had smiled, had remained so stoic while her brothers had prepared to depart for war, leading the modest MacAdam army to join that of Anker of Haddington, both Robert and John as insensitive to their mother's pain as had been a very young Eleanor. Caitir MacAdam had not cried at the hem of her sons, had not demanded God and Mother Mary to protect them—leastwise not in the presence of her sons. She'd said to Eleanor once, grimly, despondently—which only made sense now, years later—*I am nae longer only the mother of men. I am a soldier's mother. Those two people are nae the same. I envy any woman who can send them away conceitedly, full of pride for the war that calls them and the fight they give. I am not that woman.*

But she'd pretended that she was for the benefit of her sons.

"All right, Dickson," said Eleanor after a moment, her chest tight with pain. "I will prepare to leave with the others, as you wish."

"You ken where to go, aye?" He asked. "To the monastery up near Newbattle. 'Tis but a half day's march."

"Yes, Dickson."

"They'll receive ye well," Dickson said, "and ye'll get on down to Dumfries and then to yer father when the time is right."

"Very well, Dickson."

DOUGAL STOOD ONCE MORE outside the chamber where lay the sick man, awakened since Dougal had departed a quarter hour ago. He remained silent and unseen, crudely and without shame listening to the conversation within.

He'd only just returned a moment ago, having been surprised to find Rand already returned from his scouting to the north, bearing grim news. Bowyer House was surrounded. Not closely though, he'd been advised by Rand, but enough so that getting the denizens out and away was no longer an option.

"At least two dozen foot soldiers creeping about, that's all," Rand had said. "Just over the beinn and spread out by degrees to cover any northern route."

Dougal had nodded his receipt of the intelligence and had sent Rand off to take his ease for a spell.

The objective of their enemy was thus made known. 'Twas not only to secure the tower house and demesne, but they were looking to take lives. There was no reason to patrol the perimeter unless they meant to execute any person meaning to escape. If the goal had only been to seize and garrison the tower, they should have been thrilled to allow any and all to escape, their task made easy, their work done. Possibly, Dougal's earlier profane message to de Havering had incited him to denounce the charity of allowing innocents to flee unmolested. Also probable, the greater than expected resistance in today's fight had irked de Havering to the point of ruthlessness.

Dougal cursed silently. The war had cooled down in the last few years. He'd thought for sure and had discussed with others how the brutality of it had lessened, that the eager want to simply spill blood had grown old after a decade of just that. But aye, Robert Bruce crowning himself king had rather reinvigorated the English, specifically Edward I, who by all accounts was not long for this world and possibly hoped to wipe out as many Scots as he could before he went himself.

So he listened at the door to the poignant scene beyond and knew all that sentimental talk had been for naught. No one was going anywhere.

His hard heart had nearly melted for how forlorn was her voice. *Yes Dickson. Very well Dickson*—saying just what the old man wanted to hear, sacrificing her own peace of mind, willing to set herself up for a lifetime of agony, wondering how Dickson's end had come, knowing she'd left him, all to appease the old man's concern for her.

Jesu, what people did for love. Dangerous, that, Dougal concluded. Thankfully, she was nae a warrior, to whom such sentiment would prove deadly.

He turned the corner, and only belatedly chastised himself for his ignoble eavesdropping, showing himself to the occupants of the chamber, intent on putting a stop to all the quiet and needless drama between the pair.

Neither quite startled at his coming but both lifted anxious eyes to him. He passed only a glance over the man, Dickson, pleased to see him sitting up, before his probing gaze was pulled with force toward the lass.

Eleanor MacAdam's green eyes still brimmed with the tears Dougal thought he'd heard only moments ago. He studied her with different eyes now. Mother and brothers gone, she'd revealed, and a father who'd cast her off for her *wicked ways*. Aye, the grizzled old man was all she had.

"Ye have yer wish," he said blandly, wrenching his gaze from her to lay it on the old warrior. "They're watching us from every direction, have units planted all about. Nae one will go anywhere this night."

The old man paled. He was a big, wiry fellow who shrank right before Dougal's eyes, his gaze filling with dread as he turned his regard to the lass. The lass' lips quivered, her relief evident as she turned her glassy eyes onto her dear friend. She would not be parted from him.

Dickson's face turned mean with his annoyance, the sickly pale cheeks coloring near to crimson. "Aye, ye got yer wish, and now get gone," he blustered at the lass, flinging his strong arm toward the door. "Go on, then, find me something to sustain me, lest I perish from hunger while yer too busy twisting my ear with yer nonsense."

Eleanor all but leapt from the chair, not bothering to hide her glee now, despite all that Dougal's dire news implied. She bent over the old man, taking his face in her hands, kissing his cheek, all the while ignoring his grumbling.

She didn't look at Dougal as she passed by him to make herself scarce, as Dickson had just further demanded.

Dougal sighed and sat in the chair she'd vacated, the cushion warm beneath his thighs and bottom. He entwined his fingers between his legs, his elbows resting on his knees.

"They're coming through," Dickson guessed, his visage and tone returned again to a man without hope.

"Aye," acknowledged Dougal. "Ye ken we made good progress today and if it were only de Havering's force we faced on the morrow, I would feel—"

"Only de Havering's force?" Dickson questioned.

Dougal nodded. "Another comes to join this one. Hastings he is, nephew to the earl of Pembroke, and thus by way of that relation, expected to be a stronger opponent than this." He'd already explained to Bowyer's captain the larger picture, why Bowyer House's location was so important to the English cause.

"But they're nae here yet," Dickson reasoned.

"They are nae. So aye, there's still a chance we may gain more ground on the morrow. And by that I imply that we might yet reduce de Havering's force more and then, getting the lass away along with the others would nae be an unrealistic prospect." He gave Dickson a pointed look. "It *may* go that way," he qualified, "but it may nae. We canna afford to sacrifice even one more fighting man, but I did, sent out Boyd to that place near Dalkeith where we'd hoped to rendezvous with more of my army summoned from Templeton Landing. There's seventy more men, guid soldiers, to add to this cause."

"Seventy," Dickson repeated.

"Aye, seventy. Nae five hundred."

Dickson sat up straighter and leaned forward, his craggy face suddenly burning with intensity, his eyes alight. "Ye listen here, lad," he urged, his voice tight and low. "Ye vow to me, ye either get her gone or ye...*Jesu*," he rasped, clearly in agony, "or ye execute her yourself. Make it quick. Dinna leave her to them."

Dougal sat up and back, his hands sliding backwards on his thighs, putting distance between himself and the desperate man's want. *Bluidy hell.* His eyes glittered and his mouth drew hard as he stared at Dickson, silently battling with many reactions to this plea, not least of which was shock, though fury and torment warred fervently as well to be noticed.

His lip curled and he swallowed while he and Dickson exchanged defiant glares, hating the man for asking this of him. 'Twas not unknown to him, the concept. And aye, he was a sorry bastard, was considered a merciless foe, was said to have ice in his veins and black iron in his heart, but even he didn't know if he could thrust a dagger into the green-eyed lass' chest.

"There must be some secret tunnel, an escape—"

"There is nae!" Dickson hissed. "Bowyer House is rich for its arable soil and fine pastureland. The MacAdam dinna put nae coin or time into her security. Any investment went to something that would yield returns. His daughter gave him nae return!"

Dougal ground his teeth together and could not say the words, could not make the vow, a flash of green eyes in his mind's eye being a sharp attack to his gut.

"Give me yer knight's vow," Dickson begged him. "I would...but I canna, and if they but see her, take one look at her, ye ken what they'll do, how they'll use her."

He could not. He would not. Blackguard he might be, but to take the life of Eleanor MacAdam? Too long had he fought against the darkness inside him to consider that.

"I vow to ye I will protect her with my life, but I will nae take hers—could nae, nae any more than ye could."

"Ye consign her then to—"

"Nae," Dougal snarled. "It will nae come to that."

Dickson was scarcely appeased, his mien hardened and sour.

Dougal shrugged at him, shaking his head. He barely knew her, imagined no sentiment at all toward her, but he was not the blackguard he'd once wished to be, not in this regard. He would not condemn a woman to be mistreated so cruelly, not any of them inside Bowyer House.

He would figure it out. Tomorrow would tell him more, whether his gamble had paid off, the one that hoped that Hastings did not yet arrive and that they would be able to further reduce the de Havering force.

Chapter Six

Eleanor released an exasperated grumble, having come first thing to the chamber Dickson had occupied, only to find it empty. She knew she shouldn't have let him talk her—bully her—into removing herself to her own bedchamber in the wee hours of the morning. She'd hardly slept anyway, her head spinning with the recollection of every small and mammoth calamity of the day. Pursing her lips tightly, she set down the tray she'd brought for him to break his fast and went in search of him. She didn't waste her time combing throughout the keep or small yard for him but went directly to the rooftop battlements, knowing very well she'd find him there.

Upon pushing open the door there at the top of the spiral stairs, she winced when it banged into someone, and then was instantly put at ease when she saw it twas Tomag, spinning a tilted barrel on the curve of its bottom edge to move it behind the door.

"Och, lass," said Tomag, "Captain says ye're nae to be up here."

"I'll take that up with him, Tomag, thank you," she said starchily as she closed the door and walked around the corner to the front of the wall.

She found Dickson straightaway, standing side by side with the knight, Dougal Kildare, who stood half a head taller than

Bowyer's captain. Their backs faced her, and she looked briefly beyond them when she approached, finding the meadow did not stir with any movement at all.

She yanked at Dickson's sleeve, which turned first him and then the knight. But Dickson was speaking and though Eleanor opened her mouth to give him a fine scolding for putting his own health at risk by obviously not resting, she was not allowed to speak. At the same time Dickson turned and realized her presence, and without breaking stride in his speech, he held up his hand asking her to wait.

Eleanor's frown expanded and she closed her mouth with a snap. But she admitted privately to a great delight to see Dickson looking so hale and hearty, his color fine and his voice strong, seeming not breathless at all.

"Ye ken how they fight," Dickson was saying, "lords, barons, what have ye. It dinna break their hearts to risk lives, having so many at their disposal. We've nae that luxury, do we? These men are kin to us, kent all our lives, and I dinna want to lose even one. But if we dinna take more risks when they come charging this day—"

"I will nae send one man outside the gate, Dickson," was the knight's firm response. "'Tis more than only foolhardy, 'twould be a death sentence."

Dickson argued his point further by way of a story from his own fighting days, the last of those being with the larger Bowyer army at Stirling Bridge. While he went on a about a trap set by advancing men-at-arms on foot to draw forth the enemy—into firing range—Eleanor took advantage of her position to gauge not only Dougal Kildare's reaction, but the man himself.

Truth be told, it was not easy to ignore the knight in morning's light. Yesterday in the bright sunshine, shock at the siege about to befall them had befuddled her enough that she'd scarcely had time to fully take him into account. Last night, the dim glow of the fire had bathed him in soft and sympathetic light at times. But here, in the honest light of a clear morning, with no sun to blind her and no shadows to hide him, she had what she thought was her first true look at him.

She decided fairly quickly that there was no need to adjust her initial impression, that he was magnificent in a dangerous kind of way. She understood there might be some bent toward partiality in her regard, since it was she and Bowyer that he'd come to rescue, but she maintained it was true. He appeared rather thrown together, was not clean-shaven nor dressed in costly cloth arranged with any precision; his hair was long and disheveled, sweeping past his broad shoulders, and was windswept now, the breeze at this elevation waving his dark locks off his forehead and to the right. His face and forehead were not pale but golden and creased by the sun save for the scarred area, which was not the same flesh tone but darker and lighter, corded and knotted darkly in spots. Even without the scar, he would not be considered handsome, she judged—could not be, not with so fierce a façade, so rugged and filled with fury, it seemed.

He was no typical knight, was not what she might have expected if someone had told her a knight will come to save you. He was not courtly and courteous, instead employed lip curls and scowls with as much dedication as gallant knights used flowery words and utmost graciousness. He was a warrior knight, emboldened to protect and defend so much more than to woo and impress. His thick, sculpted arms were bare under a fringe of fur that was draped as a tippet around his wide shoulders, which connected over his chest by leather ties and a large, dented metal clasp. He wore no mail, no helm even, and his padded leather breastplate was aged and frayed, a few of the metal plates visible through slices in the armor, the pieces faded and dull.

Still, no one could discount the absolute splendor of the man, for how capable and strong he appeared. Seasoned, he was, she decided. 'Twas no green and novice warrior, but one who might have seen about every atrocity of war, one who may have been happy to bring much of it.

He flicked his gaze at Eleanor more than once during Dickson's speaking, snapping those gray eyes on and off her with so much intensity that she felt suddenly heated and scoured and then bereft and unseen when he returned his attention to Dickson.

And then, as Dickson droned on yet more, she felt rather ridiculous just standing there. And because the knight looked as if he were only humoring Bowyer's captain, and that he would not be applying any of the tactics Dickson suggested anyway, Eleanor didn't mind interrupting.

"Before Dickson and I retreat to the tower as I'm sure you will insist," she said, leaning a bit forward between Dougal and Dickson, her eyes on the knight, her words quieting Dickson's, "might I be apprised of what goes on here and now? The morning is fully sprung—why do they not proceed?"

Both men gave her their attention, and both spoke at once.

"We were wondering the verra same thing," said the knight.

"I'm nae going anywhere," was Dickson's concern. "And how many times will I have to direct ye to stay below?"

"Do they only await that expected army?" She asked Dougal, ignoring Dickson's disgruntlement.

He lifted and dropped his big shoulders. "One might suppose."

"And you are considering sending out a unit to engage them while they only wait?"

"I am nae," Dougal answered, his gray eyes steady on her. "Nae at this moment, unless we agree on some tactic to overtake the watch they've set to the north." He inclined his head over hers, indicating the rear of the tower and beyond. "But daylight does nae lend itself to covert forays."

"I see," she said with a nod, threading her arm through Dickson's. "Let us leave him to it, Dickson. We should get inside."

Dickson reacted as expected, scrunching up his face with displeasure while he tried to peel her fingers away from his arm. "Dinna be mother-henning me, lass. I will nae—ye dinna belong up here!"

"Do not argue with me, Dickson," she threw back at him, same as he would her were their circumstances reversed. "I belong more than you do presently. *I* can wield a bow and arrow, Dickson, and a sword if need be. Can you say the same? No, you cannot, because Curstag said to not lift anything heavier than your own hand and not to raise your arms above your heart. And since we know you weren't really fainted away near death in that bed all those hours, we both know you heard that as well."

His face turned several different shades of red and he began to bluster his outrage, which Eleanor was determined to ignore and then override. But then their petty little squabble, which had the knight's silent attention though his expression was unfathomable, was interrupted by a call from the other side of the roof.

"Kildares in sight, chief!" Someone called out.

Without a word, he spun away from them and the front wall, hurrying around to the north side. Another call was heard, someone shouting down a command to open the rear gate. "Here they come, lad! Throw it open!"

Eleanor and Dickson exchanged wide-eyed glances but wasted little time before following the knight to the far side. Even as she sprinted across the roof, so high above the ground, she could well hear and *feel* the coming of many, many horses. *Oh, we're saved completely*, she thought with a weeping joy that thrust her against the wall there. A cry burst forth at the glorious sight below, of dozens and dozens of Kildare tartan-ed, mounted men, galloping through the swiftly flung wide gate, one after another after another until the yard fairly teemed with the liberators. Many were forced to proceed fully around to the front, there being little space to accommodate so large a force.

She sent a dazzling and heartfelt smile to first Dickson on her right and then to Dougal Kildare on her left, no words necessary or even able to be heard over the cacophony of noise raised by their arrival. The smile faded, though, diminished in half and then eradicated altogether by their grim countenances.

"But we're saved," she said, breathless and confused, the words spilled as a query, wanting their bleakness explained.

"'Tis nae enough," said Dickson. "Four dozen, mayhap five."

"Sixty-four," Dougal added, his jaw tight.

Another force is expected to join this one—five hundred strong if the account be worthy. We canna defend against that many—even if the remainder of my army does arrive from Templeton Landing.

She recalled now, her delight slain as quickly as it had been born, her expression sinking to join theirs in gravity.

Possibly, their coming would only add to the number of men available to be killed.

"I'll advise Cook of their arrival," she said glumly, but with some pragmatism. "They'll need to be fed." She glanced once more down upon the troop of soldiers and then reached for Dickson's arm again, meaning to wrangle him below with her.

Sir Dougal Kildare of the piercing gray stare thwarted her intention. "I'll send him down first sign of any weakness," he pledged. "We canna have the auld fool up here and only in the way if it comes to that."

Satisfied with this, and gauging Dickson's reaction to be rooted more firmly in gratification for the knight having taken his side, being much less affronted at being called an *old fool*, Eleanor took her leave of them.

She spent the morning in the kitchens with Cook and the others, and even found Curstag there, bent over a kettle in the hearth, stirring a long spoon. Bowyer House was not stocked with any thought to feed so large a number of people indefinitely. Eleanor advised Cook she might well be working round the clock to provide sustenance for so many.

"Aye, and give thanks that we *can* provide," Cook had responded, seeming not put out. "The lads took nae one but two red deer from the forest only a few days ago."

They labored to bring to life venison stew and pasties, both recipes brimming with leeks and onions, the latter seasoned further with bacon. Since Bowyer House had no separate bakehouse, scores of small manchet loaves were made in the bread ovens in the kitchen, the chamber thankfully of good size to allow for extra hands, Eleanor, Lucy, and the expectant Ellen included.

Eleanor's pride in their production was minimized by Cook wondering, "But how long a siege can we withstand, lass, ere they famish us?"

Goldie and her lads stayed in the hall with Floireans and Henry Oliver, the bairns often occupied with Henry's hound while the adults labored quietly over small tasks. Floireans had abandoned her tatting and joined Henry in the making of short-handled, linen-covered torches, which could be dipped in pitch and made into fireballs to be lobbed at the attackers. Goldie, sometimes accompanied by her lads, made several trips to the well and back, bringing in buckets of water to have ready should any fight come to the yard itself, thereby rendering the well unattainable.

Busy was good, Eleanor knew, though it did little to stave off fear. Her mind spiraled from one dark worry to another all morning long, and worry evolved swiftly to panic when the sounds of battle could once more be heard just outside the thick stone walls. She jerked and startled at every crash and cry that sounded, deciding some new tactic was in play by the besiegers, the noises being different than the fight of yesterday.

By midafternoon, the focus of indoor preparations shifted as several hands were needed to tend the wounded as those men began trickling in. They came to the hall, the first one eliciting a shriek from Goldie, which hastened Eleanor from the kitchens. It was one of the Kildare men, with his arms flung over the shoulders of two uninjured men, the shaft of an arrow protruding from his upper thigh. Those two who conveyed him within did not wait around but sat him down at the bench and returned immediately to their stations.

Sometime yesterday, having rather dreadfully expected a rush of wounded men coming, Curstag and Floireans had gathered what supplies they might need, salves, knives, and linen strips among other things, to tend those in need. When asked yesterday what she might do to help, Curstag had told Eleanor in her crusty manner, "Keep out the way would be the most help ye can give, lass." Wondering if the same instruction would apply today, Eleanor hovered, wanting to be near should they need anything, but afraid to interrupt them in their work, about which they went with quiet efficiency.

The Kildare man sat unperturbed, as if no missile had been lodged in his leg, watching with some bemusement as the two old women waddled around him and handled the attached arrow with their crooked fingers. When neither Curstag nor Floireans could manage to wrench the shaft from his thigh, Curstag supposing it was impaled into the bone, the man gripped the short wooden dowel and removed it himself. He grimaced large, his mouth going wide as he drew in a breath through his clenched teeth, before he shook his head briskly as if to dispel the pain.

"Nicely done, lad," admired Floireans.

Catching sight of Eleanor's rapt attention beyond the old women, the Kildare soldier winked at her, one side of his mouth lifted in a crooked grin.

Eleanor's stomach churned and she rolled her lips inward, a returned smile impossible, certainly not when she was quite sure there was skin—or tissue or muscle, something solid—still attached to the slim arrowhead unearthed, which the soldier held in his hand.

"I—I'll be in the kitchens if you're sure you don't need anything," she said to no one in particular as she marched quickly away, and not that anyone today had assured her they had no present need. It was quite easy to ignore the quiet chortle of Henry that chased her from the hall.

Her escape was only a reprieve, though. Within an hour, she was being summoned, stridently, and returned to Curstag and Floireans, who were now overwhelmed with the injured. Two men were laid out on the supper boards, Curstag and Floireans working furiously over one while the other man watched from three feet away, his head turned sideways, his gaze dull. There were others in the hall as well, some already tended as told by the unbleached linen wrapped around arms and legs and one man's head and ear. Others were yet bleeding, waiting. Henry Oliver was on his feet as well, either shuffled away from the table or up of his own accord, speaking quietly with three wounded who appeared to be standing in a line.

"Another kettle of boiling water, lass!" Called out Curstag, and thankfully before Eleanor had been frozen for too long.

For just a second as Curstag turned to address her, Eleanor was shown a glimpse of the man between her and Floireans, sprawled on the board from the knees up, his legs dangling over the end. She couldn't have said if he were a Kildare of Bowyer man or if he were alive or dead—all she saw was blood; his entire torso was painted crimson with it.

She whirled around, choking down a cry of horror, and ran to the kitchens.

As the day went on, Eleanor was forced to acquire a stronger constitution, which was swiftly enabled when she was left with no choice. At one point she was made to hold the hand of a Kildare man. She watched mutely, her face imbued with sorrow, while a gush of blood from his mouth choked out his dying words. But there was no time to make death and dying personal, and little could she offer in the way of solace, for as quickly as they came, they left, either gone forever or back to the fight.

Those with lesser wounds, who were able to take up arms again, did not tarry long in the hall after they'd received treatment but retrieved their sword or bow once more and departed the hall. During certain hours of that very long day, the chamber might have been well served by a swinging door, when it seemed men were continually coming or going.

Suddenly yesterday's fight was reduced to a trifling thing; someone had died yesterday but she hadn't seen it, or him; wounds had been trivial enough that none had sought out the hall and the attendance of Bowyer's resident healers; the noise from outside had not been bloodcurdling; only hours ago she'd stood at the battlements and saw nothing moving in the south.

But there was no escaping today's tragedy. The wounded came from above and below, some having been targeted by the English archers put to work today and other injured inside the bailey, where they'd met with men attempting to gain entry through the makeshift gate.

She felt useless, was reduced to fetching and going for Curstag and Floireans, felt inept even as she was grateful they expected little more from her. But oh, she wasn't prepared, and saw things she knew she'd not soon forget.

And she was sorry that she put more value on some lives than others, that she knew relief every time another wounded man came to the hall, and he was not Dickson or Tomag or Mànas. Strangely enough and most unsettling, was how she breathed easier when it was also never Dougal Kildare coming into the hall bloody and broken.

Minutes dragged and then sped, and she had ceased to note them. By the time darkness had fallen so too had the last of Eleanor's resolve. She felt as if she were made of glass and would break at the merest touch or slightest provocation.

It was quiet now and she wanted only to lock herself in her chamber and wish the world away. Floireans asked her for more linen from which they might make bandages and Eleanor happily seized on an opportunity to remove herself from the hall. She passed by the bodies of the dead, laying side by each near the main door, without looking at their shapes under the shrouds with which they'd been covered.

Her search for clean linen brought her to the chamber Dickson had occupied yesterday and overnight, where she'd stacked a pile of clean cloths with some notion they might have been needed. Woodenly, she paused inside the door and perused the dark and bleak chamber. The fire had since died, the coals no longer glowing orange. The bed was as it had been left, the blankets shoved to one side when Dickson had risen to take up arms against the enemy, against Eleanor's pleas.

How long ago that seemed, since she was here with Dickson, and for a while in the company of the weary knight, when Dougal Kildare had come at the end of yesterday. How quiet had been their conversation, how senseless now, all those words about escaping if given the chance.

There would be no chance, she surmised now. Not for any of them.

She gathered the stack of linens from where she'd left them atop the kist at the foot of the bed and then, overcome by a fresh surge of panic, she faltered, and collapsed, her back sliding down against the trunk. She drew her knees up to her chest and buried her face in the linens, sobbing out her fear and dread there.

She would get it out here, all that she'd held in all day, she decided, and then return to the hall and be once more face to face with all the devastation of war. She grieved for those men gone, people she hadn't even known but who had fought for Bowyer. She cried for her own cowardice, for what little she wanted to see and know. She wept for her selfishness, so much of her concern being slanted toward what seemed inevitable, Bowyer and its denizens falling to the English, and what that might mean for all of them who called Bowyer House home. And then she prayed for strength, for peace, for a solution that saw no more persons slain.

Lifting her face after a long moment of silent weeping, she used the heel of one hand to wipe at her tears and then noticed a pair of boots standing near the door. Because she was drained she did not startle but moved her gaze upward, scarcely having the energy to suffer shame when she found the magnificent Dougal Kildare standing against the open door and watching her.

His eyes gleamed, but it was just dark enough that she wasn't sure if he watched her with contempt or pity. She scarcely knew if she cared but supposed someone like him didn't have time for such fragile things as pity and sympathy. Likely, he would no more accept the offering of such than he would be willing to extend the same.

Eleanor sighed. As explanation for her circumstance and her position, and while she was still unable to rouse any embarrassment about it, she said blandly, otherwise unmoving, "I'm just not...I wasn't prepared for this. I only wanted to...get that out from within." She swallowed and added, "While no one was around to see."

He nodded and his mouth moved but he said nothing. Eleanor wondered if mayhap he'd only tightened his jaw against speaking, mayhap refrained from addressing her weakness.

One more thought occurred to her. And she was just forlorn enough to mention it to this near stranger. "I had always wondered how it would go with me in a time of crisis. Would I be quiet of mind or the complete opposite—I guess I know now." She gave a brittle little laugh, a touch of nervousness devoted to her comment.

Chapter Seven

Though she looked rather forlorn, almost childlike in her distress—or fright or grief, whatever this business was—Dougal decided that she hadn't really been broken by today's ordeal. Still, and though no fire illuminated the chamber, he could see that her eyes were red-rimmed, and her cheeks and nose were likewise irritated to heightened color by her weeping. On the whole, she appeared more than a wee disheveled, her hair long ago having escaped the confines of the braid she'd made, wispy auburn locks drooping around each side of her face; her léine was untidy, both the collar and sleeve coated in what he might guess was someone else's blood; and one of her hands was wrapped in linen, the fabric soiled and tattered. Yet somehow she managed to appear quite exceptional and he, raised at the knee of a fine but tormented and abused woman, let rise undeterred inside him the inherent instinct to protect Eleanor.

Dougal stepped fully into the chamber and reached down his hand to Eleanor. She did not hesitate or question his simple intention but slid her unbound hand into his, their palms joining. Her fingers were soft and cool, and he held her hand without immediately pulling her to her feet.

"Have you injured yourself?" He asked, inclining his head toward her other hand.

The question gave her pause, and she too was in no rush to gain her feet. "Oh, that," she said in a small voice. "No, I just needed some protection against the heat and hardness of the kettle handle. Just a blister." Eleanor raised her face from her hand, tipping it up to him, innocence and discomposure shining brightly in her eyes. "And not the reason behind my insufferable weeping."

Finally, Dougal tightened his fingers around hers and pulled her to her feet. She kept her other arm and a stack of clean linens in her grasp cradled against her chest. Still, he did not release her hand, and Eleanor made no move to retrieve it.

"I ken ye've seen nae war before it came to Bowyer," he said to her. "I would take it amiss if ye were nae a wee distressed. Ye've got the right of it—get it done up here, the weeping fright, out of sight, and then ye get back to what calls ye, what needs ye, a wee refreshed."

She nodded and like him seemed to be in no hurry to put any distance between them.

She showed a wee wobbly smile and her brilliant eyes flashed at him with some spark. "I don't suppose that's how you get on, fight all day and cry all night?"

She was teasing him, he knew, attempting to make light of her own fragility, but he knew no other reply than what was truth.

"I dinna cry, lass."

"No," she said, her shoulders sagging a bit, "I don't suppose you do."

He could not say what held him close, held him rapt, what made him behave so, to be so unchivalrous as to hold her hand for so long and maintain unseemly eye contact with her. He ought not to be captivated by her, certainly not now, he thought, a frown threatening. But he was intrigued, and not only because she was bonny or because his protective instinct had surfaced at finding her so glum, but because she stared so unabashedly at him, and not only at his disfigurement. Her large eyes moved over all of his face and forehead, pausing for what seemed an eternity on his mouth, heightening Dougal's regard of her. Too often, try as they might, people could not prevent their gazes from landing and staying on the left side of his face. But not Eleanor. She appeared to struggle to remove her attention from his mouth.

Dougal was as intrigued as he was confounded.

Eventually, she tugged to have her hand freed, which he allowed. In his lower periphery, before she'd dropped her hand, he watched her fingers curl into a fist, her thumb rubbing the side of her forefinger.

"I ken it seems grim," he told her, "but truth is, we felled thrice as many of de Havering's force. I canna imagine what he hopes to accomplish come the morrow. If that other army does nae show come the dawn, I feel our chances improve greatly with one more day of fighting, certainly with the addition of the men from Templeton Landing."

Just before he'd come inside, he'd stood at the front wall and stared out into the darkness toward the south, over the meadow and into the trees beyond, and judged that he saw tonight no more cooking fires of the enemy than he had last night. Still, Hastings and his army had not come.

"I needn't ask how we fared today," she said next. "The proof came regularly into the hall for attendance." Her lower lip quivered briefly. "Some returned to fight, and some did not. I'm very sorry, Sir Dougal, for the loss of your men."

Dougal had some notion that she'd used the more formal address with some attempt to put a greater divide between them. She'd taken a step back as she'd spoken, had finally removed her gaze from his face. He wondered if just now she'd caught him subjecting her mouth to a similar examination as she had his, if she knew how fascinated—in an utterly untimely and inopportune manner—he was with her lips. Her mouth was curved like a strung bow prepared for the arrow's launch, temptation lurking in the generous pink lines. His enchantment was as inconvenient as it was both profound and bewildering. Inconvenient for its poor timing; profound for how it rattled him, clawing at him to not be disregarded; and bewildering, for she was too young, too naïve, too delicate to have garnered any of his coarse attention.

He stepped forward, hardly able to account for either his thoughts or that action, wondering what provoked him at this moment. He recognized only an intense desire to know if her lips would prove as soft as they appeared, if her kiss would taste as sweet as was her aura, if she were real. He did not examine the why behind it. Neither *why her* nor *why now*. But where the hell had it come from, such an implausible idea? Kiss her? Dougal felt as if he were under the influence of some supreme power, which governed his body as he seemed unable to do, pressing on him an urge to know just one taste of her.

"What are—why are you looking at me like that?"

Desire, always ready to sprout, thrived well in fertile soil, he reasoned. And that was it, mayhap. The fertile soil of Eleanor MacAdam looking at him—at him! At his mouth and his hand a moment ago, not at his scars. She saw him, saw the man who carried the scars and not the disfigurement as being the definition of him, or so he imagined from what little time he'd spent in her company. But he'd met her gaze, had been aware of her perusal, yesterday, today, and not once had Dougal sensed or viewed revulsion in her clear green eyes.

"I was struck—struck I say, blindly but insistently," he said harshly, a bit of disbelief coloring his tone, "by a notion that I might kiss ye." He didn't recall if ever in his life he'd forecasted his want to do so, to any woman at any time—not even when he'd been much younger, carefree, whole and unsullied by war, when the chance of a swift rejection had been improbable. Likewise, he couldn't remember a time that the pursuit of a kiss had wrought such anger within, even as he imagined that fury might be reduced if only he could control the sudden and inexplicable desire.

"Good heavens," was her appalled response. She blinked several times, her gorgeous lips parted in shock. "Whyever should you—why would you want to do that?"

Now declared, now out in the open, Dougal was imbued with a curious freedom of thought. He would never admit it of course, not in a hundred years, not to any living soul, but the sight and sound and smell of her was wreaking havoc on him, on his senses, on his very attentive cock.

But she should not know this, how captivated he was.

"I ken it might divert ye from all this madness," he invented promptly, since she hadn't moved at all, hadn't taken herself out of his reach, away from the very absurd idea.

"No," she said, aghast, shaking her head, her emerald eyes fixed raptly upon him. "No, it will only add to the madness," she said, breathless suddenly. "What has possessed you?"

He delivered another element of truth, taking another step closer to her. "Curiosity."

"You lie," she accused. "Why do you toy with me—at this moment? Now!"

A brittle and mirthless chuckle escaped him. "For the life of me, I cannae say. But 'tis nae toying with ye," he vowed, his voice low. And he believed that, thinking just now that he needed to kiss her to sabotage all the intrigue surrounding her, and his sudden fascination with her.

To him, it was at that moment—or certainly it seemed to be—something necessary, as critical as air and water and life, something he needed and wanted, to know her kiss. In the back of his mind, he wondered if he saw death on the horizon, if he wanted to know one last morsel of sweetness. War made people insensible, fatalistic; there was only now, no promise of tomorrow. Possibly, part of him hoped to be cured of the capricious desire by an unsophisticated kiss. Reasons, rational and then not, continued to swirl in his head.

But perhaps she would finally reveal her aversion and it could all be put to rest. That's what he wanted, he told himself. He took another step, removing the space she'd created by backing up. She'd stopped though, having come up against the kist.

"Go now, if ye dinna want this," he stated firmly, having yet to touch her. "If ye dinna want to be kissed, go now. Run."

"But I...I don't understand why..." she began, and left all else unsaid, a beseeching look in her bewildered stare.

But she did not run.

There was nothing to be done about the predatory gleam that entered his eyes. How they must glisten and burn in her view! They must, he knew, if they were to equal all the twisted and boundless need coursing through him now.

'Twas her own damn fault anyway, he nearly persuaded himself as he captured her arm and dragged her against him. She couldn't be who she was—so damn lovely, spirited and yet so fragile, and with that uncanny ability to see beyond his ravaged facade—and expect that he should possess enough willpower to withstand the temptation that she presented. Her fault, dammit, he seethed internally, meeting her gaze darkly, only inches between them with her bonny face tipped up to his, giving her one last chance to escape.

"I warned ye," he stated as he lowered his mouth to hers. The last glorious thing he saw before he closed his eyes was Eleanor's preoccupied nod as her lids drifted downward.

A hungry groan preceded his mouth slanting over hers. The first touch of her lips was startling for the instant and searing heat. He slid his hands into her hair and covered her mouth, enveloping her gasp, which could not have been surprise since he'd announced his intention, and therefore must have been in reaction to the heart-pounding contact. Skillfully, he tasted her with a slow stroke of his tongue. Eleanor returned the gesture, meeting his tongue with her own, both of them swiftly learning taste and feel, she so unbearably sweet he believed heaven might be just a wee bit closer now.

Dougal slid his hands down, over her shoulders and arms, and around to her back, fitting her closely against him while he devoured her with his kiss. Either she'd been kissed before or she was merely an eager student of the subject, wrapping one arm around him, her thin fingers bent into the back of his hips, just above his belt. She was not an expert, but her passion to be such was nearly his undoing, making up for her lack of experience with her abundance of enthusiasm. Heat curled low in his stomach and further south, while every nerve in his body demanded that he lay her down on that bed and make her cry out his name. He would not, of course, but then he didn't mind throwing what remained of caution to the wind, heightening his own swiftly expanded desire by bringing his hand between them, cupping her breast, lifting the glorious weight of it in his calloused palm. Only when he realized something was off, something out of sorts between them, did Dougal pause.

He wrenched his lips from hers and only a split second later realized what had befuddled him. He glanced down to find the stack of linens she'd clutched was pressed between them, now against the back of his hand. A hindrance, one he might easily have chucked aside, but which served a far greater purpose, removing his mouth from hers, allowing sanity and propriety to rear their practical heads.

He skimmed his fingers down over her linen covered and heaving breast, mournfully watching as his hand fell further and further away. Panting but meaning to regain control, Dougal hardened his jaw and released her completely. He made himself rigid, intending that he should not be persuaded to touch her again simply because her kiss-swollen lips appeared to be calling out to him. Honest to God, he'd not thought she'd have allowed him so much. He could only imagine that she'd been bewitched by the same uncontrollable instinct that had seized him, a want to know a kiss.

Wicked ways, indeed.

Truth be told, the look upon her face just then, as she apparently dealt with her own bereavement for the end of the kiss, almost convinced him to take her again into his arms. And then, perhaps his own recovery, his return to severity, was what prompted her to regain possession of herself. She straightened her spine and snapped her mouth closed, though her lips trembled slightly. Instantly, Dougal regretted most the disappearance of that smoldering, heavy-lidded fire in her green eyes. For one glorious, blink-and-you-missed-it second, he could have sworn he perceived pleasure in her gaze.

Hindsight slapped him in the face, with so much more force than what little he'd exerted to control the impulse to kiss her in the first place. And now, belatedly, came the self-directed fury. What the hell had he been thinking? His nostrils flared as he realized two unavoidable truths while they regarded each other fiercely just now. One, anything that didn't name attraction and desire as his reasons for wanting to kiss her was a lie. And two, he'd be damned if he would entertain an obsession with a lass simply because she was one of the few women ever to not be repulsed by his face.

After that, he could only imagine that if there was damage to any of his thinking on the matter, he would assert that the kiss had provoked it.

For the life of him, while his brain swirled with recrimination, he could show no other expression but rage at his own indefensible, reckless actions. Only much later, long after he'd left Bowyer House and Eleanor, would he understand that his wrath was what she saw now, what made her blanch and appear to be waiting for him to speak first, seemed to hold her breath waiting, in fact.

Dougal gritted through his clenched teeth, "My apologies, Eleanor. I should nae have done that."

Oh, and that was clearly not what she wanted to hear.

A brittle laugh erupted from her and all the rigor left her, dropping her shoulders and her hands from where they still held those linens at her chest. The forgotten fabrics, folded tightly, fell in piles to her feet. She made no effort to stop them but followed their path with her eyes. From this downcast stance, her eyes on the floor and those fabrics, she said to him, "Your greater crime, sir, is in the apology."

Dougal's brow knitted. "I will apologize when I recognize I have erred," he advised her sternly.

With a sigh—of despair or bitterness, he could not say—Eleanor went to her knees and began separating and folding again the linens. In a small voice she said to him, "I suppose regret coming after the fact must concern the kiss itself and is not specifically attached to your role in instigating it."

He narrowed his eyes at her bowed head, trying to make sense of her words, and the fact that she was returned to the demeanor he'd witnessed when first he'd found her tonight crying in this chamber; she did not cry now, not that he saw or heard, but there was a similar glumness noted. All told, not more than ten minutes had passed since she'd first lifted her face and found him watching her from the doorway. Like war itself and so many of its little skirmishes, how swiftly things could change, or be wholly upended into chaos.

Jesu, but her kiss was chaos. Beautiful chaos.

Regret coming after the fact must concern the kiss itself.

Bluidy hell, she thought he found the kiss either distasteful or uninspiring.

"Regret is attached to the timing and these circumstances," he clipped at her, "and for being cavalier—so bluidy distracted—in the midst of a bluidy siege. Dinna apply *your* meaning, *your* thoughts to my words." Regret as well, for tainting so pure a soul as hers with his base desires and undeserved yearnings. He had no business longing for anything from Eleanor MacAdam, from anyone as artless and innocent as her.

A noise outside the chamber warned him of another's presence. Dickson's voice came a second later as he neared.

"Eleanor! God's teeth, but where is that—och, and there ye are," he finished, rounding the entryway, spying Eleanor on the floor. "What are ye about?"

"Floireans begged me fetch more cloth," she said evenly, turning her face to her captain as she continued to refold the items.

"What ho? Have ye been crying?" He asked since her eyes and nose were still red. Hopefully, he would attribute the redness of her well-kissed lips to her earlier weeping as well.

Dickson slanted a grizzled frown at Dougal, about to take him to task, undoubtedly imagining he must have been the cause of her tears. His attention was returned to Eleanor when she released a sigh of exasperation.

"Yes, Dickson. I've been crying," she said tersely, stacking the folded fabrics and rising to her feet, once again clutching the cloths against her chest. "I'm frightened and at wit's end," she continued, facing Dickson, staunchly ignoring Dougal though he stood just beside the man. "I've never before watched a man die—let alone as many as we lost today. I've never had to mop up so much blood and gore and I've never known such an utter lack of hope, wondering if any of us will be alive come the morn. Yes,

I'm crying. Pardon me for needing a bloody minute to compose myself."

If anything should be gleaned from Dickson's aghast, jaw-gaping expression, one might suppose that Eleanor MacAdam had never spoken in such a manner to the man before this instance.

For one fleeting moment, while Dickson's mouth yet hung open, Eleanor looked contrite for having done so—until she slid her gaze over to Dougal and all thoughts of remorse apparently abandoned her. "Regret did not ignore me, sir," she said specifically to him, obviously in regard to his last statement. "Pray hope that it will help us to make better decisions in the future."

And with that, she turned and quietly glided from the chamber, leaving Dickson and Dougal both speechless in her wake.

Until Dickson cleared his throat and shuffled his feet, angling a sideways glance at Dougal.

"I should have ken as much," he said. "She's nae made for this—too bluidy, too foul, too far beyond the prism through which she looks at the world."

Indifferently, his brain still churning over her parting words, Dougal said, "Aye, I'd pegged her as too tender-hearted."

Dickson seized on this. "Aye, that she is." He turned and scowled at the open doorway. "Christ, she fled 'fore I asked what sent me after her in the first place." He did not share this with Dougal, however, but changed the subject. "Your man, Walter, says to tell ye he was going out with the scout tonight—Rand, I ken he's called. He wanted to ken firsthand what sits out yonder in the north. He's determined that we might covertly move these people out if they only put out a post with last night's numbers. With your men come from the Kildare keep, we've plenty to take on a dozen straggling about every twenty yards or so. We can have Eleanor and the others installed at the priory up in Newbattle before morn. Sky is covered in black clouds, canna find the moon. Guid night to travel if ye dinna want to be seen."

Still furiously distracted, Dougal nodded. "I'll talk to Walter upon his return."

Dickson nodded and left then as well.

Dougal rubbed his fingers over his mouth, staring blindly at that spot near the kist where she'd sat while presently he recalled all the wee and glorious details of that kiss, aware that even now his heart still hammered inside his chest.

He hadn't lied to her. He lamented the toll the kiss had taken on him, for making him feel like an incomparable idiot for having pursued such a glorious thing on this day, amid this battle. And yet, larger regret was tied to what had come to light in the wake of the kiss—that he was not appeased, was not satisfied simply to know her kiss, to know if she'd have rejected him, if her lips would prove as soft as they appeared. Nae, he was left wanting more. Regret, then, was knowing that one kiss was simply not going to be enough.

But aye, Dickson was right. They should be able to move the innocents out from Bowyer House shortly.

Blowing out a harsh breath, and giving himself a mental shake, Dougal left the chamber as well, meaning to make arrangements to send Eleanor away in the night.

Chapter Eight

Hours later, Eleanor was yet bewildered. Her nerves still sang and sprang inside her body, and she could no more ignore the kiss than she could contemplate thoughts of any other thing, not even the war that sat waiting just outside the gate. Still and foremost—and overriding the kiss itself, how it had intoxicated her—she wondered what had possessed him. What had occasioned the very idea? Why had he acted on it? Was it truly as he'd so blithely admitted, simply a means of diversion? Had he meant only to divert her from the melancholic state in which he'd found her?

She could imagine no answer to any of the questions swirling in her head—another repercussion of his kiss, that it raised so many more questions than it solved. And all this turmoil managed to find life inside her head even as her day was not yet done. She'd returned to the hall, finally presenting those requested linens to Floireans, who'd strangely made no mention of the delay, and then helped Moira with tidying up the hall. There was no formal meal served but a light repast shared with those wounded inside the hall and more delivered to the guards at their posts.

The southern wall, the front of Bowyer house, naturally was attended by more men-at-arms than the northern, rear wall. These were mostly Kildare men, leaving Eleanor to wonder briefly if Bowyer's untested soldiers had been rather shuffled out of the way of the men with greater experience. Possibly she found her answer when she spied, among other Bowyer men, Tomag and Mànas on the less crowded northern side. She had thought of them during the day, had been at times beset with worry over them, and thus could not prevent the wide, relieved smile she showed to them as she delivered a tray of bread, cheese, and roasted game hens.

"Must I not have thought that the blessed Lord heard me," she asked of these familiar faces, "when I prayed all day for your safety?"

"Sure and will ye nae be back at it on the morrow, lass?" Asked Tomag.

Mànas shrugged, wrestling meat from the fowl's bone with his teeth, appearing to discount the effectiveness of her prayers. "Nae much happens on this side, lass. We can hear it all behind us but have our orders, nae to leave our posting, nae to take our eyes off the landscape beyond the wall."

"But isn't that most difficult?" Eleanor wondered. "Being so close but unable to see or know what transpires? Perhaps hearing sounds that cry for help, and not moving to assist?"

Tomag, his hands filled with wedges of bread and cheese, spoke around what food already had found its way to his mouth. "Any previous dereliction might only have seen a cuff upside the head from Dickson and are we nae accustomed to that?" Tomag guessed. "But if we err now, we risk the knight's wrath or that of his man—Walter of Sandsting, he is, who rather makes Dickson seem pleasant by comparison—and then, as well, grievous harm if we cede any leverage to the English on this side for our inattention or carelessness."

"Dinna seem right, though," added Rob, one of the younger Bowyer lads, normally an apprentice to the smithy when no siege was underway, "those men fighting for our Bowyer."

"But they *can*, Rob," Eleanor remarked. "They are soldiers by profession. This is what they do. Leave that business to those who can." She did not disparage either their integrity or their worthiness by adding that likely the Kildare army would and will better defend Bowyer than its own men could.

"Aye, Dickson said just about the same," Mànas told her. "Said we stand a better chance, anyhow, with the Kildare men leading the fight."

There, so they were under no illusions then.

"Please just stay safe," she said before taking her leave of the ramparts, the tray quickly made empty by all the hands digging into it.

She ate her own supper in the kitchens, just as Cook and Lucy were tamping down fires and wiping down counters.

"I dinna ken I can do another day like this, lass," Cook cried, her eyes round while exhaustion was etched heavily in lines and dark circles beneath them. "Crashing and booming and all those men dead and I'm expected to carry on as if the sky were nae falling every hour of the day, as if the rosemary slathered all over the hens is as vital as life."

"But what else can we do?" Eleanor asked, sensitive to her fraught nerves, having suffered a minor collapse herself earlier. "We cannot leave but then we cannot give up. We take it minute by minute and hour by hour." She included the curious Lucy in her comments, intending to be the voice of reason and reassurance even as she wasn't sure she'd earned the right or had the proper mentality for it. "Look what we've done already, survived two days of a siege not any of us thought we'd see past the first hour. Cry when you need to, Cook. I have. And then we get up and get about our business. Unless we mean to give up, we must not give in."

Little appeased was the woman, was Eleanor's take on her sour reaction, snorting out her disagreement before she turned her back on Eleanor, addressing some task at the bread ovens.

Lucy offered Eleanor a commiserating smile. "She dinna want reason, lass," Lucy was bold enough to say within Cook's hearing. "She simply wants to give voice to panic."

"No harm in that," Eleanor commented. "And yet, still we must march on, the alternative being so much less appealing."

"And if it comes to that—" Cook called out, hastily turning around.

"We'll deal with it," Eleanor interjected with firmness. "*If* and *when* it comes to it, but don't give rein to such cynicism now, Cook. Rue the present, indeed, but pray do not look beyond the hour and the day. We simply cannot afford it."

Later, alone in her chamber, while she washed away the grime and filth of the day, she was again revisited by the kiss Dougal Kildare had given her. Given her? No, he had not merely given her a kiss, had not only joined his mouth to hers. He had not given, he had taken, and quite expertly. He had devoured her, had left her weak-kneed and craving more.

How strange, she mused, that so momentous a thing as the knight's drugging kiss should occur during so desperate and horrific an event as Bowyer being under siege. She almost thought it unfair, but she did not know if she should be irritated with Dougal Kildare for kissing her now, during this tragic time, or if she should be angry with the English for having upset so gorgeous a kiss with their dastardly assault.

It was, she reflected as she wiped the warm and wet cloth over her face and neck, nothing like the only other kiss she'd ever received. *The incident*, it had promptly been labeled by her stepmother, that villainous creature.

That kiss, administered by a hapless lad named Richard Scrope, and in answer to Eleanor's transparent encouragement, had been both a catalyst for her banishment from Northumberland, where she'd lived most of her life, and then so thoroughly disappointing for all that it was, clumsy and wet, and overrun by the foulness of the lad's breath, that in hindsight she thought the trade a further injustice. Essentially, she'd earned her own exile for a most vulgar and disappointing experience.

Why she'd sought out a kiss, or more specifically Richard Scrope's kiss, was a hotly debated account inside her head since that day more than two years ago. His attention had come on the heels of first, her mother's passing, and then her father's swiftly achieved marriage to Leticia Crumb, when his first wife surely hadn't yet been cold in the ground. In the uproar of both occasions, happening within weeks of each other, Eleanor had been, or had felt, forgotten, almost as if she'd been misplaced during the confusion. Even before her banishment she'd been made to feel like an outsider looking in, upon her own home, but from outside the new configuration of a different family. Suddenly, her stepmother lived in chambers where lingered still the scent of her mother; Eleanor felt lost as the oldest but least loved daughter of the house, her father's second wife bringing with her three daughters of her own, prettier, more accomplished and with greater dowries than Eleanor would ever be given; her father, never having been an overly attentive patriarch, this lessened in degrees by the loss of his sons and then his wife, had little interest in Eleanor, not even as his only living offspring.

She hadn't thought herself in love, couldn't say now if she even fancied the lad. But she was curious and she had been made lonely and disaffected by all the changes in her life, none of them for the better. She'd come to understand that her pursuit of Richard, if it should be termed as such, had only been her young heart seeking love and fulfillment. She might have found it anywhere, if her stepmother had any capacity to love, if her father had extracted greater pleasure from the company of his daughter, if she'd been allowed to be friendly with servants....

Anyway, Eleanor hadn't considered it as grand a disgrace as it had been made. 'Twas only that her stepsister, Edwina—having far too much of her mother's character, including a pattern toward dramatizing things to paint herself a victim—had witnessed the kiss and had gone running to her mother. In tears! As if she herself had been a party to the awful kiss and would forever be scarred by it.

Eleanor would never believe otherwise that the incident hadn't been overblown, eagerly seized upon by Leticia as an excuse to be rid of her. Her stepmother had wanted her gone, had called her wee indiscretion something far greater, had labeled her a whore, unfit to be in the company of her own daughters, claiming Eleanor's influence should now be considered faulty and scandalous. She'd wanted her gone and had convinced Eleanor's father that if he wanted a happy life, he needed to make her gone. And so he had.

Eleanor took a few moments to scrub her hands thoroughly in the basin of water she'd brought to her chamber. Not for the first time today, she realized that there was no way to compare that kiss from Richard to this kiss from the knight, Dougal Kildare. The two things were not comparable in any way, either in form or fashion, or in consideration of the parties concerned. Richard Scrope had been a handsome youth with a sometimes engaging manner, though he'd made a bitter habit of speaking to her as if she were younger and much less clever than she actually was. Far removed from that age and that episode in her life, Eleanor understood now he'd been most happy when preening before her, speaking of himself and his own accomplishments—*combing his own feathers*, her mother would have said. Rarely had he asked or had they discussed Eleanor. The disillusionment of his foul kiss, when finally it came—the subsequent punishment notwithstanding—had rather cured her of any imagined infatuation.

But Dougal Kildare's kiss...well, that was altogether different. 'Twas not foul or unsophisticated, and for the life of her, despite turmoil all around, she could not quite regret her part in it, even as she didn't quite understand why he might have done it. Having for years assumed that all kisses might only be as unappealing as Richard Scrope's, Eleanor was ready now to joyfully revise her opinion, having been enslaved and undone by Dougal Kildare's kiss. That, she knew now, was what a kiss should be. More than that, she supposed, if a kiss was intended to make you forget yourself, where you were, what happened around you, how to breathe.

She dried her hands on a clean cloth upon the cupboard in her bedchamber and released a sigh, admittedly dreamy, allowing herself these quiet moments to enjoy her recollection of their kiss, knowing she might have few occasions to know any other joy in the coming hours or days.

And then, as if mere thoughts had conjured him, a knock sounded at the door she'd left ajar, and Dougal Kildare asked if he might enter.

"Yes, please," she said levelly, even as her heartbeat was quickened by just the sound of his voice.

He stepped inside, around the door, and after a fleeting glance at her, Dougal moved his gaze around the chamber. He would presume it to be her own, which of course it was, but then his quick but slight frown might be wondering why it bore no mark of ownership, showed not one personal effect. Eleanor rarely thought of it specifically these days, but knew when first she'd come, having been cast out after the Richard Scrope incident, she'd thought her exile would only be temporary, that she would be recalled to the only home she'd ever known. Thus, she'd intended to plant no roots here at Bowyer House, had not personalized any part of it, and the knight saw only a sparsely furnished space, containing a narrow bed with thin blankets, not more than a pallet since it laid on the floor; a small desk for writing letters that had never been answered sat under one window; pegs had been pounded into timber columns that marked every six feet of space around the exterior wall, those dowels filled with the few gowns she called her own, those which she hadn't outgrown over the last couple years; and the cupboard where she performed her morning and evening ablutions, where sat an ewer and basin. There was nothing of herself and no softness, no tapestries, rugs, or furs to chase away the cold, no other chest or cupboard where were hidden any secret treasures, since she had none.

It was a short few seconds while he perused her chamber, but Eleanor allowed herself the same opportunity to study him. Specifically, she was searching for something in his façade that should have warned her how beautifully and seductively damaging his kiss would be. There was nothing glaring, nothing that smacked her in the face. He was big and bold, larger than life in appearance, in truth he appeared utterly wild, which perhaps should have been the telling thing. His manner certainly had given no clue—he was stingy with words and employed scowls with unerring frequency, was unrefined enough to have made the reply he had to the English messenger about what to do with that scribbled parchment of terms, and had been crass enough to have dared a kiss in the first place. He should not have been able to weaken her knees merely by kissing her. At least he didn't look as if he should.

Heated and pinkened cheeks might well become a regular thing if he remained too long at Bowyer—if they lived long enough. A flush warmed her cheeks now, realizing her study of him had outlasted his of her bedchamber, and he was simply staring at her as if he might have been apprised of her ponderings, as if he only waited until she'd finished with them. One of his dark brows was lifted ever so slightly into his faintly lined forehead.

Eleanor cleared her throat but then had her attention arrested by the transiently sheepish look about the knight's ravaged face, which heralded his address to her.

"We'll speak nae more of...what happened earlier," he said, seeming to imbue his words with more force than was necessary, as if he supposed she might have wished to address this newest *incident*, as if he expected that she would want to argue his directive. He followed that up with, "I erred. I apologized. It will nae happen again." This was delivered not directly to her, since his gray eyes had dropped.

Realizing he was looking at her nervously clasped hand, she uncurled her fingers, which then lifted his probing gaze to her.

It will nae happen again.

She was bold sometimes, she reckoned. By her recollection, she'd kissed Richard Scrope of her own accord, had sought out that encounter purposefully, mayhap or partly because she'd believed herself a wee infatuated with him. She'd made a life here at Bowyer for herself, with strangers its denizens had been to her when she'd come, without family beside her, had found some measure of happiness and indeed satisfaction in her life; she'd laid her hand over the open eyes of a Kildare man today and lowered his lids, touching a dead person for the first time in her life; she'd held two sides of sliced flesh together so that Curstag could sew the skin back together. Aye, she was sometimes imbued with mettle greater than what people might perceive of her. But she wasn't in this moment instilled with enough courage to ask him why it wouldn't or couldn't happen again.

But then, her reluctance to do so might have something to do with fear of rejection. Still, she had to bite her lip to keep from voicing any words to contradict what seemed to be a new rule of law laid down by the knight.

Oh, but she wanted to. She would beg for more, even, if she were brave enough, beg for all that he would give her. If they were bound to die, and that seemed more likely now, she would crave only beauty and joy before she went. If she were destined to die and soon, she would want first to know more of the pleasure of his touch, or a union with someone, a connection—even a meaningless one—would not want to die having not quite lived.

He could give it to her, she guessed, splendor, joy, a bond.

This jumble of thoughts had not occurred only in a split second as they sometimes did. Eleanor thought five, maybe ten seconds had passed before she realized he might actually be waiting on a response from her. He wanted a nod, or some form of assent, but for the life of her she couldn't do it. Boldness, that, which only grew, and she found herself actually beginning to shake her head very slowly while he chewed her up with his gaze.

His mien darkened at her reluctance to submit to his edict. His nostrils flared and he took a step further into the chamber.

Eleanor held her ground, almost hoping she'd provoked him to kiss her again.

But he took only that one step before it seemed he caught himself and planted his feet firmly.

And then dismissed the subject altogether.

"Otherwise, I came to say that any hope of ferreting you and the women and bairns out from the keep has been squashed," he said.

His glittering eyes were fixed on hers so severely that she might have supposed he cautioned himself against looking at any other part of her.

"I see," she said, but she did not since he hadn't explained the why of it. She wasn't displeased, however, still neither eager nor keen to leave Dickson and the Bowyer men behind.

As if she had questioned his reasoning, Dougal explained, "All but several units of Hasting's force have come. They've increased the watch in every direction. Even with the advent of my own men, we cannae risk moving the most vulnerable outside the wall."

Oh. Her heart dropped to her belly. Eleanor laid her hand over her midsection. "And tomorrow or perhaps by the next day, we will face the entire Hastings force? Five hundred strong, you believe."

Dougal nodded, his jaw tight, still or again. "But all hope is nae lost," he said. "Every night, God willing, we will still have the opportunity to consider getting you and the others away. So long as we hold the gate, that option remains viable. Once the gate and walls are breached finally—and they will be eventually—that is nae longer an option for us."

"And by then it will be too late anyway, correct?"

He refused to commit to an answer, unless she might read anything from his grim expression.

"But surely women and children will not be..." she started and then stopped when his mouth pursed with more severity. "Oh, we are not safe," Eleanor presumed. "They will not practice civility? Will Goldie and her lads and Curstag and Floireans, and poor Henry Oliver be subjected to the ravages of war?"

"It's simply nae a chance either Dickson or I are willing to take," he said, giving no firm evidence in his belief. "If it were Pembroke himself advancing, we might count on such courtesy, but his nephew I dinna ken by either name or reputation. Or, if their terms of surrender had included provisions for you and the civilians to vacate—why does that make you smile?"

Ill-timed laughter bubbled up in her throat. She couldn't help it. How ridiculous she was! Unable to curtail her inappropriate amusement, she asked of him, "Mayhap if the terms of surrender had been considered—or perused, at the very least—before they were shoved up someone's behind, we might know what they would have been?"

A warm smile lit up his face.

Eleanor was captivated, even as she supposed he might be as surprised as her by his own reaction.

Though he was a dynamic man, his countenance was not beautiful, but severe and pensive, downright monstrous some might say. He was set alight with a vitality and intensity that seemed to heighten one's awareness of his person, but so much of his surely once handsome façade was reduced by the wreckage of fully one half of that precious flesh. And yet, when he smiled, when he flashed those white teeth, he was at that moment very handsome, so much less a monster.

"I will nae be fetching it, lass," he quipped, "if that's what ye'll be asking."

"Well, you did—essentially—give the order to put it there."

"And there it will stay."

Eleanor's smile remained.

Before he had kissed her today, she could have said with certainty that the idea had never occurred to her that he might or that she would like him to. But earlier he *had* kissed her, had shown her a wee bit of heaven, and now he smiled at her, and Eleanor teemed with a new certainty that she wanted him to kiss her again.

And yet, much like the unfortunate timing of the kiss, even this lightness felt so misplaced during so great an upheaval, certainly with the news he'd just shared, that a larger army came, thus reducing their chances of survival. Her smile faded.

Mayhap he read her mind.

"It's nae improper, a wee smile," he counseled, "even now. We seize on whatever we might to cope with the stresses of the day."

"But not a kiss?" She boldly challenged, finally managing to make proper mention of it, and only because he'd skittered around it with his first words to her tonight. "A kiss is misplaced amid the atrocities of today," she remarked. "You said as much."

"Aye," he acknowledged, taking another step into the chamber, "and for the reason stated, because it's too damn distracting. I canna have my head beguiled by your kiss so that all other considerations are pushed aside or are given so much less attention."

She nodded, not willing to give voice to more thoughts on the subject, afraid if she opened her mouth again, she might argue against his logic, in essence for another kiss.

Nevertheless, she was made spellbound by his words. *Beguiled by your kiss.*

Dougal took another step closer to her. "Eleanor, I dinna want ye to—"

He stopped, jerking his head to the right, toward the door, where came noises of someone's swift approach.

Dickson came only seconds later, bursting into the chamber. He was followed by the Kildare captain and both men wore matching and decidedly lively grins.

"*Jesu*, lad," said Walter of Sandsting, after a quick nod at Eleanor. "Ye will nae believe who comes." He said no more but hitched his thumb over his shoulder at the open portal. "Found this one banging on the postern gate, as if Bowyer House were open to weary travelers."

In through the door came a man about the size of Dougal Kildare, with black-as-pitch hair and eyes that sparkled and undoubtedly bedeviled, being that he was the most handsome man Eleanor had ever seen.

Her eyes widened at the same time Dougal barked out a stunning chuckle and exclaimed, "God's bluid! The devil has come to save us."

Chapter Nine

"Bluidy hell, but ye're a sight—scarcely expected but so verra welcome," Dougal said to his long-time friend, eagerly pulling Caelen MacFadyen into a tight bear hug. "Tell me, I beg ye, that ye travel with your full army."

Caelen showed a broad grin when they parted. "Ye ken I dinna leave Turnberry without them. We've been trailing Hastings for nigh on a week, assuming they'd lead us to Pembroke, and that we could either waylay them in their efforts to find the king, or simply annihilate Hastings' force ere they could."

Dougal blew out a relieved breath, fully appreciating the good fortune and timeliness of this encounter. Aside from the king himself, there were few chiefs he would wish at his side at a time such as this. Caelen MacFadyen, with whom Dougal had fostered as lads under the tutelage of Alexander of Menteith when that man was the Sheriff of Dumbarton, sat nobly at the top of such a list. He'd only just spent time with Caelen at the king's coronation but had thought he'd understood that Caelen had other plans upon his departure from Scone. "I ken you were headed further south."

"Sure and that was the plan," said Caelen, who looked as hale and hearty as ever. "But then ye ken I'm nae one to rebuff any opportunity to gainsay English plans. We only stumbled upon Hastings and his army but imagined them up to nae guid, moving north as they were." He cocked his thumb at Dougal's captain, rapt with attention and excitement at Caelen's side. "I said to Walt we'd been dogging Hastings, had a full-on skirmish yesterday. What has come of Hastings' army—Walt says mayhap three or four units only arrived tonight—that's all that's left after we finished with them."

Dougal was yet befuddled with the godsend of his coming, his smile unmovable.

Caelen continued, "My sense is they're going to pull de Havering into their fold and make for Pembroke's gathering. Ye and I will likewise join forces and shadow those bastards—pardon, lass," Caelen murmured, presenting one of his mercurial grins to Eleanor before returning his regard to Dougal, "until they've got Robert Bruce in their sights ahead of them and no escape but only us behind them."

His acknowledgment of Eleanor recalled her silent but attentive presence to Dougal.

"Eleanor MacAdam, meet Calen MacFadyen, knight of the realm, mormaer of Turnberry Castle," he said, moving his hand from one to the other. "This is Bowyer House, a MacAdam parcel, which you've just saved from near-certain ruin, my friend, or from a merciless occupation at the least."

Dickson, at Dougal's side, clapped him on the back, his thrill palpable, his grin as wide as any other.

"Rest easy now, lass," Caelen said briefly, his tone light, adding a wink in her direction and saying, "The MacFadyens have come to save the day."

Though the urge was strong, Dougal refrained from rolling his eyes. 'Twas not unexpected, such behavior from Caelen, but he wasn't sure he wanted his friend practicing his skill on

Eleanor. Because he was gifted with an enviable handsomeness and an abundance of effortless charm, Caelen turned heads with alarming ease. Though he had never said as much, Caelen was miserably married, Dougal believed, though he didn't know if that meant he was faithful or not to the woman. Having once met the man's wife, Dougal couldn't imagine that Caelen—that anyone!—could be happily wed to the wretched woman. And because Caelen was often *too* eager to pursue fights and battle with the English and never expressed any desire to reunite with his bride, Dougal thought he had the right of it: the man would risk disease, dismemberment, and death rather than return to his bride.

Dougal's jaw hardened. He meant to stake no claim on Eleanor—on any woman!—but damn, he didn't want her head turned by Caelen MacFadyen, was not sure he could stomach being a spectator to that.

"Truly, sir," said Eleanor, her eyes bright with relief, "'tis an honor. Your timing could not have been any more favorable." As if an afterthought, she lifted her hand before Caelen's attention might have been transferred to another, quickly adding, "Sir Dougal was our first godsend, of course, and has fought admirably, valiantly to keep us safe. Sure and certain, sir, we'd have been overtaken on that first day without his timely arrival as well."

Her wording, how quick she was to alleviate Dougal of any sense of failure, might have spoken volumes to certain ears. It was quite clear she wished it to be known that she did not devalue his efforts, and wanted others to think well of him also. One might, if they were of a mind, read much into that.

Dickson might have, if anything should have been made of his suddenly narrowed eyes, passing over first Eleanor and then Dougal, as seen out of the corner of Dougal's eye.

Dougal promptly brought the matter back to the fight. "How are they going?"

"*Jesu,* they're nae light," said Caelen, shaking his head, "having artillery and machines, loaded down with foot soldiers and cavalry, but damn if they dinna move fast. They ken the land well, moved swiftly over hill and glen, crossing burns and traversing gorges with relative ease."

"That dinna bode well for us," Walter remarked.

Despite the noted admiration in his own words, Caelen shrugged. "They canna move as we do, which was why we did eventually catch up with them. And fighting as they did, eyes toward retreat and nae the enemy at hand, indeed bodes well for us." He paused then, and while the others in attendance gave weight to his words, Caelen glanced around, seeming to realize for the first time that they stood inside someone's bedchamber. One perfect black brow arched upward and he considered Eleanor with a critical eye before turning his regard to Dougal.

And he was just enough of a bluidy demon that one corner of his mouth turned up into a smirk while sparks of mischief danced in his eyes. "Have I or we interrupted something?"

Dougal favored him with an unamused glare while Eleanor readily assured Caelen that he had not.

"Not at all," she said, too swiftly and with pinkening cheeks, so that Caelen's smirk increased as did Dickson's suspicious scowl.

"I had just now come to inform the lass," Dougal said, certainly more for Dickson's benefit and not Caelen's, "that I imagined little hope to ferret her or any of Bowyer's residents out and away from the siege."

And now it was Caelen who slapped a hand on his shoulder, and his mien was once again serious. "Ye ken it's an honor to aid ye, my friend, and at the same time, thwart any plans laid to work by Longshanks."

Though nothing could compare to being delivered from the certain calamity that was their fate here, the other consequence of Caelen's coming with his formidable army thrilled Dougal as well.

"But aye, to put Pembroke's fellows to a run, nipping at their heels," Dougal said, including Walter and Dickson in his observation as he glanced at them as well, "suits me far better than any other challenge I can imagine."

"We might nae pounce on them as they sit there, then," Caelen said, nearly phrasing it as a question, "but give them the morn and the head start, hope they lead us straight to Pembroke."

"Aye," agreed Dougal, "does us nae guid to slay them here and now. We might better use them as trackers, escort us back to the main army, the king's greater enemy."

When nods were exchanged all around, Eleanor spoke up, addressing Caelen with admirable generosity. "What can I do for you, sir? Need you food or ale or water? Or have your men any need we might humbly attend?"

"Nae, lass," Caelen replied. "We are well-fed and yet in high spirits for having won the day—on several fronts now, since running into my auld friend here." Once more he met Dougal's eye, his cheerful gaze equal to the substance of his tone and words. "Perhaps enjoy a night of leisure, lass, as ye likely have nae since the siege began."

"Aye," said Dougal. "Come, my friend. We will greet the quiet night from the ramparts and catch up on affairs of concern." He held his hand up toward the door, not sure if he were more irked by the enthralled attention Eleanor gave to the undamaged knight or for the lengthy perusal to which Caelen was subjecting Eleanor, seeming to truly notice her now as a woman, a young and very attractive one, and not only as the daughter of Bowyer's titleholder.

Walter and Dickson departed first, and only when Caelen had bowed his head at Eleanor and moved to follow, did Dougal address her himself.

"All is well, Eleanor," he said, unwilling to investigate the pleasure derived from having her pretty green eyes returned to him. "Ye may indeed rest easy this night. The MacFadyen is faithful to his word; if he perceives nae lingering danger to us, we should presume ourselves spared."

She tilted her head to one side and showed Dougal a mournful pout. "I will not rest easy, Sir Dougal. We have your men to bury on the morrow if the English are thus persuaded to abandon their mission."

"Aye, and we will attend those men," he acknowledged. "But ken the threat is gone. We will be as their shadow, chasing the English and danger away from your door. They will nae be out of our sight to further harass you."

Eleanor nodded and a new ruefulness overtook her face—or did he only imagine that, when coupled with the next words she spoke?

"You will leave, then? You and your army, and pursue war with de Havering and now Hastings, far and wide if need be?"

"I will."

"Very well," she said quietly and walked toward the door. "There are no words to express completely how grateful I was—am—for your coming to Bowyer, for what you've done and lost to keep her safe. You have my most heartfelt thanks. I wish you Godspeed, sir," she said, though she should have expected to see him at least one more time before he left.

Dougal nodded curtly, understanding he was being dismissed, knowing it was likely for the better.

He inclined his head at her and offered a low, "Good night, Eleanor," before he passed by.

Her low voice reached him once again just as he'd gained the stairwell, a dozen feet away, just before he slipped into the dim interior there.

"He should have kissed me farewell."

Dougal's brow knitted dramatically, shocked at her words. But when he turned to address them and her, the door to her chamber was closed. But had she allowed him to overhear her musing? His hand gripped the doorjamb of the stairwell, his knuckles white while he contemplated if he would pursue an opportunity to respond.

To kiss her?

Jesu, but dare he? No, 'twould not be right, to have apologized for having done so already and then repeating the same mistake. Yet...mistake? No, certainly it had not been that, not in form or content, not for how it had made him feel, but only for the complication of it. She wasn't someone with whom he might only trifle, and he didn't keep company with women for any other reason.

He pulled his hand from the doorway, fisting it at his side as he descended the stairs to join Caelen and the others below, presumably in the hall.

He should have been thrilled—and he was; they were saved—but his nerves were yet on edge. He should be sipping ale, mayhap wine if Bowyer House could afford it, celebrating their current, vastly improved circumstances. Possibly, even if Caelen hadn't come, Hastings might have taken de Havering's force away, abandoning this wee task of taking and holding Bowyer in favor of the larger prey, convening with Pembroke's militia and chasing after the newly self-crowned king of Scotland. Might have, anyway, but Dougal was damn pleased he did not have to suffer through hours waiting to find out. Whether they came at the gate on the morrow or not, they had no chance of overpowering all the men convened here, which now included the MacFadyen force.

Always, highest on England and Edward I's agenda was the complete and total subjugation of Scotland and all Scots. They meant to achieve this in the grandest way possible, knowing that greater conquests would further corrode the already impaired morale of the Scottish citizens. So aye, going off to find the head of the snake, Robert Bruce, should rightly be expected as their next move.

He should have been thrilled, but instead he was thinking about what Eleanor had just put in his head when she'd bid him farewell. Assuming the siege was sacrificed, he would leave on the morrow to follow the enemy away from Bowyer, presumably in pursuit of Scotland's king. He must protect his king.

A million things might happen to prevent him from ever seeing Eleanor MacAdam again. Indeed, he considered the chances miniscule at best. He could perish in the war, be taken as a prisoner again, or find himself on distant shores as Wallace had been for several years; she might wed and leave Bowyer, or she might be recalled to Northumberland by her sire. He meant to impress upon Dickson that it had just been proven that she wasn't safe here and should reside elsewhere.

He could think of only one thing that would assure he did ever see her again: the desire to do so.

But he knew himself, knew what he was, inside and out. It would be in his best interests and hers to suppress any such absurdity.

DESPITE THE GLAD HEART wrought by the advent of the MacFadyen chieftain, which effectively ensured a favorable end to the short-lived but brutal siege, Eleanor passed a rough night. She was, she didn't mind admitting to herself, very sorry that Dougal Kildare would soon take his leave.

She tried to convince herself that her sorrow was not only in relation to his kiss, and the subsequent lack of opportunity for another. She wasn't sure how successful she was in that endeavor. Though she'd been in awe of the man and his impressive presence, how he'd leapt so spiritedly into the fray of the siege—indeed, had taken control—she wasn't sure she would have been left with so much regret if he were about to leave but *hadn't* kissed her. She might have only fondly recalled for days or weeks the intimidating knight who'd come to Bowyer's rescue and then was gone. She might have gone on believing that he was as ferocious as his ravaged face suggested, as he'd initially been so severe and curt with her.

But he had kissed her. And she convinced herself in the wake of that momentous occasion that just as his kiss had weakened her so gloriously, so too it had altered her perception of him. Truly, he had nearly been a monster prior to last evening, at times a harsh or indifferent man, one to whom she might suppose only war brought any satisfaction. Possibly that was what she was expected to believe, based on the persona he put forth, the one he'd mayhap invented to suit his appearance so perfectly.

But he wasn't a monster.

She wasn't sure why she might imagine Sir Dougal would revisit their kiss with as much delight as she did, particularly when he'd specifically said it had been a mistake, one he did not wish to repeat. But certainly he thought about it, did he not?

When she woke in the morning, before the dawn had come, noise from outside her window drew her there, to the ledge of the thin aperture. She rubbed sleep from her eyes and mechanically began unraveling the braid in her hair, which would need to be combed out before being plaited again. Possibly the voices below, or the jangling of harnesses or the whinnying of horses had been what roused her. In the still gray, pre-dawn light, she saw that the MacFadyen's army was indeed numerous, the squat bailey teeming with horses and soldiers, all of whom appeared to be readying to depart.

Beyond the stake wall and the makeshift wagon gate, in the meadow south of Bowyer House, nothing moved but a creeping, ground-hugging fog. This, coupled with the fact that no one directly below her in the yard seemed to be hurrying with any desperation, Eleanor assumed the English had indeed vacated this mission, off to a greater objective than the wee MacAdam tower keep.

Sleep and peace were quickly ushered away, replaced by a racing pulse and suddenly constrained throat. She found Dougal Kildare almost immediately in the throng, the gloomy morn unable to conceal his figure, standing taller than almost any other man, head and shoulders above more than half of them. He spoke with Tomag, one arm lifted and pointing up at the ramparts directly above him, his gaze further left than where Eleanor's window was, from which she spied. He stood in profile, unknowingly showing her the unscarred half of his face, and she cursed the distance which offered so little detail. Even as she wanted to stare unobtrusively at him, to commit his visage to memory, already lamenting all the instances she might have done so but did not, Eleanor knew she wanted more to be within reach of him.

She spared only a moment more, moving her eager gaze rapidly over all the milling and moving soldiers and horses. Dickson was there, directing traffic and giving orders, telling Mànas to direct some of the Kildare army and their steeds out from the congested bailey by way of the postern gate. Possibly, he was reluctant to dismantle and remove the wagon gate and its hastily concocted anchoring, worried that it might be premature.

Eleanor moved away from the window and dressed hurriedly in the shadows of her chamber, the fire having died hours ago. She garbed herself in her last remaining clean léine and kirtle and quickly donned her short boots, cursing her fumbling fingers that refused to comply with as much speed as she would have liked. She straightened and realized in her haste, she'd buried the hem of her léine in the back of her boot and wrestled briefly to free that. She grabbed the nearest wool shawl and draped that over her shoulders, flipping her hair out from within.

Sure and she had no misconceptions and didn't for one instant believe that she wasn't ridiculous, scurrying around to make herself presentable as if she, rather advanced in years and with little to recommend her, should capture the prolonged attention of so valiant a knight as Dougal Kildare. And she wasn't vain, but then neither was she simple-minded. She had so few tools at her disposal, that she combed her hair out and left it loose and curling around her shoulders, hoping he perceived his last glimpse of her as a memorable one.

But she did not spend any inordinate amount of time on her appearance. These knights and their armies need not practice any courtesy, delaying their departure to give a fine farewell to anyone at Bowyer, not if they meant to keep close in the shadow of the English. She would expect no such dalliance merely for the sake of needless decorum. They owed Bowyer House no more than what they had already given.

She dashed from the chamber and down the stairs, relishing the idea of one more glimpse of the formidable knight, Dougal Kildare, compelled not only to show herself in the yard simply to give a proper fare thee well, but with some hope that he might smile once more at her, that he might leave her with something to cherish, a new memory, one not tainted by a battle looming in the background.

The door to the hall was open, men coming and going yet, suggesting their departure was not only seconds away.

She had time.

Eleanor squeezed between the press of bodies and horse-flesh, smiling absently at those she passed, her gaze darting always back to Dougal. He was no longer speaking to Tomag but facing what she might presume was his own horse, a big bay destrier, securing his saddlebags.

"Sir Dougal," she said, quite pleased to have put out a voice unwavering.

He cocked his head first, but turned almost immediately, his back now to the huge steed. Dougal's gray eyes appeared nearly black in the bleak light before dawn. It did not escape her notice that he ran his gaze over the length of hair falling over her left shoulder before he met her eyes.

"I dinna ken if ye slept yet or nae," he said, " but I was hoping I might see ye ere we took our leave."

"Did you?" She asked, powerless to keep hope from shading her tone.

"Aye," he said. "I've spoken at length with Dickson in the last hour about propping up defenses here, but he and I agree wholly that it might be safer for ye to return to Northumberland."

His concern was unexpected, but only because she hadn't considered the possibility of it. It was not unwelcome but then it was not what she might have wished to follow his admission that he'd hoped to see her before he left.

'Twas to be an impersonal farewell then, Eleanor realized, a hint of disappointment revealing itself to her.

"I am not welcome there, sir," she said carelessly. "We will be fine here."

"Nae welcome in yer father's house?" He questioned, his frown—the most familiar thing about him—returned.

Eleanor shook her head, drawing her shawl more tightly about her, finding not the warmth in his gaze she only now realized she'd anticipated. But she gave no explanation to his query. He was leaving, their time was done, his question and any answer she might have given unnecessary. He would not get to know her story nor she his.

When he accepted this, and pushed no more for clarification, they exchanged a quiet and—as she imagined it—a profound look, before he reached for her hand, which Eleanor willingly gave to him, releasing the edges of the wool wrap.

He stared at her hand, tracing his thumb over the back of it, compelling Eleanor's gaze to follow his. His hand was larger, stronger, darker than her own, which seemed frail and limp in his light grasp, so much so that she straightened a bit and stiffened, invigorating herself to steeliness. He thought her weak only, thought only of the protection she needed, thought not of her.

"Keep well, Sir Dougal," she said, her voice scarcely breaking. "I will not ever forget what you have done here at Bowyer House, or how auspicious was your coming."

"Nor I, lass," he said, staring with a greater intensity at her now.

Eleanor's lips parted, a reaction to the severity of his present gaze as he looked her over, from one eye to the next, at her nose, her lips. Whatever polite amiability he'd first shown had evolved and she thought her sparse words put him in mind of what he'd lost here at Bowyer, his good men. Eleanor hastily added, "May they rest in peace, sir, and know we will cherish them. And may you swiftly forget all of Bowyer that it would only distress you to recall."

Dougal gripped her hand tighter, and for the barest moment he pulled her near. But not close enough, and not with enough pressure that anything but her hand and arm were moved before he must have thought better of it.

"Impossible, Eleanor," he said, his voice harsh once more, as if the words were gritted from between his teeth. "That I should forget even one moment."

That was for her, about her, about them, she knew, or inferred by the growing huskiness of his voice, as if it pained him to speak now.

"Dougal...."

She realized she'd spoken that single word. That was her breathless voice, delivering the lone word as a plea. That was her, returning the warmer, firmer grip of his hand and tilting her face up to him.

"Keep well, Eleanor MacAdam," he said, giving her hand a final squeeze before he released her altogether.

"Please keep safe," she urged. But oh, how ridiculous she was! For the tears that threatened.

She nodded jerkily, attempting to smile, wishing he had.

Five minutes later, she watched the Kildares and Mac-Fadyens ride away from Bowyer House, leaving the yard vacant and almost completely without sound.

How strange, how utterly peculiar, she thought, that she should know more sorrow watching Dougal Kildare riding away than she had when her own father had turned his back on her in this very yard four years ago.

Chapter Ten

I t was a fine day, with islands of clouds wafting overhead, changing shape as they sailed about the sea of blue sky. A capricious breeze rustled leaves and lifted loose strands of Eleanor's hair off her face as she and Lucy walked toward the village. Eleanor carried a basket laden with dried meat, fresh-made cheese, a crock of honey, and a small joint of roasted pork that would undoubtedly last him for several days. Henry was Bowyer's only pensioner, and though his fighting days had been with another lord, the mormaer of Man, amid a different war, he was Bowyer's own now and she was happy to make sure his needs were met.

She was fairly certain that Lucy regularly accompanied her simply to escape the drudgery of her kitchen duties. Though the girl was kindly toward Henry, she didn't much care for his hound, was always skittering away from or around the dog though he rarely moved himself. And then, Lucy had once expressed that it was difficult to be social with others when she was forever bound to the kitchen's *dreary dankness*—her words, to which she'd added at the time, giggling profusely, "But ye might as well apply that to Cook's manner also."

Though she suffered bouts of laziness and she talked entirely too much—*blathering* is what she did, according to Dickson—Lucy was a fine lass about whom Eleanor never had cause to grumble.

"Sees me every night in the hall," Lucy was saying now as they climbed the hill on the west side of Bowyer, which separated the tower house from the village. "He must ken he gets the lion's share of ale and his favorite, whenever we serve it, the beans with the bacon the way he likes them. I dinna shill so much onto other trenchers," she said, referring to Tomag, who was either ignorant of her singular attention or chose to ignore it for the obvious reason, that he did not return her interest.

"Perhaps he only needs a further, more blatant nudge," Eleanor suggested.

"Bah," scoffed Lucy, squinting her eyes toward the village as they crested the beinn. "Guid crack upside the head is what he needs. I dinna ken how much more apparent I can make it."

Lucy carried on as they descended the small hill, telling the story about when Tomag had carried her from the well to the hall. Lucy had, by her own account, overfilled the bucket she'd fetched, the weight of it causing her to stumble and fall, crashing onto the bucket itself before landing awkwardly on her arm.

"'Twas my arm that was sore and nae reason for him to have carried me," she said. "But he did—carry me, that is— and went back and fetched that bucket and fresh water himself."

This occasion might have been what had provoked Lucy's sudden notice of Tomag, whom she'd known all her short life. Before that day, more than a year ago now and by her own admission, scant attention had she given the lad. This tale, by the way, was one that Eleanor will now have heard more than only once or twice. Because she was familiar with this particular narrative, and in which she was convinced Lucy put too much stock, Eleanor allowed her mind to wander.

Six weeks had passed since Bowyer had been besieged by de Havering and his English army, six weeks since Dougal Kildare had ridden away. Scarcely a day passed that she did not think of him, wondering how he fared, if he lived yet. Thoughts of him occupied not only her feelings—mayhap irrationally—but her restless mind as well. On the meanest days, she was quite sure he must have perished. Certainly, he would have returned had he lived. He'd felt it, too, had he not? The connection between them. It would have brought him back to her, wouldn't it? Oh, she knew she was foolish, mayhap not so unlike Lucy, giving too much credibility to what little they'd shared, how short had been their acquaintance. Perhaps he made a regular habit of nearly se-ducing young women in any keep he was bound by honor to de-fend. Maybe he left a trail of inspired but broken hearts all over keeps and villages throughout Scotland.

Bowyer and its residents had recovered from the wee assault laid by the English. Though they'd lost not one man to the fight-ing, and only a few had suffered modest wounds, likely none would soon forget what had befallen them, or might well happen again. War had finally come to their little corner in Midlothian. To that end, Dickson had made it his life's mission to outfit Bowyer in such a way that there would be little need to only await a savior such as Dougal Kildare and Caelen MacFadyen had been. He had two main objectives—"And I dinna care what yer sire says, either about the necessity or the cost!"—the first being constructing an actual wall. So now the Bowyer guards, tenants, and those with regular occupations had become stone masons in their spare time—of which there was little with the

late summer harvest nearly upon them and their own labors re-
quiring so much attention. They'd begun with the gate, naturally, constructing an actual one, and the frame to which it was
secured. And section by section, they built a stone wall around
it. They sourced the rock themselves, using two oxen Dickson
had purchased. They chipped and chiseled and dug the stone
out from the quarry beyond the wee loch in the northernmost
acreage of Bowyer. It was loaded onto the very wagon that once
had prevented the English from walking straight into the bailey,
the vehicle since repaired, and the oxen pulled it back to Bowyer,
that trek the most painful thing to behold. 'Twas a slow oper-
ation, limited by the lack of time in a man's day and the actual
number of men being available to devote to Dickson's mission.

It was further slowed by the fact that Dickson was adamant
that at the same time they began work on a means of escape,
which he foresaw as a tunnel burrowed beneath the keep, and as
was his hope, reaching as far as a quarter mile away. Left to their
own devices about this laborious endeavor, after Dickson's initial
instruction, Mànas and Daniel worked exclusively on this. The
latter had once remarked upon the slowness of their progress to
Eleanor, saying, "Like as nae, lass, nae only me and my bairns but
my grandbabies, too, will work in that shaft beneath the earth."
He then reminded Eleanor of his age, being not yet a score of
years, still unwed and not yet the father of those bairns.

"I might well *nudge* him about the head," said Lucy now
as they came abreast of the nearest cottage, which was Henry's.
"Nudge him with the back of a guid wooden spoon. Mayhap
with the big black kettle."

Eleanor grinned, her attention returned to the frizzy-haired
lass with the droopy but always gleaming brown eyes.

"Why don't you tell him?"

"Tell him what?" Lucy asked, her face scrunched up.

"I'm not sure," Eleanor admitted. "Either that you wanted to spend time with him, or that—"

"Tell him I want to throw my legs over his shoulders."

Eleanor coughed out a shocked chuckle. "Good heavens, Lucy!" She cried. Though she didn't exactly know what was meant, she understood a saucy implication. Eleanor might well be a few years older than Lucy, but at times such as these, she felt decidedly unworldly.

"What? Like ye dinna ken the same with the knight, the Kildare? I saw how ye looked at him—and he at ye. Saw yer farewell, anyhow, him holding yer hand like he dinna want to ever let go—ye dinna want him to leave, did ye?"

While she wasn't pretentious by any means, Eleanor also wasn't in the habit of exchanging so much personal information with the servants of Bowyer House, aside from Dickson, of course, from whom she kept few secrets.

The door to Henry's small croft opened. He stood in the middle of the opening while his hound slowly meandered around him and across the walk to Eleanor, who scratched at the scruff behind his ears as Lucy sidestepped him completely.

"Good day, Henry," Eleanor said to the old man. "You heard us coming, I presume?"

"Heard this one's jaw flapping," he said, a crooked grin lifting his thin lips. *This one* was only and ever Lucy, who he liked very much to tease. His grin evolved into a full smile when Lucy reached up on her toes and kissed his cheek as she passed him.

"We brought ye savory treats, Henry," Lucy said. "Wait until ye see."

Eleanor pressed a kiss to his weathered cheek as well, knowing he loved both the sweet attention and the company. Lucy, in her matter-of-fact way, didn't wait for Henry to close the door and find his seat, the comfy chair near the small hearth that had been built for him, but took his hand and dragged him within, leaving the door open. Henry had no need of the natural light or even tapers, but Eleanor and Lucy did.

They had barely unearthed all the goods from the basket, had exchanged but a few pleasantries with Henry when Eleanor heard her name being shouted.

"About as subtle as an arrow through the eye, that one," said Henry.

That one, as called by Henry, never referred to anyone but Dickson, who owned the voice behind the hollering.

Eleanor poked her head outside the door of Henry's cottage, just in time to see Dickson riding his favorite mare into the village, down from the hill.

"Good grief, Dickson," she called out. "What are you about?"

"'Tis nae often," he said, his face red from exertion, "but regular enough we get a missive from yer sire, lass." He reined in abruptly at the end of the short walkway in front of Henry's place. "But nae ever before now has he included a note just to ye."

"Father wrote to me?"

Dickson grumbled, "Says nae one word about the siege we withstood on his behalf—in his bluidy stead, burying bodies we oughtn't have been—though I put down to parchment all the bluidy particulars. But he pens a missive to ye instead."

Eleanor rushed forward, steadying herself against the horse, her fingers gripping the bridle. She wasn't filled so much with excitement at the rare occurrence, as she was with dread. *Dear Lord, what if he were recalling her to Northumberland? I won't go.*

"Ye're nae going to like it, lass," he predicted, reaching into this tunic to withdraw the parchment, which he promptly handed to her.

"Please don't say he wants me to..." she said absently, her eyes already scanning the short note, which took up no more than a quarter of the single page. "To my well-beloved daughter," she read aloud, her voice a murmur. Somehow she managed to refrain from snorting out her disdain over so patently false a salutation. "I greet thee well," she read on, "and advise you to think upon the counsel of your father and make haste to Northumberland. I have, in your stead, arranged for your marriage. John Chishull of Horsely awaits your arrival on the 27th, and no later, for the nuptials to take place. Written in haste the Thursday after the Ascension," she continued with the scribbling of her father's closing, "from Northumberland by your father, Anker MacAdam." Confusion and shock drained all the color from her face and saw her turning over the paper, as if more might have been written elsewhere though not on the facing page. She read the words again, only now dimly conscious of Lucy coming to stand by her side, trying to peak at the letter without being overtly obvious, and even though to Eleanor's knowledge she couldn't read, certainly not the shoddy scratch of Anker MacAdam's English.

Ignoring the maid, Eleanor lifted her pale face to Dickson, who gazed down at her with a certain, uncommon sympathy that brought Eleanor closer to tears.

"He intends to marry me," she said, the shock of it evident in the breathless quality of her voice. "To an Englishman. He wants me to leave Bowyer," she went on, as if Dickson had not himself read the missive and instruction, as if Eleanor had not just now read it aloud. "Leave Bowyer...and live in England," she said, her tone suggesting her father had in fact asked her to wed a toad and live on the moon.

"Aye, lass," Dickson said, his tone a mix of wrath and pity.

"Och, Eleanor," said Lucy, "who is this man, John Chishull? Do ye ken him already?"

"I do not," Eleanor said. "I'm to wed a man I've never met." She consulted the missive again. "On the 27th of this month. Or shortly thereafter, I would imagine." Her voice grew smaller and smaller as the particulars of the letter sank in, as her future began to unfold in her mind, mired in joylessness, too far from Bowyer and the only people who cared for her.

"He dinna ken what yer about," Lucy said, slapping her hands on her hips. "Yer sire, that is. Dinna care that ye nearly were kilt—all of us. Ain't seen none of him since he brung ye here. How's he ken what you're doing? Tell him ye wed already, what's he ken?"

Eleanor offered a smile of appreciation to Lucy but feared it might actually be mistaken as a grimace for how wretched were her thoughts.

"Now see here, lass," said Dickson, his tone much milder than the situation warranted, in her estimation. "Ye ken he only wants...aye, and we'll have some time...that is, ye'll—aye, and come on back to the keep and let us consider our response. He'll expect a missive saying aye, we're coming."

Eleanor began to slowly shake her head. "I won't, Dickson. I will not."

"All right, all right, but let's talk about it. C'mon now."

Eleanor cast another forlorn glance at Lucy, and beyond her, to where Henry Oliver stood in the door of his cottage, his mouth open, though Eleanor could not decide if he exhibited shock or dismay.

"Go on then," Lucy urged, pushing Eleanor's arm. "Go on with Dickson and sort this out. I'll keep company with Henry for a while. Ye're nae leaving today—nae at all if I read yer face right. Ye'll see the old bird again."

Eleanor gave a nod to Lucy, and then to Dickson, who returned the gesture and set his horse apace with her when she began to walk up the lane.

"Dickson," she said before he might have tried to soothe all the tumult inside her, "I'll meet you back there. I won't be long. Just...just leave me to my thoughts as I walk." When he hesitated, surely about to argue this, Eleanor implored, "Please. I'll be along shortly."

He acquiesced with little grace, scowling at Eleanor before he turned the horse around and sped away.

John Chishull of Horsely awaits your arrival.

A husband. An Englishman.

And this after she and Bowyer had just withstood a siege by more of his ilk, she thought uncharitably.

Honest to God, she'd believed her father had forgotten all about her. And oh, how that had pained her heart. But now, well now she wished her father had continued to ignore her existence, had persisted in pretending he had no daughter at all.

She did not take herself further away from the village, to be alone with her overwrought thoughts, but walked slowly back to the keep. She used the minutes wisely, exerting less energy on distress and exercising more effort toward imagining a way out of this sure catastrophe.

By the time she reached the tower house, Eleanor had formed her own plan to circumvent her father's arrangements for her. He had, in effect, abandoned her; he didn't get a say in her future. She was going to make sure of it. But then her fresh idea was not only to thwart her father's plans because of the pain of his desertion. No, her just-imagined scheme came with its own ulterior motive, one borne of her surely foolish infatuation with Dougal Kildare.

She marched straight into the old steward's office, which was Dickson's own these days, though he'd said time and again he was no steward but only acted the part as needed, essentially making up the rules as he went along.

"Can you take me to find the knight, Dougal Kildare?" She asked straight away when Dickson lifted his face to her from behind the steward's desk.

"What the—? Ye want the knight to protect ye from yer own father? Lass, that's nae—"

"I want to ask him to marry me," she clarified, raising her chin, expecting either shock or a clear annoyance for her certainly unexpected request.

Dickson did not disappoint, somehow managing to lift his brows in surprise while he scowled at the same time.

"Ye wot now?"

"I'm going to find Dougal Kildare," she stated boldly, "and ask him to marry me instead."

Dickson sputtered and spewed naught but air and spittle for a full three seconds before he managed to produce actual words. "Are ye bluidy mad? Have you gone daft then? Finally?"

Wanting to maintain what little composure she still held on to, Eleanor informed him, "Of course, I knew you would hate the idea and I know you will try and talk me out of it. But know that it is my will and my right to make decisions regarding my life. You can either help me find him, Dickson, or turn a blind eye to my schemes. I will not, I vow to you, return to my father and that evil Lucinda, and marry some pasty-faced Englishman, not after what they did here at Bowyer." She inclined her head in a provocative nod, accentuating her avowal.

As expected, Dickson was not yet done with his bellyaching. He went on fully for another two minutes, listing everything that was wrong with her plan, not least of all wondering why she should think the knight would *want* to wed her. "And more than that—before we'd even get to *that*," Dickson hollered, "do ye ken how dangerous the territory is now? How do ye presume to travel safely from here to there—and bluidy hell, how would we even begin to find one knight in all the thousands of acres in the Highlands?"

Calmly, Eleanor answered only the last question. "I thought we might simply seek out the king. News sometimes travels to loyal parties," she said confidently. "Might we make inquiries about the king's last known whereabouts? Should that not be the place to start? Sir Dougal did say he expected to join once more with Robert Bruce."

"Ye want to turn us in to tramps?" Dickson countered. "Camp followers? Chasing Scots' armies?'

Displaying none of the impending triumph that she felt, she asked, "Does that mean you will help me?"

"Well, bluidy hell," groused her dear friend, "obviously I canna leave ye to your own wits—look what ye've just done, what schemes you've concocted, left alone with yer thoughts and this trauma for mere minutes, imagining yerself returned to England and that harpy of a stepmother. If I'm nae there to temper all the bad ideas, ye'll nae live long enough to invent any guid ones."

Eleanor withheld the smile that wanted to come. "But this is a good idea, is it not? I don't know any other person, even casually, to wed, someone strong enough to stand up to my father if need be."

This gave Dickson pause. He stared thoughtfully at her, his square shoulders drooping a bit. "I dinna ken what marriage to a man such as him might mean, lass. Christ, who kens if he's even of the marrying ilk. If ye're seeking happiness and dinna I wish that for ye, I'm nae sure he's the one to give it to ye." He rolled his tongue over the inside of his lips before continuing. "He's all about war, fighting, freedom, righting wrongs—nobly, to be sure, but it dinna lend itself to the tenderness needed to make a marriage work. If ye only seek protection, safety, removal from yer father's clutches and his schemes, Kildare is the man for that role, I should imagine."

Frankly, she hadn't thought *that* far ahead, to what being wed to Dougal Kildare might actually entail. Likewise, she hadn't given so much thought to the very real possibility that he might refuse her. Just now, she focused on something else, the pain and heartache that had provoked this desperate plot. "This is just further proof that I mean nothing to my father, Dickson," she said, attempting to keep any hint of melancholy from her tone, allowing a bitterness to taint her words instead. "He doesn't care about me, as evidenced by the cold years I've been left here, without one written word from him until this, directing me to come wed some stranger that will likely only benefit him and certainly not me. I feel like...I think Sir Dougal would not be unkind. Absent mayhap. Aloof, I'm quite certain. Unfathomable mostly. But at least I would go into the marriage—should he agree—without expectations. I have some idea of his character. What little I know suggests a man of honor. I firmly believe I would be safe and well-cared for, not abused in any fashion." She bit her lip before she said, "I can eke out a...a good life with that."

Dickson nodded slowly, his tired eyes suggesting he was unconvinced.

Eleanor tilted her head at him. "I'll go, with or without you. You know that." A thought occurred to her. "Actually, it might be better—for your future relationship with my father, that I do go alone. He won't be able to blame you for—"

"Dinna speak nonsense," Dickson clipped. He waved a meaty paw, dismissing her. "Go on, then. Pack yer bags. Tramps we'll be."

Eleanor swiveled toward the door, allowing a victorious and thankful smile to slowly emerge.

Chapter Eleven

D ougal thought himself not so unlike Caelen MacFadyen, seeking out any little battle or fight or even smaller but industrious ventures, whatever might keep him away from home—the longer the better.

Adhering to a certain sense of honor, Caelen had made no declarations himself, but Dougal still believed that his marriage, or more specifically Caelen's wife, was something to be avoided at all costs. In Caelen's case, apparently the prospect of death by the sword was more appealing than getting on with that union, making bairns and a home at Turnberry with the woman. Dougal couldn't know for sure, but he might guess that from the tales of Caelen's involvement in one skirmish after another and by the man's own vague admissions, that he'd spent only days or weeks at home in the past few years, but not any more than that all told. There had been some tales carried through the wind of the camps that Caelen had rather been forced to wed, having been caught in a compromising position with the woman who was now his wife.

Sorry fate, that.

For his part, and though Dougal was never overwhelmed with any thrill or delight at the idea of going home, 'twas not any disagreeable wife waiting there that kept him far gone. Nae, 'twas the house itself and all the memories attached to it, recollections of his brutal father and a mostly joyless childhood, so much of it lived in fear. His tiresome uncle, Padean, was yet in residence, unless the gods might have bestowed favor upon Dougal and taken that man from the earth. His mother was his only joy at Templeton Landing, but even she, since his captivity and disfigurement, was sometimes difficult to bear. He could scarcely stomach the constant pity gleaned in her gaze. And he never wanted to be too long in her company so that she had time to see or realize his true character, how similar to his father he was after all, black heart and all.

His mother, Aimil, was at once the weakest and the strongest person Dougal had ever known. Whether his conception had been a matter of force or not, she had never said, but enough whispers and innuendo had reached Dougal when he came of age to understand it, that he supposed 'twas not love made that brought him to life. Indeed, when Aimil had announced her condition, so Dougal had been told, his father's wife had ordered the milkmaid whipped in the village, either supposing her guilty of spreading falsehoods or assuming her wicked, for having lain with her husband. And though there was an unwritten law that did not permit a woman to be lashed more than a dozen times, the lash had met Aimil's tender back more than twice that, at the insistence of Tearlach Kildare's wife. Tearlach himself had not intervened on the maid's behalf. How his mam had withstood such torture, and in her condition, Dougal could to this day not comprehend.

He'd spent the first few years of his life all but confined to the one room hovel in which his mother lived, she being too afraid to make his presence known, he being the very image of his father. Of course, living in the shadow of the keep, it did not take long for Tearlach to come face to face with his son. He had not sought him out in the first decade of his life, but once met, once Tearlach had beheld the intensity of the gray-eyed stare of the lad, once he'd discovered that Dougal was by far bigger and brawnier than any other his age, once he'd exchanged enough curt conversation with him to understand his mind was sharp, the laird had been intrigued. And then, having an uncommon appreciation for the perpetual chip Dougal wore on his shoulder, which Tearlach might have mistaken at the time for fearlessness and not the opposite—Tearlach Kildare, after all, and according to his mother, was the devil—Dougal had been invited regularly to the keep, and to the training. When the youngest son of Tearlach had died of a fever none could alleviate, Tearlach had begun to look at Dougal through a different lens, having only one legitimate son remaining, and he worth about as much *as a chamber pot woven of cotton*, Aimil had often noted. Dougal had then, at the age of twelve, and in spite of his mother's begging him otherwise, had found a seat at the laird's table, and then a place within his inner circle. He'd been fostered out to squire with another laird as any legitimate son might be. By that time, knowing the wheels could not be stopped from turning, Aimil had changed her tactic, had begun to pester Tearlach to acknowledge Dougal officially, to write letters to the bishop. Dougal would never believe this alone, his mother's pleas, had been what had mattered to Tearlach.

His mother was sweet and loyal but not particularly clever, was not possessed with so much charm or wit, though by all accounts she was undeniably beautiful, which surely had been the sole impetus for the chief taking notice of her and then taking her. She was weak and run over by first her overbearing parents and then the laird, and only found strength, immeasurable when needed, when it came to protecting her child. For her son, she would do or brave or dare almost anything. He'd always hoped she hadn't sold her own soul to see Dougal receive what she thought was his due.

Truth be told, he wished he'd listened first to his mother, when she'd begged him to get away, as fast and as far as he could, as soon as he'd been old enough to do so. He felt, soon after being taken under his father's wing, so to speak, as if the darkness had actually begun to invade his heart then. Tearlach Kildare was an abomination, with no perceptible redeeming quality, not one. Aside from the fact that he died ere he turned fifty, he did no other favors to the world or any person in it.

Dougal had taken the lash himself—thrice as many blows as his mother had, in the very spot she had, near the post in the middle of the lane in Templeton's village. His father had administered the blows. The infraction had not merited a whipping at all, let alone one so merciless, the cause so worthless that time had erased it from Dougal's memory, any recollection of it. His father had only wanted to test his mettle, to see if he were any more a man than his other sons. Dougal still bore the scars from that experiment, and knew he could look back at that moment as the instant rage had been born inside him.

He should have left. A hundred times, he regretted that he had not. As it was, by the time Dougal was old enough to understand what his father was, it was too late; his mother by then would not abandon her own aged parents and Dougal could not abandon her. And when his father was finally dead—long time coming, to Dougals' mind—he'd accepted the lairdship solely to prove to himself he was not his father. A byproduct, not an unhappy consequence, was installing his mother as mistress of Templeton Landing, since Tearlach's wife had preceded him to hell by several years.

So aye, memories didn't make any return to Templeton Landing a joyous occasion. He had at one time imagined that with his father gone, with his stepmother deceased as well, with his mother's future secured, there might have come a time when he did want to be home. He was still waiting for that sense to overtake him.

But return to Templeton Landing he would, since Pembroke's pursuit of the king, with an army now said to be ten thousand strong, had become indefensible. Robert Bruce, his reign yet in its infancy, his hands dirtied by his own treachery to obtain the crown, had not yet the support of his constituents to take on Longshank's man in the field.

Having convened with the king, Dougal and Caelen had been part of the early rebellion, which Aymer de Valence, the Earl of Pembroke had been assigned to squash. Dougal and Caelen had followed de Havering and Hastings force to the larger English contingent. Pembroke had made quick work of capturing the bishops of Glasgow and St. Andrews, two of the king's key supporters. And things had only gone downhill since then. Despite the slowly growing numbers of patriots come to join the fight against the English, Pembroke's army was simply too large to withstand. Slowly growing was the rebellion, since Pembroke had also managed to secure the aid of those Scots loyal to John Comyn, whom Robert Bruce had murdered in late winter, inside the sanctuary of a kirk no less, thereby removing any threat to his wearing the crown.

Summer had come and with it fine weather, but the tides of war did not turn as did the warmer breezes wafting across the land from the sea. Pembroke delivered devastating losses to Bruce's combined army at Methven in June with an early morning surprise assault. After that, as part of their lengthy retreat, they'd faced off with the MacDougall clan, allies of the slain Comyn. Dougal and Caelen had grown increasingly perturbed by the dwindling size of the king's army, of which they were now part, and with the lack of preparedness of those that did remain. He'd swear half these men had never raised a sword before this season of war. In such conditions, outnumbered and unprepared, their army had rapidly dispersed, the king barely escaping with his life.

With hope to have assumed the crown without bloodshed so swiftly eradicated, with the future of the Scottish crown yet in peril, Robert Bruce had relieved the majority of his army from their present duties, advising that he would take some time to regroup, and possibly consider more diplomatic entreaties. He'd been vague in his discourse, giving Caelen and Dougal and several other knights and nobles leave to seek their homes for the winter, giving no exact accounting of his own immediate plans.

Caelen, normally fairly even tempered unless provoked, had not long been departed of the king's company before he treated those around him to a blistering of the ear, wanting to stand and fight instead, rather than disassembling as the king favored. Dougal had parted company days later with a still sour Caelen at Beinn Bhuidhe, knowing he would see him again, God willing standing once more aside the king, sword in hand.

Despite the hardships faced, since the last few months had seen him either fighting for his life or running to escape death,

Dougal still managed to think on Eleanor MacAdam—every day, sometimes hourly it seemed, certainly during those times when his mood leaned toward things to mourn, the end seemingly getting closer and closer.

Like an itch he couldn't ignore, his mind repeatedly scratched at the memory of their kiss. In the past, he'd found that unkind thoughts or memories only needed constant action in order to avoid them. He kept his hands and mind occupied, thereby allowing himself little time to ponder all the misfortunes of his life. Strangely enough, surprise attacks, constant and demoralizing retreat, and simple actions of his sword did not seem to be doing the trick now. Despite every effort, he could not banish her from his mind. He would have thought that as he was striking his sword into the heart of the enemy, come at the back of the king, that as he saved his king's life, that he would not see a flash of green eyes, would see honor and glory instead. But aye, each time his own life was closest to being snuffed out, 'twas curiously when she was closest to him in recall.

Unable to make sense of it, and reluctant to apply the wrong reason to it, Dougal tried his damnedest to ignore it completely. When that failed, he gave in reluctantly, deciding instead to enjoy the fall. He allowed himself his memories of her, without attaching any other meaning aside from what it was: a pleasant interlude passed with a bonny lass amidst the ugliness of war; a stirring kiss had been met and known and he would carry that with him until the next one came along. *You should have kissed me farewell, sir* uttered in her soft voice had haunted him for days and weeks.

He had cause to wonder that if not for his responsibility to his army, to see to their needs and wants first when no battle was nigh, if he might have returned to Bowyer House, to Eleanor. As often as this notion teased him, Dougal was able to waylay any such idea by reminding himself that he was no good for the likes of Eleanor MacAdam.

He sat now with his beleaguered and further depleted army closer yet to home, but still with a day of travel ahead of them. They set up camp near an ancient and ruined broch and cooked some rabbits Luca had shot with his bow. Aside from horns filled with ale this morning as they'd passed near Dornie, other provisions were scarce, and for that, reaching Templeton Landing would be welcome.

For lack of any other industry, Dougal had unsheathed his sword and sat near the cooking fire sharpening its blade, a necessary task and useful practice that always managed to bring him peace.

As were so many of his men, he was dressed in many layers to combat the chill of autumn. The ground was not yet frozen, but regularly he was able to see his breath when he woke in the morn. Like Walter and many others, Dougal had begun to wear his larger fur, the one that was the size of a great cape, which rarely allowed him to suffer from the cold.

Walter sat beside him presently, rubbing his hand up and down the top of his left thigh. He'd sustained an injury during the Methven debacle that Dougal worried had not healed properly and would only continue to cause him trouble. He had some idea that Walter was concerned about it as well. At the very least, long days in the saddle were no more a thing to be taken for granted, but looked upon each morning with dread. Yet another reason to be thankful for their close proximity to home.

He mentioned this to Walter. "Morag will ken what to do for the aching," he said, speaking of Templeton's ancient healer.

"Pray better she has something to cure what ails the rest of them," Walter said, inclining his head toward the general population of their withered army.

"I ken they want the fight," Dougal acknowledged, "as does any right man when freedom is at stake. But the king is nae wrong. All year we've been fighting with more audacity than with any guid sense and coordination. 'Twill nae carry us far."

Walter shook his head, his feelings on the matter well known. "We should've pushed on, made a stand against Pembroke, pushed through until we were close enough to impale Longshanks with yer nice shiny sword. They're only going to garrison more and better over the winter, obtain a greater foothold here."

"If reports are true, we might fare better waiting out the winter," Dougal countered, "and learn in spring that the decline of Longshank's health had nae been exaggerated, that he is nae more of the earth."

Walter snorted. "Och, but we dinna ken we'll have an easier time of it with the crown on his son's head."

"The prince is nae his father," Dougal said. "He dinna have Longshanks infuriatingly sound head for strategy, and certainly he is imbued with neither the boldness nor the arrogance to wage a proper war. I ken we'll fight easier against the son."

Rand rode into camp at the moment, coming swiftly enough that Dougal and Walter bounded to their feet. The lad tied the reins of his courser to one of the stakes to which Dougal's tent was attached.

"Might better have employed such speed and cunning 'fore Pembroke broke our ranks," Walter grumbled.

Upon his approach, Rand took note of the sword in Dougal's hand but possibly not the sharpening wedge in his other hand. The lad's smirk was mysterious, and truth be told, more animated than Dougal would have thought possible of the lad, who normally maintained a bland, steady demeanor.

"Ye'll nae believe it, so I'll nae say it," said the lad, uncommonly cryptic. "Nae need of yer sword, though," Rand said next. "'Tis nae the enemy who comes."

"Who *does* come?" Dougal asked with little patience for the scout's unusual game-playing and demeanor. A scout was trained to relay information quickly and succinctly, nae tease the listeners with riddles.

Rand turned and pointed off into the gloaming, where a line of trees met with the clearing in which they camped.

Rand's smile faltered briefly when no one came through the trees, not soon enough to have asserted timing better suited to his alert. Vaguely, the lad pointed toward the towering pines, his shoulders sagging with perhaps a wee annoyance.

And then—just as Walter barked out, "God's bluid, lad. Did ye lose them? Whoever is expected to show themselves and help me make sense of that manky expression yer wearing?"—several shadowy figures were noticed moving among the pines in the twilight.

Dickson was the first person Dougal recognized, the sighting of Bowyer's captain causing Dougal's heart to drop well south of his chest, instantly supposing some peril had befallen Eleanor.

And then he saw her.

Eleanor.

"Well, I'll be damned," Walter breathed.

She rode a white mare and was cloaked in a voluminous mantle, her russet hair spilling out from the hood. Even before she was close enough to know for sure that they were, he felt her eyes upon him. She removed one hand from the reins and laid it over her heart, seemingly overcome with some emotion to have found or stumbled upon the Kildares, relief or joy Dougal could not discern.

Blindly, greatly distracted, Dougal sheathed his sword and tossed aside the sharpening stone.

He scanned his gaze over the entire party, all Bowyer persons, he recognized, and then approached Eleanor just as she alighted without assistance.

The sight of her—here, so close to home—stunned him, as did the response of his heart. It skidded and crashed to a halt. And then, as if he were made of weakness, as if he indulged in foolishness, his very next thought was to question if his constant ruminating over her had actually and somehow called to her, summoning her to him.

I'm bluidy losing my mind.

Later, he would blame shock for not realizing that he'd spoken those words aloud.

"Ye'll nae be alone in that journey, lad," Walter murmured, obviously as stunned as Dougal.

He and Walter stood shoulder to shoulder, his men gathering close as well, not without their own curiosity. Dickson and Eleanor approached the pair, but Dougal had eyes only for her, could not say even if Dickson appeared healthy or otherwise. She wore still her summer face, her skin gorgeously bronzed, highlighting her green eyes. He thought mayhap she appeared thinner, but he could not be sure, the cloak hiding all other evidence aside from her face and cheeks, which he judged leaner, mayhap a wee sunken.

"Eleanor, what are ye about?"

Though he'd addressed Eleanor, Dickson and Eleanor both answered.

"There was nae stopping 'er," said her faithful protector, "and who's to say she's nae in error of judgment with this scheme?"

"Good heavens, but we've looked everywhere for you," said Eleanor at the same time. "We've been searching for weeks and weeks." She laughed then, as if she perceived some irony in the as-of-yet unexplained circumstance. "Who'd have thought the last place we looked might better have been the first place we searched? Oh, but are you coming or are you going from Templeton Landing? We are close, are we not? To your home?"

"But Christ, I'm bone weary," Dickson continued, seeming to aim his comments more toward Walter, while Eleanor's regard was strictly for Dougal. "Several fortnights, that's us on the road, and I can tell ye, nae fib, this party's nae easy to travel with."

When they quieted at the same time as well, no one said a word for one, two, three seconds. Dickson looked with some expectation at Dougal and his captain and some of the army, mayhap having expected a different welcome. Eleanor appeared all at once breathless and excited and then so damnably exquisite, the proverbial sight for Dougal's weary eyes. Walter's face was screwed up with so much confusion as to have rendered him speechless.

And Dougal could not take his gaze off Eleanor.

But he recovered first. "Eleanor, what the...what are ye doing here?"

She laughed again, mayhap experiencing her first pang of nervousness for all the watchful and curious gazes aimed at her. "Oh, well, looking for you." She cleared her throat, seeming to compose herself, reining in her noticeable pleasure at finding him. "I was looking for you," she repeated.

"Aye, and now ye've found me, might ye express to me why you traversed the war-torn country to seek me out?"

She blinked rapidly, possibly disturbed by the bite in his tone, caused by his utter confusion.

"Um...yes, of course, but might we speak in private? 'Tis rather a matter of a personal nature."

"Your person or mine?"

"Excuse me?"

"Personal to ye or me? Ye can say what ye want 'fore my men. Nae secrets among the men of an army, lass."

She looked decidedly uncomfortable, but having since discerned that she was under no imminent threat, Dougal's ire was piqued. She had no right to invade his camp, raise his awareness and his heart level, looking like an angel come calling, smiling as if she had not caused a tumult inside him, as if her mere presence did not scream at him that he'd been a fool to pretend he hadn't wanted to stay longer at Bowyer or return to Bowyer and know her more.

"Very well," she said, her lips thinning a wee bit. "I came to...that is, I sought you out with the intention of requesting—"

"*Jesu*, have ye brought yer maid?" Barked Walter, interrupting Eleanor's stammering, as he perused the full party who'd come. "And all the clumsy lads from Bowyer?"

Scowling anew, having had eyes only for Eleanor, Dougal swung his gaze round to the watchful visitors.

Indeed, Dickson and Eleanor traveled with another dozen people. The maid, whose name Dougal had never known, looked decidedly uncomfortable atop the small palfrey.

Dickson took exception to Walter's boorish query. "God's teeth, but I was nae going to be traipsing around the country with nae support. And the lass could nae be moving about with only us, an army, and nae chaperone—as her maid is—for propriety's sake. *Jesu*, man."

Tomag, as well, protested the slight. "Ye say clumsy, old mon," he directed to Walter, "but was that nae me standing aside ye, foiling the blow meant for ye, 'cause age has slowed ye down, made yer reflexes nigh useless?"

The two men jawed back and forth for several seconds. When Walter and Tomag had exhausted their squabble, the winner possibly determined by who scowled most fiercely at the other, Dougal pointedly lifted his brow at Eleanor.

"Are you sure—I'd really much rather speak privately with you—" she implored once again.

"Eleanor," Dougal growled, meaning to get on with her business before he sent her on her way.

There were several—many—reasons to know joy at the sight of her, no matter what cause had brought her to him. But more significant than any of those matters of desire and want, which were grounded in weakness, was the larger truth: she stirred him in ways no other woman ever had, and had managed to do so in a relatively short amount of time; she was as a beacon of light to the darkness in him. She was decent and innocent and so very breakable. He *was* the darkness, would taint and tarnish all that bright light around her. No matter her reason for being here, no matter what his heart said about her arrival—he simply did not have the luxury of allowing his senses to exert power over his decisions—he had no business sullying so good a heart as hers. Send her away, he would, and quick.

Eleanor bit her lip and took one step closer to him, possibly hoping that she would not be overheard, at least not by *all* the dozens of people standing in attendance.

"Ye'll nae have any response if ye dinna put out the request," he said to her, his patience wearing thin.

"Yes, of course. Very well," she said, her cheeks appearing suddenly burnt by the sun, so red did they become. "I wanted—*need*, actually—you to marry me."

He stared at her, unable to speak, trying to process her words.

He'd not misheard them, he didn't believe.

His blood ran cold. She might well have skewered him with his own blade, so vast was his sense of betrayal.

Did she mean to cry foul, insist he'd abused her? Had she believed their kiss a grievous crime?

"Sir Dougal?" She urged, her voice small, the fine color draining from her bonny face in response to his stormy countenance.

His lip curled. He turned to Dickson and snapped, "I'll give ye five seconds to get her out of my sight."

Chapter Twelve

Eleanor was stricken mute, exchanging a dumbfounded look with a gape-jawed Dickson as Dougal Kildare stalked away from her, away from the entire engrossed audience. Belatedly, realizing all the eyes that had widened and tracked the angry knight's departure now turned to gauge her response to what had turned into a fantastic debacle, Eleanor felt the scorching heat of a flush climbing again up her neck and cheeks. Bad enough that he'd forced her to make her request in front of all these people, but so much worse—more confounding and beyond mortifying—was his inexplicable rage as his reply.

"Och, but he dinna answer ye," Lucy remarked, her tone filled with her own surprise.

"Answer enough, I guess," was Tomag's response to this.

Walter of Sandsting attempted to defend his laird's behavior. "Now, and it's been a spell since we've ken genteel company, lass. Sure and dinna ye take him aback with so... puzzling a request. Now ye give him time—"

Walter stopped abruptly when Eleanor marched away, in pursuit of Dougal.

Dickson barked out, "Dinna be chasing after him! He dinna deserve—"

"*I* deserve the courtesy of an explanation, Dickson!" She called over her shoulder. "Give me five minutes."

Despite his swift and angry stride, Dougal had not gone far into the woods.

"Sir Dougal! Wait!" she called out, scrambling around trees and over brush, twenty yards, thirty, and then more, deeper into the thickening trees.

And perhaps he regretted his swift and wrathful departure, so that the sound of her voice caused him to wheel around and begin stalking her, bearing down on her with long, aggressive steps.

"Is this a jape?" Dougal asked in his deep baritone before he'd reached her, looking more a furry and furious beast than mere man at the moment.

"No—good grief, why would I spend so many weeks upon horseback, traipsing across the country to jest about something like that?" She drew up sharply, his approach quite intimidating for the breadth and size of him, for how lethal he appeared right now. Indeed, his scar seemed to have come to life, the white ropey skin reddened and pulsating.

"For the life of me, I dinna understand it," he clipped. He pointed angrily at her from two feet away while his eyes blazed with fire. "So help me God, if you've spread lies, purporting that I'd violated ye—"

"What? No! Sweet St. Andrew! Why would I do that?"

"I dinna ken," he shouted. "Same as I dinna ken why you would ride far and wide, tracking me down, to ask—bluidy hell! Explain yourself."

Memory had proven unreliable, she realized. In her mind since he'd left Bowyer, she managed to use hazy and beautiful brush strokes on his image, having washed all the scowls from his face. She'd spent too much time recalling that expression he'd worn just before he'd kissed her, as if he'd been cast under some tender spell, not so far dissimilar from the look he'd given her just before he'd ridden away. But this, now, was a fine reminder of his rage, which must surely simmer always close to the surface to be raised fully formed and so menacing with such singular speed.

"Well, I might have," she returned, her own ire lifted, "perhaps immediately after my... I guess it was my proposal, but you looked ready then to do me harm, and then you stalked away."

"I am unmoving at the moment," he said through his teeth, placing his hands on his hips. "Clean up this mess. Make damn sure it makes sense and then get the hell out of my sight with this shite."

Unable to comprehend how and why he was being so cruel to her, Eleanor was at a loss. Though she was fairly certain she'd exaggerated in her own mind—for nostalgia's sake and because it pleased her—what he might have thought or felt about her, it had never occurred to her that he loathed her. He did now, she was fairly certain. An entire storm of hatred had taken up residence in his vicious gray eyes. He was exactly the monster he appeared.

She could have been knocked over with a feather, so startled was she by this turn. Of all the responses she'd expected, this ungodly and callous rage had never entered the realm of possibilities. Honest to God, she'd expected as the most plausible negative response an immediate but curt refusal, at worst mayhap presented with a scornful snicker. But not this.

"Did...did you only trifle with me?" She asked as this just occurred to her, her voice cracking. "Is that what you do? Play savior and protector to garner attention and admiration? Have you women scattered all over the country, awaiting your return?

Mayhap a kind word or...or even a stolen kiss?" Possibly, she believed her first query might have some truth to it; that was the one she wanted answered. The questions that followed were simply her giving voice to the hurt she felt. Men of that ilk, who did indeed trifle, must by necessity have the required temperament for such an endeavor—gallantry, a distinct lack of earnestness, an easy nature better suited to wooing—or so she would imagine. Dougal Kildare might be labeled gallant, but certainly he knew no lack of sincerity, and no one in their right mind would portray his character as pleasant and sociable.

Dougal lifted his hand from his hip, his fingers rigid as he pointed to the left side of his face. "I have this, Eleanor," he seethed. "I have nae the leisure nor the means to *trifle* with people."

His reply only furthered her confusion. If he hadn't trifled with her, then what did his present anger signify?

Mayhap it didn't matter. Perhaps an enigmatic man such as he, with the clearly horrific history as suggested by his scarring, might never be understood.

Before she further humiliated herself by shedding tears in front of him—over him and caused by him—which might in fact have been mustered by the troubling realization that any tender regard toward her had only been a figment of her imagination, Eleanor gulped down a swallow and decided to extricate both of them from the unsustainable situation in which she'd thrust them.

"I am deeply sorry to have troubled you, sir," she said, imagining that her voice couldn't have sounded any smaller or more flat. "I have made a grave error in judgment. I—I thought you were...it doesn't matter. I will make haste to remove myself from your unkind presence." *Unkind* was as far as she would go in slighting him for his savage conduct.

As he had done to her, she turned her back to him and stalked away, not even bothering to lift the hem of her skirts as she tromped through autumn's crisp and unyielding underbrush. She'd walked but a dozen feet before she heard the growl behind her and then footsteps that crashed through the foliage quicker than her own. Eleanor braced herself but was still startled when his hand clutched at her arm.

"Bluidy hell, Eleanor," he fumed as he whirled her around.

She tried to shake off his hand and cried to him, "Will you cease with your foulness!"

"What did ye expect my reaction to be?" he snarled, his grip firm still. "Ye still have nae accounted for yer arrival nae yer mad appeal. And how the hell am I nae to imagine it is a trap set and snared, or a bluidy jest?"

"How can you think that of me?" Hurt and anger now warred within her.

"Explain," he hissed, "so that I can understand."

"I will not!" She insisted, angling her face up toward his, the cords in her neck risen with her heated words. "You've made your position clear and thus are not entitled to my reasoning, as it is no longer any concern of yours." Suddenly Dougal wasn't the only one who found it necessary to grit words out from between tightly clasped teeth. "Let me go."

"Just give me—"

The unmistakable sound of metal scraping against metal turned both of them around. Dickson came, scrambling through the dense woods, sword in hand. Several others followed in his wake.

"Git your filthy paws off her," he raged. "So help me God, I'll smite ye where ye stand."

"Dickson, please!" The last thing she wanted was bloodshed. Oh, but this was simply awful, not at all how she'd expected or imagined this meeting might have gone. It was all just a farce now, a sad and pathetic farce.

Dougal released her arm, his own hand instinctively reaching for the hilt of his weapon. But he did not draw his sword, in fact appeared more annoyed than alarmed at Dickson's defensive advance.

Dickson was scarcely appeased, stepping closer to the pair. His top lip, under a week's growth of stubble, twisted unpleasantly. "I ken it would cost me my life, but it would be my pleasure to take yers first, yer intercession at Bowyer House notwithstanding." He lifted his sword, positioning the tip of the blade directly in front of Dougal's face, not a foot of space between. While he maintained steady and unfriendly eye contact with Dougal, he barked at Eleanor. "Go on then. We've said what ye wanted. Received his bluidy reply. Nae guid was ever gonna be had, I said as much."

Before Eleanor moved, Dougal Kildare aimed a fresh hostility at Dickson. He projected his face forward, closer to the blade and growled, "Ye bluidy fool, carting her all around a war ravaged land and for what? For some bluidy game? A childish whim? Ye want to protect her, try keeping her contained there at Bowyer."

"Dinna be telling me how to do my business—"

"Sure and someone has to!" Dougal tossed back, flinging his hand out to underscore his wrath. "How bluidy hard can it be to tell her no? To keep her in check?"

Walter joined the argument, taking the knight's part of course. Tomag surged forward then as well. More swords were drawn, the arguments evolving to shouts and indictments and character assassinations, the heat markedly increasing. And when the first shove occurred—Dickson wisely not using his sword but his hand to push at the Kildare laird's chest—all hell seemed to break loose. More shoving took place and punches were thrown. Walter and Eleanor, intent on diffusing the situation, only tried to remove Dougal and Dickson from each other. Her own cries for them to stop went unheard. Her main concern was Dickson's heart health, his face a ghastly shade of red for all his roaring. But the first push had brought more Kildares into the fray, and that roused the few Bowyer men to defend their captain and mistress, and pretty soon, Eleanor was at the epicenter of an all-out brawl, so small amid all the puffed chests and towering anger and huge bodies. So then it was no surprise when someone drawing their arm back clocked her in the face with their elbow.

Eleanor cried out, and squeezed her eyes shut at the flash of white-hot agony. So acute was the pain that her knees buckled instantly, as if she could not withstand it, *and* grasp her injured nose, *and* stay on her feet, not all those at once. She felt the blood oozing immediately and fell, wincing yet more when she crashed straight to her bottom, landing hard on the unforgiving ground. This did, however, effectively serve to stay all the frenzied action around her.

With the press of bodies so tight around her, and she having been rather lost in the shuffle, Eleanor didn't know who'd hit her until she heard Dougal Kildare's voice. "*Jesu*, lass. I'm—ah, Christ. I'm sorry."

Her eyes were still squeezed tight, trying to fend off the burning tears, but she knew Dougal was close, just beside her, mayhap had dropped to his knees or his haunches.

"Ye bastard!" seethed Dickson from overhead. "Now look what ye've done!"

"Good lord," Eleanor cried with frustration, her voice sounding as if she were suffering a long and nasty bout with a cold. "God's bones," she said crudely, at wit's end, "just stop it, all of you."

"Eleanor, let me see," Dougal demanded, trying to pull her hand away from her bleeding nose.

The throbbing was nearly unbearable. She forced her eyes open and pushed at his big paw with her free hand, afraid he might inadvertently cause her more pain. Already her stomach turned with the severity of it.

"Don't touch me," she said, but not with greater animosity for the fact that he'd just given her a bloody nose, but simply as a general plea, and because it ached so badly. "Just...leave it."

"Here now," said Dickson, bending at the waist, at Eleanor's side, the fight and its hostility forgotten. "C'mon then. We'll get ye seated and we'll be off. He's done his last bit of harm then."

"Leave off, Dickson," clipped Dougal, his gray eyes shining with concern, having met and now holding Eleanor's watery gaze. "Give her a moment."

With one hand covering her nose, her fingers bloody now as well, she still held up her other hand in front of her face for protection against any other accidental jostling.

"I know you didn't mean it," she allowed generously in a trembling voice, "but please don't touch it. The pain is making me sick in my stomach."

His next expression, all that raging fierceness gone, was one of utter anguish for the harm he'd caused her.

"Eleanor, I dinna mean to—" he began, his voice ragged. "I would nae ever raise a hand against ye—"

"I know, Dougal," she said weakly, suddenly feeling as if she might empty the sparce contents of her stomach.

Oh, what a day.

AS ELEANOR APPEARED about to swoon, Dougal gently put his hand on her shoulder to steady her. He glanced up at Dickson.

"Where is her maid?"

Dickson, still holding his sword—to the old man's credit, he hadn't raised it for actual use during the short scuffle—straightened and called for Lucy.

"Clear out," Dougal ordered the crowding throng, mostly lads involved in the wee melee. "Go on. 'Tis done."

"Aye," said the lad, Tomag, derisively, "and we'll nae soon be forgetting how ye managed to end it."

Walter took charge of that one, herding him and others away, grumbling to Tomag, "Ye dinna want to be nipping at that bear, lad. Go on then. Yer captain remains. She's in nae danger."

Tomag was not yet done with his contempt. "Danger's come and gone, just smacked her in the face."

"Get out of here ere I move ye with my boot up yer arse," Walter encouraged gruffly.

While that wee drama unfolded beyond them, Dougal returned his attention to Eleanor, who sat on the ground in astonishing disarray. The hood of her mantle had fallen, and her hair had not escaped a dishevelment, being a bit fluffy and untidy round her head. Tears slid from her eyes and washed down her cheeks, making a trail through the dust of the day's ride. Not only her hand but her cheeks were covered in blood and when she finally, now, pulled her hand away, Dougal grimaced anew at the damage done to her perfect face. Recalling her earlier command that he stop using foul language, he only cursed internally at seeing her petite little nose awash in blood, which still oozed from one nostril.

"It's straight yet," he said levelly, "dinna look broken." Aye, but she'd have a bruise, no doubt, for many days.

Bluidy hell, but he'd made a muck of it. He was still mightily enraged by the entire fiasco, the yet-unexplained reason for her request, but he never would have wished harm upon her. Anything but that.

"Eleanor, I do apologize. I was keeping my eye on Dickson's sword, making sure he did nae raise it." He had also been very aware of her presence, elbowed and shoved until she was at his side, but when the actual fight had broken out, he'd thought her well removed, clearly not close enough to have received his elbow in her face.

She tilted her head, her eyes widening with furious disbelief. "Keeping an eye on Dickson and his sword while you yourself were raising your fist to swing."

"I was nae," he argued with the truth. "I was catching Tomag's flying fist."

Her indignation evaporated as swiftly as it had come, her shoulders slumping. "I'm sorry for the trouble I've brought." With less care, she wiped her hand across the bottom of her nose, sending a streak of blood across her cheek.

Lucy's shriek arrived before she did. "Och, ye beast! What have ye done to her? Dickson, dinna only stand there! Take yer sword to the monster or as God as my witness, I—"

"Lucy!" Eleanor called. "Lucy. Stop. 'Twas an accident."

Dougal rose to his feet, just in time to meet the suspicious glint in the tiny maid's eye.

"Says who?" She snipped. "Him?" She asked, pointing with her thumb at Dougal.

Ignoring this, Eleanor reached up her hand. "Help me up."

Dougal gritted his teeth, furious that he stood right here, had just knelt at her side for more than a minute and she'd not asked him to assist her. "Dinna move yet, lass," he cautioned. "The bleeding will nae stop with any skulking around."

"She dinna skulk," Lucy sneered at him and knelt at Eleanor's side.

Without preamble, and as if she were a mam to many snot-nosed bairns, Lucy lifted the bottom corner of her apron and applied it to Eleanor's bloody nose.

"Stop swiping at my hand, lass," directed Lucy curtly. "Like as nae, we canna stop the bleeding with nae pain nor difficulty. Sit tight and bear it, will ye nae?"

Hands on his hips, his mood scarcely improved, Dougal saw only the back of Lucy's dark head and little of Eleanor's face. He turned and exchanged a long-suffering look with Walter, who stood at Dickson's side, the latter with his frowning gaze trained heartily on his charge. Already, Dougal was thinking they would not soon be rid of the party from Bowyer House. He couldn't simply place Eleanor in the saddle and wish her well, sending her on her way, with naught but hope that the motion of the horse didn't open up her nosebleed again.

The one he'd started.

Son of a—

"Ye dinna need him anyway," Lucy said next to Eleanor. "I've been saying to ye for the last month, while we're gallivanting all over God's cold soil, ye might just as well wed one of the lads. Dinna matter who it is, so long as it's nae the toady Englishman yer da expects ye to wed. Cannae make vows with that one if ye're already bound to another."

"Hush now, Lucy," Eleanor murmured.

But the maid did not.

Dougal's scowl only grew as he listened to what the maid clearly wanted him to hear.

"Ignoring ye for all these years, yer da," Lucy went on. "Unnatural, that is, the way he forgot all about ye—get yer hand off mine; I'll pinch until the bleeding stops. Dinna care nae one bit about our near death experience. Dinna answer Dickson's note," she prattled on with her griping. "Nae one question about how we fared. Just says aye, come hither, lass. I can be done with ye once and for all. Come meet yer husband."

"Lucy, that's enough," Eleanor said, her tone tinged with warning, some of which might have been lost in the odd and deep nasally sound.

"And nae just any Englishman," said Lucy, the back of her head bobbing up and down with her tirade. "Nae, but this one's cruel, and dinna we learn that down near Crieff, when we ran into that merchant and asked what he ken of him, yer intended bridegroom, John Chishull. But dinna fear. As the merchant said, his thirst for war and brutality will nae doubt see him kilt ere the marriage gets too old."

"I'm warning you, Lucy," Eleanor said now, her tone more desperate. "That's enough."

"'Tis nae enough and aye, I'll speak my mind," Lucy groused. "Yanking me north and south for nigh on a month an' dinna I have every right to say enough is enough. Will we nae get on back to Bowyer now, which we should nae ever have left? And ye can say vows with Dickson or Henry Oliver and it dinna make nae difference. Why we had to chase after this one, ye never did make clear to me."

Chishull? Son of a bitch, indeed. Dougal knew well the name. Her father wanted to pawn her off on that wastrel? His crimes against Scotland and her people had been well and horribly related over the years. He'd once been Longshanks sheriff at Dumfries, his tenure there not unremarkable for the brutality of those months there. His removal had only come about after he was nearly killed by locals, much as de Hezelrig had been slain by Wallace at Lanark for his unjust crimes against guid Scottish folk.

He pictured Eleanor under the thumb of one so cruel, pictured her porcelain skin marred by bruises that were deliberate and not merely an accidental jab to the nose. He was still pissed at her coming, and at her astonishing request that they marry. Christ, but how much had she read into their one and only kiss? Or rather, how poorly had he hid himself from her at that moment? Had his heart been laid bare for her to see?

But son of a bitch. He was going to have to wed her, wasn't he?

Dougal sighed audibly, turning Lucy's head around and pricking Dickson's ears as well, he saw in his periphery.

Eleanor pushed Lucy's hand and apron away, her green eyes fixed with apprehension on Dougal. Her nose did not continue to bleed now, though it looked quite red and sore still.

Dougal shifted his regard to Dickson again. "Might better camp with us this night."

"Aye," said Dickson.

"We'll make Templeton on the morrow," he said next. "Ye and yer party can recuperate there for a few days."

That was all he could give now, unwilling yet to commit to that which seemed unavoidable.

Without another glance at Eleanor or her luminous green eyes, Dougal took himself off, further into the woods.

Chapter Thirteen

Not quite how she'd planned her reunion with Dougal. Not at all, actually.

Over the last month of searching high and low for him, sometimes seemingly lost for days in an endless sea of green and brown hills, Eleanor had envisioned many scenarios as his reception of both her and her proposal. Never had she imagined this,

They should have given up weeks ago, should have returned to Bowyer and she should have merely faced her fate. The day of reckoning, the 27th, had long since passed. It had been Dickson who'd furthered their weary march and search. One day, after they'd scoured a tiny hamlet near Crieff for news of the Kildare army, he'd become suddenly hellbent on finding the knight. 'Twas only later that Lucy had learned from Tomag that instead of finding information on the whereabouts of Dougal Kildare, Dickson had apparently stumbled upon information about her intended, John Chishull. Having learned of the man's proclivities for violence, Dickson had become earnest in his attempt to locate Dougal Kildare. Apparently, the devil they knew was preferable to the one they did not.

All for naught though, and ingloriously so.

She sat round one of several small fires strewn about their loosely orchestrated camp, her gaze darting repeatedly on and off Dougal. *On*, whenever he was engaged with another, and she was free to look her fill. Oh, but she'd forgotten the intensity he carried with him, how impressive a figure of a man he was. *Off*, when he lifted his imperious gray gaze to her and she was compelled to feign regard for something or someone else, not so much interested in being caught watching him.

And she did her best not to cry. Not an easy feat with Lucy chirping at her side, in her ear, replaying the events of the day, highlighting all that had gone wrong, as if Eleanor had not seen and born witness to it herself, as if she'd not been the recipient of so grand a set down. Two set downs, she supposed, considering her still aching nose.

"Tells ye nae, he will nae wed ye and then wallops ye in the sniffer," Lucy was saying. "I'm tempted to sneak inside his tent and thwap his head with my angry fists while he sleeps."

"Similar to my own displeasure at the idea of wedding Chishull," Eleanor said quietly to Lucy, "Sir Dougal is entitled to want more or better or different for himself."

"Sure and is he nae?" Lucy returned. "But ye ken there's a kinder way to go about it."

Eleanor couldn't help but laugh at this. "Lucy, there was nothing kind about me hopping on a horse and speeding away from Bowyer to escape my own intended fate."

"Aye, ye've got the right of it," agreed the maid. "The whole thing, both ends of it, stinks of wretched misery. I dinna envy ye, lass. I did, for a long time, ye the daughter of the house, keeper of Bowyer, and with yer once fine clothes and bonny hair. But ye can have it all. Give me the drudgery of my labors and my own mind to make my own choices any day."

Eleanor nodded thoughtfully, supposing her choices were fewer and fewer as the days went on. Like as not, her father would be furious with her, with the date of her scheduled wedding come and gone and she not there, but in all probability, he would, after a fashion and after an enraged scolding, only betroth her to another, someone not of her choosing, and with no concern for the man's character or Eleanor's happiness.

When the night had grown old and the late rising moon was high in the sky, Eleanor excused herself from those closest to her. Exhaustion riddled her body and mind and she wanted only to hunker down and court sleep, but was compelled first to see to her needs. She passed by a neatly placed row of canvas tents, not unlike ones she'd seen now several times upon their travels over the last month, having visited several different army camps. She'd seen armies of all sizes, supposing that the Kildare force fit somewhere in the middle. She'd thought it odd that as she'd met more people and more places in the last month than possibly she had all her twenty years, she'd not met anyone in those travels who had captivated her in the same manner as Dougal Kildare did.

Little good her infatuation would do her now, though.

She'd only gone far enough to have privacy, not more than sixty or so yards into the woods, but was then alarmed when she sensed a presence in the shadowy trees upon her return. Footsteps came closer and while Eleanor froze with caution, the figure moved into a shaft of the pale moonlight, instantly recognizable.

Dougal.

"Eleanor," he said.

Said by way of a cautious greeting, she might have supposed, wondering if he'd intentionally sought her out now. She released the breath she'd briefly held and stepped out of the shadows, closer to him. Her pulse did not settle though; she would never *not* be fascinated by him, by the low rumble of his voice as he said her name.

He did not move, neither to step off the sparse path to allow her to pass nor to move on past her, if his intent had not only to seek her out. And because he did not speak immediately and the quiet unnerved her, Eleanor spoke first.

"I could not help but notice that some faces are missing," she said. "You've lost more men to this war."

"We have," he said and then observed, "and they were nae laid to rest as kindly as those interred at Bowyer House."

"I'm sorry about that," she said. "Does that make getting home more difficult then? Having to notify their kin that they're gone?"

"Aye," he agreed. "But they'll ken. They'll all gather round as soon as the army is sighted, and they'll ken when the horses march up the lane and over the bridge and they dinna see their son or brother, husband, what have ye."

"I imagine with the war dragging on so many years, you cannot recall the last time you returned with the same number of men with which you left."

He shrugged and scratched at his scarred cheek. "Even 'fore the war, we might have lost a man on any outing to either mishap or misadventure, to a hunting accident or skirmishes with rival clans."

"My world view is limited," she reminded him. "Improved—or increased, at the very least—since last we met, but I know little of such things, for which I now have a greater realization and appreciation."

"Hmm," he said. "It's nae exactly an ideal time to be touring Alba, lass."

"Yes, well, needs must and all that," was all she said to that.

"I ken if ye simply ignored yer sire's summons, he'd have come for ye or sent for ye," Dougal guessed.

"One of those. And I didn't want Dickson to be blamed or held accountable for what is my recklessness."

"But he will be, lass. If your father or his agent get to Bowyer and dinna find him there..."

"No," she said, shaking her head. "We've already agreed to fib if need be, and tell my father that I left alone, of my own accord. Dickson's absence, should it be noted, was to be explained by pretending he was out looking for me, daft girl that I am."

"How did ye talk the auld man into it, your mad scheme?"

Because his quiet, light tone suggested some belated amusement, more in regard to poor Dickson's predicament, Eleanor was able to grin. "I simply told him I was going—that is, that I planned to look for you. I told him I was going whether he liked the idea or not. Of course, short of putting me under lock and key, there was no way he could have stopped me. He wasn't happy, I'll tell you that."

He rubbed his hand once more over his left cheek.

"Does it pain you? Your scars?" She asked boldly. What had she to lose? He'd already subjected her to his enormous rage and had then rejected her. He'd even whacked her in the nose, albeit accidentally. What more might he do for her very forward query?

"Ye're a bold one, Eleanor MacAdam," he commented, though she wasn't sure she detected any derision in his tone. "I ken I heard one time some mention of your *wicked ways* getting ye banished to Bowyer in the first place. I guess yer boldness should nae surprise me."

"Who told you—ah, Henry Oliver," she guessed. The old man had more than once referred to the Richard Scrope incident as being incited by her *wicked ways*. She'd always believed he'd just been teasing her. "Good Lord, what did Henry tell you? Is that why you kissed me? Because you'd heard about...?" Eleanor left that trail off, his lifted brow and curious expression telling her he might not have the full story, only Henry's opinion on it.

"I guess that answers any questions I might have had about the definition of *wicked ways*."

Oh, but this was a different Dougal Kildare, playful and without so much severity, as if he would bite her head off. But why now, why after he'd rejected her so harshly?

"*Is* that why you kissed me? You believed that because of my purported wicked ways, that I'd have allowed it?"

"I kissed ye because ye needed it," he said simply. "As did I."

"You needed the kiss, but not a wife?" She asked, unable to hide her exasperation at his purposefully vague and wholly unsatisfying answer.

Rather than answer either parts of that question, he asked instead, "Have ye really been gone from Bowyer for a month?"

She nodded, finding little comfort in the fact that likely he could not see the stain of a blush on her cheeks in the darkness, which signified her acute embarrassment, having chased a man across the country during wartime simply to have him refuse her. Like she had to her father and possibly Richard Scrope, she'd overvalued her appeal to Dougal Kildare. She was trying very hard not to become morose, to entertain self-pity, imagining that no one loved her.

She'd already decided in the last hour that she would instead focus on formulating another scheme to evade her father's plans for her. Industry was so much better than wallowing in her tiny misfortunes.

"I should...get back," she said, even as she acknowledged that she didn't want to relinquish this moment, his private company, his present agreeable mood.

"Take my tent tonight, lass," he said as he finally moved to his left, off the barely discernable path. "Ye and yer maid. It'll only get frostier as the night wears on."

She couldn't hate him, never that. But she felt as if she should harbor some resentment toward him for his incivility this afternoon. Perhaps she was childish to think as much, and behave so, wanting nothing from him, not even his tent, if he wouldn't give her what she needed. "That is very kind of you, sir, but we will be fine, as we have been for weeks now." Whether or not it was guilt that prompted the kindness, she had no idea, but she did know that it was not her job to give relief to his conscience. "Good night, sir."

She'd walked a good dozen steps or more before his voice reached her.

"Guid night, Eleanor."

ELEANOR REGRETTED HER own stubbornness, for refusing Dougal's offer of the use of his tent when it began to rain shortly before dawn. She and Lucy, huddled together as they had been overnight for weeks now, scrambled to lift their blankets up and over their heads. Because of the cold and her overactive brain, she'd barely slept all night. The light rain and dampening chill didn't help matters and Eleanor found herself, despite her exhaustion, wishing for dawn to break. She might as well just get on with the day, whatever it might bring.

When the day finally dawned, and despite the remaining dreariness and still annoying rain, Eleanor rather jumped to her feet, eager to get going.

Dickson quite easily thwarted her intent to lose her glumness.

"God's teeth, but ye look like shite," he said as soon as he saw her face. "Only get worse, I imagine, over the next few days, when the rainbow of colors spring from the bruise."

Wonderful. "And good morning to you, Dickson," she said, brushing past him to find privacy once more before she was forced—her own fault, she understood—to spend another day in the saddle, where she would have to listen to Lucy grouse endlessly about their circumstance and her own dislike of riding. The maid was priceless in her own way, but her habit of counting the days gone from Bowyer, always with some anecdote, had really begun to get on Eleanor's nerves.

"Thirteen days now," she'd said two weeks ago, one of her narrations that had stuck in Eleanor's head. "I once had my monthly for thirteen days. Me mam wept every day, convinced I was nae long for this earth, that I must be dying. My brother—Samuel, ye dinna ken him—he was thirteen when he died, that's what had me mam so riled with dread, supposing she was 'boot to lose another bairn."

"Twenty-one days now," Lucy had said just last week. "I'll nae be twenty-one summers for another four years, mayhap five. Me mam would ken for sure. Did ye ken there were twenty-one apple trees outside that hamlet where we met that merchant from Crieff? Aye, I counted them. I wondered why they planted twenty-one. Why nae grow an even number, so ye can say I've got a score of apple trees?"

Tomag, either to relieve the tedium of their journey over the weeks, or to make fun with Lucy, had begun his own tallying. "Three days now Lucy has nae failed to impress us with her ability to count." Or, "Seven days she's ridden on that horse and called him a fine mare and still she dinna ken he's a gelding."

Lucy had not understood his gaming with her, had debated each fake issue he'd raised, which had meant that Tomag had ceased to be entertained by himself and her.

The Kildare army and the party from Bowyer House were on the move again shortly after dawn and a light repast of what remained of both parties' provisions, at this point hard cheese and crusty bread. They headed further into the Highlands as the sun found its way directly above them, clearing gray clouds and brightening the day.

Dickson rode out front with Walter, those two never seeming to be at a loss for words but then also happy to ride side by side without conversation for long stretches. Trading war stories when they did speak, Lucy had supposed in a whisper midway through the day. Dougal Kildare was seen and then not, at times leading the party, too far ahead to be the object of Eleanor's attention, or sometimes riding out at great lengths until he disappeared altogether. At one point, he'd stopped his huge destrier on the fringe of the muddy road, watching as the party slowly marched past him, acting as a mother hen or what he was, the leader of this army, wanting to make sure all were accounted for, the party collectively well-disposed. His gaze met and stayed with Eleanor far longer than it had with any other ahead of her, she convinced herself. It meant nothing, though, his silent scrutiny, his gray eyes more unfathomable than usual at that moment. Still, they had the power to unnerve her, or stimulate her, whatever it was that caused her breath to catch and her pulse to race whenever he stared too long at her.

As the sun began its afternoon descent, they finally arrived at Templeton Landing, Eleanor's first view of Dougal's home being from the valley which surrounded it as it sat upon a promontory with taller, rolling hills beyond it.

The sheer size of Templeton Landing awed her. Bowyer House might fit two or three times into the perimeters of this great walled fortress. The keep itself was squared and cornered with four rounded towers, the entirety of it surrounded by a wide parapet. The curtain wall was three stories high and the gatehouse at the center of its front was taller yet, squared and not rounded as were the other turrets. As they neared, the banner waved by a forward marching soldier in Dougal's army instructed that the portcullis should be raised and soon hundreds of hooves of dancing horses could be heard echoing over the timber bridge which covered the moat. Inside, the bailey was crowded with residents and serfs, welcoming home their loved ones and friends.

Soldiers jumped from their mounts, taking up wives and children into great hugs, while young lads from the stables saw to their horses and pages secured their arms. Women cried at this homecoming, children screamed their joy; brothers, sisters, and mothers fought to find their man among the army.

Eleanor wondered who might welcome Dougal. True, no resident ignored his presence, most extending greetings of welcome to him, yet there was not a single person who seemed to wait only for him. No one set of arms and eyes sought him out, wanting only to touch him to assure themselves that he was real and here now. She thought it odd that this had not occurred to her, that he might have someone waiting on his return, might have refused to wed Eleanor for want of another. Even as she chided herself for only belatedly considering this possibility, she saw no one rush to greet him.

She didn't wait on anyone to help her dismount, having done so herself for the last month. A Kildare soldier took the reins from her, assuring her he'd square away the care and housing of the Bowyer steeds.

Eleanor did not advance toward any person or the keep itself though her gaze did once more seek out Dougal. She saw him in quiet conversation with three young women, presuming these were kin to one of his men lost either at the siege at Bowyer or sometime in the ensuing months, amid the further skirmishes they met. She recalled that the first man to be slain at Bowyer was named Niall, and that Dougal had said he had sisters who would rather know he slept eternally in company rather than alone upon some unnamed hill. The women were similar in height and figure, tall and lithe each of them. One appeared struck mute as stone with grief, her hand over her mouth, her eyes fixed wretchedly upon her laird. Another wept quietly, her face in her hands, Dougal's consoling hand upon her arm possibly unnoticed. The third young woman presented a stiff exterior, her chin lifted and her gaze defiant, as if she would refuse to believe the truth. Only her quivering chin gave any evidence of acceptance. As if she felt eyes upon her, or mayhap having been advised her loved one had died defending Eleanor's home, she turned and stared directly at Eleanor for a moment. Eleanor did nothing with her own expression, letting the woman see her sorrow.

She wondered exactly how many of these painful conversations the laird would be required to have today.

Lucy sidled over to Eleanor, her brow knit, and her lips pinched. "Like we're plump hens whose necks they mean to wring, the way they're eyeing us," she hissed to Eleanor.

A swift glance around to others milling about the courtyard made Eleanor, too, feel conspicuous, doubly so since she knew her nose was unsightly now after yesterday's mishap. The many eyes upon them, not all of them gauged to be charitable, had her rather bracing herself when she noticed Dougal striding toward her.

He spared not one morsel of attention for Lucy but kept his piercing gray eyes trained on Eleanor, who could not help but know a sympathy for him, for being the bearer of mournful news to those women.

"Are they Niall's kin?" She asked, inclining her head toward the trio making their way now arm in arm out of the yard.

Perhaps he was only amazed that she recalled the lad's name, so that his face briefly registered a wee surprise before his customary frown returned.

He nodded. "Aye, his sisters, sorry for his demise and I dinna ken 'twas any comfort after all to ken he laid next to yer *màthair*." He lifted his hand toward the expansive keep. "I'll show ye to the hall, and have a chamber prepared for ye. But I want to find my own *màthair* first, if ye dinna mind waiting."

She assumed Dougal's courtesy to her was merely because she was not a soldier, and possibly because she was a woman. If it had only been Dickson and Tomag and others of their ilk arriving and hoping to find ease here at his home, he might have left them in the care of another, might have directed them to the gatehouse and its barracks.

"Not at all," Eleanor replied. "We don't need any special treatment."

How strange, she thought, she'd crossed the country to find him, had asked him to marry her, and didn't know anything about his family. Her curiosity over his mother was overwhelming. She wondered first what manner of woman raised a man such as this knight and then Eleanor's brow knit, questioning why the woman had not been present in the bailey, opening her grateful arms to her returned son.

At Dougal's direction, she and Lucy preceded him into the keep, advancing up a short flight of stone steps and passing through an open and arched doorway, which delivered them directly into the great hall. They moved only far enough inside to allow others, Dougal directly in their wake, to enter as well. Otherwise, both Lucy and Eleanor were in awe of their first glimpse inside Templeton Landing. The hall was vast, surely one hundred feet in length and almost half that width in depth, with three different hearths on three different walls. The ceiling was vaulted and fitted with impressive trusses, ten inches thick it seemed, and not crudely hacked but finely carved. The two short end walls were plastered and painted, the long exterior walls being of pale red stone.

Dougal strode across the hall to where the high table sat, and where sat a corpulent man dressed in finery such as Eleanor had only ever seen in England. Though Templeton Landing was certainly grand, it was rustic as befitted its northern location, and the man's silks and fur-lined garments stood out with striking incongruity so that he appeared almost absurd.

"Och, and the prodigal son returns," called out the man, his fleshy jowls moving and swaying with his speech.

Eleanor didn't know the man at all to judge his tone, but she sensed no warmth in the questionable greeting, and supposed much should be made by the fact that the man did not rise to greet the laird, did not even release the greasy bone of meat from his fleshy hand.

He was, in fact, surrounded by food, platters and bowls and goblets, though Eleanor in the middle of the hall was not close enough to say on what he dined. Some long ago caution uttered by her father returned to her: *Beware the man who dines alone; he shares the table with a fool and trades ideas likewise.*

Perhaps because of the dubious reception, Dougal did not return a greeting, even a vague one, but asked straight away, "Where is *màthair*?"

"Sure and she had been feeling poorly," said the man, whose identity was yet unknown to Eleanor.

Briefly, he stretched his gaze beyond Dougal to where Eleanor and Lucy huddled and listened, unobtrusively, but not with any intent to hide their lurking. Eleanor didn't know if his eyes were swollen or just bulbous, rather prominently projected outward with heavy lids rather than sitting within the face. Likewise, she didn't know what he might make of her appearance. The curtness of Dougal's voice as he addressed the man suggested she might not care what he thought of her.

Eleanor inched closer, taking note of the way Dougal's broad shoulders stiffened.

"Padean," Dougal growled, "where is my *màthair*?"

Rather defensively, sensing Dougal's rising ire, the man flapped the hand that held the half-eaten bone of meat.

"Settle lad, she is nae deceased yet," he said and spent an infuriating moment removing some stuck food from between his teeth with one of his pudgy fingers. "But grant me pardon for worrying she might infect all of Templeton with whatever ails her—fever or some such. Ye would hae done the same, isolated her away from the healthy populace."

"I'm about three seconds away from shoving that bone all the way down your throat," Dougal said, his voice dangerously low and slow. "Where is my *màthair*?"

"Returned to the hovel whence she came," said the man, making no effort to disguise his glee, for what he'd done to Dougal's mother.

"God's bluid," Lucy whispered at Eleanor's side. "Evil, right here before us."

"God damn ye, Uncle," Dougal seethed now. He pivoted on his heel and headed toward the door, possibly not recalling Eleanor and Lucy's presence, and certainly unaware of their wide-eyed shock. "Make yerself scarce, Uncle," he called over his shoulder. "I'd strike ye down now if she dinna need my attention more."

The hair on the back of Eleanor's neck stood up, both in reaction to the lethal quality of Dougal's voice and for concern for his mam, who had apparently been treated as a leper, sequestered outside of her own home.

Eleanor moved to follow Dougal, and because Lucy's arm was threaded through hers, the maid was essentially dragged along with her.

She said nothing to Dougal, put out no queries, only thought she might be of service to him or his mother, but that he would refuse her offer if she voiced it.

She and Lucy skipped to keep up with Dougal's angry and lengthy strides, and it did not go unnoticed that his hands were fisted and swinging at his side as he crossed the bailey and exited through the gate.

They stayed many lengths behind him and likely his present fury and concern for his mother did not allow for awareness of others.

"Fie, and we ken we had troubles," Lucy remarked in a whisper. "Uncle might've been enjoying his last supper, the way I see it."

Chapter Fourteen

He'd known Padean's character was unsavory at best, that treachery was second nature to him, but honest to God, he'd never have imagined that he'd risk Dougal's wrath—indeed his very life—by playing foul with his mother. God help him—only He could—if his mother had been further mistreated than merely being removed from the keep because of some supposed contagion.

He'd kill him.

With his bare hands.

He felt desperate now, his stomach and jaw both clenched, and his furious stomping around the north side of the keep and through the wooded vale and up and down the hill over which the lane wound wasn't helping. His mother's constitution had never been robust, and Dougal prayed that she suffered now one of her regular bouts with congestion and cough, nothing more, and that Padean was only taking advantage of that to remove her from the keep as he'd longed to do forever.

The village came into view as he crested the wee beinn, the breeze previously thwarted by the same hill now slapping Dougal in the face as he descended. 'Twas almost a year he'd been gone, but little had changed in the village. The fields were as barren as when last he'd seen them, the growing season come and gone while he'd been away. He marched along the lane as it twist-

196

ed through an untidy grouping of cottages, some appearing ignored over the last year, one with its door hanging askew, only one hinge attached, wrinkling his brow yet more.

Bluidy hell, the only reason he'd not tossed out Padean previously was because he was, or had been, despite every other indecent and infuriating characteristic, well-versed with the running of Templeton, and the needs of the village—though those seemed to have been overlooked presently.

He would be home for a spell now, mayhap all winter, and would set matters right, beginning with his mother's care.

The house in which Aimil had been born and raised sat at the end of the row of thatched roof hovels and homes—the designation sometimes dependent upon its occupants—the lane being locally referred to as Eithrig's Path, named ostensibly after one of Templeton's first settlers, from more than a century ago around the time the keep had been constructed, back when the village was only one road and not several.

Aimil's parents, Dougal's grandparents, had years ago succumbed to old age, or as Dougal sometimes thought, to their bitterness. Little had he mourned them, being rather pleased at the time and since that his mother had been relieved of their acidic company. He'd always thought Aimil's light weeping at their passing had been more dutiful than genuine.

The croft and cottage had briefly been leased after Aimil had moved to the keep, the arrangement short-lived after the tenant, Alpin Anndrais, had been lost at Falkirk and his expectant wife had perished in the subsequent birthing weeks later, without having yet been informed that her husband had preceded her in death. The bairn, a healthy lad, named after his father, had been taken in by a childless couple of middle age—Dougal initially believed as a future workhorse, though his mother had assured him otherwise—and the house had remained vacant ever since.

A linen-covered basket sat on the ground just to the left of the door, seemingly untouched.

He didn't knock at the house but wrenched the door open, having to put his shoulder into it for the way it stuck on the ground as it always had—its greater-than-expected resistance to opening suggesting disuse; no one was tending his mother, he would guess.

The interior was nearly pitch black, windows shuttered and no fire lit. Dougal's fury soared anew.

It stunk of filth and sickness, not so unlike a boggy battlefield when the fighting was done.

The figure of his mother was discernable on the narrow cot in the far corner only by way of the light allowed entry by him having left the door open.

"*Jesu*," he gasped, going immediately to his knees at her side. "*Màthair*," he called her, fleetingly wondering with great alarm if she were indeed already dead.

His voice turned her head, giving Dougal instant relief.

She was tiny and crumbled upon the bed, her léine and kirtle soiled, her once lovely black hair knotted and tangled all around her head. Her skin was disturbingly colorless though it shone with perspiration. Dougal laid his palm against her brow just as she opened her eyes.

"Aye, and I ken ye'd come one last time," said his mother, her voice fragile, scratchy from disuse he might guess.

"I am home, *màthair*," he said, kissing her cool brow. Her fever, perhaps coming and going, had recently broken, he would guess.

"Gone too long," she said, showing strength beyond what she seemed capable of, lifting her hand and laying it against the smooth side of Dougal's face.

He laid his hand over hers. "Home again with ye."

He didn't question her about her illness, or the length of her banishment here. Her eyes were glassy, didn't quite fix properly on his face, her smile otherworldly for her weakness, in that she was barely conscious.

I will kill him, he thought without remorse, saving shame for himself, for having left his mother at Padean's mercy.

This had been Dougal's longest, continuous absence from home, having been gone this past year. Likely his uncle might have thought Dougal had become a victim of war, thought he'd finally met his maker. Padean would have imagined that Aimil had no one to speak for her or protect her, and that Dougal would never learn of his conduct toward his mother. He couldn't imagine any other person who would have challenged his uncle to gainsay his handling of the situation, having essentially tossed her into her childhood home to die. White-hot rage surged anew in his chest, blinding him to courteous matters such as showing mercy himself or even waiting on further explanation from his uncle for this evil management. There was no justification for such cruelty as this.

Shadows filled the doorway, darkening the one room cottage, turning Dougal around with a start.

Eleanor and Lucy had followed him and stood there now. What remained of daylight was at their backs and yet he did not mistake the intensity of their pity. Dougal laid his mother's hand upon her chest and stood.

Eleanor and Lucy stepped further into the hut, the latter covering her nose with her hand, her brow wrinkled.

Without preamble, Eleanor asked, "What can we do?"

"I—I dinna even ken where to start..." he said, using a voice he had not heard since his childhood, feeble, uncertain.

"Aye, but we do," said Lucy, moving away from Eleanor to the windows that had been added in the last few years to the hut, where she moved aside the oil cloth and opened shutters, allowing more light to spill into the cottage.

"Your *màthair*?" Eleanor guessed, laying a lingering and sympathetic glance on the wrecked figure on the small, raised bed. At Dougal's nod, she returned her gaze to him and spoke assertively. "You will want to deal with your uncle, I presume," she said, showing an uncanny ability to read his mind. "Do that, Dougal. The man deserves your wrath. And rest easy in one regard concerning your dear *màthair*. Lucy and I will see her as right as we are able."

"Shove that bone as ye threatened him, sir," clipped Lucy, eyeing the knight's mother with distress. "As far and viciously as ye are able. Nae fit for this earth, that one. C'mon, Eleanor, we'll get the wee lamb right as rain."

Still reeling from his mother's condition and the pair's very generous offer—Aimil might well be contagious, whatever ailed her—Dougal murmured, "What will ye need?"

"Send someone to us," Eleanor answered promptly, her green eyes snapping with decisiveness. "Ye needn't be running and fetching, but send someone who can, someone you trust to do so earnestly and speedily."

"Eleanor, ye should nae have to—"

"Pray save all concern for your mother, sir," she invited, briefly laying her hand upon his arm. "Now go. Truly, you're only in the way."

Believing their concern genuine and that any care would be given tenderly, joined with Eleanor's practicality and Lucy's umbrage on his mother's behalf—and knowing inherently that he would trust Eleanor with his own life if need be—Dougal did feel comfortable enough to leave the women to the monumental task of recovering his mother.

"I'll return shortly," he said. "I'll send down a few of the lads now."

He turned and exited the hut, his departure stalked by Lucy's bloodthirsty instruction, "Show 'im wot the inside of hell looks like, sir!"

He lacked no appreciation for the complete about-face of both lasses. Yesterday, Lucy would have been happy to show Dougal the bowels of hell. And for the same reason, his savage dismissal of Eleanor's request that they wed, Eleanor had been quite sore with him, he was sure. How fine they were then, to dismiss what sourness they'd known when faced with far greater a calamity, to come to his aid with neither hesitation nor question at so unfortunate a time.

"GOOD GRIEF, LUCY, BUT where *do* we begin?" Eleanor wondered.

Lucy planted her hands on her hips and surveyed the unkempt cottage, which appeared to have been vacant for some time before Dougal's mother had been so callously dumped here.

"Aye, it's like Cook always says," Lucy announced with an authoritative nod. "We canna work in these conditions. We must right the wrong first, which is to say while we're waiting on kettles and water—peat and fire starters, too, it seems—we will tidy the place so that we can labor easier when we've all the proper tools."

"But sit with her and hold her hand, Lucy," Eleanor directed. "She's still reaching for her son, doesn't know he's gone just now." Indeed, though the woman appeared not so much cognizant, hardly able to keep her eyes open, her hand lifted to where Dougal's face had been close only moments ago.

Lucy grimaced and drew out a faltering "Ahhh." She wrinkled her nose. "I dinna do well with coddling, lass. Ye ken that. Ye sit with her. 'Tis yer man to whom she belongs."

"He is not my man, Lucy," Eleanor balked, an instant frown falling over her brow. "God's bones, but don't speak as such."

"I'm jus' sayin', if it were Tomag's mam, I'd nae expect ye to sit and hold her hand."

Eleanor rolled her eyes. "It doesn't matter which of us tend to her, Lucy. I only didn't want ye to be left with the heavier workload."

"I'd much rather be scrubbing and tidying, lass," Lucy assured her.

Reluctant to argue the point further, certainly not when the woman might have been without attendance for days or more, Eleanor sat on the side of the small bed and took the woman's nearly lifeless hand in hers. There was no kind way to think or say it, but that the woman stunk terribly, that she might well have soiled herself, being clearly unfit to rise and tend her own needs.

"Oh, the poor thing," Eleanor cooed, brushing her thick but tousled hair away from her face. "Shh," she urged, gently when the woman's brows lifted at the soft touch.

While Eleanor sat with Dougal's mother, who did settle to peacefulness while Eleanor stroked her brow, she and Lucy quietly discussed their plan of attack regarding the woman's care. Since neither was a healer, nor could claim more than basic knowledge of such things, they decided they would request from Dougal or whomever came next that one be sent for. Before Lucy had made too much headway with the cleaning, Eleanor put a stop to it.

"This is ridiculous, Lucy," she said. "And Sir Dougal for obvious reasons wasn't thinking clearly, but we need to return this woman to the keep, where she will be more comfortable, and supplies and aid will be closer."

"Aye, that's the right of it," Lucy agreed, looking with some relief around the cluttered and abandoned house, where dust and filth covered almost every surface. "We'll be able to give her a proper bath and clothe her in a fresh kirtle and cover her with clean linens. Aye, that's what we'll do."

And she went to the door and leaned against the frame, presumably awaiting whoever the knight might have sent to assist them, meaning to change their direction. "I'll tell them to bring a litter instead."

Only a moment later—Eleanor hadn't expected that Dougal would have delayed sending aid to his mother—riders on horseback came, the sounds of hooves beating against the ground suggesting at least two or three, the noise amplified in the quiet of the evening and the still village. Lucy waylaid them before they might have come into the cottage, advising them to return with some means to transport the woman to the keep.

Reluctant to abandon her position aside the woman, Eleanor heard only the murmur of whatever response was given from whomever had come. Apparently some dissent, as judged by Lucy's return reply, which was easily heard as she stood only a few feet outside the door.

"I dinna care who told ye wot," Lucy snapped. "I just said to ye she's to be moved to a more kindly circumstance and ye're to make that happen by bringing a litter. Now git. Take it up with the laird if ye ken ye will challenge me."

Eleanor pictured Lucy's fists plopped onto her hips as she sometimes did when her dander was risen.

The maid did not come again inside the cottage, but Eleanor could hear her grumbling to herself just beyond the door, as she busied herself with sweeping the stoop. "Telling me wot I should be about, and they leaving the miserable woman to rot away all by her lonesome. Hmph."

It wasn't long before more riders were heard and the doorway filled with another's presence. Dickson had come, and with him Tomag and one of Dougal's lads.

"Aw, *Jesu*," grumbled Dickson as he closed in on Eleanor and her charge, a hard grimace worn and filled with fierce compassion for the still and small figure in the bed.

"The Kildare laird just pounded the piss out of his uncle," Tomag said, all good humor despite the sorry glance he also sent to the woman.

"Literally?" Eleanor asked, her eyes widened. She'd expected that merely because the man was Dougals' uncle—mayhap his mother's brother?—that his threat had only been figurative.

Tomag grinned, as if he were greatly impressed. "Exactly, lass. Fists to his face, and a kick to his ass at the end, sent him sprawling down the steps out of the hall. Landed in fresh horse shite, dropped there upon our return, I guess."

"Gave him the never darken my doorway bit," Dickson provided, shrugging as if the spectacle had been dulled by such an uninspired threat. "Uncle promised he was nae done with either Templeton or yer knight. Called him a bastard, few other names—dinna ken when to shut his trap until the laird knocked at him again. Saw one of his teeth go flying."

"He'll be missing that with the next bone he gnaws at," Lucy said, with no small amount of satisfaction. Her smirked enlarged into a true smile. "Och, and the knight rises in my estimation with each beastly growl and fat man beaten."

"And that's the difference," Dickson advised them, "'tween a bailiff with guid intentions, as best as he's able, myself included—only trying to see the job done fairly and rightly—and those with their own agendas. The laird's away and that fat man dinna care if he ever returned, dinna care for naught but himself and his gullet. Like as nae, has lined his own buried coffers with the laird's coin, mark my words. I ken his ilk."

"Certainly we are missing much of the story," Eleanor suggested, "including the specifics of the reasoning behind the man's abuse of the laird's mother."

The Kildare lad, who'd come with Dougal to Bowyer House for those few days when they'd been under siege months ago, Arthur by name, quiet as he'd ever been by Eleanor's reckoning, and thus whose presence was rather overlooked presently, filled them in.

"But he is a bastard, Sir Dougal—pardon, lasses—as the former laird, his sire, was nae wed to his *màthair* there," he said, tipping his head toward the neatened platform bed and the woman in it.

"Bastard is he?" Remarked Dickson, chewing on this, his bushy brows knitting.

"Aye," said Arthur, who appeared very earnest, explaining, "but nae in the figurative sense, though his temper flares fast. But in the actual sense, since his parents were nae wed."

"How's he laird then, and nae the uncle?" Dickson asked. "Uncle is his father's brother, aye?"

"Yes, sir. But that was her doing," said Arthur, again indicating Dougal's mother with a tip of his head. "She made that happen, though I dinna ken the particulars. But ask any here, they'd want the laird's sometimes explosive fury rather than any part of his uncle's evil-doings. Dinna trust that one, nae one bit. Do right by the laird, give it yer best and yer all, dinna shirk or scrimp, and he'll treat ye fairly though ye wouldn't...well, ye might nae guess that...er, either by looking at him, or—pardon, lass—by his reaction to the announcement of yer intention of yesterday."

Eleanor managed a lackluster grin to show no hard feelings for his observation.

"But then, the mistress here—that is, the laird's *màthair,* she dinna fare so well when the laird was gone. Padean—that's the uncle—he made sure of that. Treated her nae better than the milkmaid she once was, gave grief to any who dared otherwise, but she'd nae ever say as much to her son, and Padean gave it a rest when the laird was in residence."

Any further discussion on the matter was thwarted by the arrival of yet more persons, as heralded by further noise outside.

Dougal Kildare himself had come and strode purposefully into the tiny and now cramped cottage, seeming surprised at first to find it filled with more Bowyer folk than Kildares, and second, to find Eleanor sitting on the bed and holding his mother's hand.

They shared only a brief glance before he transferred his seemingly anxious regard to his mother.

Looking for any evidence that he had indeed *pounded the piss* out of his uncle, Eleanor only found it in his hands. His chest did not heave yet from his reported exertions; his face was not ruddy in the same manner; but his hands were reddened and possibly swollen, and thus Eleanor supposed neither Tomag nor Dickson had exaggerated the tale of what he'd done to his uncle.

The removal of the woman from the soiled bed was made effortlessly by Dougal lifting his mother onto a stretched canvas litter he'd provided and which Dickson and Tomag maneuvered into place beneath her.

'Twas a slow march back to the keep then, with Dougal and Tomag bearing the litter, Tomag kindly walking in front, his hands holding the arms of the device behind him so that Dougal could keep an eye on his mother as they walked. Eleanor and Lucy walked on either side, both with a hand on the side of the litter, a safekeeping measure. Dickson led the party, as he was accustomed to doing.

Dougal advised Eleanor, and by way of proximity, Lucy as well, "I dinna ken that anyone inside Templeton will consider her any better than my uncle had."

Eleanor did not advise that Arthur had moments ago said just about the same thing.

"And ye might simply snarl at them to do yer bidding," Lucy supplied as an idea, but then qualified, "but luckily for ye, ye dinna need to. Ye leave her in our hands, better cared for she'll be than at the mercy of any of these people, who left her out there all by herself. I want to meet and have words with any of them, who ken where she was and how she was suffering and continued about their business. Might better leave that to me, sir. Naught I like better than telling people how wretched they are and wot it'll get 'em."

They moved off in different directions. Dougal following Tomag's lead along the path through the short woods at the front of the stretcher, while Lucy needed to go wide right around a fat conifer and Eleanor subsequently skittered off the path on the left as a cluster of trees was also in her way. Thus, she could not see what expression Dougal might have made to Lucy's wee rant on his mother's behalf. Many things might be said about Lucy—she was sometimes too frank, could on occasion annoy a person with her endless prattle, and often thrust her nose into business that was not hers—but one could never assume that she was not made of compassion and an inherent want to take up the cause of the weak or maltreated.

No sign of Padean Kildare remained either in the yard or the hall, though several others milled about, casting sidelong glances at the coming party and the unconscious woman brought on the litter. With Dougal giving direction to Dickson in the lead yet, they climbed the stairs to the second floor and entered a chamber at the end of a long passageway, Eleanor and Lucy bringing up the rear of the marching line.

Dougal's mother was installed in a higher, larger bed there, the frame having four posts and sumptuous coverlets. The chamber was of a generous size, with a kist of gleaming wood near the foot of the bed, and a taller, round top cupboard against a far wall, that piece being nearly grotesque in size, the top of it nearly touching the timbered ceiling.

While Tomag bent to light a fire when the litter was empty and Dougal and Eleanor hovered over his mother, Lucy ticked off instructions to Dickson.

"Make yerself useful, ye and yer scowl," she said pertly, "and get them in the kitchens to boil some water. Kettles to keep here, one hot, one cold. And more of the same for her bath. Dinna take any of their slackness if they mean to gainsay ye."

"You...um, took care of your uncle then?" Eleanor asked of Dougal, more as a distraction to alleviate the growing concern etched in his gray eyes.

"He is nae more for Templeton," Dougal said, his mien darkening simply at the mention of the man.

"How awful he is," Eleanor remarked, "for having treated your dear mother so poorly."

"But ye have nae, nor Lucy," Dougal said, finally lifting his eyes, meeting Eleanor's. "How do I thank ye?"

Eleanor tilted her head to one side. "How do I properly and effectively thank you for what you did at Bowyer? We have only the words and the authenticity behind them. I don't doubt your gratefulness as I hope you never did mine."

"But after yesterday, and the way I—" he started, seeming suddenly sheepish, a wholly unfitting look for him.

"Another—separate—matter entirely, and it has no bearing on this one, sir," she promised him, and she meant it. It wasn't as if she would have withheld care of his mother—or any person in need—simply because he'd rejected her proposal. And the truth was, and though she didn't in any way imagine it might change his stance on the matter of them marrying, Eleanor rather liked being of service to Dougal. She was pleased to set his mind at ease. Their history was short and mostly tragic, and she could not claim to know him well, all things considered, but she didn't doubt that he was pleased that she was here now, able to offer what she could.

She would find over the next few days that she was pleased to have an occupation, some industry to keep her busy. Presently, she considered it justly her penance for the havoc she'd obviously wreaked on the knight with her cross-country chase and—as hindsight had shown—ill-advised proposal of marriage. But mostly, and as she would for any person so frail and unjustly treated, Eleanor wanted to offer some measure of comfort to the woman, as none in residence seemed either capable or willing to do so.

Why the woman had been sequestered inside her old home, if the fear were only contagion, seemed to be rooted in some larger issue, which Arthur had hinted at, and one that scratched at Eleanor's curiosity, though not enough to question now, when her life seemed indeed to yet be in peril.

She said instead to Dougal, "I had wondered...she would have been at the gate to celebrate your return if she could have."

"Always."

Chapter Fifteen

By midnight on the day of their return home, Dougal was finally able to relax, though the term was relative. Having arrived home only signified the end of that journey but plunged Dougal now into the affairs of the demesne, most critically, his mother's condition. Knowing he would be of little use inside the sickroom, he only poked his head in hourly or thereabouts, receiving the same update each time from either Eleanor or Lucy: no change.

Walter himself, whose leg was yet in need of attention, had gone personally to search for Morag, who was not specifically Templeton's healer, but the closest one to serve as such.

He'd met earlier with Yopin, Templeton's steward, and had watched as the aged man carefully included the banishment of Padean Kildare from Templeton in the file in which he kept a record of all the castle's grievances, settled or otherwise. In a different ledger he neatly scratched the names of those men lost, men Dougal had called forth to follow him to war, men of his own blood or dependence. 'Twas a long many minutes watching Yopin apply those names to the vellum journals and, as ever, Dougal was mournful of that which the continued battle with the English took away from Scotland.

He'd been fully apprised of what Templeton had seen and endured and produced over the last year, the discourse of Yopin so ordinary that Dougal wondered if the man ever wearied of its monotony. There was an unbroken sameness of topics, reports, and events—the small money matters of castle life, the tiresome daily cares, hearing the same complaints, remedying the familiar wrongdoings. The man was well-suited to the tasks of his role, his nondescript face being regularly without expression.

Dougal had since met with each family of every man fallen, receiving tight-lipped resignation, open and wailing grief, and from the mother of Peter Redhaugh a ruthless appraisal of Dougal's capabilities for having not brought her son home. From the smithy he learned of the work needed and completed on the forges that made the iron. Gabriel, captain of the huntsman, advised of the red stag and deer population, the forest teeming with them, despite the growing number of wolves in the area, which had garnered much of his attention over the last twelve months.

And so on had progressed his evening, receiving one report after another, from tradesmen, tenants, and some of the household staff. And not one of them had either made mention of his mother and her illness or inquired about her current condition. The great pride he normally took in Templeton and all its inhabitants was soured and more than only a wee bit by this lack. But then, roles were rather set in stone here in the Highlands. You were born and died in the same class, and any deviation from this raised brows and invited umbrage; if you managed to elevate yourself, those to whom you were now equal or greater disparaged your ascent, and those left behind scorned you for your new rank, their resentment rooted in envy. Dougal had only escaped such pique because he had immediately proven himself as laird, fair and just, and life at Templeton so far improved from the castle his father had handled. Thus, he'd not been unaware of the resentment his mother had faced, for having been lifted from milkmaid to mistress of the castle, but even hindsight wasn't able to provide him with any clue that these people would have treated her no better than a hound in her time of need. He was sorry then that his own attitude toward the population in general dropped an alarming degree for their behavior, no one save the very young escaping his silent and seething fury.

Having no more that might be done today, any other person he might have wished to confer with no doubt abed at this hour, Dougal returned to his mother's chamber. Somehow he was not surprised to find Eleanor still at her side, in a circumstance not unfamiliar to Dougal, having once found her keeping vigil over Dickson in much the same manner. She was asleep now as she had been on that occasion.

Not that he'd had any doubt, but he saw that his mother had indeed been well-attended. She lay sleeping still, or again, appearing freshly groomed, her hair washed, combed, and braided, the tail of which rested over her shoulder and across her chest. A small golden fire burned in the hearth, coloring her cheeks in a soft orange glow so that he could not say if her earlier distressing pallor was improved or not. But on the whole, and at only a glance, she appeared at least restful in her slumber and so much improved merely for being clean and away from the chaos and filth of that hovel to which she'd been exiled.

Having satisfied himself that her chances of surviving whatever ailed her were greatly increased, Dougal turned his attention to Eleanor. As he had once before and unwilling to resist the temptation now, he watched her sleep. As he'd regularly been, he was entranced by her loveliness, and then put in mind of her genuine care of people, for having remained with Dickson when he'd been ill—*he is everything to me*, she'd said—but now having stayed with a person she'd not yet formally met, and solely because her heart was good.

She was the savior now, their roles reversed.

There was no large and comfortable armchair here in this chamber of which she might have made use and so she'd pulled the short stool close to the bed in which his mother lay and sat there with her upper body laid forward on the bed, her arms crossed under her head. Her face was turned toward him and the door, the soft firelight unable to conceal the fact that her nose was still red, mayhap swollen as well. Not surprisingly, it did little to detract from her beauty. Her hair, since unbound from the braid she'd worn all day, lay in waves around her shoulders and down her back. Her lashes fanned across her cheeks and her lush lips were closed, soft and tempting even in slumber.

I wanted—need, actually—you to marry me, she'd said yesterday.

'Twas no game she played, he now knew, only her contemplating self-preservation, mayhap wed to the devil she knew and not the one she did not.

Wed to Eleanor with her tender heart, he mused. Eleanor, who seemed never to hold any grudge against him for any wrongs he'd committed against her, of which there were now a few.

He moved further inside the chamber and around the bed. He might have sat with his mother on the side opposite Eleanor, thereby not disturbing her. But he wanted to disturb her, both to satisfy his own selfishness, to have her company, and because he would not allow her to sleep all night either in this chamber and certainly not in that position. He walked quietly around Eleanor and perched himself on the soft mattress next to his mother, his back to the headboard, his hip near his mother's shoulder, his gaze on Eleanor as she did rouse now at the shift in the mattress.

She came awake swiftly, straightening on the stool, appearing shamefaced as if he'd take her to task for having dozed. She rubbed sleep from her eyes and when wakefulness was full upon her, gave her regard only briefly to him before subjecting his mother to a greater study.

"Did she wake at all?" He asked. "Say anything about what her sickness might be?"

"She roused during her bath, sir, but was not quite coherent," Eleanor answered, her voice husky with sleep, "not even enough to question who were the two strangers administering to her. But I do feel as if she's improved. I don't know if she had a fever prior, though your uncle said she might have—but Lucy and I both agreed she was without a fever all evening."

"I liked it better when you called me Dougal," he said, a wee surprised that was his next concern. He supposed he could now afford to be familiar with her. His mother's condition, though wholly unknown, was indeed vastly better, and he knew he was soon to be Eleanor's husband. Still, even as he said this, and with the latter thought in mind, he cautioned himself that he should make no further overtures toward agreeableness. He would wed her, but it would be with conditions to keep her protected from the murkiness of his heart.

Eleanor, too, was caught unawares by this. She did not remark upon it though but kept to the matter at hand. "The lad, Arthur, said the healer could not be found." Posed more as a question than a statement, possibly wondering what Dougal would do about this.

"Morag often travels great distances to minister and is sometimes gone days at a time. Walter took a party to the convent near Farne. The abbess there is not unknown to either me or Templeton and might allow Sister Eveline, their own healer, to make a short trip here to see *màthair*."

"That would be of great benefit to your mam," Eleanor said, slanting a look again at his mother. "Until we know what ails her, Lucy and I cannot imagine what might be done for her."

He availed himself to yet another greedy study of Eleanor, her soft auburn hair now cascading all around her shoulders while her eyes shone emerald in the dim light.

Dougal cleared his throat softly, the action drawing Eleanor's fine gaze, as statements or ideas of import might generally be preceded by such an introduction.

"Ye dinna meet with Father Siward," Dougal said, "as he, too, is gone from Templeton, presently. He is at a conference of clergy in Nairn at present but expected within a sennight." He searched her gaze, wondering if she had any idea where he was going with this. She held her eyes fast to his, as if to keep his gaze from piercing her too deeply. "Upon his return, I will ask that he wed us."

Eleanor's responding expression was, he thought, more bittersweet than either relieved or pleased.

Her lips parted and she licked them, beckoning his stare to the temptation of that action, so that he was visited by a swift and powerful recollection of their kiss.

"I did not assist with your mother hoping that would change your mind on the matter," she said evenly. "My problem is not yours, sir. You appear to have enough of your own."

Her care of his mother had nothing to do with his decision. "I ken yesterday I would wed ye, before we left the camp."

"Because you overheard what Lucy said?" She guessed after a moment. "Dratted girl, with her loose lips."

"Ye canna wed Chishull, lass. If he plays the husband as he plays the soldier, ye would nae be kindly treated."

"The problem is still mine alone, sir, and not yours to fix."

She pulled her gaze from him and set her elbows on the mattress, leaning forward, as if her attention and focus were solely for his mother.

Because he could imagine no other reason aside from injured pride—stirred by his fierce refusal of yesterday—to have her balking now, Dougal asked, "Then why did ye come to find me?"

It was a moment before she answered, and when she did, she did not look at him, but kept her regard fixed on his mother's face. "Imagination, ignoring all input from the organ of sense, had played me false, sir. I thought...that is, I believed...I did not expect either your outright refusal, or one so savagely given. But then, the manner in which it was delivered advised me that I had in my mind overstated your opinion of me."

In the dimness of the chamber, he only knew that she wore a blush now because her cheeks were the same color as her sore nose.

"I handled it poorly," he allowed without shame. "I was stunned, in fact."

"Yes, I could see that you were," she said and swallowed a lump in her throat, or possibly more words that would have informed him of her view toward his reaction. "Truly, though, sir, I will not hold you to your acquiescence now, being that I am unable to determine if it honestly comes as a result of you feeling as if you owe me something."

"It does nae."

Ignoring this, she went on. "I hadn't thought it through, as I am sure you will have guessed. I don't really know you well enough to have done what I did. Honestly," she said and grinned sheepishly, "Dickson should have reeled me in as you suggested long ago. Even as we crossed the country, I was sure you must already be wed or had a sweetheart, which might have...been why you regretted so instantly....that kiss."

"I regretted the kiss for the reasons stated," he said levelly, "the sorry timing of it, since we were at that time under siege." He chewed the inside of his cheek, watching her critically, but could make nothing of her expression, which he might believe she intended purposefully to keep neutral. "I crossed the bounds of both guid sense and propriety, pouncing on ye as if ye were...as if ye might have welcomed it."

Of course she had, had kissed him back with brilliant eagerness, which had not ever been far from any part of his frequent recollections of the too-distant event. But he said as much now almost hoping to elicit some reaction from her.

Eleanor did not disappoint. Though she still refused to look directly at him, her cheeks turned even pinker, and she spent a long moment chewing on her bottom lip, all very telling.

He knew already, from what she'd said then, that night, that she had indeed welcomed his scandalous attention, the kiss itself, had once said that he should have kissed her again, as a farewell.

While he needed to put her in mind of their kiss so that she recalled that while she was attempting to let pride dictate her answer now, he knew he'd be a fool to ever kiss her again. 'Twould not be enough, he knew that already. One taste had been but a tease, had left him craving more, so much more. He would wed her to protect her, to keep her out of Chishull's hands but his own were no cleaner. His history was no less bloody or dirty, soiled by death and destruction and little remorse did he suffer over any of that, save until he'd met Eleanor, with her blithe spirit and pure heart. Aye, he would wed her, but he would not befoul her either with his base needs or his blackguard's heart.

After a moment, in which time her chest appeared to rise and fall with greater agitation, Dougal said plainly, "We will wed when the priest returns."

"Do you *want* to marry me?" She asked, sounding dubious, as if she already believed she knew the answer.

"Yer situation, lass, does nae afford one the benefit of that consideration."

"It's not about want," she clarified, looking no less suspicious about his intention.

"Do ye *want* to be wed to Chishull?"

Eleanor shook her head.

"Then we will wed," he said. "But with a stipulation."

"A stipulation?" She repeated.

"We will wed for practicality's sake and nae anything else. I nae ever had any intention of tying myself down to either Templeton or a wife. We will be wed in name only—"

"In name only? Without.... But what of...children?"

"There will be nae bairns, Eleanor. Aye, I'll wed ye. I dinna want to see ye fall into the hands of some pernicious Englishman," he said. He didn't want to think about any other man's hands on her. "I will nae ask after your father's mindset, to regard his daughter with such coldness, knowing there is nae accounting for our parentage, my own sire being a special sort of evil. I'll give ye my name and the protection that comes with it, but nae more than that."

Eleanor straightened on the stool, her back so stiff one might suppose an iron rod had been affixed to her spine.

"May I ask why?"

"Nae. 'Tis nae yer business to ken."

"But as your wife—"

"In name only," he reminded her. "This or nae anything at all, Eleanor."

"With that as a condition," she declared, "I suppose I needn't have crossed the country to find you. For only a man's name, and being then unavailable to wed another, I might have wed Dickson or Mánas or any other man at Bowyer House, or any stranger I'd met in our travels."

"Ye have that option," Dougal reminded her coolly. "I'm nae the one who needs to wed."

"I have one question," she said after another long pause in which she considered his reply. At his subsequent nod, she asked, "Did you not...enjoy kissing me?"

Dougal's jaw hardened instantly. But he supposed a lie would only wound her internally and because of his stipulation, the truth would have no bearing on their marriage. Therefore, he answered honestly though without the flourish that a kiss such as hers was likely due. "I liked your kiss well enough."

Eleanor sighed, her expression easing a wee bit.

"I will need some time to consider," she said next, her gaze meeting with his neck and not his eyes.

"Aye, and go on then," he said gently. "Seek yer bed. I will keep watch with *màthair*. I do thank ye, Eleanor, truly, for the kindness ye've shown her."

Eleanor nodded. "I wish I knew more or could do more. Lucy and I discussed how woefully inadequate we felt today. Still, I do believe she rests easier now."

"Aye, as ye should. Did they ready a chamber for ye?" He wouldn't put it past the household staff to have not. Sullen and spiteful wenches, they could be.

She grinned, her first smile tonight. As always, it transformed her, lighting her bonny face to radiance.

"Lucy took care of that and who would challenge her? She and I will share a chamber, if you don't mind a maid in the family quarters."

At the quick shake of his head—he would begrudge either of them nothing after what they'd done for him—Eleanor stood and pointed to the table just beyond his left hip.

"There is broth there, should she wake," she said. "Between Lucy and I, we managed to feed her half that cup." She pointed further to the cupboard at the far side of the room, where sat an ewer, basin, and a stack of cloths. "For her forehead if a fever does come." She met his eyes then, found him staring at her and her lithe figure and not at the necessities or which she spoke. "But Dougal, pray do not hesitate to wake me if there is any change. Not only do I not mind, but I would want to be here."

Good or bad, he thought she might have meant.

Aye, he would wed her, she and her tender heart.

"Guid night, Eleanor."

AT THE DOOR, ELEANOR turned and laid one last glance upon Dougal and his mother, smiling a wee good night before she closed the door part way and walked wearily down the corridor.

I liked your kiss well enough.

Rubbish, was Eleanor's assessment of that.

He'd hated that she'd asked the question in the first place, hated that she made him even consider lying to her. She could see that in his face at that moment, as he'd clenched his jaw and glared at her. He did not regularly engage in fibs, she knew, so there was truth in there, but he'd minimized it on purpose, so said the aforementioned clamped jaw, despising that she'd pulled that out of him.

But that was all she needed.

Aye, she would wed him.

Because he did indeed enjoy her kiss and he would, like her, be hard pressed to avoid another, certainly if they were to be wed and in constant and close proximity.

Wed in name only? No, she would not agree to that.

But then she would rightly be stuck with it, if she were wrong about him.

But she didn't believe she was. Whatever his actual reasons for insisting on such a qualifier, she would never believe otherwise, that he wouldn't want more kisses, and even more than that with her. She was naïve, she knew, utterly unsophisticated all things considered, but she wasn't wrong about this, she believed.

Eleanor entered the chamber Lucy had shown her briefly earlier, the one the maid had assumed for them when no one had offered them one. She closed this door fully and tiptoed across the chamber in the darkness, supposing tomorrow was soon enough to sort out what few possessions she'd traveled with over the last month; she would sleep in her léine and kirtle. And though she hadn't slept in a real bed, indoors, more than only a few times over the last month, and she wanted to flop down gracelessly onto the thick mattress, she climbed gingerly into the bed, not wishing to disturb Lucy.

She snuggled not only under laundered sheets and blankets but gratefully under the furs that also covered the bed, luxuriating instantly in the feel of it.

Almost immediately, Lucy, on her stomach, lifted her head and turned toward Eleanor.

"She sleeps yet?"

"Yes, and her son sits with her."

"God bless him," Lucy murmured, laying her head down again on the soft pillow, facing Eleanor.

"I'm going to marry the knight," she whispered to Lucy, neither willing nor able to keep hope from her voice.

"I ken ye would," Lucy said groggily. "Or rather, I kent he'd come 'round."

"Will you stay here with me, Lucy?" She didn't add, *because I need you*, didn't want to put that pressure on the girl, wanted it to be her choice.

"Will Tomag stay then as well? Dickson? All of them?" Lucy asked.

"I will beg Dickson to. And like him, Tomag has left behind no kin at Bowyer. He might find Templeton to his liking."

Enough time passed before Lucy spoke again that Eleanor actually thought she might have fallen asleep again.

"Aye, I'll stay with ye. Even if Tomag dinna remain, I dinna ken Bowyer will ken anything but trouble going forward. Dangerous place, that, war getting closer as we ken. And then ye'll need me, to wrangle these people into amiability—nasty bunch, these folks." She rubbed her nose with her finger and then said, "But I'll stay happier if Tomag is here as well."

"I'll talk to Dickson on the morrow," said Eleanor. "Or later today," she clarified, guessing it must be after midnight by now. She yawned and closed her eyes, though her brain was restless still.

In all honesty, Eleanor never had been able to make sense of Tomag's feelings for Lucy. The maid was correct, in that she'd made it fairly obvious that she would gladly receive any overture from the lad, but he'd never done anything with that. Not anything to Lucy's satisfaction. And yet, he was attentive to the maid, never uttered a cross word to her, seemed to not only enjoy her company when forced into it but sometimes to seek it out himself. Eleanor was hopeful, then, that the lad would choose to remain at Templeton Landing with them.

Only a moment did Eleanor devote to the maid and her expected beau, her mind turning once more to Dougal Kildare. She didn't actually need any time to consider her response, but she did want to discuss it with Dickson. She knew she would say yes. She hadn't spent the last month in rain and cold and upon the hard ground and inside seedy inns because she didn't want to marry him.

She fell asleep, nearly smiling.

She was going to marry the knight with eyes as gray as faded armor.

Chapter Sixteen

I t was a long-standing habit of Dougal's upon his return from any lengthy campaign that he spent time with the people for whom he fought. He'd made a practice of doing as he had yesterday, seeking out persons and information, or sharing news, even grim, as he was able. Likewise, he generally made himself available fairly soon after his return to any who might need to seek him out. Because of this and wanting to be close at hand should his mother wake today, he remained at the high table in the hall after he'd broken his fast, having requested that Yopin sit with him both to record any formally made complaints and to weigh in on matters of which Dougal would know little, having been gone so long.

The normal relief and exuberance he might experience for being home had yet to settle within him, but he attributed his weariness to being the result of the dramatic events of only the last few days since he'd not lifted his sword to fight in more than almost a month at this point. These included, of course, the advent of Eleanor MacAdam and her stunning proposal, his violent altercation with Padean, and not least of all his concern over his mother. Moreover, having spent the night at her bedside, forgoing a good night's sleep in his own bed, had resulted in a sleepless night. He was determined today to have a pallet installed in her chamber for his overnight use, unwilling to ask either Eleanor or

Lucy to remain with her but knowing he would need to sleep better if it might take her more than only a few days to recover.

He'd been relieved of his overnight vigil by a bright-eyed Lucy, who advised first that Eleanor had just woken and would be along shortly, and then had proceeded to shoo him out of the room, saying, "We dinna hae nae other business calling us," she said. "We'll sit here. Ye, the laird, just returned, must have persons seeking ye out, with their little grumbles and gripes. Get to it."

The grumbles and gripes had been about as petty as Lucy had suspected. Those which included charges of theft brought by one against another were of particular annoyance to Dougal. Templeton was not rich by any means, but no one was going hungry or without a roof over his head; there was no cause for thievery save for greed or envy—things Dougal had gone to war to fight against and not for. Having heard more than a dozen petitions, some infuriatingly long-winded, Dougal had had enough by midafternoon and asked the steward to announce to those who remained waiting that they would have his ear on the morrow. He and Yopin then debated for a quarter hour is sinfulness caused idleness or the reverse, wondering if those regular petty criminals only needed to be punished by adding a workload to their regular jobs or tasks.

He poked his head into his mother's chamber after that, or he tried to. Lucy met him at the door, barely cracking it open. "I'll just let ye see that we're nae up to nae guid, barring ye entry," she said, pulling back the door a wee bit more until he saw Eleanor's figure outlined near his mother, who was as she'd been all night and since he'd recovered her from the cottage, lethargic, unresponsive.

The blankets had been pulled back completely, folded neatly at the foot of the bed. His mother lay only in her shift upon the linen covered mattress.

"We ken we'd move her arms and legs, *excite the humors*, Curstag says," Lucy went on. "She's always telling us when in doubt to do as much. It canna hurt but then yer mam's limbs are bare and ye dinna want to be seeing that so ye canna visit now."

He could do no more but nod, a bit overwhelmed by their industry. They were not only keeping vigil, but they were actively attempting to recover his mother, a stranger to them. A tightness, not wholly unpleasant, seized his chest. He met Lucy's gaze, while her brow was lifted, possibly waiting for Dougal to remove himself from the doorway.

"Ye and Eleanor are fine persons," he said, even as he felt it was utterly inadequate as an expression of gratefulness.

"Aye, and we do the best we can, sir," said Lucy, sans any humility. "Otherwise, what's the point?"

Dougal nodded and took himself away, processing Lucy's parting words. A good reminder, even if it had been delivered by a cheeky lass half his age.

He next found Walter in the smithy's barn, making a request for armor plates to outfit a new brigandine. After greeting Wedast, the smithy, Dougal requested a conference with Walter and his officers atop the battlements. Meetings such as this were regularly held outside the keep, where there would be no other ears to spy upon their gathering. Twenty minutes later, Dougal was surrounded by Walter and his officers, Elon, Luca, and Boyd. Having happened upon Dickson and Tomag inside the bailey, and considering them equal to Walter and Boyd, he invited them to join the discussion as well, figuring they might be permanent residents themselves if Eleanor was to be his wife.

"Twenty-seven lads left with yer uncle," Walter said first thing, his snarly mien stating clearly his opinion of the characters of those men.

The breeze atop the wall was stiff, the group gathered closely so that they weren't forced to raise their voices overmuch.

"I dinna ken how or why they might expect to be paid," Boyd remarked, likewise shaking his head with disdain for the treachery of some.

"Ye watch now, lad," Walter cautioned. "Padean dinna cajole them with his charm. He's up to something, has promised them part of it if they keep with him. Mark me on that, will ye now?"

"Ye ken he'll make a play to overtake Templeton?" Elon asked, nearly aghast at the idea.

"He dinna pilfer arms and an army simply to fetch his victuals," Walter snapped.

"But what might the man expect to do," asked Tomag, "with few more bodies than might make one unit?"

"Padean's got marks everywhere," Walter enlightened them. "He'll call in all debts, bring in fighting lads or the money to hire them." He shook his head once more with disgust. "I swear he believed ye dead and gone, lad, dinna see this coming."

"I did nae either," Dougal admitted, having already tortured himself with searching for any indication in their history of the level of Padean's greed and treachery.

"Do ye ken those lads left with him, already imagining his plans," Dickson asked, "and expecting they want to be on the side that might emerge victorious?

Dougal nodded, having considered this as well.

Dickson screwed up his face over this conjecture and commented. "Dinna ken what that says about their faith in ye."

Walter clarified. "They dinna discount the fight in the lad. But they suppose Padean's malice is greater. He's the devil, will stop at nothing, dinna mind how many he loses, who gets hurt, he'll have his way. They count on him to come out on top for that alone, supposing evil dinna die."

I should have killed him, Dougal lamented, knowing he hadn't been thinking clearly enough, his mother's plight unraveling him a wee bit yesterday, to have dealt properly with his uncle.

They discussed tightening the posted watches, mayhap moving them around as their schedule and location would be known to their new enemy.

"Count us in," offered Dickson, who then elbowed Tomag. "Eh, lad?"

"Aye," said Tomag, nodding. "I'm fair sick of battles made by greed, but damn they'll keep at it if we dinna stop them."

"That's it, lad," Walter approved.

"Excuse me," called a small voice behind them.

The circle of men all turned, finding that Eleanor had come to the battlements. The wind fought with her braided hair, winning in small increments, pulling long strands out and away from her face.

She grinned briefly at the party in general before she met Dougal's gaze.

"Might I have a word, sir?"

"Aye," he said, separating himself from the group. "*Màthair?*"

"Is fine," she was quick to supply. "Better, in fact, at least in one regard. She woke several times and seemed more coherent but she's so weak for...well, from having been ignored and thus not sustained by either affection or sustenance, that it will be a while before she rouses more vividly."

She tucked one of those wayward strands of hair behind her ear, to little effect; it escaped again almost instantly and was blown straight out from the side of her face. Though the day was overcast, her eyes were fabulously green.

"I didn't mean to interrupt, and mayhap my timing is poor," she prefaced, "but I did think you would want to know your mother had roused a bit. Mayhap you would want to visit with her now."

"Aye, I will and ye dinna interrupt. We were just finishing here," he said, pointing his thumb over his shoulder at the waiting men. When Eleanor seemed not so much interested in either taking herself off, having delivered this pleasing news, and did not turn as if she would lead him to his mother, but only stared at him with an anxious face, Dougal's heart dropped. "Is there more, lass?"

"Um—oh, no, not about your mother," she said nervously. "But I—mayhap this timing is poor as well—but I have given thought to what we discussed last night...."

Dougal lifted his brow expectantly, sensing by her exceptional stammering that she had decided against becoming his wife. He told himself in that split second 'twas for the better; he meant to protect her from Chishull and any other wicked man her father might betroth her to, but wasn't sure she would be safe from her own husband if it should be him.

She dropped her gaze briefly to his chest before meeting his eyes again and stating in a firm voice, "I know you did not and would not have sought the match, but if you are still willing, I would be very...grateful to marry you."

And he knew right then that everything he told himself was a lie, knew that immediately and irrevocably by the way his heart surged in his chest. He wanted her for his wife, no matter what pain and promise it would cost him to have her near but remain stalwart in his intention to not sully her with his blood-stained hands and heart.

"I am willing," he said simply. "You have decided my terms are nae disagreeable?"

"'Tis not ideal, truth be told," she said, showing him a bittersweet grin. "Not what I would have imagined of my marriage. But I am willing to exchange vows with you with those terms in place."

Dougal narrowed his eyes briefly over this, at her wording, but decided she appeared anxious enough that the phrasing might have been unintentional, and he should read nothing into it.

"Might I beg one other favor aside from your hand in troth?" She asked. "Of course I'll want Dickson to stay and Tomag if he will, but might I also send to Bowyer House and invite to Templeton anyone willing to travel? The thought of Goldie and her lads, or dear Henry Oliver, even Cook and Curstag and Floireans, I cannot bear it, to think of them subjected to another siege—without at least Dickson there to prevent harm to them, they are at the mercy of the English, and you have said yourself—"

"Settle, lass," he interrupted, taking the hand she'd lifted in entreaty as her fretfulness grew. "We have space aplenty, and they are welcome." She could ask that they house Longshanks himself and Dougal might well find a way to make that happen.

Her shoulders sank with her relief. And the next smile she showed him was brilliant for its sunniness.

He gave a fleeting thought to this here now, how she'd been briefly unsettled but how easily she'd been soothed, and his own simple part in that, and what he felt, having rid her of distress in that regard, how glad his heart was then.

"Oh, thank you. See?" She asked, her sunny smile intact. "Already you are very good at husbanding."

Dougal barked out a small, rare chuckle and asked her to escort him to his mother.

ELEANOR SAT AT THE raised table in the hall, feeling decidedly conspicuous despite the fact that she had been invited to the family table and did not sit there alone. Indeed, more than half the available chairs were occupied, by Dougal immediately next to her, and Walter and Boyd beyond him. Dickson sat to her right and the steward, Yopin, to whom she'd been introduced only moments ago, sat next to him. Despite the addition of Eleanor and Dickson to the seating, there were several empty chairs, one belonging normally to the laird's mother, and another for the priest, who had yet to return from Nairn.

It had been so long since she'd dined in such a manner, in so vast and crowded a hall. She didn't miss those suppers, the last occasion having been at the house in Northumberland with her father and stepmother and her daughters, the company of which had not ever made for a genial mealtime.

She was nervous now, her hands beneath the table and scrunching the blue wool of the skirts of her léine. Dougal had requested her presence at supper with the intention of introducing her officially and stating their intention to wed. He'd said this as he'd left his mother's bedchamber earlier, his coming rather disappointing as his mother had once again been fast asleep.

Eleanor had asked first that she inform Dickson first before any announcement was made, but Dougal had told her he'd already spoken with Bowyer's captain, who gave him a bit of grief but seemed genuinely pleased with the news.

When Dickson had sat down next to her just now, he'd winked at her and said in a low voice close to her ear, "I kent he must've been barmy the other day, so quick with his refusal. Good sense returned, all is well."

"But you will stay here with me, Dickson, will you not?" She'd asked, that being her greatest concern.

"Aye, lass. Nothing to haul me back to Bowyer," said the old man, allowing Eleanor's nerves to relax over that matter. "Lad says there's always work needs doing, roles need filling. I'll get on aul right."

Eleanor had squeezed his hand, so pleased with his commitment.

On the subject of Dougal's mother, Aimil Beaton, and after Dougal had taken his leave, Eleanor and Lucy had revisited their earlier conversation, that something other than lack of care and sustenance must be ailing the woman. 'Twas too deep and lasting a sleep to have been only that, unless she'd been placed or sent to that cottage more than only a few days before they'd discovered her. While Aimil had roused as Eleanor had reported to Dougal, her speech had been indecipherable, most of it nonsensical, as if she'd not known who she was or where she was. Between Eleanor and Lucy's attendance, they thought they'd managed to force her to ingest enough broth and herbed tea that she should have been stronger already. They'd also agreed that until the healer came, they would not alarm Dougal with their inexpert opinions.

As it was, Lucy remained with the woman and Eleanor had freshened up for supper. Of course her options were slim, having only traveled with one satchel over the last month, but she'd pulled out the blue léine, had brushed it clean as best she could, and sat here now, aware of all the eyes watching her. Nervously, she moved the hair off her shoulder. Lucy had convinced her to leave it down and flowing—*virginal*, the maid had mouthed to Eleanor though there had been no one around to hear. Eleanor had thought a more practical and tidy knot would better suit the occasion, but after Lucy had rolled her eyes and fussed so much, Eleanor had compromised, pinning back only the sides and leaving the length to fall down her back.

Dougal, in extreme contrast to her mean appearance, was magnificent. He hadn't dressed formally, and perhaps that was decided purposefully in some deference to what might have been obvious to him, that she hadn't formal wear in her possession presently, but he was grand and handsome all the same. He wore freshly laundered breeches and tunic and tall boots of soft brown leather. His red plaid was draped over one shoulder, the pleats perfectly aligned with equidistance between one and the next, the length of it contained inside a fine belt of leather that was not the same one he'd worn all the days she'd known him.

She'd known him but for only a few days at a time but had noticed that he had not ever let his facial hair grow out. She'd thought perhaps he shaved regularly because possibly hair did not grow on the scarred side of his face. But tonight he was without any stubble at all, his jaw square and firm, the skin on half his face completely smooth save for what lines and wee wrinkles he'd already earned in this life. She thought he might have trimmed his hair, or had someone do that for him, the dark locks reaching his collar still but not much further, the front and top brushed back off his forehead. His eyes, when he'd met her at the bottom of the stairs, had smoldered with pride, likely renewed by being home and properly outfitted.

She'd once thought him not quite handsome, had thought that even without the scar, he was too severe, his scowls too beastly, his lip too often curled with disfavor, to have been considered handsome.

But he was very handsome, she revised, warmed by his piercing regard, intrigued and tickled by the nearly pleasant smile he offered her before he'd led her to the table.

She supposed that beauty was biased and interfered with by emotions. Honestly, the more time she spent with him, the more smiles he showed her, the more handsome he became to her.

"Dinna be nervous, lass," he said at her side while they waited for the hall to fill.

Eleanor offered a wee grin for his consideration, his awareness. "I don't suppose it's every day that the laird announces his plans to wed. And rather suddenly, so soon after the upheaval of our return, your uncle's departure, and your mother's ailment."

His response was just peculiar enough that Eleanor studied him more. Dougal Kildare was a man who made constant, intense, and sometimes frightening eye contact with a person. But for one quick flash of a moment at the beginning of her statement, he'd blinked his eyes away from her.

Oh. She tilted her head and considered him. "Oh, but you have previously announced your betrothal," she guessed, correctly as told by his next expression, a hardening of his features that advised she should not inquire about it. And yet she was to be his wife, she should know some of her husband's history—even if he expected to marry in name only. "Were you wed? Was there an actual wedding that followed the betrothal announcement?"

Dougal shook his head. "Nae. She took one look at me when I returned from my captivity and cried off."

"What a wretch," Eleanor seethed on his behalf, though the feeling was genuine. How shallow a creature she must have been! "I'm sorry. Was that an arranged marriage?"

"Nae," he said stiffly. "Or rather, it had started that way."

Eleanor's heart sank. He had loved her, whoever she was. And she had broken his heart.

"Where is she now?" Pray do not say she resides still at Templeton.

Dougal shrugged. "I neither ken nae care."

Which spoke more of bitterness than disinterest.

Eleanor faced forward, watching people take seats at the benches flanking the trestle tables, while servants filled horn cups with ale. The high table had been served wine in metal cups.

Did he love her still? The woman who had broken his heart? Had that anything to do with the terms he set forth for their marriage? If so, did that mean his heart was reserved yet for his previously intended bride? Or had she so damaged him that he might imagine love beyond the realm of possibility? Had that woman ruined any other's chance with him because of her small-mindedness?

A forlorn sigh escaped her at the same moment Dougal stood, meaning to address the assembly.

Adopting a placid expression, Eleanor glanced first up at him and then fixed her gaze on a spot above the sea of faces in front of her when he began to speak.

"'Tis guid to be home," he began, his voice strong and clear, carrying easily to the far end of the hall, to the dozens and dozens of listeners. "'Twas nae an easy rode traveled, nae any part of it in the last twelvemonth. We lost guid lads, too many gone. Ye ken their names and faces—keep them well in yer heart, recalling to salute their sacrifice." He cleared his throat then and continued. "The Kildare army was proud to witness the coronation of our king, Robert Bruce. 'Twas nae so much pomp and spectacle as it was reverence and pride—we will take back what is ours."

A cheer went up, which Eleanor deemed perfunctory. They—these denizens of Templeton—were simply miserable wretches, all of them, or they were waiting on words more pertinent to them: in regard to Padean Kildare and mayhap even an explanation about the identity of the woman inexplicably seated at their laird's side. She lowered her gaze, beginning to see faces, some of which were indeed trained on her, though more sat still with their laird, unfathomable, dull, every one of them.

"Proud fight we made," Dougal said next, "Some guid, some nae so much. 'Tis a sad day when our own king is hounded round his own country by men of the same, whose allegiance should be inherent and stalwart. But spring will come and with it new opportunities to extract or annihilate any who stand in the way of true freedom for Scotland." He tapped the fingers of his right hand on the gleaming surface of the uncovered table, his height perfect that his wrist was not bent to do so. "Yopin has been given the full accounting, the tale recorded as part of the chronicles of the Kildares' history, should ye desire specifics about the skirmishes, conversations, and parties met." He drew in a deep breath before he spoke again. "And that brings me to the matter of Padean Kildare, no longer welcome here at Templeton. I'm sure the tale has reached yer ear, mayhap embellished or patently false. Ken this: He deceived my trust and sullied the Kildare honor—which I have striven to demonstrate and elevate and by which I expect ye all to adhere—by his foul practice with my own *màthair*. He is exiled from Templeton and notice has been sent to our mormaer, the MacRory on Mull, and to our own bishop. I ken my uncle was nae alone in his treachery, but many of ye here are guilty of the same indecency, any of ye who ken of Aimil's illness, of her own banishment, and did nae one thing to right that wrong. I dinna recall every face I've slain," he said, his voice low and grumbling with fury now, "nae the voice of every adversary, nae even all the names of those who have done me wrong," he seethed. "But I ken who ye are, ye who ignored the plight of my *màthair*, chose the ease of remaining in Padean's graces rather than challenge his abuse. I will nae forget yer name nae yer misdeeds, mark me on that."

The hall had generally grown quieter as he'd begun to speak, but there was still the occasional cough, and a child's whine, and once a stifled sneeze from someone at the back of the chamber. At this moment, and during his brief tirade, delivered with such menacing solemnity, Eleanor was certain no one even breathed, so still was the hall.

Dougal then rapped his knuckles once, twice on the table and moved on, his voice returned to what it had been when he first addressed the people of Templeton Landing, strong and clear.

"And now I will introduce ye to my betrothed, Eleanor MacAdam, late of Bowyer House," he said without preamble, lifting his hand and turning slightly toward Eleanor. "She will become my wife and ye will welcome her and her party as if they were yer own, for they shall now be."

A bit of an edge had crept into this last bit, the threat unmistakable: do not treat her as you have my mother.

The hall remained utterly silent.

And Dougal sat down and smiled at Eleanor as if he had not just made at least half the people in the hall gulp down swallows of dread. Having been disregarded and ignored already in her short tenure by more than only a few people here, Eleanor smiled beautifully at her soon-to-be husband.

Well done, sir.

Chapter Seventeen

The healer Morag finally showed herself the next day, almost at the same time as the nun, Sister Eveline, was brought in from the abbey in Farne. While the nun was profuse in her apologies for having delayed her coming by one day for personal reasons, the healer, Morag, made no such statement so that it was generally assumed that she'd been about her business, in another shire and with a different sickly soul.

The two women examined Aimil at the same time, conferring quietly with each other, while Lucy and Eleanor watched from the doorway, Lucy nibbling on her nails with some anxiety.

Dougal was not presently inside the keep but Eleanor had begged Tomag to fetch him, assuming he would want to be present for the consultation and determination.

It was good that the two women, both learned in art of medicine and healing, their lessons having come by different routes, agreed without issue over the diagnosis. The matter itself, what ailed poor Aimil, was not good at all.

"Poisoned?" Eleanor repeated, aghast, exchanging a horrified look with a wide-eyed Lucy.

"Aye," said Morag, who wore a shock of white hair that contrasted sharply with her generously lined olive skin.

Eleanor blinked rapidly, the startling news rendering her otherwise speechless.

The nun, Sister Eveline, who might well be very old but whose face was nearly wrinkle-free, and was pale as snow save for two bright red spots in the very center of her rounded cheeks, nodded her agreement. "Slow administration perhaps, that she did not die suddenly. But the lethargic convulsions you described, coupled with a here-and-then-gone fever and the way she labors for breath."

"Hemlock, mayhap," Morag supposed, "or monkshood."

"But who would do such a thing?" Lucy asked, outrage overtaking her shock.

Morag tilted her head dispassionately at the maid. "The one who wanted her dead." She shrugged then. "Much easier to conceal than a dagger in the breast. I'd put my coin on the elder Kildare, Padean," she stated baldly. "Nae but evil in that one and have I nae seen it a time or two?"

"I've met him myself once," Sister Eveline said, nodding to underscore Morag's finger-pointing. "He is not a godly man."

"*Jesu*—pardon, sister," Lucy said, "but the laird'll kill him now for sure."

Indeed. Eleanor thought she might actually help him. "Oh, dear Lord," was all she could say, unable to comprehend either the evil or the tragedy of such a plot. She covered her cheeks with her hands, tears springing to her eyes, her gaze falling on the woman in the bed, who appeared so light and tiny, so vulnerable with her son being gone. Instantly her heart ached for Dougal, imagining he would blame himself and for just that reason, that he wasn't here to protect her. For a flash of a moment, she considered begging these women to lie, to tell him anything but that his mother might have lived had he been here to tame his uncle.

But no, she could not lie to him of course.

Another thought surged inside her and she dropped her hands, lunging forward a step toward the healer and the nun.

"But now we know what ails her," she said breathlessly. "Can it not be fixed? Might she be saved?"

Morag shook her head, her lips pursed with pessimism.

Eleanor looked to Sister Eveline, her beseeching gaze imploring her to contradict the hag's response.

"Killed her from the inside out, lass," said the nun, with far more solemnity and sympathy than Morag's practical, indifferent manner. "Her body is shutting down, one organ at a time. Frankly, I don't know how she is...alive even now."

They heard Dougal before they saw him, heard him coming along the corridor, barking at someone to delay their leavetaking until he was ready to send them off.

Eleanor turned to face the door, her breath caught in her throat, wondering if it was incumbent upon her to relay the awful news. She sensed rather than saw the other women turn as well.

His normal gait was swift and sure and so the door was pushed fully open almost aggressively, but then he was brought to an abrupt halt by the faces staring at him. His face wrenched with pain when he met Eleanor's eyes, likely reading some pitiful truth in her watery gaze. Only briefly did he acknowledge either Lucy or the healers before laying his pained gaze upon his mother. But he did not move away from the door, further into the room. He seemed only to be trapped, mayhap wondering if he removed himself without speaking, without hearing what surely the faces before him said, it would not be true, would not be happening.

Morag, having an identical forthwith disposition as Lucy, but lacking all of the maid's ability to mine empathy, was the first to speak.

"Poisoned, laird," she said, nodding for good measure. "The worst is over. Death will close it out now."

He said nothing, but did slowly advance into the chamber, his gaze still on the figure in the bed, his countenance a mix of fury and grief. He stopped beside the bed, still six feet away. His jaw moved back and forth.

"Are ye sure?"

Sister Eveline answered, wringing her hands at her waist. "We are in agreement on the findings and sadly, that she cannot survive it. I am sorry, laird."

After a slow nod, he used a voice as soft as Eleanor had ever heard from him. "Leave us."

There was a brief moment filled with an exchange of worried glances between the four standing females before Sister Eveline moved first, inclining her head and mumbling a whispered pray that God take Aimil well in His hands, before she exited the chamber. With a slight twisting of her thin lips, Morag shrugged her shoulders and followed. Lucy threaded her arm through Eleanor's, tugging a bit while Eleanor wrestled with indecision, not wanting to leave him.

But he hadn't spared her a second glance, his regard only for his mother now, that she consented to Lucy's prodding and departed as well.

In the corridor, they encountered a man of small stature, no bigger than Lucy, dressed in the customary vestments of a priest. He spoke presently and quietly with Sister Eveline, Morag seen further down the passageway. As the murmuring nun and the nodding priest blocked much of the corridor, Lucy and Eleanor paused to wait. But when Sister Eveline was done speaking and continued on, and the man strode toward them, he only inclined his head serenely as he passed, entering the chamber where Dougal's mother would die.

Thirty minutes later, having waited in the hall, Eleanor watched the priest descend the stairs and leave the keep.

She chewed her lip, debating going to Dougal or not. Theirs was a new relationship, hardly able to be defined as only a betrothed couple, their history being both short and complex, and so much of her emotion toward him generated by gratefulness and the stirrings of his kiss.

And yet, she was his betrothed, would be his wife one day—however he saw fit to hinder their union with his terms—and Eleanor determined she should be at his side. At least, she thought she should try, rather expecting that he might not welcome her presence. But she returned to the chamber, quietly closing the door behind her, and surely he realized her presence though he did not acknowledge her even as she sat on a small stool near the hearth, not wanting to intrude fully but needing him to know she was here.

After the first night spent at his mother's bedside, Dougal had for the next one moved in a larger chair, one with a back and arms that was infinitely more suitable than the stool to catch a wee bit of sleep as needed. He sat there now, having moved it closer to the bed, one arm and leg butted against the bed frame and blankets. He was leaned forward, his elbows on the bed, and held his mother's pale and tiny hand.

Eleanor sat quietly, watching emotions play across his face. When, after many minutes had passed, and she judged his face without either rage at the crime committed or sorrow for the imminent loos of his mother, indeed when he appeared almost to smile, she dared to ask, "What do you think on?"

He did not answer for a full ten seconds or more so that Eleanor wondered if he would at all.

Finally, he said, "I was recalling a certain walloping she gave me."

To her amazement, a small chuckle did follow.

Considering his stubbornness and temper, and his use of *certain* to signify there had been several, Eleanor asked, "One in particular?"

"Aye," he said, straightening, shifting his upper body toward Eleanor a wee bit. "Nae any of them were undeserved," he conceded. "But this one might have been the last one. I dinna recall the infringement, what crime had wrought the punishment, I only recall her being too short. She could nae reach high enough to cuff me upside the head, was slapping at my arms and shoulders. And then she stopped and bristled with her anger and bade me duck my head so she could reach. I remember it struck me as ridiculous and I burst out laughing. Nae, I was nae going to help her, I laughed at her." He paused, his lips unmoving, curved with the memory. "She chuckled then, too. She kent it was useless. She said, *Be a guid man, Dougal, so I dinna have to carry around a squat stool just to knock ye straight.*"

As sometimes happened with the sharing of memories, the emotions tied to the moment could not properly be conveyed. While Eleanor thought the tale charming in its way, she was struck more with what it said of his relationship with his mother, that he yet answered to her when he was tall enough not to. But more so, she was intrigued by his easily related statement, *I burst out laughing,* hardly able to imagine the Dougal Kildare she knew as being a lad who so easily laughed, and at something so ridiculous, as he said. This fascinated her; so he hadn't been born surly.

"Small but fierce," Eleanor guessed of the woman, encouraging more conversation from him.

"Aye, fierce," he nodded. "Nae for herself, but always for me."

"Her only child?"

He nodded.

"Did you grow up there?" Eleanor asked. "In the cottage where we found her?"

"Aye, until I was ten and two and the laird could nae ignore that I was his image in youth. I ken she wrestled with that. She wanted him to acknowledge me, his firstborn, but she ken what he was—Padean has nae anything on my sire's devilry. Straight away, I was sent away to foster at another house, so I always believed her regret was instant." He was thoughtful for another moment, chewing the inside of his cheek. "When I returned, I lived in the keep, under my father's thumb, which was nae to her liking at all." His face then wrenched with pain, as if he fought strenuously against tears. "She begged me to leave, for us to get away. But I wanted his attention, however cruel it was, wanted to prove myself to him. I was worthy, I would show him."

A product of his environment, torn between two strong-willed parents.

She didn't ask after the grotesque scarring on his mother's back, which had been noted each time they'd bathed her. The scars, though vast and once deep, were old and pale, the flesh disfigured as was her son's face. Eleanor wasn't sure he knew of her suffering on that account and did not want to add more pain to what he knew now.

But oh, how her heart ached for him, for having revealed that his mother had wanted to be gone from Templeton, but that he had refused. His guilt now, for what it had cost them, must be immense. She did not put forth any pathetic prattle, that he'd done what he thought best, that he couldn't have known it would turn out this way. Little consolation such inanities would be, almost insensitive for their worthlessness.

"She did nae have an easy life," he mused with some mournfulness.

Mayhap he did know of her scars then, Eleanor considered.

"Does she have gray eyes like you?" She asked. "Is that where you get them from?"

He shook his head, his eyes yet on his mother. "Her eyes are green. Much darker than yours but lit with the same fire ye often are."

He sounded weary and after a few minutes in which he offered no more, and though she remained, she said nothing else, just kept watch over the man grieving his parent.

AIMIL BEATON DIED PEACEFULLY in her sleep the following afternoon. Only then did Dougal leave her bedside.

In the hours preceding, Father Siward, Eleanor, and Lucy had been the only ones inside the chamber with Dougal. Eleanor had been pleased with the priest's regular visits. He'd not only administered last rites and had said many prayers, but he engaged often and well enough with Dougal, sharing memories and narratives of Templeton, that Eleanor was left to assume that despite his youthful appearance—she wouldn't have guessed him any older than Dougal, who surely was no more than a score and ten—he'd been the cleric here for many years. Perhaps his serene manner had rendered him ageless, she guessed. In any event, she appreciated both the man himself and his tranquil and obliging company.

That evening, after Eleanor and Lucy bathed Aimil one last time, and as they began to shroud her for burial, they heard the soft braying of a horse and then the constant and rhythmic ringing of a bell. A peek out the window showed the priest astride a narrow-backed palfrey, a lantern held aloft in his hand, while a young lad plodded along ahead of him, tolling the bell incessantly. The ragged coarseness of the lad's garb stood out in marked contrast to the lavish robes of the priest on horseback. The quiet murmuring of the priest's prayers was only a hum to listening ears.

Outside the door in the dim corridor, Walter had taken up the position of sentinel, standing with his feet apart and shoulders squared, his sword held in both hands, the tip of the blade on the floor between his legs. He would remain there overnight, a high honor conferred to the laird and his mother.

Inside the chamber, Eleanor sewed small and tight stitches around Aimil's head and hair, the latter being confined necessarily in plaits. Lucy worked around the bottom half, joining the top and bottom sheets for burial. The shroud was not only plain cotton but a fine woven linen of pale blue. When they were done, and as a practice mentioned by Lucy, they embroidered Aimil's name into the sheet, in a vertical line along her hip.

Dougal sat watch over his mother overnight once again and in the morning, Father Siward arrived, dressed in his finer funeral vestments. The body in its grave-clothes was placed on a bier covered not in the Kildare tartan but with an unadorned pall of ivory, and carried through the keep and outside, into the rainy morning, away from the bailey and across the bridge over the moat. Father Siward led the procession, followed by Dougal, who walked as a solitary figure dressed in his best clothes. The body of his mother, borne by his most faithful soldiers, was carried in his wake. Eleanor, Lucy, with the steward, Yopin, beside them, walked thereafter and were trailed by the general mourners, that is the remaining population of Templeton.

They marched straight up the lane and turned into a small, wooded vale, and then over the hill, and down into the village and then beyond, cresting a smaller rise outside the edge of the cluster of cottages, where they finally stopped. The view was fine, the knoll tall enough to see both the keep in the distance and the cottage where Aimil had once lived, and wide enough that several aged and wind-dulled grave markers sat already.

The striking rain, driven by high winds that sometimes sent it sideways, put Eleanor in mind of her own mother's funeral. The mourners had been few then, the parish decimated by the sweating sickness that had taken her mother—ah, the cruel irony of that, it being her mother's first visit to Bowyer, having pestered her husband to take her to his birth place. They'd stood then much as these people now did in similar conditions, the rain plastering hair to heads, the wind pushing skirts and any loose fabric angrily to the east. Most were forced to keep their heads down and angled away from the pelting rain, while the priest battled to keep the pages of his psalter dry and unflapping. Uncannily, Eleanor recalled most from that service the vibrant violet of the priest's stole, how it had seemed so out of place among the sedately garbed attendees.

'Twould have been both inconsiderate and disrespectful for the weather to have dictated the length of the service, which was not reverently quiet as Father Siward was forced to shout to be heard above the wind and rain, and so the mourners, genuine and otherwise, huddled together for nigh on half an hour before the body was kisted into the earth, her final resting place.

They dispersed quickly then, the majority of the funeral guests, scurrying down the hill with greater speed than they'd ascended.

Dougal stood at the graveside, staring down into the hole in the earth, his hand resting on the hilt of his sword, the scabbard beneath it a striking ornamental one he did not normally wear.

Eleanor pulled the cowl of her hood tighter around her head, holding it securely at her throat and with a nod of her head, advised Lucy to return without her just now. The maid did not go far though, stood at the base on the wee beinn with Dickson and Walter, waiting on the laird.

Moving to stand close to and noticed by Dougal, Eleanor afforded him a few moments of quiet and stillness before she stepped forward yet more, sliding her hand between his arm and torso, laying it on his forearm.

"Come," she said gently. "The funeral meal awaits."

Dougal turned his gray eyes onto her. The rain did not allow her to know if he cried or not, his face fully moistened and stricken by water. The redness rimming his eyes was possibly a symptom of exhaustion for the long nights spent at his mother's bedside. For a moment, his steaming breath was all that moved between them.

Ah, but he was tortured she could see in his gaze. So much pain was etched there, in the striking gray of his eyes, in the cinched lines around them, in the twisted tightness of his mouth.

"You are not the cause of her death, Dougal," Eleanor said, having no doubt about what his anguish was about.

"Am I nae?" He asked.

Boldly, Eleanor pivoted from his side to face him and clenched at the plaid and tunic covering his solid chest. "You did not kill her or cause her death," she said vehemently. "Wed yourself to the cause of vengeance, as I know you will and as your uncle deserves if he truly is the culprit here but relieve yourself of blame, Dougal. *You* cannot live like that."

"I dinna ken how to escape it."

She would have never suspected that he would show vulnerability but appreciated that he felt comfortable enough to do so with her.

"You don't escape it, Dougal. It has no right to pursue you. Living your life as you saw fit, certainly choices made in your life and as laird to Templeton should not be imposed as suffering upon you now. Guilt, like vengeance, is a choice, Dougal. Think you your mother would want this for you?"

He considered this, but said nothing, did not even nod to acknowledge the wisdom of her reasoning. He laid his hand over the one on his arm and turned to lead her away from the grave.

"I have to find him, though," he said as they walked down the slope.

Yes, he did. While she believed heartily that the guilt was misplaced, Eleanor knew the want for justice was not.

Padean Kildare needed to pay for what he'd done.

Chapter Eighteen

The rain stayed only long enough to see Aimil interred in the earth, tapering off until the air was bone dry by midday. The wind remained though, relieving trees of sodden autumn leaves and howling through the next several nights. A missive came from Caelen MacFadyen, which huddled Dougal and his officers together for more than an hour but over what news was never shared with Eleanor. And though no words had been spoken between Dougal and Eleanor about the matter, Dickson one day informed her that Tomag and Daniel and several others were taking a wagon to Bowyer House with the intent to collect Henry Oliver and any other who might choose to move north to Templeton Landing.

Eleanor had been pleased about this and would have announced her gratefulness to Dougal if she spent any length of time in his company. He was brimming with vitality for his new vocation, finding Padean Kildare and making him pay for his crimes. He came and went, and Eleanor never quite knew when to expect either his departure or his return. He was cordial, polite even, but fiercely distracted during those rare and fleeting moments in her company.

"People mourn in different ways," Lucy had theorized. "He'll satisfy his grief at the end of his sword."

Eleanor supposed Dougal, accustomed to action, always with some task or goal in sight, might indeed grieve better on the move, with an objective at hand. She knew for certain that his misplaced guilt would certainly not be assuaged if he did not avenge his mother.

Suppers inside the keep were quiet affairs, the hall only half filled on certain days. Templeton's people made no overtures toward Eleanor or any person from Bowyer, though she suspected the lads in the army had an easier time of it, forced into proximity with their Kildare counterparts. Dickson certainly seemed right at home, one day heard upbraiding a young soldier upon the ramparts over which he was charged to supervise in the laird and his captain's frequent absences.

Dickson had work then to keep himself active, and the lads from Bowyer were often included in Dougal's forays, but Eleanor and Lucy, no longer needed to care for Aimil, had little to occupy them. Their overtures in the kitchens had not been received kindly. Aye, the women there, including the cook who was as tall as Dougal with shoulders just as wide, had been respectful of Eleanor, soon to be their mistress, but they had mostly been diffident, the lack of welcome perceived more than expressed.

Accustomed to the friendly staff at Bowyer, in whose company Eleanor had never felt misplaced, she knew she would eventually expect and effect change there in the kitchen and throughout the keep but decided she needed to wait until she was officially wed to do so. Having no choice but to occupy themselves, Eleanor and Lucy decided they would subject Aimil's bedchamber to a thorough and invigorating scrubbing, the chamber scarcely having been entered, let alone tidied, in the four days since she'd died in the bed.

They stood in the doorway, debating if it might be considered an intrusion, they the outsiders taking on the chore.

Ever practical, Lucy marched forward, bucket of steaming water in hand. "We're nae the outsiders," she insisted. "And nae only because ye'll wed the laird. 'Twas ye and me that sat hour by hour with her, bathed her, loved her, fretted over her. We're going to fix these people, Eleanor," she went on, "they and their odd ways, but nae today." She shook her head and grumbled, "Leaving this disturbance untouched for so long. Shameful is what it is."

Their next debate ensued within the hour, half of the chamber scrubbed, the tall cupboard wrestled out of its normal spot, moved between the two long windows where it fit so perfectly they wondered if it should be left there.

Lucy grimaced. "Scrubbing is one thing, but dare we rearrange? The laird might nae wish the chamber to be lessened of any trace of his mother."

"I suppose," Eleanor cited, "that if she'd died peacefully, naturally, that would lend itself to that argument to keep the chamber as it was. Mayhap because her death was neither kind nor natural, we should obliterate any memory of it."

Lucy was convinced and they got back to work, in the end moving almost every piece of furniture in the room.

When they were done, and perspiring and weary, Lucy grinned at the room and their achievement and decided, "And the old cottage from where she came next. If our folks from Bowyer are coming, they'll need somewhere to hang their hats and lay their heads."

And so they did the very next day walk about to the village, buckets, mops, and cloths in hand, ready to tackle the derelict cottage at the end of the lane. They tore open the shutters once more and removed every stick of furniture from the hut, stacking it on one side of the door in the wind-swept grass, and set about with the task of first scouring the whitewashed wattle and daub walls and scrubbing the timber-laid floor.

Just after the noon hour, Dougal and his small unit of soldiers returned from their daily jaunts to locate Padean. Eleanor puzzled over their early return, wondering if they'd found the man and had exacted justice. She did not go outside the cottage but peeked through the short front window, deciding Dougal's mien as he rode by did not look fiercely satisfied enough that she might suppose his uncle had been dealt with.

An hour later as she stepped outside to begin washing the crude furniture itself, Eleanor again caught sight of Dougal. This time, he was without his steed, walking along the lane with an anxious lad who couldn't have been more than seven or eight years of age. Excited indeed was the lad with the cropped black hair, skipping at the knight's side as they strolled, his mouth moving continually while he held in his hand a wooden sword, occasionally parrying with the air in front of him.

Dougal exchanged dialogue with the lad, the murmur though not the words carrying to Eleanor. Not wishing to be caught gawking, she turned half sideways, watching in her periphery as they neared, saw Dougal grin at the lad and then wink at something said.

A surge of immense pleasure welled up inside her, for how patient and attentive was the knight to the admiring boy. This joyful emotion was swiftly squashed, however, the woman in her bemoaning the fact that if Dougal Kildare had his way, it would never be her own child clomping so happily beside him.

They turned off the main lane before they reached her, following the side road out to the loch she might guess, not knowing what else might be found in that direction. The cloth in her hand and the grimy furniture forgotten, she stared at their backs until the cottage across the way cut off her view, lingering over the swell of emotion in her chest caused by from so ordinary a thing, a man walking along with a boy.

The day moved on, Eleanor and Lucy eventually making their way back to the keep in time for supper. Knowing that Dougal had returned, she was rather surprised that he did not appear in the hall at that hour, which meant that they hadn't dined side by side since his mother's funeral meal. She didn't believe it was intentional, and didn't quite suppose that he was avoiding her, but she was teased by both of those ideas. In dark moments, she wondered if he was rethinking his acceptance of her proposal but was able to quickly shoo away such dastardly thoughts, considering herself unnecessarily uncharitable in those moments. People mourn in different ways, as Lucy had said.

In the evening, she and Lucy decided they would avail themselves of the luxury of a bath and then disturbed harried kitchen lads to trudge upstairs with the big wooden tub and buckets of steaming water. They made several trips to fill the bath, and then one more to deliver cooler water to temper the heat. They took turns, helping each other wash their hair, and sought out their bed almost immediately after, the bath having soothed them expertly.

The keep at night was incredibly silent. Almost eerily so. At Bowyer House, the horses and livestock were housed more closely and any of their whinnying, clucking, or snoring might have been regularly heard during the night. There was a loose shutter also in her chamber at Bowyer and even the slightest wind whistled regularly through it. Outside that same window there was a constant quiet tapping noise, never identified, and with her so long that when one night it had stopped, Eleanor had risen to investigate, unable then to discover its source and then lack. But always, there were little noises throughout the night, things familiar and which brought some measure of comfort for their constancy.

Templeton was soundless. No water dripped from eaves, no pigeons roosted in nooks or crannies, shutters did not slap or whistle. The stables and barns were far enough removed that no beasts were heard. The night watch on the wall, if they spoke at all, did so in such hushed voices as to go undetected. If mice scampered about this keep as they sometimes did at Bowyer House, she did not hear them. Not even Lucy, sharing the bed with Eleanor, made one little sound, her breaths soft and slow.

No sound at all, Eleanor had realized as she lay beside Lucy unable to sleep. No sound at all until the floor boards creaked outside the door as someone passed. She listened, deciding someone either crept along stealthily, meaning to go unnoticed, or the boards only creaked here and there, and not with every step. Because they were on the second floor, which housed only the family apartments, which presently meant chambers were occupied by only her and Lucy and the laird himself, her brow furrowed, wondering who was about what.

More curious than frightened, Eleanor slipped out from underneath the blankets and padded on bare feet across the chamber, putting her ear to the door. When no other sound was heard, not even any further groaning of the floor, Eleanor cracked the door and peered out into the corridor. She saw no one but heard something else, what sounded to her like the closing of either a shutter or cupboard door, coming from one of the chambers closer to the stairs.

She pursued the sound, tiptoeing along the corridor, not entirely surprised to find Dougal inside the chamber that had been his mother's until only days ago. Moonlight was the only illumination, painting him in blue-gray shadows, but bright enough to reveal that he also prowled around barefooted, wearing only his breeches, not even any shirt.

"Dougal?" She whispered.

He turned from the cupboard, the one she and Lucy had repositioned between the windows. Mayhap he'd investigated inside, to see if its contents were altered as well—they had not been; for lack of any idea what to do with Aimil's personal belongings, her kirtles and hose and gowns among other things, they'd left everything there as it had been.

"You couldn't sleep?" Eleanor managed somehow, her gaze arrested and smitten by the gloriously naked chest he turned at her while she forgot for the moment her own inappropriate garb, she in only her thin shift.

'Twas not lean, supple grace that was his bare chest, but impossibly wide and square shoulders and powerful, rippling muscles, adored by moving shadows as he stepped away from the armoire. Eleanor lost the ability to think, could hear his voice but not the words, staring with hunger at his magnificent body.

"What?" She blinked after an embarrassing moment, and tried to focus, wrenching her gaze upward to meet his. "I'm sorry, you couldn't sleep?"

She thought he might be grinning, or about to, but mayhap the shadows played with her perception. His voice when he answered was thoughtful possibly, though scarcely amused.

"Nae. This was ye and Lucy's doing? The tidying?"

"Yes," she said, able to maintain eye contact with him. "I hope you don't—are you upset that we've rearranged it all?"

Dougal shook his head and glanced briefly around. "It dinna matter now."

She couldn't be sure, but she had some idea that his placing his hands on his hips now, though the action was not unknown to him, might have been purposeful, as if he wanted to bring her attention back to his chest. Eleanor bit her lip and refused to be tricked into gawking at him, if that be the case. But she did still steal glances, noting the fine sheen of short hair which nearly completely hid his nipples, and the way it tapered down to a thin line that disappeared beneath the waistband of his low hung breeches.

"How are you...?" she began next, unaccountably nervous, folding her thumbs into her palms, folding her fingers over them. "We haven't hardly spoken...are you all right?" How untimely, she thought, her sudden edginess, all roused by his naked chest, when she should instead be concerned with his emotional state and not his splendid physical state!

"I apologize for the inattention, lass," he said, quite agreeably. "I have been focused."

"It is not myself I am concerned with," she told him. "I was...I didn't know if I should be doing anything for you, or what manner of attendance you might need during your mourning."

"This was helpful," he said, moving his gaze once more around the chamber. "And I saw ye and Lucy attended the neglected cottage, and I thank ye."

Eleanor nodded. "I saw you walking with a dark-haired lad," she said. "He seemed quite thrilled to be in your company, or simply to have your attention."

Now Dougal nodded. "That is Alpin Anndrais. His father was with me at Falkirk, was until he was killed anyhow. His mother was heavy with him at the time, lost her life in the birthing."

"Oh, he is...an orphan?"

"Technically, aye. But Peter and Jonet—they've the cottage across from the one ye cleaned, where *màthair* was found—they took in the infant, raised him as a son."

"You say that haltingly," she commented. "Raised him as a son? Lovingly? Or otherwise?"

His broad shoulders lifted and fell. "They dinna mistreat him, I'd nae allow that. But there is nae warmth, nae the affection that comes through blood. But his father was a guid man, an incomparable warrior, gone too soon—slain on that day, from which too few of us escaped unscathed." He paused and crossed one arm over his chest, scratching idly at the opposite shoulder. "I want his son to ken his da, that he was a guid man. I suppose part of me believes he needs more consideration, more affection."

This wee narrative raised several observations in Eleanor's head. The one that screamed the most, that he himself would be such a fine father, was the one she kept to herself. For now.

What she did voice was perhaps a bolder query. "Is that where your scars come from? Falkirk?"

He nodded grimly, the line of his mouth tightening.

"And it's not something you would want to talk about?" She guessed.

Dougal shook his head, his gaze hard on her.

She backed off, returning to the subject of the lad, Alpin. "Affection is not borne of blood, as well you know. You've mentioned your own sire and not in any rapturous terms, and you know of course how quick my father was to cast me out and then proceed to pretend I didn't exist until I could be of use to him."

"Affection is nae implicit at birth and by the parent, but aye, it should be."

"Agreed. And thank God for our mothers."

"Amen."

He was amiable, practically garrulous, and there was not a furrow or scowl to be found anywhere, at least none that the moonlight showed. He was half naked, wonderfully so, and the night was quiet, the air cool, but her body was on fire with need. So then Eleanor asked the one question she'd wondered about for quite some time.

"Do you ever think about that kiss? Or about kissing me again?"

His answer, when it came a full ten seconds later, in which time neither of them moved even one muscle, was uttered through clenched teeth, she was quite sure.

"All the time."

Even as joy burst inside her for this reluctant admission, she knew a sorrow that he would deny himself and her, because of the outrageous terms he'd set to their betrothal, the meaning behind which she'd not been afforded the courtesy to know. Some part of her believed that if his reasons were legitimate, if they had merit, he would have disclosed them, and thus they must not be, since he had refused to tell her why he expected to be married in name only. Subsequently, Eleanor believed she had the right to show him the error of his way, how ridiculous was his expectation that they would not touch or kiss or share any such intimacy.

The very way he'd gone rigid just now, coupled with his admission, told her it wasn't something that came easily to him, denying them.

She stepped forward, having hovered in the doorway this whole time, more greatly delighted that she wore only her shift than she was concerned about the impropriety of it. Dougal did not move but to become even more rigid, his arms flexing while a cord stood out against other lines and scars on his neck.

"Eleanor," he growled as a warning.

Which did nothing to stop her forward progress. Unless he removed himself from the chamber or bodily prevented her from touching him, she was going to kiss him. She would show him how silly was his stipulation, how pointless it was.

She stopped when only inches separated them, when the hem of her shift grazed his shins. She raised her face, but he did not lower his head. She laid her hand on his cheek, her palm meeting with the steel of his jaw. Lifting herself on her toes, she pressed her lips whisper-soft against his mouth.

"Kiss me, Dougal," she pleaded against his warm, unyielding lips.

He didn't move.

She was possessed then, with need and ideas that might never have occurred to her if not for the desire coursing through her. Never could she have imagined a time when she would lay her hand against a man's chest. In a million years, the act of lifting her leg, entwining her foot round his calf, would not occurred to her. But these ideas came to her, and she acted on them, all but draping herself against him, until she was sure he hadn't the will to refuse her.

And so he did not.

All that coiled energy, by which she'd been often so intrigued, was let loose.

Dougal seized her roughly and brought his mouth down on hers, his kiss savage, filled with fire. His hands clamped at her arms, holding her to his kiss, his tongue demanding entrance, he meaning to punish her for tempting him, meaning to frighten her, she might guess.

But God help her, there was a splendor in the violence of his submission, which thrilled her for what it said, that his terms were not even to *his* liking, but provoked by some absurd and insignificant cause. Part of her wanted to weep openly, her seemingly long-held dreams come to life in his arms.

But then all reason quickly fled as Eleanor forgot everything but her own aching desire. She moaned into the kiss, wrenching her arms from his grip, flinging them around his strong shoulders and neck.

He is meant to be mine and I his, clamored around in her brain. It allowed her to lose any inhibition, which need had greatly reduced already. She was awash in sensations, pleasure, arousal, heat. He pressed his body against hers, held her fast at her hips, his lean fingers digging into the flesh beneath the linen of her shift. Her breasts were crushed against the rock hardness of his chest. Eleanor whimpered her delight and swirled her tongue around his, slanting her head to accommodate the greed of his kiss. He pulled her closer yet, his hand stroking up her back and tangling in her loose hair.

She moved her hands as well over his hard flesh, across his thick shoulders and over his muscled arms, around his lean waist and lower back. His skin was hot to the touch, every inch of him molten and coiled steel. He bent her backward over his arm and trailed his lips along the column of her neck before surprising her by scooping her up in his arms and carrying her out of that chamber and into another. His bedchamber, she presumed, though it interested her not at all. Only he did, and his kiss.

Without great care but then not lacking any gentleness, he laid her down on his bed, the coverlet cool and soft beneath her. He joined her immediately, laying half atop her, his thigh wedging itself between her legs. Every nerve in Eleanor's body was on fire, the flames shooting higher when he skimmed his rough palm down over her neck and collarbone before his hand slid over her breast and downward. From the underside of her breast, he cupped all of it and raised it upward, his fingers squeezing all around it. He met her lips again with his own and groaned into the kiss that followed just as he grazed his thumb over her nipple.

Eleanor gasped at the sensation, how it ignited a thread of fire from her breast to her very core.

"Sweet St. Andrew," she cooed, nearly dizzy when he did it again, the sensation completely foreign and yet so lush for its magic. Her heart pounded with joy, and then wonder overtook her when he lowered his head and lavished her breasts with the same expert attention he'd given to her lips.

Her body went stiff at the first touch of his lips to her nipple, with naught but the thin fabric between them, and then she went limp, luxuriating in his touch, the way his teeth tugged at her hardened nipple through her shift.

And then he stopped, just stopped moving completely, until he raised himself and kissed her lips but briefly before collapsing against her, his face buried in her hair.

He said nothing and didn't move for an excruciatingly long moment.

"Dougal?"

"I dinna want to do this, Eleanor," he groaned raggedly against her temple.

The torment she heard in his savage voice finally gave her pause. Whatever his reasons for wanting so lifeless a marriage, she was wrong to force it upon him, to pretend the reason didn't matter just because she didn't know the details, or because she believed he truly did want this.

She closed her eyes tightly, pain denouncing all the pleasure he'd brought. A tear squeezed out and slid down and into her hair.

"Then don't," she whispered, her voice breaking. She pushed at his chest. "Don't." He moved his face, his lips grazing her temple, likely encountering her salty tears. He placed a kiss there, where her hair was wet. "Stop," she begged, unable to bear tenderness from him now but then resentment from him later.

"I can nae," he ground out and took her lips once more in a searing kiss while Eleanor's heart ached and soared at the same time. "I can nae stop, Eleanor."

Chapter Nineteen

Dougal could scarcely imagine a person or happening that could have induced him to stop now. Sadly, his wish to resist any intimacy between them, to have her remain unsullied by his bloodstained hands and heart, was not greater than his need for her now. He deepened the kiss yet more, as if he would rebuff any possible insistence by his honorable self to leave her pure and whole.

He kissed her neck, licking at her throbbing pulse all the way to her ear and then downward, pausing to kiss the hollow where her shoulder met her neck.

Eleanor ran her hands over his back, over his shoulder blades, tracing his muscles and scars. She did not flinch from the feel of the twisted flesh beneath her fingers, the remnants of Tearlach Kildare's rage and a myriad of other lesser ones, unkind trophies of war—Dougal never had decided which source was the more brutal, which one stung him far greater than only physically. Fleetingly, he gave thought to the fact that he wasn't self-conscious about his scars presently even as Eleanor was introduced to so many more just now. He hadn't been in a long time.

He moved his hand again, over her belly and onto her breast. He leaned down and kissed the tip, compelling it to a tight peak.

The linen of her shift was darkened, wet from his attentions, clinging to her nipple.

Wanting to see her splendidly naked as he knew she would be, Dougal disengaged himself, rising from the bed and pulling a startled Eleanor to her feet as well.

"I want to see you," he said by way of explanation. "All of you."

She was dressed in only her shift and he in naught but his breeches and he felt as if they were supremely overdressed for what plans he had for her.

Dougal slid his fingers beneath one wide strap of her chemise, the backs of his fingers touching her bare velvety flesh. He skimmed his hand up and down for a moment before he tugged the strap away, down her slim shoulder. Gently, he coaxed first one side and then the next down and away. It was agonizing, how slowly he slipped her free of the garment. A wave of heat stroked him, growing in multitudes as her breasts were bared and then her belly, until her shift hung at her hips. Dougal left it there for the moment, his chest heaving slowly as he stared at her. He'd lit no fire in this chamber and still her skin gleamed, glowing like the finest porcelain in the pale blue moonlight.

Her breasts were round and firm, fuller, larger than he'd imagined—aye, he most certainly had—her nipples a dusky rose, their taut peaks a shade darker. The colorful tips beckoned to him. Dougal lifted his hand again and brushed the globe of her breast with his palm, his exploration as reverent as it was disciplined. He had no wish to frighten her with the audacity of his hunger.

Eleanor gasped but held still, panting through her nose while they stood only inches apart. Heat radiated from her, the heat of desire and thrill, same as what attacked Dougal.

She is mine, he thought. *This resplendent creature with the delectable body and the generous heart is mine.*

The arrival of that thought, this knowledge coming, was intoxicating.

"Ye have magnificent breasts, Eleanor," he said. "Mayhap the most perfect breasts I've ever beheld."

Her kissed-drowsy lids lifted. "Are you...my God, are you comparing me to another? To several others?"

He sensed more incredulity than reprimand in her tone. But he was not comparing her to or recalling any other. There was no comparison. But aye, even a favorable assessment likely did not sit well with her.

"I'm nearly a score and ten, lass," he qualified. "I've lain with other women."

Not like this, though. Not with Eleanor. He'd not ever gotten naked with someone as desirable as she. Hell, he couldn't remember the last time coin hadn't been exchanged for the right to touch a woman intimately. In those cases, they served as vessels, and Dougal could recall neither face nor figure. He knew 'twould not be the case with Eleanor. Even were he not intending to wed her and reside with her for all the rest of his life or hers, he thought it unlikely that he would not ever be able to recall her figure or bonny face. She was exquisite, made more beautiful by her desire.

"I feel as if cold water has been tossed between us," she lamented breathlessly, her hands fidgeting and then fisting at her sides.

But Dougal only grinned, taking one of her hands and pulling her against him, meeting her searching gaze. He brushed back the tangled hair from her brow. "I ken I have the means and the need to bestir ye again."

A small and wobbly smile answered before she did. "Oh, thank God."

"Have you thought about this? With me?" He wondered huskily, lowering his hand between them, letting his palm slide up and down over her hardened nipple.

Eleanor closed her eyes, her head falling back. "I have...only with you."

Likely, her voice was not her own, the sound completely foreign to her for the husky quality of it. Dougal was only further enamored.

Dougal moved his large hand to her other breast and that nipple offered the same welcome, tightening for him. Eleanor shivered with delight. "For hands so large and strong and calloused," she murmured dreamily, "your touch is as silk."

He bent and took her lips again.

"I have thought about this with you," she said, breaking the kiss, their lips only a breath apart. "But as my thoughts were limited by...my lack of experience—which is based on almost entirely the heat and wonder of your previous kiss—I'd not ever given thought to tender versus feverish. Truth be told, I don't know what to expect but that you will bring me pleasure."

He sensed a question in her statement. "Pleasure I will give ye," he assured her. "Pleasure ye will give me."

The next kiss was bold and wild, his tongue darting inside her mouth, his hands lowering from her breasts to slide the fabric completely away from her hips, until it dropped to the ground at her feet, and she was naked before him.

She was magnificent, her lithesome body pure and graceful, lean but curved as well, enough that his fingertips tingled with anticipation. His gaze, darkened with desire, moved slowly downward, past her soft but flat belly and the dark curls at the enticing juncture of her thighs, over smooth and supple legs and to the floor, where she'd just lifted one foot nervously over the other.

Dougal inhaled and exhaled slowly, adoring her with his eyes. And while he was very sorry that she did not first meet his cock when it was flaccid and posed so little threat, he wasted no time but doffed his breeches and braies in one swoop of his arms, kicking them aside.

He straightened in front of her, watching as her eyes widened and her lips parted as she looked him over. But he did not give her time to become anxious by the breadth of his desire but laid his hands on her hips and pulled her flush against him. They gasped together, a low growl and a breathless and startled moan, as soon as their flesh met.

Everything beyond a kiss, all he'd known from her before now, brought Dougal new and extraordinary delight. Their chests and legs and stomachs were pressed together. Reveling in the naked heat of her, his senses reeling at all the soft womanliness pressed against him, Dougal groaned once more with satisfaction.

She lifted her arms and wound them around his shoulders, clinging to his nape as he ravaged her mouth with his tongue.

Her breasts were crushed to his chest and his growing erection jutted formidably against her belly. Every sensation was at once tantalizing and excruciating.

"Lie down with me," Dougal urged, coming up from the soul-shattering kiss. Dragging her hand away from his neck, he moved toward the mattress and brought Eleanor down with him. "Lie back," he directed when she sat next to him and when she did, he stretched next to her on his side.

For a moment, he only stared at her at length, from her face down to her toes and back again. He set his hand over her breast and brought the nipple to hardness again, watching her as she did him. The moonlight was not so faint that he wasn't aware or made harder by the shy but curious light of her gaze. He followed his hands with his mouth, his lips finding the flesh of her breast, his tongue scraping gingerly over her nipple. Eleanor released a breath, the sound airy, suggesting the pleasure was unexpected.

Eleanor lifted her hands to cradle his head against her, shifting, angling toward him, so trusting and open, arching her back so that her nipple met his tongue. His hands moved as well, his caressing fingers gliding along the outside of her thigh. His body quickened as his palm stroked over her leg toward the center of her. When his fingers slipped between her thighs, the excitement felt in her was almost intolerable. He burrowed his fingers into the curls covering her womanhood, and she moaned once again while he brought to life a throbbing pulse beneath his fingers. He grew bolder, explored deeper, and Eleanor let her legs fall open to him, lost to the magic of his touch.

"*Jesu*, but you are so wet for me," he whispered heatedly as he slipped one finger inside her, exploring her with smooth and tantalizing strokes, sliding in and then out.

"I must be dying," she said weakly while he learned her most secret and vulnerable places. "If I weren't speaking, I'm not sure I'd know if I were breathing any more."

"That's a glorious smile," he said just before he leaned forward and laved his tongue over her swollen nipple once again.

Small, exquisite convulsions of need stroked every inch of her, and Eleanor lifted her hips, rising to meet his fingers when they plunged and lowering her hips when he withdrew.

"Aye, that's it, love," he murmured against her breast.

Suddenly, Eleanor was writhing against him, straining upward toward his fingers and his hand, where his palm was torturing the thatch of brown hair between her legs. She whimpered, clutching blindly at him as she rocked against his hand and was shown what he knew must be a flaming rapture. She quivered with a moan, embracing the ecstasy as it washed over her until she was numb and motionless. Dougal shifted and wrapped his arms around her, holding her trembling body, kissing her hair.

When she could speak, she tried to form a question. "Dougal, what...?"

Dougal landed another peck on her cheek before he loosened his hold, laying half atop her. "'Tis one way to give and receive pleasure, lass."

"One way?"

"Aye, lass. There are hundreds of ways to achieve that release."

"You're going to kill me, then, like this?" She asked, her voice still small, drained.

He took it as it was meant to be, just her astonishment speaking. He picked out a pale grin in the dim light.

Dougal captured her hand and brought it to his still hard cock. "More pleasure here. Feel how hard I am for you, how much I want you, Eleanor."

"We're not done, then," she guessed with some astonishment.

He shook his head as he closed her fingers around him. "Nae, love. We've only just begun."

He showed her how to stroke him and whispered what he was going to do to her and with her. She didn't blush, might have been beyond that already, was mayhap more eager and curious than troubled by apprehension. In fact, she surprised him with her response to his recital.

"Don't only tell me," she begged, "show me. I want to feel you, this, " she said, squeezing her hand firmly around his shaft, "inside me, Dougal."

These raw and needful words stroked his already enlivened senses and body. "Aye, lass. I need to feel you around me."

Dougal moved, settling his hips into the cradle of her open thighs, his erection seeking entrance. He was wild with expectation and need, and this was magnified tenfold when Eleanor shifted beneath him to accommodate him. "Slowly," he cautioned. "I dinna want to bring you pain, though there is nae getting around it." He sank slowly into her, filling her, his hands fisted on each side of her head.

Eleanor gasped again. "There is... 'tis not pain but fullness."

For now, he thought. He'd seated himself only as far as the barrier of her innocence would allow. It was here and now, if he had any reserve strength to resist her, to save her—an unlikelihood, at best—that he briefly thought he should, could still, stop.

Instead, Dougal bent his face low and kissed her savagely at the same time he shifted his hips back and surged forward, pushing through her barrier. He caught her cry in a kiss. The fingers at his waist dug into his flesh.

"Give it a minute," he rasped against her lips, otherwise unmoving.

Her panted breaths were blown against his mouth until Dougal distracted her with another kiss. There was just enough space between them that the short hairs of his chest teased her nipples with even the slightest movement, causing Eleanor to seek more. Experimentally, she moved her chest, which moved her hips ever so slightly. Dougal growled low in his chest and lifted his hips, stroking smoothly and slowly forward again.

Eleanor tensed, holding her breath while Dougal made tentative forays,

He went rigid inside her, stretching her until she was wonderfully and nearly unbearably tight around him.

"Sweet saints," he breathed, "but ye take me so bluidy well."

"Like a hand to a glove?" she asked. "'Twas as I just thought."

"Aye, hand to a glove, lass," he repeated, unable at the moment to give any other thought to words as responses, not when his cock was so gloriously encased inside her tight sheath.

He moved again, withdrawing with excruciating slowness before submerging himself deeply again. He did this again and again until he imagined the pain either lessened or forgotten, and the flourishing ache grew tenfold inside him.

When Eleanor lifted her hips to meet him, he increased the tempo, alternately kissing her and fondling her in places away from where their bodies were joined. She now had some idea about what would come, likely recognized the resurfacing desire inside her, and moved her hands down to cup his solid buttocks, silently begging him to seek more, go deeper, move faster. Dougal's brain and body were alive, every bone and muscle, every nerve quivering with raw energy and yearning.

She cried out this time with her release, rocking her hips against him as her climax coursed through and over her.

He wanted it to never end, wanted to know this divine feeling for hours and continued to move until he could no more. He closed his mind and abandoned all sanity save the blinding intensity of this, with Eleanor, until his own release could not be denied, and he buried himself deep and stiffened, grunting and breathing some curse before collapsing against her while their bodies throbbed.

He was only vaguely aware of her voice murmuring in his ear, was only dimly conscious of the sheen of perspiration that made his skin slick. His eyes were closed, unable to be open, it seemed. For long moments, they did not move, their fused bodies spent and sated.

Finally, Dougal shifted, but only to raise his arms to support himself while he lifted his face above her. He was yet on top of her, his manhood yet sheathed so marvelously when he laid his lips in a lingering kiss upon her cheek.

A slow and drawn out sigh oozed from Eleanor. Her beautiful smile was so close. He hadn't words for what he felt just now, couldn't pinpoint each and every emotion that thrilled him and satiated him. Whatever the whole of it was, it was fine and perfect and somehow caused no dread. Eleanor lifted her hand and laid it against his cheek, and he wished he could see her eyes clearly just now.

Instead, he placed small kisses about her face, on her other cheek and her nose and near her temple, where he was surprised to encounter the saltiness of tears. "Why do you cry, Eleanor?" He hadn't sensed sadness at all, nor any regret so soon.

"I...have no idea," she said and laid her hand against his cheek, mayhap as some assurance that the tears should be of little concern to him.. "I hadn't expected... that is, I didn't know it felt this..." she stammered and paused. And then she said, "I didn't know anything and yet I did not expect this, such fire and such exquisite delight. I had no idea it was so...consuming."

Consuming? Aye, it was. As was he, consumed by her.

Though he was in no hurry to part from her and this, what they'd shared, he knew his weight was not inconsequential. Gingerly, he withdrew from her and rolled to his side. In the same motion, he took her with him, wanting her in his arms.

They settled easily, naturally, he on his back and she on his chest. He used his foot to hook and move the fur at the end of the bed, lifting it until he got his hand on it and draped it over their bodies.

He thought only a moment had passed before Eleanor was asleep in his arms.

Dougal sighed and quickly fell asleep himself, too sated to even beat himself up over this, how quickly he'd caved against his plans to never touch her again. Too tired to consider what had struck him so ardently, how worthy and good he felt every minute that he'd touched her.

I WILL NEVER BE THE same again.
   I am a different person now, she thought.

Dougal had been gone from his bedchamber when she'd finally woken, at an almost indecent hour. She had some hazy recollection of him kissing her before he'd left. He'd said, "I dinna ken when I'll return." Or, she thought that was what he'd said. She couldn't be sure. She couldn't remember or had been too sleepy to process it in the first place.

'Twas an awkward circumstance, having done that earth-shattering thing with him and then...nothing. He just...left.

She wanted to see him, and kiss him, wanted to be kissed, wanted to see if he would smile now, more, better, easily.

But he wasn't there.

Though she felt no shame for what she'd done, she'd been a little nervous about facing Lucy, as the maid would surely have noticed her absence and might have a fairly good idea where she'd spent the night.

But Lucy was not found in their shared bedchamber when Eleanor had slipped inside, but that was not surprising, the hour being so late. Eleanor had washed and changed, secretly reveling in the soreness of her body.

She'd been surprised to find Lucy inside the kitchen, apparently having made a wee bit of headway with the household staff. She and another young woman had their heads bent over whatever simmered in the kettle in the main hearth, Lucy saying something about rosemary and thyme flavoring meat most delightfully for pies. Because they were in mixed company, Lucy gave only a sly and knowing grin but no actual grief.

Though the servants were outwardly more friendly with Lucy, their equal by class, Eleanor stayed for quite a while in the kitchens on the ground floor below the hall, not minding that no grand overtures were made toward her and not wishing yet to force her presence so heavily upon them. She did make herself useful, familiarizing herself with the kitchens and its connected chambers and then standing once for more than an hour cleaning and cutting cabbage, happy to be left to her own thoughts as she was. These mostly revolved around recollections of the night past and every scintillating touch from Dougal and so much hope for their future.

By early afternoon, the kitchen becoming steamy enough to curl all the short wispy hairs around her brow and forehead, and with no other task available to her, Eleanor took herself away, stepping outside into a clear, sunny day, immediately spying Dickson upon the battlements. She lifted her skirts and made her way up the stone steps that abutted the inside of the gatehouse, shielding her eyes from the sun as she climbed and looked upward.

She went first straight ahead to the outer wall, which much like Bowyer House overlooked a nondescript meadow of grass, sliced in half by the road to the gate. Beyond, however, the vista was magnificent, distant cloud and tree covered hills found in every direction. In the foreground but beyond the wind-swept grass, one of Templeton's many lochs shimmered under the midday sun.

"Och and what have we?"

Eleanor smiled, turning around at Dickson's voice.

"Am I allowed up here, Dickson?" She asked cheekily, in reference to the last time they stood atop any ramparts, those at Bowyer and while under siege. Oh, but how long ago that seemed already!

"Aye," he allowed, "but mayhap only in my company or the laird's. These lads are nae so tame as wot we got there at Bowyer."

Eleanor grinned at this as well, but she wouldn't tell Dickson, who was forever obsessed with the security of her chastity, believing few men above pouncing on her, that the prize was gone.

"Dickson, I know you're happy to be in the thick of things up here, but exactly what do you do all day upon this wall when no threat is nigh?" She glanced around, seeing only stone and soldiers.

There was some nostalgic charm to his instant scowl, never taken half as seriously as Dougal Kildare's.

"Wot ye mean wot do I do? Same as I did at Bowyer." He pivoted and thrust his hand out, indicating the ten-foot wide width of the walkway. "Plenty of space here. And training is constant, so long as we have half the men watching faithfully. I can instruct on so many of the hand-to-hand techniques up here." He stepped closer and lowered his voice, putting four fingers to the right side of his mouth. "I dinna mind telling ye—and cheers to yer bridegroom there—these ones are sharp. I'm digging deep for something they dinna ken."

"If that displeases you, Dickson," she said, "I believe that the teaching may actually be your life's goal and wish and not only having the most perfectly trained army."

"Aye, ye might have the right of it, lass, but the lads here—mayhap under threat—are playing along nicely with me."

Her grin improved. "How kind of them." They faced the outside now, quiet for a moment until Eleanor asked, "Where is Dougal today? About his hunt for his uncle?"

"Nae more hunting, lass," he said. "They found him, nailed it down yesterday, his location."

She gasped at this, fearing a confrontation or battle, and then recalled something she'd thought of yesterday and had meant to ask Dougal but had forgotten. "Dickson, are they sure it was Padean Kildare who poisoned his mother? What proof have they? What if it wasn't him? What if she weren't actually—"

"Now, hold on there, lass," Dickson interjected, lifting his hand, swatting it downward several times to beg for calm. "He dinna go about headlong and heedless now. Nae, the truth come out. Did ye ken a wretched women in the kitchens when first we came—eyes like a hungry toad, lips so thin ye'd swear she had none?"

Eleanor shook her head, not able to place such a caricature. "I don't know her."

His eyes widened and he said sternly, "And ye will nae. Flòraidh she was. Gave up the plot when the cook said she was acting squirrelly after the uncle was tossed out, and the laird directed his attention there—*Jesu*, dinna he tell ye this? Anyway, Flòraidh said the poisoning had gone on for months, all under Padean's direction, with his coin. She swore up and down she dinna administer it, but the lad was nae so sure. And why'd she run? Aye, she did," he said at Eleanor's now widened eyes. "Asked to settle her affairs ere she was sent to the sheriff in Nairn. Ducked out on nae one but two lads who are only now aware of the secret stairs leading to and fro the servant's dormitory. Gone, she was, until they caught up with her—and that's where they came upon information to find the uncle now. God's bones, lass, but what do ye and he talk about if nae that—aw, bluidy hell. Guess that look right there tells me there is nae much talking."

He rolled his eyes, which amused Eleanor but only because he seemed more surprised than actually upset.

Dickson released a long breath and laid his palms against the waist-high wall. "Ye could've done worse—Chishull for one," he said, tipping his head at her while he stared straight ahead. "I'd nae let this one within ten feet of ye if I didn't trust him with ye. But Christ, Eleanor, he's a cold one. That's nae for ye—are ye sure about this? We could head out west. Tomag reminded me of—"

"I want to be here," she said firmly. "With him." When he said nothing, she asked quietly, "You could be happy here, could you not?"

"I can make happiness anywhere, lass," he said without hesitation. "I just...guid man he is—honor, boldness, cleverness, all affixed properly, more than most in some regards...."

"But?"

Dickson turned, slanting a look of puzzlement upon her. "He dinna smile, lass. No humor at all in that one. Ye're nae a cackling hen, always giggling and tittering like some half-wit bird, and was I nae always grateful for that, but Eleanor, he's a grim creature, dark and dangerous. And ye...ye are nae made that way."

Considering the assessment unfair, Eleanor was quick to defend Dougal. "Dickson, think of every circumstance in which we've known him." She ticked them off on her fingers. "Under siege at Bowyer. Us accosting him on his journey home—obviously he was shocked by my proposal. Then here at Templeton, his mother ailing and then...gone. And his uncle responsible. He hasn't had much reason to smile, Dickson. But he has, recently. At me."

Dickson nodded, and even as he said, "Aye, if he's capable of it, ye're the one to bring it out of him," Eleanor thought he wasn't convinced.

"I only want ye happy, lass."

"I know. I love you for that, among so many other things. Dickson, if I'm not—happy, that is—I'll let you whisk me away."

"And I will." He winked at her. "If the toady-eye Flòraidh with nae lips could evade him, I ken we might as well."

Eleanor stayed only a few more minutes with Dickson upon the wall before making her way to Dougal's chamber, which she tided, belatedly recalling the blood-stained sheets, which she scrubbed as best she could herself before bringing them and the ones from the bed she and Lucy shared down to the laundress.

Dougal did not return that day or the next and Eleanor could not help but begin to worry.

Lucy came upon her—must have searched her out—standing in the turret of the northwestern tower, watching the hills for his return.

"Well," said Lucy, "if I dinna have a brain in my head and kent what ye were about, gone all night 'fore he left, yer daft grins and constant nail biting, and watching out every window, would have told me."

Eleanor turned, meaning to take umbrage at so bold a statement, but could not remove any expression from her face, either her concern, nor the blush that came and would advise Lucy she had the right of it.

Frankly, and with little care that she shouldn't be discussing something so private with the girl, Eleanor asked, "Have you done this before? Is it supposed to be...I know he is intent on finding his uncle, but...should he have left? Then? Right after...?"

"Och and we're nae going to start with this, I dinna mind telling ye. He's the laird," Lucy reminded her sharply, impertinently. "Padean Kildare poisoned his mother. Aye, he needs to get that taken care of. Ye're nae going anywhere but Eleanor, ye had better get used to his absences. Long ones, I should ken. This one'll nae be long though, I ken."

Eleanor chewed her lip, not appreciating that reply, not one bit.

But Lucy was correct.

In an era when soldiers and armies might be gone for months on end, when Dougal himself had last been gone from Templeton for almost a year, this absence was relatively short.

He returned, he and his entire party intact, after three days.

Eleanor and Lucy had been in the fields just outside the village, picking the last of the blueberries, when they heard them come. Eleanor had hiked up her skirts and had run the entire way back to the keep, smiling and laughing the whole way, Lucy stumbling and laughing right behind her. Though the coming party was small, not more than a score of men, the yard was crowded with so many others wanting to greet them that Eleanor had to push her way through a rowdy throng to find Dougal. She couldn't find him immediately and then saw only the back of his head as he entered the keep. For one brief second as he turned, she thought he must have seen her, or the arm she waved over her head at the opposite side of the yard, stalled near the gate. Perhaps not though since he pivoted again and disappeared from view.

Lucy pushed at her back as Eleanor worked her way through the bodies and horses.

He was seated at the high table by the time Eleanor finally reached the hall. Seated, she thought, not bounding up the stairs searching for her. But no, he could not, not with so many courting attention, mayhap the full story of his mission. He smiled and clapped the steward, Yopin, on the shoulder, the ease of that small interaction—his grin specifically— answering any questions she would have had about Padean Kildare. Imprisoned. Or dead.

But her concern was for Dougal.

She knew a swift joy at only the sight of him, whole and well. She'd not forgotten how handsome he was, how the sight of him stirred her blood, more so now after what they'd shared immediately before he'd left.

Eleanor strode forward, nudging Walter and Boyd a wee bit so that she could stand directly before the laird at the table.

"You are returned," she said, showing no cleverness, only a breathless joy at seeing him.

The ease about his features dissipated, his jaw hardening, his gaze flitting over her, not meeting her gaze for more than a split second. He said nothing, only clamped his lips and nodded at her.

"And you met with success?" She said. This nervously, his puzzling attitude unsettling.

"Aye." He said, inclining his head in thanks to the kitchen lass who set a tankard and platter of bread and cheese before him.

And then his eyes found hers again. They showed no matching joy. No delight to see her, not even a quiet or hidden one, as far as she could tell. And she understood instantly, saying absently around a forced smile, "Very good. Welcome home," before taking herself off, away from the iciness of his stare.

Oh, but she was crushed! To have ached for this man, who lifted cold, hard eyes to her, eyes that did not soften, did not lighten at all when they fell upon her, ones that were not at all reminiscent of his languid and loving looks of several nights ago.

Eleanor ducked inside the corridor off the hall. As soon as she was out of sight she put her back against the wall and covered her mouth, catching her startled and pained cry in her hand. She understood exactly what she was meant to know. She was nothing to him. That night had been a mistake to him, one he had no intention of repeating. He'd not thought of her, had not missed her, hadn't ached for her in his absence.

All of her joy, sprung so swiftly and abundantly upon his return, diminished in an instant.

Lucy found her only a second later.

"Dinna cry here," she said practically, her mouth thinned grimly, taking Eleanor's arm, dragging her up the rear, spiral stairs. "*Jesu*, that man."

Chapter Twenty

Truth be told, she rather sulked the rest of the day, keeping to the chamber she shared with Lucy, unwilling to show her tear-stained face, but then somehow managed to retain hope that he would seek her out. She imagined a dozen different reasons he might give for his chilling indifference, deciding which of them might justify such boorish behavior, and which she would take issue with.

To no avail. He did not show. He never came looking for her.

The next morning, with her chin held high, she sought him out. She deserved an explanation, just as she had but never satisfactorily received after his offensive reaction to her proposal of several weeks ago.

She searched the hall and yard, his chamber, and the ramparts, but he was not found. And because she didn't know better, she almost imagined he might purposefully be avoiding her. When no one could rightly say where he was, she was prompted by desperation to search every chamber in the keep and every building on the grounds.

Inside the kirk, in which she did not actually expect to find him, she found Father Siward.

Frustrated at this point, and having roughly pushed open the thick arched portal, which scraped noisily against the slate floor, Eleanor could not then escape the priest's notice, as he was seated in the first of the dozen pews, alone, having no occupation that she could discern, mayhap only disturbed from prayer.

"Pardon me, Father," she said, her voice small for her infraction, barging in so clumsily. She began to back out.

"Come, lass," he invited. "You do not intrude."

Eleanor gritted her teeth, not wishing to be waylaid from her search. But then she scarcely wished to be considered impolite. She closed the door and approached, cautioning herself not to be rudely inattentive while her mind was elsewhere.

Father Siward patted the space beside him on the bench seat. "Sit, my dear."

It had been some time since Eleanor had attended Mass or had practiced her religion, a ritual gone with her devout mother. But she crossed herself before she sat, bowing her head awkwardly at the sparse altar. She stared first straight ahead, trying to recall if there were some other sacred gesture she was forgetting; mayhap she might have genuflected fully. After a small moment of chewing her lip, she turned to the patient priest.

"I hear felicitations are in order," he said, pulling his mouth wide in a friendly smile.

Befuddled, Eleanor said blankly, "You do?"

Father Siward's smile expanded. "Aye, lass. The laird informs me that ye will wed."

"He does? And may I ask when this was brought to your attention?" Timing was a matter of critical importance.

The smooth flesh at the top of the priest's nose crinkled slightly. "Several days ago," he said mildly. "Before he went off on that horrid business regarding his uncle."

"Father," she began, turning on the bench to face him better, "I understand that ended...well. In the laird's favor?"

He cocked his head at her and asked just what Dickson had. "Did he not tell you?"

"No, and we'll get to that. What did happen?"

After releasing a surprisingly gusty sigh, Father Siward told her, "He killed him, of course. I'm sure there was another, non-violent solution, and I fear 'tis only more blood on the laird's hands, but there it is. Padean Kildare, despite his despicable reputation—or perhaps because of it; fear is a great impetus—was a well-connected man. Any sheriff's trial, even one before the king—Padean's late wife being a distant cousin of de Brus—might not have gone the way intended, as justice should have been served. As it was, we'll never know what the laird might have done. On the run and desperate, Padean sent those men with him to set a trap for the laird and his party. It backfired spectacularly, those men culled from Templeton's ranks advised they would suffer no ill-consequence if they deserted their arms." He shrugged, as if the matter had indeed been simple. "They agreed and left Padean to his own devices, save for his closest minions, who stood as sentinels, ordered to fight—certain death in the face of both the laird's fury and for being outnumbered as they were at that point." He paused, seeming to choose his words carefully. "Suffice to say, Padean was not without his own resources, sword and dagger in hand, and our laird was given no choice, truly, in the slaying. It only pains me for his soul the great satisfaction I know he derived from—his words—*sending the infidel to hell*."

Eleanor's shoulders slumped. "There really is no escaping violence, even from within one's own home."

"Dangerous times indeed," Father Siward agreed. "But tell me, my dear, why you wouldn't have asked this of your betrothed."

"I'm not sure we are still betrothed," she revealed, worrying the hands in her lap. "Or rather, I believe he might have changed his mind." She chanced a glance at the kindly priest. "Did he mention how the betrothal came about?"

Father Siward grinned again, relieving Eleanor of any concern about what he must think of her, being so pleasant in his manner and reception.

"He did, lass. But I cannot conceive he has changed his mind." He stared thoughtfully at Eleanor for a moment, quietly drumming his fingers along the wood of the top of the pew, where he'd stretched out his arm. "You may rest easy in that regard, lass. Dougal Kildare doesn't do anything he doesn't want to. If he agreed to wed you to offer you protection, he meant it. He's not capricious," he said, shaking his head.

"Yes, but that's just it," Eleanor divulged—she felt very comfortable disclosing all the facts to this man, whom she could never imagine would think to use it against her in any way. "He didn't want to wed me, told me straight away no. I'm not sure what changed his mind—unless it was a misplaced sense that he owed me something for making his mother's last days as tolerable as possible—but he did. But then he...he stipulated that he would give me his name but...ah, not anything else." Her cheeks flamed and she wondered if she'd said too much. "At any rate, I thought... well, that we'd made some progress...in that regard before he left to pursue Padean, but I was wrong. He's back and he's as cold as ice, hasn't said hardly one word to me. So I don't think there will be a wedding after all. He's got so much anger in him," she concluded, wondering how much of that the priest may be aware of.

"His rage is not inexplicable, of course," said the priest. "'Twas not easy to grow up here for a third of his life living in the shadow of Templeton, and then—as an afterthought, as he perceives it—to be invited to dine at the laird's table later, and only when those that would have replaced him, the legitimate sons of the old laird, proved too weak, great disappointments and not only because they died." He pursed his lips, thoughtful again, before saying. "If you have not heard, his father was evil—our laird and no one else misremembers that. I know he struggles, fearing he might be too much the image of that man. But he is not. Dougal Kildare is many things, a most complicated man, but he is not evil. Perhaps he is still that lanky lad seeking acknowledgement, love, whatnot, from his father. He never found it, of course, and that's some of his bitterness, misplaced though that is. The scarring did not help in that regard, seeking love," said the priest, his mien sorrowful as he reflected. "I sometimes wonder if he intentionally doesn't ever put himself in any position to be rejected ever again. His mother loved him to be sure. Indeed, she was devoted to him, but I was sometimes concerned that her methods were not always...undertaken with her son's best interests at heart. But I'll say no more on that—Aimil was indeed a good woman."

So much to consider and contemplate, but Eleanor felt a little funny discussing Dougal with the priest, and this being their first real conversation. "I feel a little awkward, almost treacherous," she said with a slight wince, "to be speaking to you about this, rather behind his back."

"But you should not," Father Siward insisted. "First, you are to be his wife and have a right to know his history. Next, I tell you nothing that is not commonly known. In the end however, there is more, so much more that will have to come from him." He studied Eleanor for a moment, narrowing his eyes with the examination. "You love him?"

The question surprised her, but her answer did not. "I...want to," she said, not entirely sure. "I...I have deep feelings for him and plenty of hope, which I can't seem to squash no matter what he does to pound away at it." She smiled wistfully, her mind engaged with that aforementioned hope. "I think I would be very good at it, loving him, if he would let me. I think part of me is afraid as well, having in my own history a wee bit of rejection." At Father Siward's look of concern, Eleanor dismissed this swiftly with a wave of her hand. "It's nothing. I have Dickson now, I'm fine." She stopped and considered what more she might say on the matter. "I do not think he doesn't deserve it—that is, there is much worthy of love, but he pushes me away at every turn."

"No one said anything worth having would come easy," counseled the priest. "I cannot say for certain but mayhap he only tests you. He was betrothed once before," he added, slanting a cautious look at Eleanor. "Very well, you do know about her. She failed the test, straight away. Perhaps he only needs to believe and understand that he is not being judged, either by his father's standards or as his son, or by the scars he wears more with shame than pride."

"With shame? Why is that?"

"That I do not know. Lass, I will advise you as I am sure your own dear mother would or any good woman: follow your heart but remember, first and always, your own worth. You are an exceptional young woman."

"You are wonderfully kind, Father Siward," she told him, truly touched by the generosity of his statement. "So very considerate to sit and—"

The wrenching open of the kirk's door, the scrape against the floor unmistakable, stilled Eleanor's voice and turned both their heads.

Dougal had come, his magnificent figure silhouetted in the doorway against the bright daylight beyond the dimly lit kirk.

Father Siward squeezed Eleanor's hand in her lap before he stood.

"You must be searching for your betrothed," he presumed to Dougal, mayhap with intention, Eleanor thought.

Dougal moved within, his silhouette becoming only a dark shadow at the back of the small kirk.

When he said nothing, though Eleanor could well feel the intensity of his gaze upon her, Father Siward took her hand and pulled her to her feet.

"I would offer to stay," Father Siward said quietly to her, "But I have every confidence, lass, that you can manage him well enough on your own." He released her hand and moved up the aisle toward the laird, to whom he said, "I suggest an open air walk about, on such a fine day."

And with that, he circled around the back of the pews and exited the church through the south transept. For a fleeting moment, Eleanor felt abandoned. She stared longingly at the shadows into which the priest had vanished.

"Aye, let us walk," Dougal said.

With a curt nod, provoked by his brusque tone, she walked past him and stepped outside, the sun momentarily blinding so that she raised her hand to her forehead. The wind was fierce, noisy and flapping, as if it had wings. She paused, awaiting his instruction regarding destination then moved on when he indicated the lane, which she knew ended not far beyond the kirk, but that there was a slim trail along a low stone fence for at least a quarter mile until the trees closed in on the fields of winter crops planted only recently.

"Did ye discuss with Father the wedding then?" Dougal asked when they had taken their first steps alongside the fence.

Eleanor stopped, stunned by how bland and simple was his query.

Lest he intended to merely walk on without her, Dougal was forced to stop as well. He lifted a brow at her shocked expression.

"Discuss the wedding?" She fisted her hands at her side. "What wedding?"

"Do ye jape with me?" He asked. "Do ye ken another? Our wedding," he clarified, his ire so easily roused.

"Our wedding is it?" She threw at him and then stalked away in frustrated befuddlement, further away from the village and the keep.

"Eleanor!" He called out, managing to catch up with her quickly enough. "What is this?"

"What is what, Dougal?" She asked, marching on, having to raise her voice above the wind. "Our wedding? That one you barely mentioned to me so that I had no idea Father Siward had even been made aware of it. Our Wedding? The one that hangs in precarious balance, given your unaccountable behavior after your return? The wedding you didn't want in the first place?"

Her stomping was so furious, her pace matched well to her tone, that very soon they were quite a distance from the kirk. Eleanor did not stop but invaded a thicket of trees, following a bare and twisting path.

"I advised the priest of the upcoming nuptials," Dougal barked at her, never more than a pace behind her. "Was I to bring it uselessly into conversation every day?"

"Admit it, Dougal, you're regretting your consent, wanting to change your mind." She stopped abruptly again, facing him, a wee breathless for her tramping along so furiously. "Is this how it's going to be? That you don't share or take time to advise me of your plans—any of them, including the date and time I should have made myself available to be wed? And I have to suffer judgment from more than one person because my *betrothed* does not share conversation with me, and I must inquire of what had transpired regarding a life and death confrontation with the man who poisoned his mother! And then yesterday—that *coldness*—is that how it will be? Distant? Aloof? And that—that!—" she cried, "after....after the other night?" She queried, thrusting her arm wildly into the air. "My God, how can you be so hot and cold?"

His nostrils flared, as if he were incensed that she dared to bring up the other night.

"I'd advised ye of the terms acceptable to me in a marriage," he said, his voice as icy as his heart, she decided. "Despite the lapse of that night," he continued, "my feelings on the matter have nae changed."

Lapse? Lapse! Eleanor scoffed in disbelief, this tinged mightily by the agony caused by his careless words. Just when she thought she couldn't be further shocked or riled to any greater frustration.

"You cannot put the spilled milk back in the bucket, Dougal," she told him. Her chest heaved and the wind blew her hair all around. Eleanor ignored this and stomped away, further into the woodland. "I don't want a marriage like that," she grumbled over her shoulder. "I rescind my proposal."

"God dammit, Eleanor," cursed Dougal, once more close on her heels. "So what? Ye'll just leave?"

Tears threatened but she lifted her chin, even though he likely could not see this defiant pose as she marched along. "I believe I have no choice." She continued walking, having no idea where she was going. The small forest thickened, rising up as a rolling hill and then descending low into a glade of pine and birch and what she thought were rowan trees. She stopped walking, her consciousness struck by the beauty of this area of towering, ancient pines and the sun-dappled, fertile carpet of mosses, bluebells, and wood anemone. At the edge of this clearing was a small brook with swiftly moving water that oddly made no sound.

Eleanor paused, staring at the sparkling clear water. For a brief moment, she was attuned to her quiet surroundings, realizing her hair was no more tossed about by the wind. Immediately she felt drained of emotion, certainly the most powerful ones, and sagged a bit with a reprieve from sadness.

Dougal paused beside her.

"What do ye want from me?" He asked quietly.

"Tell me why," she said blandly, her gaze on her surroundings and not him. "Why—especially after the fact—would you want a fake marriage?"

She sensed instinctively that he wouldn't tell her anything. Resignation filled her.

He thought a tersely offered, "It is to protect ye," would suffice.

"Protect me from what? And how? By withholding...everything?"

"Ye'd have my name," he said plainly.

"I can have Dickson's name or Daniel's," she reminded him. "Or Boyd's. If that's all I wanted."

He walked toward her, and she braced herself, but he only sat on an overlarge gray rock, the boulder seemingly misplaced in this lush green clearing.

Eleanor turned to face him squarely. "Why would you deny us what we shared that night?" She asked, her voice breaking. "Do you call that a mistake?"

"I've told ye, Eleanor. I'm nae guid. My heart is nae....fit. Ye'll only be hurt."

"Rubbish," she accused. "At least be—" she stopped, clamping her lips, hating that she was reduced to this, nearly begging for affection from him, for anything. After a deep and calming breath, she said to him, "I have recently been reminded that I should follow my heart, Dougal. If I knew yours better—understood it at all—I would follow mine more easily. As much as I don't deserve to marry someone of Chishull's reputation, so too, I deserve more than someone who doesn't see my worth. I want someone who would be pleased to have me by his side, completely and in every manner, and not just as...as chattel or whatever your terms would make me."

He nodded, his lips pursed, his hands on either side of him on the surface of the rock, bracing himself it seemed.

But he said nothing.

And Eleanor was then flooded with more awareness of their strangely silent surroundings. "What...why is it so quiet here?"

Dougal laid his gray eyes on her with disturbing intensity. A moment passed, long enough that Eleanor raised her brow at him before he answered.

"'Tis the windless woods."

The windless woods.

Eleanor glanced around, contemplating his response, that designation, and her surroundings.

Yes, it was.

There was no wind, no sound at all. How peculiar.

And yet something stirred in the air and within Eleanor. She gasped softly and laid her hand over her heart. She perceived a hollowness in the air even as it filled her, as if they'd intruded and had roused a sleeping monster, which now gently agitated the air around them.

"'Twas my refuge as a child," Dougal surprised her by revealing.

Eleanor returned her attention to him, to find him watching her thoughtfully. Possibly he'd not taken his gaze off her in the last moment.

"From your father," she guessed, recalling Father Siward's cryptic words, and a few of Dougal's as well.

He nodded and then removed his stark gaze from her, moving it around the scenery. His fingers scratched noiselessly at the rock beneath him.

Eleanor thought he might have revealed more—anything—for he seemed to be suddenly in a mood more somber than aggrieved by their quarrel.

He did not, only nodded again, slowly, and said, "Aye."

"I know so little of you," she remarked, imagining that he might prefer to keep it that way. Yet another reason why a marriage between them would likely not succeed. Even without those damnable terms to keep distance between them, he would remain closed off, keep her forever at arms' length. Resignation settled heavily within her. She could not fight against his demons. "I didn't only randomly pick you as a potential husband," she confessed after a moment, which brought his piercing gaze back to her. "I chose you and chased you because you stirred something deep and abiding in my chest, even before...before the other night. I can't explain it, the how or the why of it. But I wanted *you*, Dougal, to be my husband. I cannot say it was love or is love—what do I know?" she asked with a broken laugh. "Save that I know now being married to you on your terms, in name only, would break my heart."

And what a shame that he did not give her the courtesy of a reply, seemed only to sit and wrestle with something inside himself.

With everything said and done, and so much more left unsaid by him, she decided she owed him nothing, not even the kindness of a farewell.

Eleanor turned and walked away from Dougal, away from the eerily silent woods, tears finally falling.

DOUGAL WATCHED HER go, both incensed and remorseful.

She *was* worthy of someone better than he, and didn't he know it.

He fisted his hands on the stone upon which he sat and blew out a tormented sigh.

Unaccountable behavior, she'd called his coolness toward her.

Truth was, that tantalizing night with Eleanor had given him hope, the commodity so rare he'd been unable to name it for hours and hours. In hindsight it was easy to think, *I should never have left her bed*. At the time, he'd risen with a renewed purpose, wanting to find Padean and seek that prescribed vengeance so that he might return to Eleanor and revel again in her passion awakened, a discovery that was not so much surprising as it was glorious.

Find Padean he had, but what had transpired when they'd met had served as the cold ice of a reminder that evil lived not only in his avaricious uncle but in himself. No wild, internal struggle had taken place, no noble virtue had emerged to temper his killing of Padean. He had not even tried to fight against the evil inside him at the time but had been thoroughly pleased when Padean had asserted a fight, such as it was, so that Dougal could slay him without remorse.

And yet shame had not escaped Dougal but was instead tied to his feelings toward Eleanor. He remembered staring at his hands—even as Padean lay dead at his feet—at the sword in his tight grip, at the blood that dripped from his blade. A flash of recent memory had assaulted him at that particular moment, the image of his hand gentle and eager upon Eleanor's soft flesh. This contrasted sharply, excruciatingly, with his own vile nature, and he'd shaken with violence. Conflicted inwardly, he understood that inside him, in his flesh and in his heart, dwelt no good thing.

He had no right to Eleanor, to any joy with her; he'd earned no such thing.

Despite every instinct inside him that begged him to pretend he was made otherwise, that he was without sin or malevolence, he could not in good conscience subject Eleanor to the whims of his inherent malice, how swiftly it flared, screaming to be assuaged when the fits beheld him. She might as well wed John Chishull, for all that she would in either case have a husband who shunned honor and nobility when it suited him, when war called or vengeance screamed to be had, or mayhap at other, improperly uninitiated times.

I chose you and chased you because you stirred something deep and abiding in my chest.

How long before she realized what he really was? How long before she trembled at his touch, not with yearning but with fear, with disgust? Would that not be the gravest travesty at all, to see revulsion in her warm and loving gaze?

Once more, he let his gaze wander around the windless woods but felt not the usual compensation of its tranquility.

Chapter Twenty-One

Somehow he wasn't surprised that she did not make herself available for any further conversation. She did not appear in the hall at last meal and was not found anywhere inside the keep in the hours before she might have retired. By then, she was ensconced with Lucy in their shared bedchamber and the opportunity to relieve himself of torment, to tell her his truths—as she did deserve to know—had past for the day.

He waited until morning, and when she didn't show herself in the hall to break her fast, and he saw no sign of Lucy either, Dougal went about his day, knowing he would seek her out at some point, as he had yesterday.

He spent several hours with a group of tenants in various meadows, discussing improvements to the irrigation processes. Though upgrades were necessary, the work would have to wait now until spring, when every chance of frost had come and gone. He was standing there, with half a dozen farmers, atop a mossy hillock, when he spied a pair of riders heading south along the lane, away from Templeton. His brow furrowed with puzzlement, Eleanor's slight figure unmistakable as one of the riders. He thought the other must be Dickson, that person's shape larger, and Dougal unable to imagine that her captain would allow her to ride even leisurely without him by her side.

Though he entertained a fleeting but credible notion that she might be leaving him, leaving Templeton, Dougal somehow managed to refrain from mounting his waiting steed and racing after them. She would not depart Templeton without a goodbye, he was convinced, despite...everything. Undoubtedly, she would not abandon Lucy and the rest of the Bowyer House party, departing with only Dickson.

Precious little peace came with this confidence, knowing she would certainly leave, eventually. There was nothing to keep her here if he would not—could not—give her the marriage she wanted. More havoc was wrought by this, his mind and heart flirting with the burgeoning idea that he couldn't rightly live without her, that he didn't want to.

I chose you and chased you because you stirred something deep and abiding in my chest. Powerful words indeed, though Dougal qualified them with the truth, of which she had not been fully apprised. In all probability, if she knew his true character, she would not have uttered so provocative a statement.

An hour later, as if the constancy of his thoughts had conjured her, Dougal happened upon Eleanor. More curious yet, he came upon her in the windless woods. On this occasion, he was only cutting through the forest, returning from a visit with Asgar Mead, who kept a croft well outside the village, and beyond the largest of Templeton's loch. Dougal had paid his respects to the old man, a former bailiff at Templeton, who lived now on the generosity of others, of which he'd told had been hard to come by while Padean had overseen the keep and demesne.

He saw her mare first, or the white coat of her mare, and frowned with unease at the riderless horse until he noticed Eleanor. She sat very close to where they'd stood when talking yesterday, in the tall green grass a wee bit removed from that old rock that had long ago seemed so mammoth to a young Dougal but now only was large enough to comfortably hold one person seated.

She sat with her legs crossed and her arms settled into the grass behind her. When she realized Dougal's approach, she lifted her hands and dusted them off on each other before laying them in her lap. She watched him dismount cautiously, mayhap with a wee bit of resignation...unless that was in reality displeasure he read in her green eyes.

Dougal dismounted, leaving his destrier loose near her tethered mare. Whether or not she expected or wanted his company was not a concern presently. Assuming as he did that she would depart Templeton soon, he knew he owed her some manner of explanation. He valued her enough to understand this.

He walked toward her, neither having said a word yet, and was struck by an untimely urge that he wanted to not only sit next to her and have conversation with her, but he wanted more than that to take her in his arms, to hold her again, to feel her arms slide around him as she'd done before, far too rarely to suit his yearning for her.

He did not, though. And when he did not sit beside her but chose to stand before her, subjecting her to a thoughtful and open perusal, believing it might be one of his last opportunities to do so, Eleanor rose to her feet and lifted her chin.

The first words said between them were hers and were preceded by a short and bitter laugh.

"We've come to this, then. Everything has been said? Or we only presume no more words are either necessary or merited?"

Though he perceived some rebuke in these words, he did not take issue with it. "I wanted only to look upon ye."

Eleanor tilted her head at him, a question in her gaze, in the slight arch of her brow.

"Ye will depart, will ye nae?"

She nodded. "Soon."

"Ye would do well to remain," he said mildly, knowing he had no right to expect more from her when he'd offered so little. "'Tis safer here, so far north."

"Your concern for my safety is admirable, but unnecessary," was all she said.

He placed his hands on his hips. "I feel we dinna satisfy each other fully in yesterday's conversation."

"I've said my peace, Dougal," she informed him, a wee bit starchy.

"I've nae said mine," he drawled despite his racing heart. "Ye wanted an explanation and I ken you are owed that. It didn't spill out, Eleanor, will nae come easily even with a day to prepare it."

"Prepare it? Invent it, you mean?"

She was entitled to her indignation, he conceded.

"Ye asked about the why of it," he said, "why I would nae want to be wed properly to ye. But I would, Eleanor."

Her perfect pink lips parted while a certain befuddlement overtook her features.

"Ye give me hope and I canna recall when last—if ever—I ken it," he told her. "'Twas nae only an excuse, a way out, to say I was trying to protect ye. 'Twas nae a lie when I said I was nae guid. I'm nae a...I've a blackness in me, lass. Been with me my whole life, the anger ye've seen is only what boils on the surface though. More of it roils inside me and makes me unfit." He spoke candidly, the words flowing, her attentive regard somehow soothing. "My sins are numerous and gruesome, my heart as unclean as yours is nae. I'm nae only the product of a monster but am one myself, Eleanor. Do ye ken why I have these scars?" He stopped and shook his head and then spoke firmly, without hesitation. She had to know. "The English dinna do this and my sire dinna do this. I did this. I have—had—such rage back then." He sighed and continued. "'Twas at Falkirk, though. The fight was lost. Retreat was called, men left for dead, running for their lives. But I could nae. Would nae. I stopped, there in the field, fell upon any wounded Englishman I could find, happy to slit their throats," he said, recalled to the savagery of the day. He blinked, returned to the present, aware of Eleanor's chest heaving as she listened. "Fire was everywhere, from their war machines or fiery arrows, I dinna ken. But there was me, lass, so busy with my hatred I ken nothing but that. Kill them all, was what I wanted. Never saw the horse and rider coming at me, shoving me away from the last life I took, knocked me right into the fire." He laughed bitterly, remembering that he'd felt nothing after the initial scorching and searing heat. He'd wanted only to find the one responsible and visit the same horror onto him. "He came at me again, believing me finished. I waited. He was no match for my sword or my rage. But I dinna kill him swiftly, honorably. Bluidy buried his face in the same fire that caused this," he said, pointing to his face, his voice ragged, the stench of those moments never far from his recall. "Risked capture, being kilt, just to visit vengeance and hatred upon him, a lad doing his job, only what was required of him. I'm nae guid, Eleanor, I have that sickness in me, I ken I do. I canna sleep sometimes for hearing his screams. *Jesu*, it tears me up inside, to live with it."

Having said that, nothing had changed, but in the telling, the constant heaviness inside him seemed suddenly lighter. The burden of the years carried less weight inside him, he supposed.

"Revenge is nae sweet, lass," he summarized. "Seeking it and fulfilling the need of it made a monster of me, more so than only any evil visited upon me by my own sire, more than only the scars ye see."

Eleanor drew a deep breath, taking her bright green eyes finally off him, her cheeks puffing a bit as she exhaled.

"Do you believe yourself evil?" She asked after a long moment had passed. Her tone was unfathomable, her gaze searching as she brought it back to his.

"I am. I must be."

"And this...the monster that you perceive yourself, that is what you wish to protect me from?"

"Aye."

Eleanor made some sound of agreement, but the tone of it wrought a frown from Dougal.

"Very well, and thank you for explaining this to me, Dougal."

Lifting her skirts, she turned to leave.

"Eleanor? That is...? You have nae anything else to say to me?"

Pivoting again, she faced him, and he wondered if she were horrified by what he'd revealed, if that's what her compressed lips and stormy gaze now meant.

"No," she answered tightly. "I understand now. And you might have saved us both the trouble, might have disrespected me less by favoring me with the truth, Dougal. Just say, *I don't want to be wed to you, Eleanor. I have no interest in being your husband or taking you to wife.*"

What the—

"Instead, you use that truly horrific event from your history as a way to wheedle out—what? Gracefully? Pride intact? Do you imagine I needed my feelings spared? I can tell you I do not. In this instant you are indeed a monster. The truth would have served you more positively. I'd have greater—"

"What the bluidy hell are ye going on about? The truth? 'Tis as I've said. I was made to look like a monster because I am one—"

"But what does that have to do with me, or being wed to me? Why does that mean you cannot?"

Frustrated by her annoyance, which was to his mind wildly misplaced, he raged at her, "Did ye nae hear what I said? I killed men for nae other reason but to make them dead. I got this," he said through gritted teeth, pointing to his cheek, "because an ungodly rage overtook me, and I visited needless evil upon others."

"Was it awful? Beyond your imagining? The battle that day?"

Though bewildered by her change of tone and trajectory, Dougal answered mechanically. That battle, more so than any other, and not only for its result but for how it all played out, was the substance of his nightmares. "Aye, the worst I had ever seen, before or since. Spearmen, bowmen, infantry, horses, five thousand strong," he said, staring sightlessly as he spoke, "and nae enough to prevail. The cavalry fled ere the battle was met. We took refuge in the schiltrons, but they were quickly weakened by the English arrow storm. Our archers scarcely proved effective against the well-armored enemy. We retreated across the River Carron, northwest of Falkirk, and held the ford with a small guard, but nae for long. They...they just kept coming. The water turned red, I recall, colored with the bluid of all those fallen, three, four times as many as they lost." He blinked and finished with, "Ye could nae take more than a few steps at a time without encountering a body."

After a moment, Eleanor's voice pierced his consciousness, the gentleness of it pulling him from that memory.

"Dougal, if a spider bites me, I'm going to stomp on it. If a man put his hands on me without my consent, I will smack him. Indignation or fear or fervor would make me crazed, I might imagine. Is that not the way of it? Is that not war? Killed or be killed?"

He thought instantly she was minimizing it only for his benefit. She didn't fully understand.

But she persisted. "Did you feel only hatred for your mother? Was that rage you visited upon me in your bedchamber?" She waved off his want to reply immediately. "I understand. It was overdone. Overkill? Is that not what they say? Is that not part of war as well? Have you killed in such a manner since then? Is not the very fact that it gnaws at you indicative of remorse? Do evil people know remorse?" She bit her lip and then posed another question. "Is it possible that your idea of yourself as evil is tied to—would you know such remorse if your reflexive actions then had not resulted in you being scarred, having to carry it around with you all the rest of your life?"

He might have argued each or every point she'd raised, but the truth was, it was ingrained in him, that what he'd done had been far and above what was called for in battle. And still, "It does nae make me a suitable prospect as a husband."

And yet a greater truth seized him now. Eleanor was not repulsed by the truth but defended his grotesque actions.

Before he might have questioned why, how, she gave him an answer.

"I do not fear you, Dougal," she said. "I do not see you as evil. Never once have I been afraid of you. You are not that man, Dougal." She took a step closer to him. She laid her hand upon his forearm. "You're the man who rode heedless into the fight at Bowyer House. The one whose face wrenched with pain when he found his mother near death in that cottage. You're the man who gives time and attention to Alpin Anndrais because he lost his father. Dougal, the man who caressed me and loved me the other night knew no hatred, no rage. He showed tenderness and love, I'll never believe otherwise."

"What I did to Padean, though—"

"He poisoned your mother, Dougal!" Eleanor argued fiercely. "If you hadn't slain him, I might have myself."

In the wake of that small eruption, Eleanor sighed. Dougal stared at her, contemplating all that she'd said, how she looked at him now, not with revulsion but as if she waited for something, something more from him.

But dare he hope that...well, that there was hope?

A weak and obviously forced smile turned up the corners of her lips when he had no other words for her.

"Again, I do appreciate that you shared that with me," she said. "I'm sorry that you..." she stopped and shook her head, without completing that thought. Lightly, she squeezed his arm before dropping her hand away. "I imagine that Dickson will have everything in order so that we might depart first thing in the morning." Another pause, and then, "Farewell, Dougal."

His heart aching, he watched her walk away. A sharp, burning pain stabbed his chest.

"Dinna go," he heard himself say and didn't for one second regret the words or his lack of control over them.

Eleanor stopped, still several yards from her mare, but did not turn. She lowered her head, her gaze likely on the ground in front of her.

"Stay," he said.

Her head moved slowly back and forth and then stopped, turned to the left so that he saw only her profile and barely that. "This is not for me, Dougal. You and I are not...well-suited."

Ah, so she wasn't so unaffected by what he'd revealed.

Her next words had him quickly rethinking this assumption.

"You will not allow us to be," she said.

Dougal frowned and strode forward, now on a mission to make her stay, understanding that he couldn't watch her walk away, couldn't let her simply walk out of his life. If she believed him without true evil, then he and they had a chance.

Possibly sensing his short pursuit, Eleanor turned abruptly but held her ground, did not back away despite his angry stride, which was actually more grounded in desperation.

"Eleanor," he began.

"No, Dougal," she interrupted, her green eyes shiny with tears. "I don't want to be—"

"Stay," he insisted. "Marry me." *Don't leave me.*

"I cannot be wed to someone who dictates how they will have a marriage," she said, tears spilling now, "without any input from the other concerned party. It isn't fair and reeks of arrogance, that you would consider your wants and needs but not mine."

"I did what I thought was best." He had been protecting her. He truly believed her too good, too fine for someone like him.

She was as valiant as any knight, as tender as any loving mother; she was dutiful in the best way but not to the point of helpless submission, and he knew firsthand how loyal she was to those she loved. And mayhap—in all likelihood—she was worthy of someone of greater character and honor than he, but damned if he would let her go now, when she'd just revealed how generous was her heart, that she didn't or wouldn't hold his sins against him, between them.

"That much I do believe. You do care about me, Dougal. But I fear you won't let yourself fully succumb to any grand feeling for me, any depth of feeling, for fear of what it might do to either you or me." Her voice broke when she said, "I-I would have burned with pride to be loved by you."

Dougal growled fiercely and tugged her hard against him, bringing his mouth down on hers. He did not coax or cajole, there was no need, no need to breach defenses when Eleanor was clinging to him, returning his fiery kiss with equal or greater fervor. The hand he placed at the back of her head trembled against her hair, and Dougal realized he'd been terrified that she would actually have gone through with it, would have left him.

He paused the kiss and chuckled a bit sheepishly as more weight was lifted off him, reduced by the passion of her kiss. *Wouldn't allow himself to fully succumb? Had no grand or deep feeling for her?* This concern, he felt very confident dispelling. God knows he'd fought hard but with so little success to keep her from reaching his heart. "I dinna mind telling ye, lass, *succumb* does nae seem to be an option. It runs over me and rules me, it bedevils me, and there doesn't seem to be a bluidy thing I can do about it." But damn, if there weren't so much relief, so much joy, attached to the possibilities now presented to him. To them. "If ye say ye might or could love me, Eleanor, I will give ye my heart, all the world, whatever ye desire. I will strive everyday to be the man you would—"

Eleanor laid her fingers against his lips. "You are that man, Dougal."

He kissed her again, her hair, her temple, her cheek, her lips. At her mouth, he lingered longest.

He was not *that man*, he still believed. But he would be or would become him. Anything was possible now.

Epilogue

His superstitions, which she did not learn about until many months into their marriage, were silly, she thought. The order in which he donned his clothes, the manner in which he pleated his plaid, the precision with which he settled his sword at his hip, three inches inward from his side, would have no bearing on the outcome of any fight. But because she knew they were important to him, she laid out his clothes in a suitable way, to accommodate his pattern of dressing.

So many years had passed, so many times she'd readied his gear for travel, for war, that tears no longer stung her eyes. Not that she didn't feel them inside, wrought by dread and fright and love, but she learned to put them in their place, which had no place in his presence so close to his departure.

She'd teased him once, possibly the last time she'd cried at his leavetaking, that if he didn't love her so well, little would she mourn their parting. He'd loved her then, in that moment, had spared quite a bit of time to linger over her, both of them quickly made naked and amorous. She would never believe her third child hadn't been conceived then. He'd thought the same, had returned to find her belly protruding once more, had grinned devilishly at her, teasing her he was happy to have left her with so fine a parting gift.

A sigh escaped her, mayhap that was the yearning to weep expressing itself.

As always, she thought: how would I survive without him? Why would I want to?

Still, she liked to think she handled it fairly well these days, having reluctantly grown into the role. Same as she had so many others—mistress of Templeton; mother to a future laird and several knights, mayhap a priest if she would be so blessed; friend, mentor, confidante. *We adapt as necessary*, Father Siward had told her years ago, mayhap on that first occasion she'd sent Dougal off to fight, within months after they'd wed. With Padean gone and then Dougal's absence, she'd been forced to be laird and steward and bailiff, too.

She'd learned quickly and had settled into a life that was filled with joy beyond her imagination.

Dougal had settled, as well. It was rare, had been years in fact since he'd displayed anything more than mild annoyance in her presence. Though she did not deceive herself that his rage was not put on full display inside any battle or brawl and though even his mild annoyance could be intimidating, she did not bemoan the exit of those ferocious scowls he'd employed so often when first they'd met.

She sat on the kist at the end of the bed, as she had a hundred times before. Sometimes, 'twas only to catch her breath, the toll of bringing four bairns to life in six years sometimes overwhelming. Occasionally, small and necessary sewing tasks were speedily completed just here. Three years ago, she'd sat just here and had wept like a baby when Dickson had finally succumbed permanently to that heart that had wanted to quit long before, but which he'd forced to keep going. She missed him still, her true father. She'd wept for a long time, until Dougal had come and had laid her in the bed, curling up behind her, keeping her warm and loved while she'd cried.

Henry Oliver, who'd come to Templeton in a cart with his peregrine on his shoulder and had lived comfortably here for the last ten years, had died this spring. His falcon, whom he'd raised since she was a chick covered in creamy-white down, had flown in circles round the hill where he'd been buried for three days before disappearing. She hadn't been spotted since.

Eleanor sat now upon the kist for no particular reason, only in some reflection, for which time was rarely afforded.

Lucy had the lads with her and her brood, a trio of lasses. She would keep the children away and busy until it was time to say their farewells to their fathers. Tomag had ascended to Dickson's role, which was equal to Walter's but greater still since Walter's fighting days were well behind him now. The old captain would keep company with Eleanor and Lucy and their bairns while the laird and the army were away. Walter would ask Eleanor if any of her four boys were old enough yet to hear stories of battles fought and gone, long behind them now. Eleanor had decided earlier this week she might tell Walter now that Ewan, her oldest at nine, might be ready to be entertained by Walter's surely embellished tales.

Her husband of nearly a decade found her there, on the kist, her shoulders slumped, her thoughts melancholy but not dangerously so.

He entered slowly and went to his knees before her when she lifted her dry eyes to him.

"Ye're nae weeping at my leavetaking," he remarked, "so then I guess you're again with child, hence the lethargy. Were ye debating whether or nae to tell me ere I left?"

Eleanor smiled serenely at him, even as she was sorry that she'd caused him even this little worry. She lifted her hand and laid it against this scarred cheek, as she'd done a thousand times before.

"I am not expecting another bairn," she said softly. She met his gray-eyed gaze, no less piercing than it had been a decade ago, his regard no less stimulating. "You are a good man, Dougal Kildare, a great father and husband."

"I ken it's hard to send me off, love," he said, "but if ye ken it's any easier from my point of view, leaving ye and the lads, ye have erred in yer thinking. I ride off and ken a tightness in my chest and I ken it's fear, but nae of death, but of nae ever seeing ye again."

She sighed and moved the hair off his forehead. "Would that we never had to be parted."

"I'll haunt ye, I vow." He said, his tone suddenly mischievous.

Eleanor shook herself, adopting a forced smile. "First, do not die that you are forced to haunt me. Promise me."

"Aye, lass. Dinna die." He tapped his forefinger to his forehead. "Got it."

"But yes, please do haunt me if that's all we have."

"Aye, noted."

Eleanor's shoulders dropped again. "I dinna mean to bestir you with my own melancholy. I was only reflective today. I am blessed, Dougal, in so many ways. I love you and I thank you for all you have given me over the years."

"We've more to come yet, love."

They stared into each other's eyes in silence for a long moment, memorizing details, things that changed over the years, new lines around the eyes and lips, the graying hair at his temple and the wee patch where her hair naturally parted, a new scar upon his right cheek, earned at Bannockburn, not pale yet like the others.

"Have I earned it, love?" He asked. "Any of the joy ye give me?"

Curious at his sudden somberness, Eleanor tilted her head at him. "I knew you weren't listening. I've just said..." she began but stopped when he shook his head, not of a mind to endure her teasing, or possibly fearing a lack of time.

"I take nothing away from my *màthair*, lass. She did the best she could, gave me more than most would have managed. But there was no joy. There was duty and honor and what she thought was owed to me."

"She did her job, Dougal, and keep that at the forefront—she did what she thought was best. We've learned ourselves, we have to make up so much of parenting, having no guide but instinct. She loved you, though, surely you—"

"She did. I nae ever doubt that. But the bitterness, the ability to hate, some of that came from her as well."

Eleanor's heart clenched. "But we have so much joy, Dougal."

"Aye, we do," he agreed immediately. "But it's ye, love. Ye are joy. And have I earned it?"

Her answer came easily, known first in the sweet tenderness in her chest. "Every day," she said, leaning forward to take his face in both her hands. "Every hour, every year, always." She kissed his lips and felt his hands reach for her hips.

He glanced around, as if he were about to shed light on a secret. "Saw the lads well occupied with Lucy way out yonder. I'd wager guid coin that I can love ye now, ere they return, leave ye naked and sated and nae worried at all about what I'm doing riding away from ye."

"I don't make wagers I know I cannot win," said Eleanor, coming to her feet. She smiled at her husband, adoring his returned grin, and removed her apron, turning her back and lifting her hair so that her husband could untie the ribbons of her léine. "The lads have certainly forced us to speed things up," she said over her shoulder.

"God, I love you," said Dougal, pressing a kiss to the shoulder he'd just bared.

The End

Other Books by Rebecca Ruger

Highlander: The Legends
The Beast of Lismore Abbey
The Lion of Blacklaw Tower
The Scoundrel of Beauly Glen
The Wolf of Carnoch Cross
The Blackguard of Windless Woods
The Devil of Helburn by the Sea
The Knave of Elmwood Keep
The Dragon of Lochlan Hall
The Maverick of Leslie House
The Brute of Mearley Hold
The Rebel of Lochaber Forest
The Avenger of Castle Wick

Heart of a Highlander Series
Heart of Shadows
Heart of Stone
Heart of Fire
Heart of Iron
Heart of Winter
Heart of Ice

Far From Home: A Scottish Time-Travel Romance
And Be My Love
Eternal Summer
Crazy In Love
Beyond Dreams
Only The Brave
When & Where
The Highlander Heroes Series
The Touch of Her Hand
The Memory of Her Kiss
The Shadow of Her Smile
The Depths of Her Soul
The Truth of Her Heart
The Love of Her Life

www.rebeccaruger.com

Printed in Great Britain
by Amazon